image® COMICS PRESENTS

INVINCIBLE™

THE DEATH OF EVERYONE

CREATED BY
ROBERT KIRKMAN
& CORY WALKER

image®

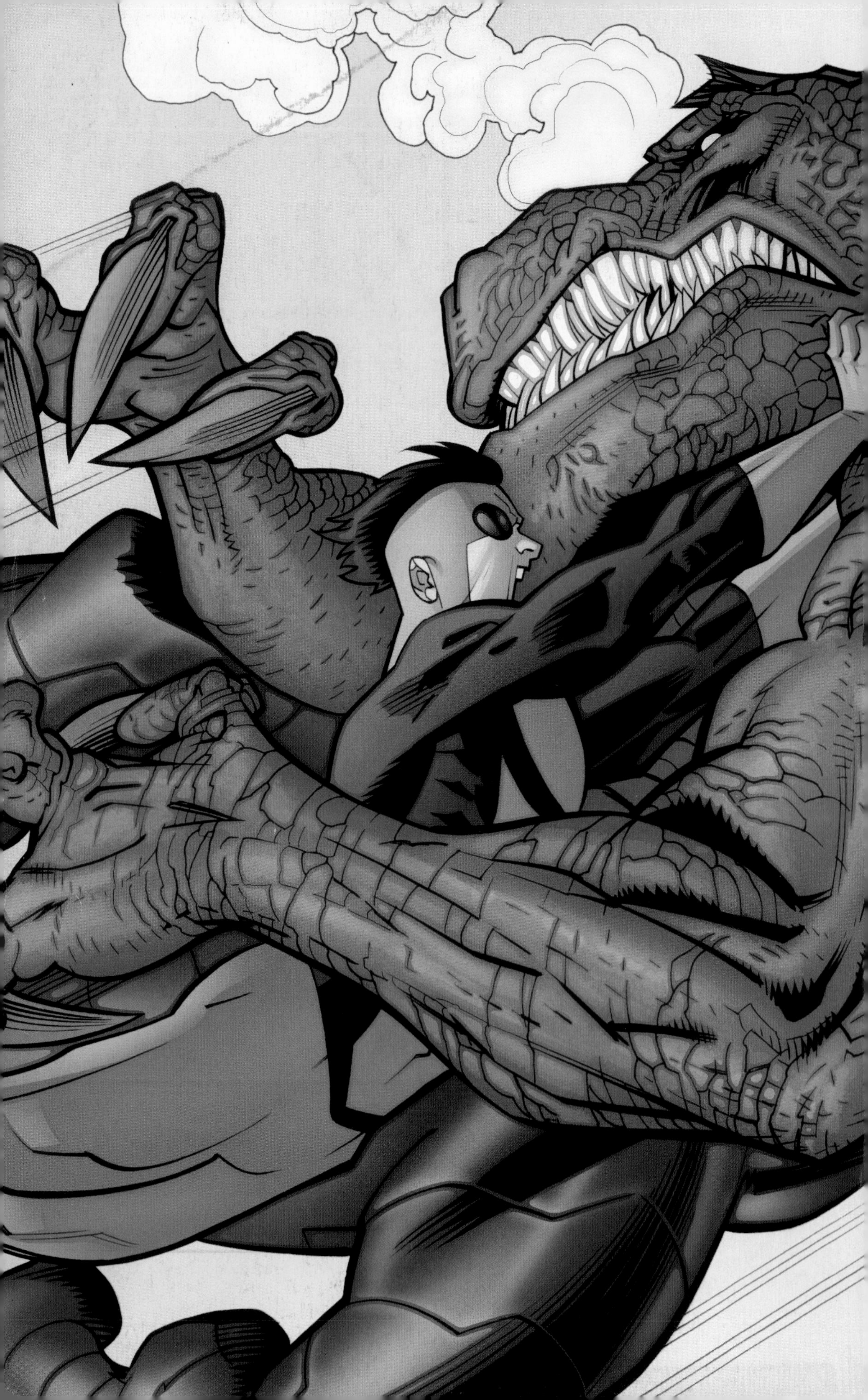

writer
ROBERT KIRKMAN

penciler
RYAN OTTLEY

inker
CLIFF RATHBURN

colorist
JOHN RAUCH

letterer
RUS WOOTON

editor
SEAN MACKIEWICZ

cover
RYAN OTTLEY
& JOHN RAUCH

INVINCIBLE, VOL. 18:
THE DEATH OF EVERYONE
ISBN: 978-1-60706-662-0
First Printing

Published by Image Comics, Inc. Office of
publication: 2001 Center Street, 6th Floor,
Berkeley, California 94704. Image and its
logos are ® and © 2013 Image Comics,
Inc. All rights reserved. Originally published
in single magazine form as INVINCIBLE
#97-102. INVINCIBLE and all character
likenesses are ™ and © 2013, Robert
Kirkman, LLC and Cory Walker. All rights
reserved. All names, characters, events
and locales in this publication are entirely
fictional. Any resemblance to actual persons
(living or dead), events or places, without
satiric intent, is coincidental. No part of
this publication may be reproduced or
transmitted, in any form or by any means
(except for short excerpts for review
purposes) without the express written
permission of the copyright holder.

PRINTED IN U.S.A.

For information regarding the CPSIA on this
printed material call: 203-595-3636 and
provide reference # RICH – 504714.

SKYBOUND ENTERTAINMENT
www.skybound.com

Robert Kirkman - CEO
J.J. Didde - President
Sean Mackiewicz - Editorial Director
Shawn Kirkham - Director of Business Development
Helen Leigh - Office Manager
Brian Huntington - Online Editorial Director
Feldman Public Relations LA - Public Relations

For international rights inquiries, please contact: foreign@skybound.com

IMAGE COMICS, INC.
www.imagecomics.com

Robert Kirkman - Chief Operating Officer
Erik Larsen - Chief Financial Officer
Todd McFarlane - President
Marc Silvestri - CEO
Jim Valentino - Vice-President

Eric Stephenson - Publisher
Ron Richards - Director of Business Development
Jennifer de Guzman - PR & Marketing Director
Branwyn Bigglestone - Accounts Manager
Emily Miller - Accounting Assistant
Jamie Parreno - Marketing Assistant
Emilio Bautista - Sales Assistant
Susie Giroux - Administrative Assistant
Kevin Yuen - Digital Rights Coordinator
Tyler Shainline - Events Coordinator
David Brothers - Content Manager
Jonathan Chan - Production Manager
Drew Gill - Art Director
Jana Cook - Print Manager
Monica Garcia - Senior Production Artist
Vincent Kukua - Production Artist
Jenna Savage - Production Artist

image

CHAPTER ONE

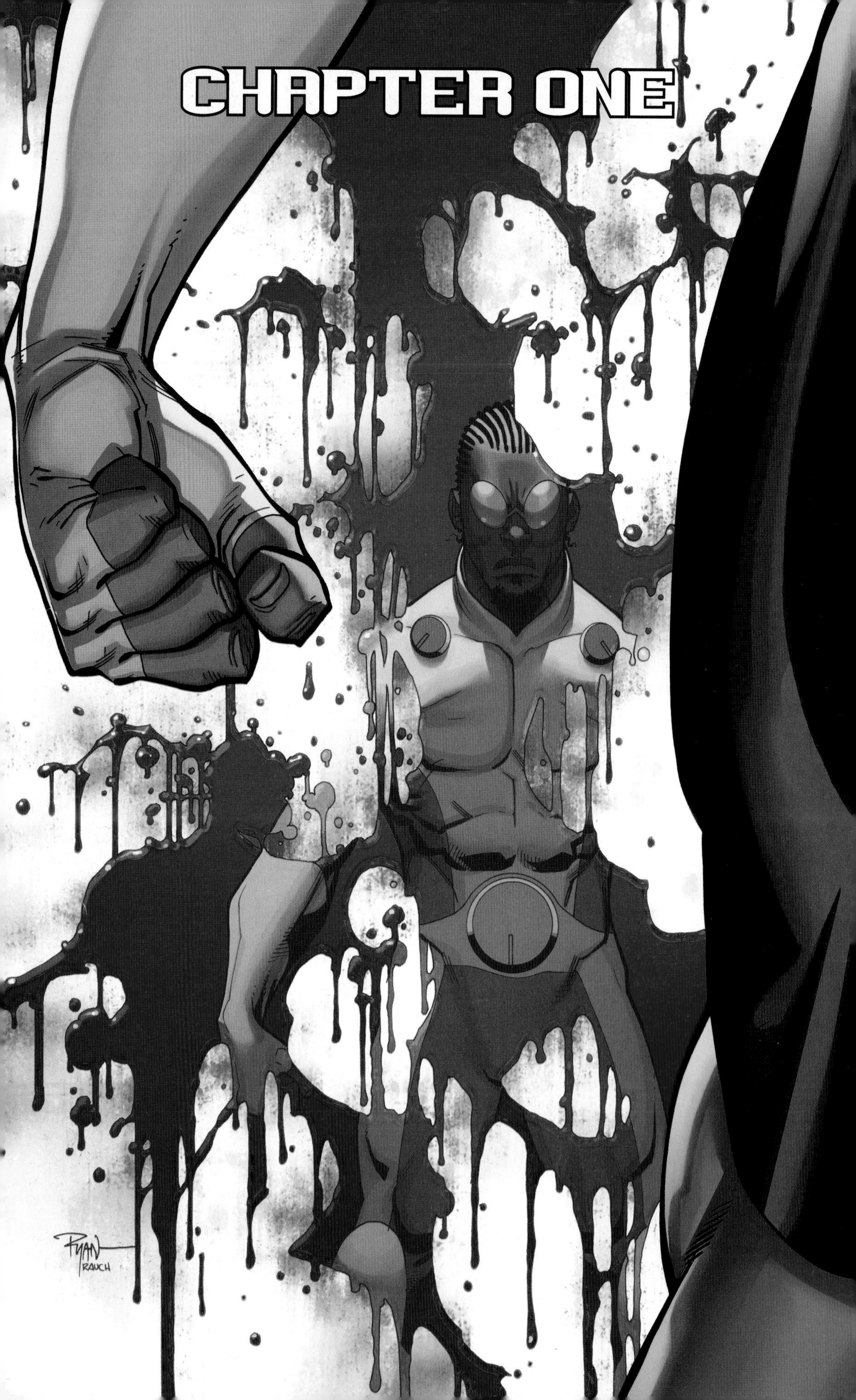
RYAN
RAUCH

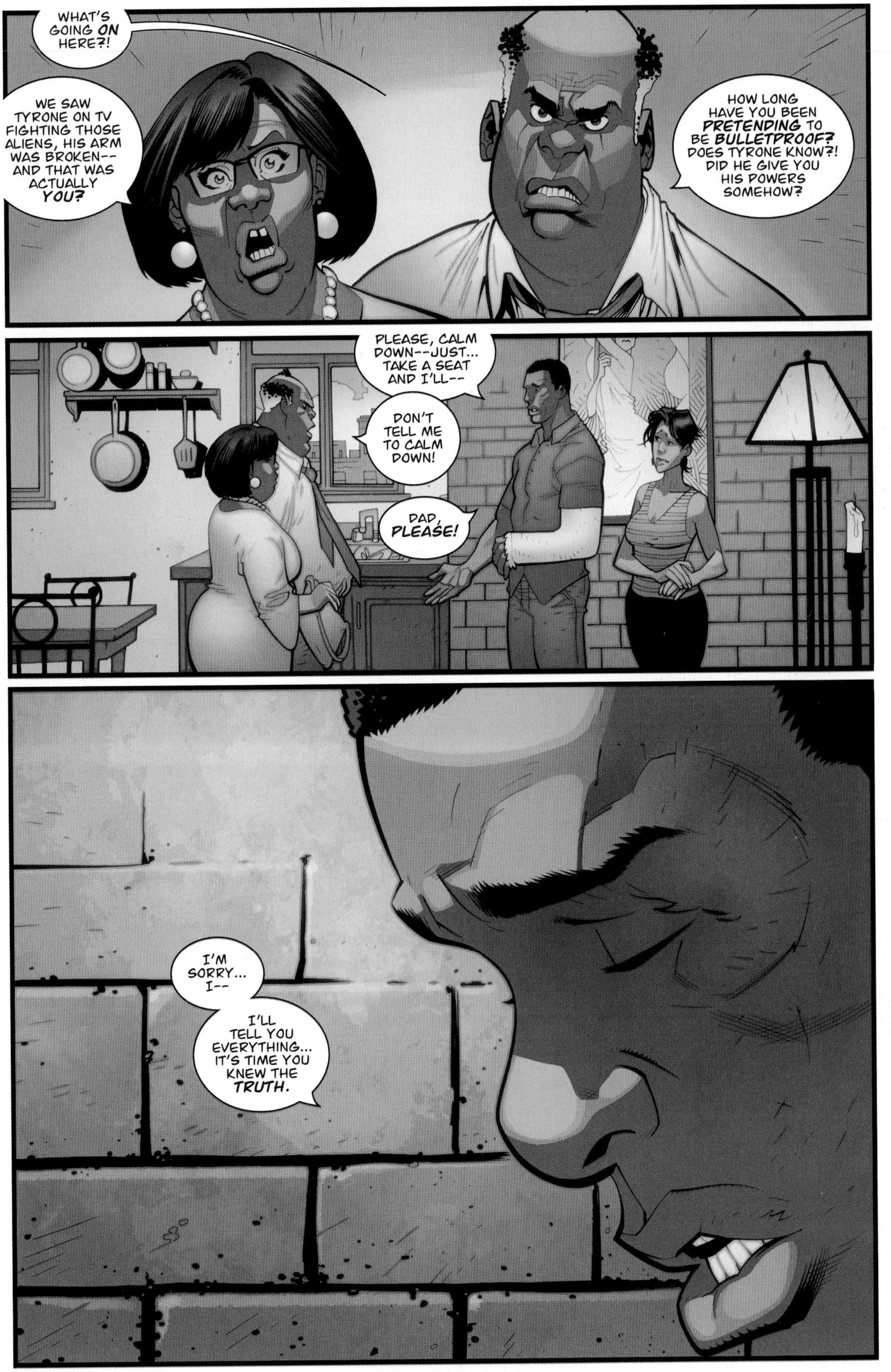
WHAT'S GOING ON HERE?!
WE SAW TYRONE ON TV FIGHTING THOSE ALIENS, HIS ARM WAS BROKEN-- AND THAT WAS ACTUALLY YOU?
HOW LONG HAVE YOU BEEN PRETENDING TO BE BULLETPROOF? DOES TYRONE KNOW?! DID HE GIVE YOU HIS POWERS SOMEHOW?
PLEASE, CALM DOWN--JUST... TAKE A SEAT AND I'LL--
DON'T TELL ME TO CALM DOWN!
DAD, PLEASE!
I'M SORRY... I--
I'LL TELL YOU EVERYTHING... IT'S TIME YOU KNEW THE TRUTH.

YOU GUYS HAVE NO IDEA HOW HARD IT WAS... GROWING UP IN TYRONE'S SHADOW.

HE WAS *BRILLIANT*... ALWAYS WAS. I DON'T DENY THAT.

WE WERE DIFFERENT PEOPLE, HE AND I. TWINS, YES... BUT *VASTLY* DIFFERENT.

HE USED TO SAY HE WAS THE *BUILDER* AND I WAS THE *DECORATOR*... BUT I DON'T THINK HE MEANT IT TO SOUND SO CONDESCENDING.

AT COLLEGE, WE SORT OF LOST TOUCH. TYRONE WAS OFF DOING HIS OWN THING.

HE GRADUATED EARLY... BECAME A WORLD-RENOWNED AND WELL-RESPECTED SCIENTIST.

AND I WAS DOING MY OWN THING.

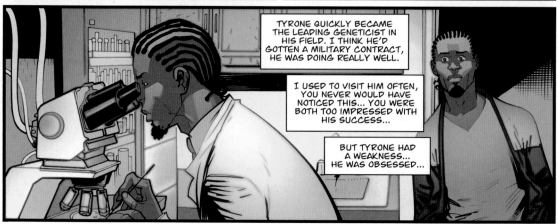

TYRONE QUICKLY BECAME THE LEADING GENETICIST IN HIS FIELD. I THINK HE'D GOTTEN A MILITARY CONTRACT, HE WAS DOING REALLY WELL.

I USED TO VISIT HIM OFTEN, YOU NEVER WOULD HAVE NOTICED THIS... YOU WERE BOTH TOO IMPRESSED WITH HIS SUCCESS...

BUT TYRONE HAD A WEAKNESS... HE WAS OBSESSED...

...WITH **SUPER POWERS.**

HE WAS SPENDING EVERY WAKING MOMENT STUDYING SUPER HEROES AND VILLAINS, TRYING TO DETERMINE THE SOURCE OF THEIR POWERS, SO THAT HE COULD **RECREATE** THEM.

I NEVER REALIZED HOW OBSESSED HE'D BECOME, HOW FAR HE WAS WILLING TO GO, OR HOW MUCH HE ALLOWED HIS QUEST TO CHANGE HIM.

UNTIL ONE NIGHT WHEN WE WERE HAVING DINNER TOGETHER AT HIS HOUSE... ALL HE COULD TALK ABOUT WAS HOW CLOSE HE'D GOTTEN.

THE LAST THING I REMEMBER FROM THAT NIGHT WAS HIM TELLING ME I WAS A BIG PART OF HIS PLAN...

...AND THEN FEELING A LITTLE WOOZY.

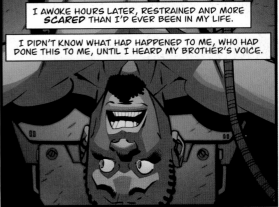

I AWOKE HOURS LATER, RESTRAINED AND MORE **SCARED** THAN I'D EVER BEEN IN MY LIFE.

I DIDN'T KNOW WHAT HAD HAPPENED TO ME, WHO HAD DONE THIS TO ME, UNTIL I HEARD MY BROTHER'S VOICE.

HE SAID I'D NEVER REALLY DONE MUCH WITH MYSELF, AND THAT MY SACRIFICE WOULD BE A NOBLE ONE. HE REMARKED THAT IT WAS ALMOST AS IF I WAS **BORN** FOR THIS PURPOSE...

...THAT HE'D BEEN PROVIDED A PERFECT GENETIC DOUBLE TO TEST HIS PROCESS ON.

HE'D COME UP WITH A WAY TO GET POWERS... AND I WAS HIS GUINEA PIG.

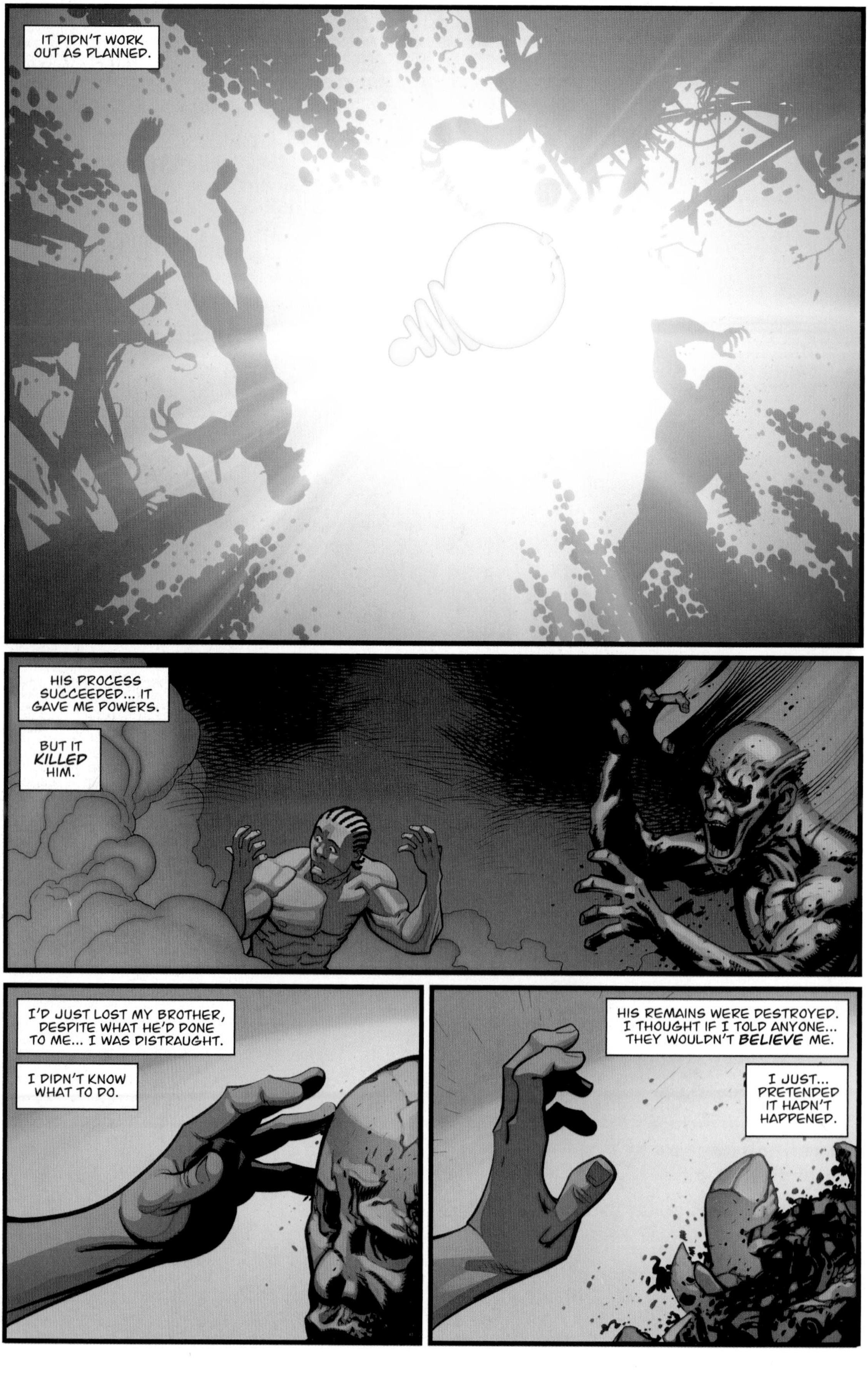
IT DIDN'T WORK OUT AS PLANNED.
HIS PROCESS SUCCEEDED... IT GAVE ME POWERS.
BUT IT KILLED HIM.
I'D JUST LOST MY BROTHER, DESPITE WHAT HE'D DONE TO ME... I WAS DISTRAUGHT.
I DIDN'T KNOW WHAT TO DO.
HIS REMAINS WERE DESTROYED. I THOUGHT IF I TOLD ANYONE... THEY WOULDN'T BELIEVE ME.
I JUST... PRETENDED IT HADN'T HAPPENED.

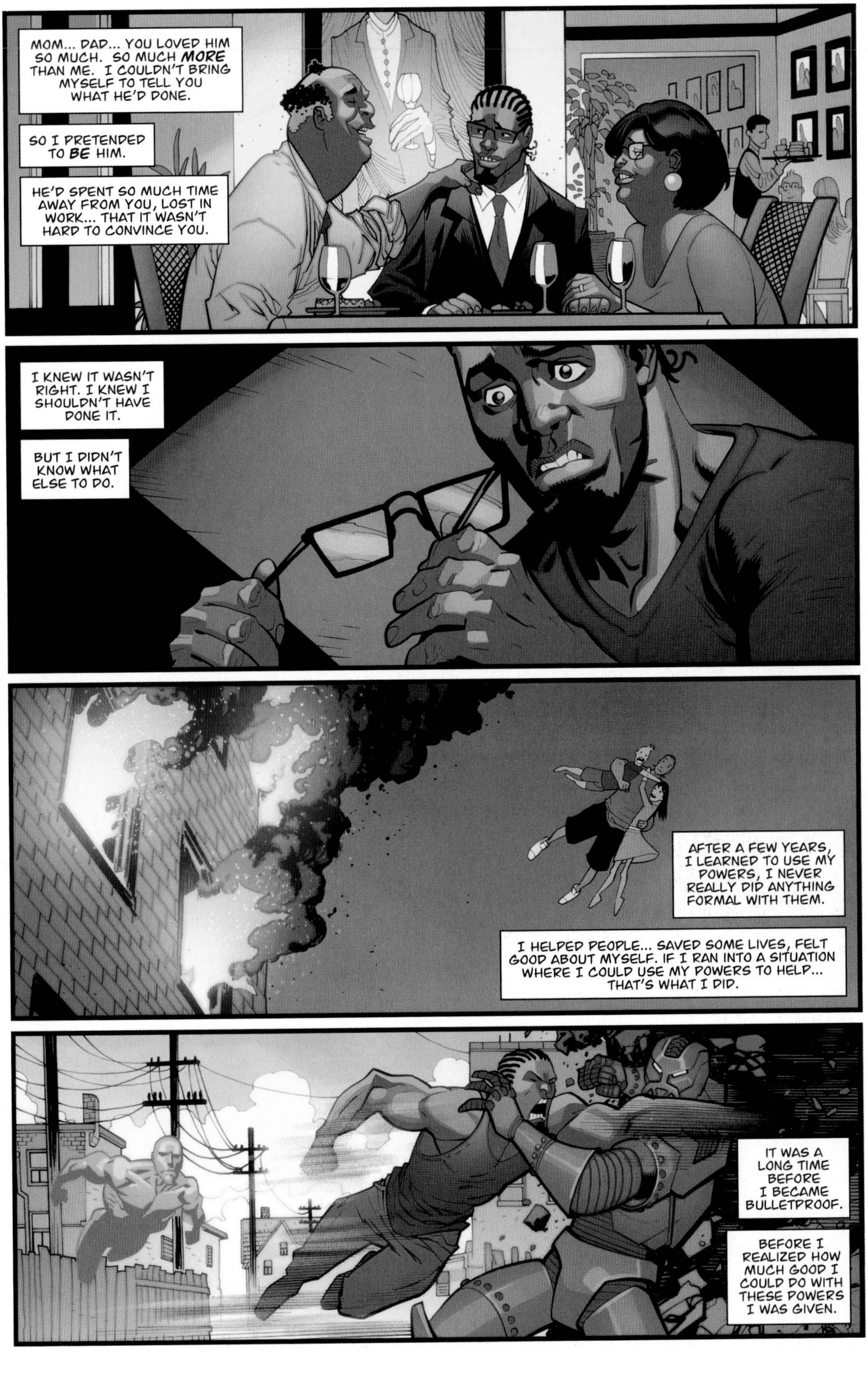
MOM... DAD... YOU LOVED HIM SO MUCH. SO MUCH MORE THAN ME. I COULDN'T BRING MYSELF TO TELL YOU WHAT HE'D DONE.
SO I PRETENDED TO BE HIM.
HE'D SPENT SO MUCH TIME AWAY FROM YOU, LOST IN WORK... THAT IT WASN'T HARD TO CONVINCE YOU.
I KNEW IT WASN'T RIGHT. I KNEW I SHOULDN'T HAVE DONE IT.
BUT I DIDN'T KNOW WHAT ELSE TO DO.
AFTER A FEW YEARS, I LEARNED TO USE MY POWERS, I NEVER REALLY DID ANYTHING FORMAL WITH THEM.
I HELPED PEOPLE... SAVED SOME LIVES, FELT GOOD ABOUT MYSELF. IF I RAN INTO A SITUATION WHERE I COULD USE MY POWERS TO HELP... THAT'S WHAT I DID.
IT WAS A LONG TIME BEFORE I BECAME BULLETPROOF.
BEFORE I REALIZED HOW MUCH GOOD I COULD DO WITH THESE POWERS I WAS GIVEN.

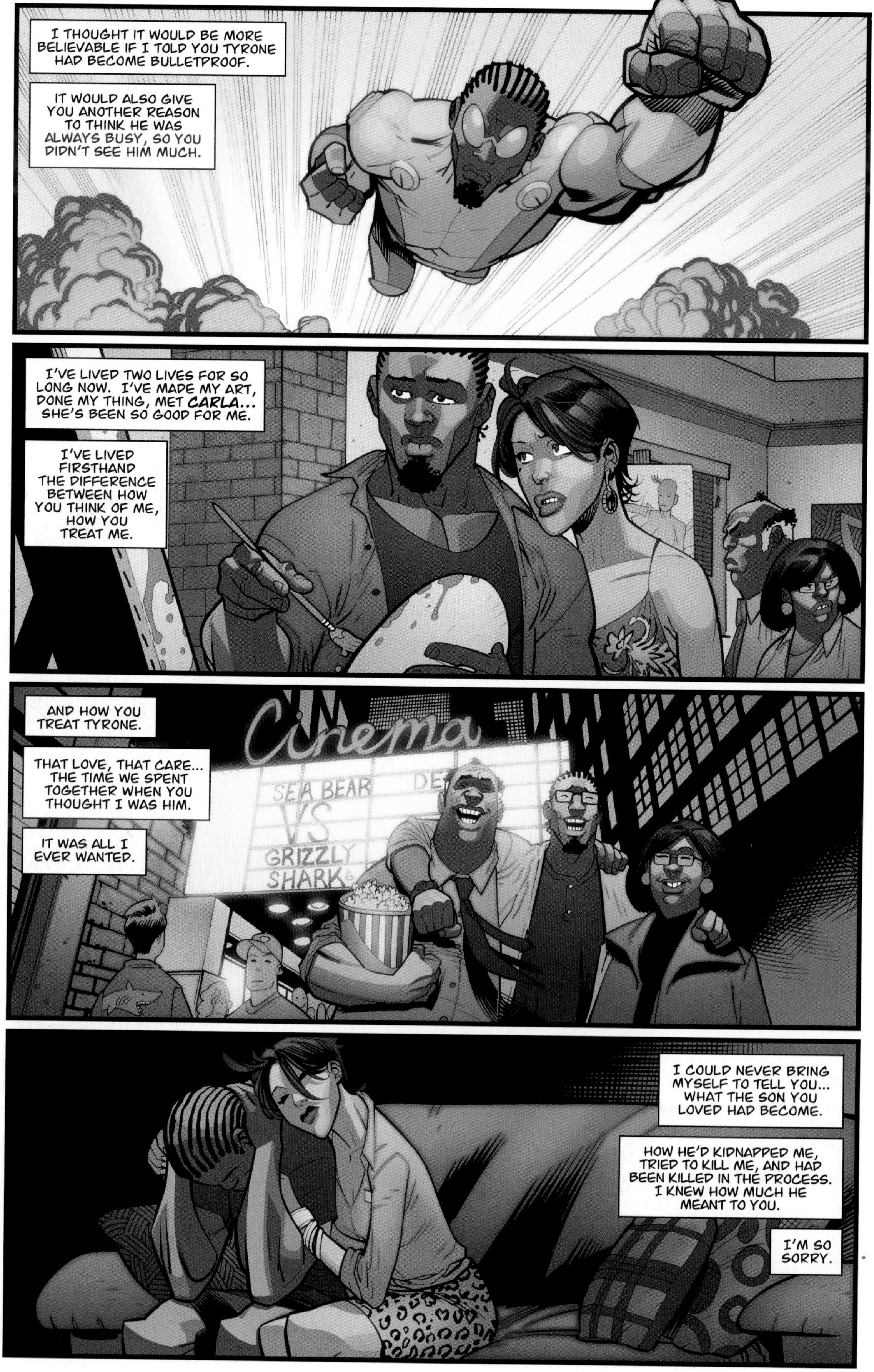
I THOUGHT IT WOULD BE MORE BELIEVABLE IF I TOLD YOU TYRONE HAD BECOME BULLETPROOF.
IT WOULD ALSO GIVE YOU ANOTHER REASON TO THINK HE WAS ALWAYS BUSY, SO YOU DIDN'T SEE HIM MUCH.
I'VE LIVED TWO LIVES FOR SO LONG NOW. I'VE MADE MY ART, DONE MY THING, MET CARLA... SHE'S BEEN SO GOOD FOR ME.
I'VE LIVED FIRSTHAND THE DIFFERENCE BETWEEN HOW YOU THINK OF ME, HOW YOU TREAT ME.
AND HOW YOU TREAT TYRONE.
THAT LOVE, THAT CARE... THE TIME WE SPENT TOGETHER WHEN YOU THOUGHT I WAS HIM.
IT WAS ALL I EVER WANTED.
Cinema
SEA BEAR VS GRIZZLY SHARK
I COULD NEVER BRING MYSELF TO TELL YOU... WHAT THE SON YOU LOVED HAD BECOME.
HOW HE'D KIDNAPPED ME, TRIED TO KILL ME, AND HAD BEEN KILLED IN THE PROCESS. I KNEW HOW MUCH HE MEANT TO YOU.
I'M SO SORRY.

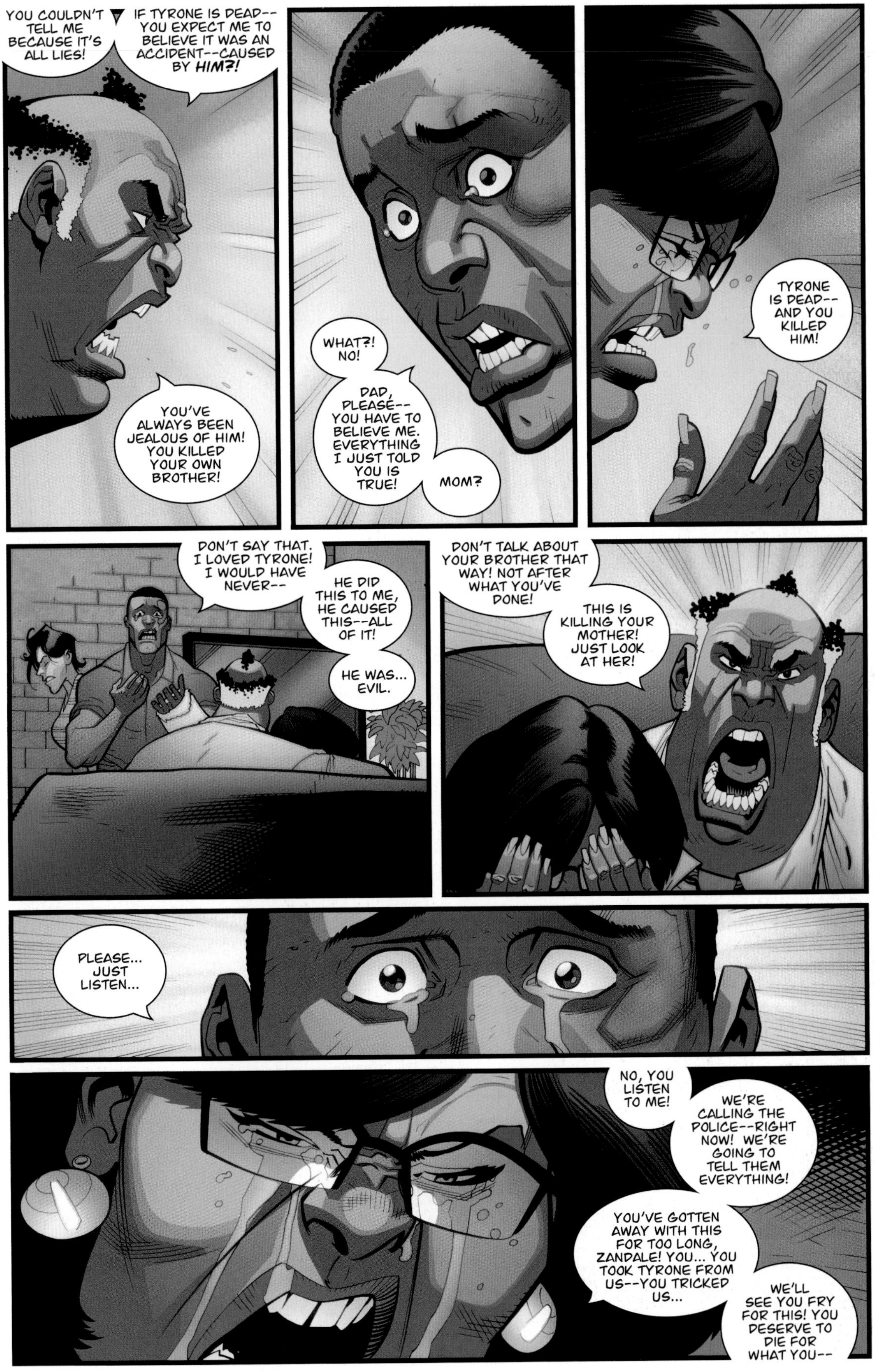
YOU COULDN'T TELL ME BECAUSE IT'S ALL LIES!
IF TYRONE IS DEAD-- YOU EXPECT ME TO BELIEVE IT WAS AN ACCIDENT--CAUSED BY HIM?!
YOU'VE ALWAYS BEEN JEALOUS OF HIM! YOU KILLED YOUR OWN BROTHER!
WHAT?! NO!
DAD, PLEASE-- YOU HAVE TO BELIEVE ME. EVERYTHING I JUST TOLD YOU IS TRUE!
MOM?
TYRONE IS DEAD-- AND YOU KILLED HIM!
DON'T SAY THAT. I LOVED TYRONE! I WOULD HAVE NEVER--
HE DID THIS TO ME, HE CAUSED THIS--ALL OF IT!
HE WAS... EVIL.
DON'T TALK ABOUT YOUR BROTHER THAT WAY! NOT AFTER WHAT YOU'VE DONE!
THIS IS KILLING YOUR MOTHER! JUST LOOK AT HER!
PLEASE... JUST LISTEN...
NO, YOU LISTEN TO ME!
WE'RE CALLING THE POLICE--RIGHT NOW! WE'RE GOING TO TELL THEM EVERYTHING!
YOU'VE GOTTEN AWAY WITH THIS FOR TOO LONG, ZANDALE! YOU... YOU TOOK TYRONE FROM US--YOU TRICKED US...
WE'LL SEE YOU FRY FOR THIS! YOU DESERVE TO DIE FOR WHAT YOU--

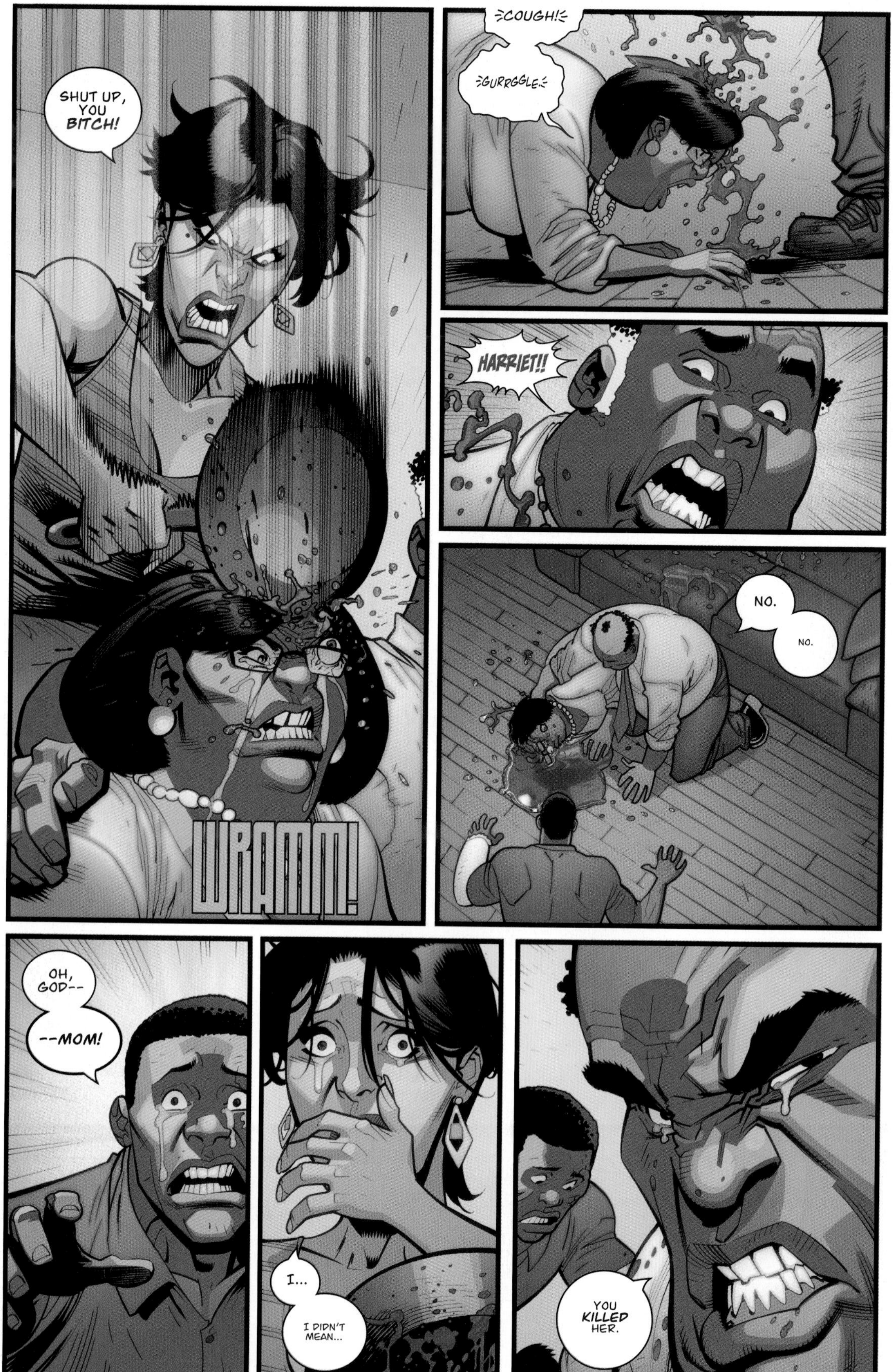
SHUT UP, YOU BITCH!
WRAMM!
COUGH!
GURRGGLE
HARRIET!!
NO.
NO.
OH, GOD--
--MOM!
I...
I DIDN'T MEAN...
YOU KILLED HER.

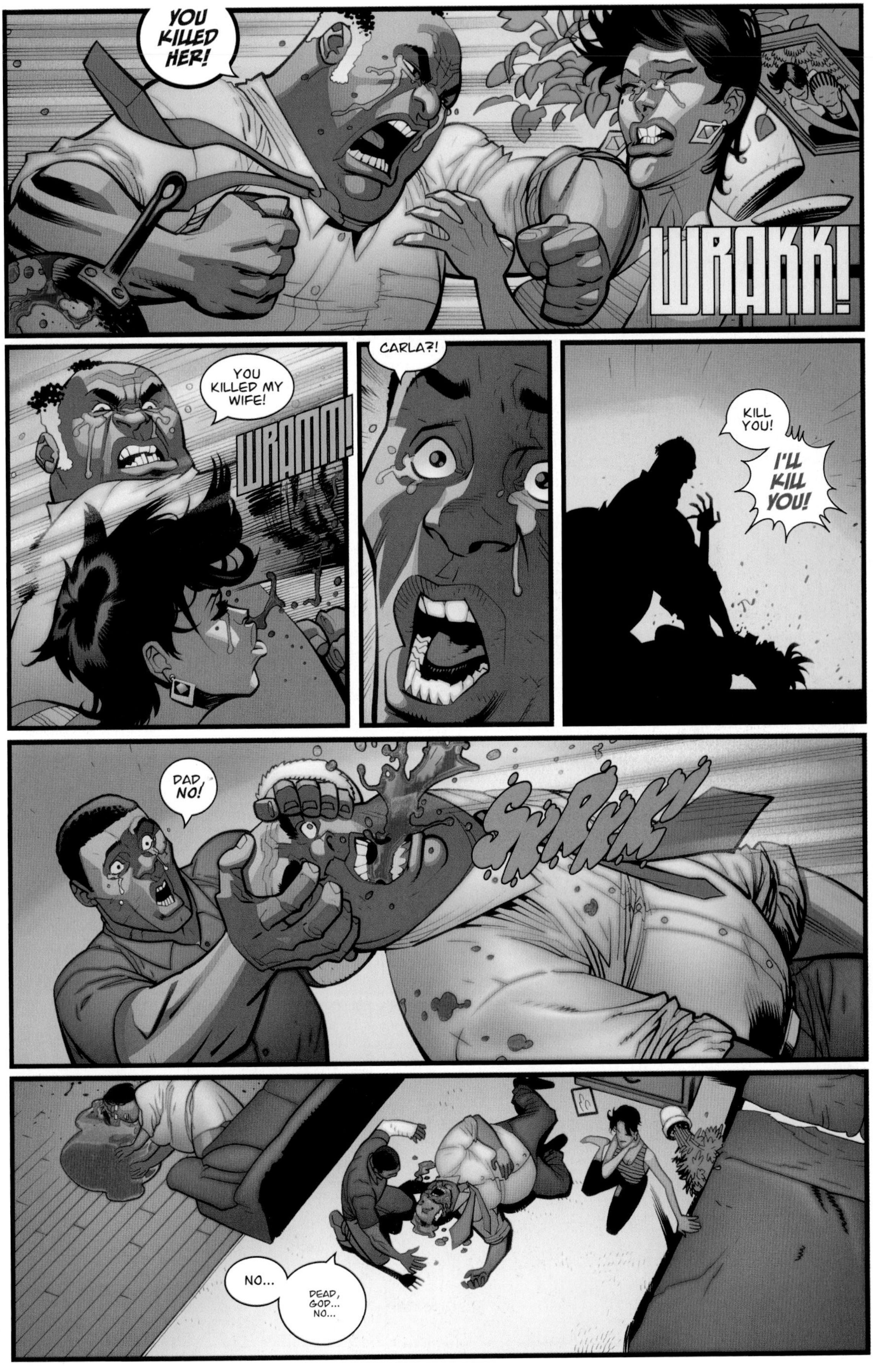
YOU KILLED HER!
WRAKK!
YOU KILLED MY WIFE!
WRAMM!
CARLA?!
KILL YOU!
I'LL KILL YOU!
DAD, NO!
NO...
DEAD, GOD... NO...

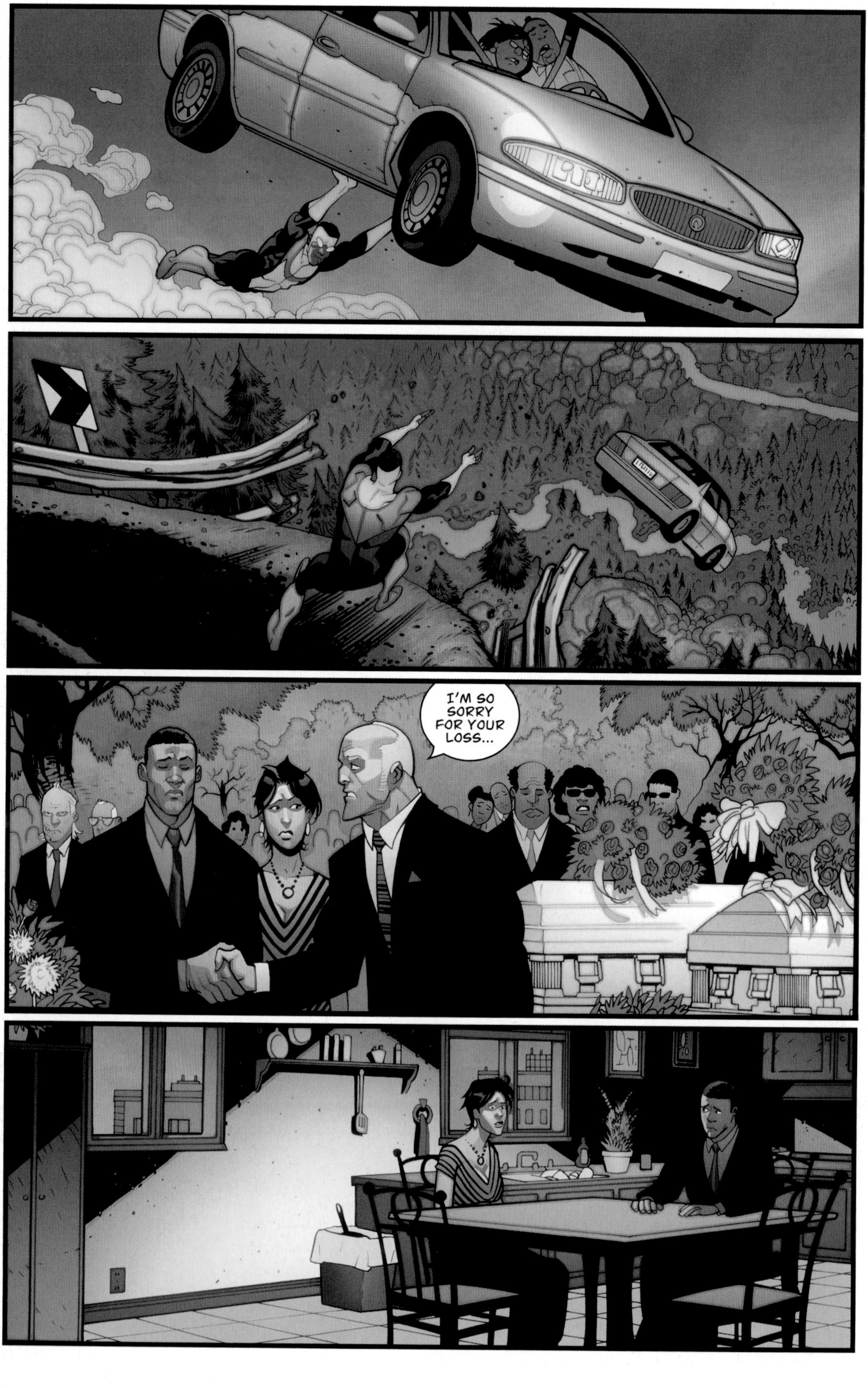
I'M SO SORRY FOR YOUR LOSS...

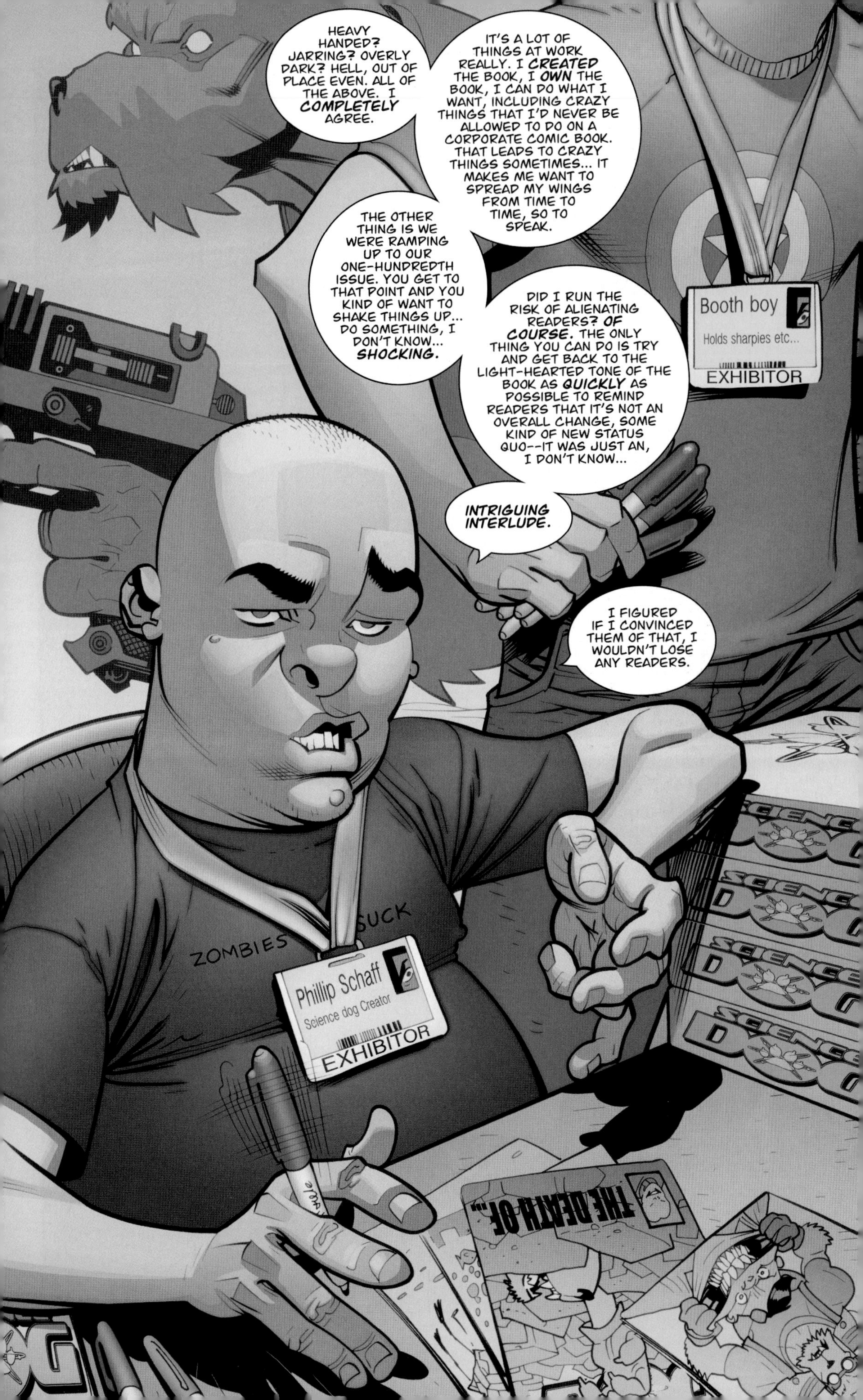
HEAVY HANDED? JARRING? OVERLY DARK? HELL, OUT OF PLACE EVEN. ALL OF THE ABOVE. I COMPLETELY AGREE.
IT'S A LOT OF THINGS AT WORK REALLY. I CREATED THE BOOK, I OWN THE BOOK, I CAN DO WHAT I WANT, INCLUDING CRAZY THINGS THAT I'D NEVER BE ALLOWED TO DO ON A CORPORATE COMIC BOOK. THAT LEADS TO CRAZY THINGS SOMETIMES... IT MAKES ME WANT TO SPREAD MY WINGS FROM TIME TO TIME, SO TO SPEAK.
THE OTHER THING IS WE WERE RAMPING UP TO OUR ONE-HUNDREDTH ISSUE. YOU GET TO THAT POINT AND YOU KIND OF WANT TO SHAKE THINGS UP... DO SOMETHING, I DON'T KNOW... SHOCKING.
DID I RUN THE RISK OF ALIENATING READERS? OF COURSE. THE ONLY THING YOU CAN DO IS TRY AND GET BACK TO THE LIGHT-HEARTED TONE OF THE BOOK AS QUICKLY AS POSSIBLE TO REMIND READERS THAT IT'S NOT AN OVERALL CHANGE, SOME KIND OF NEW STATUS QUO--IT WAS JUST AN, I DON'T KNOW...
INTRIGUING INTERLUDE.
I FIGURED IF I CONVINCED THEM OF THAT, I WOULDN'T LOSE ANY READERS.
Booth boy
Holds sharpies etc...
EXHIBITOR
ZOMBIES SUCK
Phillip Schaff
Science dog Creator
EXHIBITOR
THE DEATH OF...

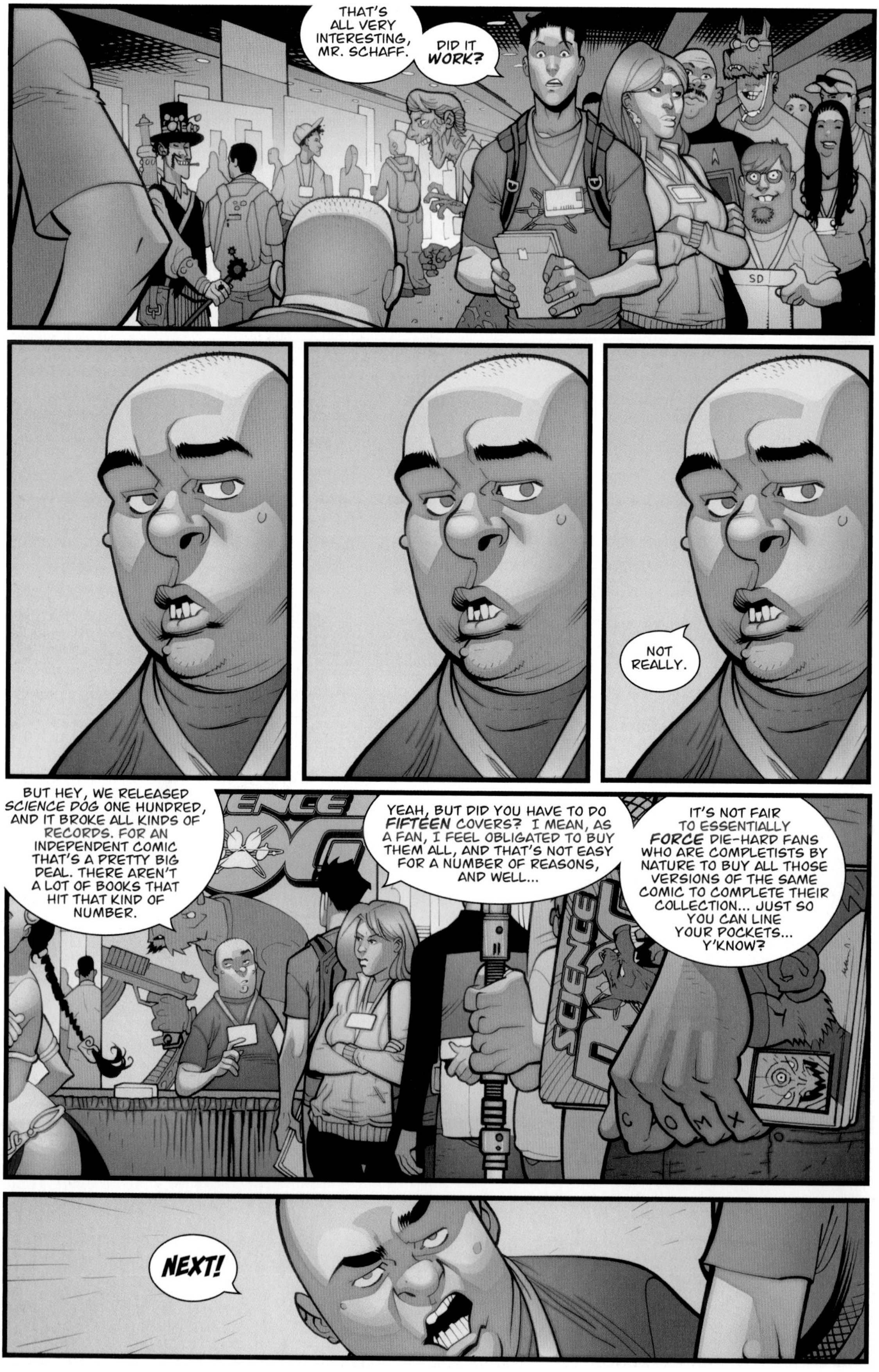
THAT'S ALL VERY INTERESTING, MR. SCHAFF.
DID IT WORK?
SD
NOT REALLY.
BUT HEY, WE RELEASED SCIENCE DOG ONE HUNDRED, AND IT BROKE ALL KINDS OF RECORDS. FOR AN INDEPENDENT COMIC THAT'S A PRETTY BIG DEAL. THERE AREN'T A LOT OF BOOKS THAT HIT THAT KIND OF NUMBER.
YEAH, BUT DID YOU HAVE TO DO FIFTEEN COVERS? I MEAN, AS A FAN, I FEEL OBLIGATED TO BUY THEM ALL, AND THAT'S NOT EASY FOR A NUMBER OF REASONS, AND WELL...
IT'S NOT FAIR TO ESSENTIALLY FORCE DIE-HARD FANS WHO ARE COMPLETISTS BY NATURE TO BUY ALL THOSE VERSIONS OF THE SAME COMIC TO COMPLETE THEIR COLLECTION... JUST SO YOU CAN LINE YOUR POCKETS... Y'KNOW?
NEXT!

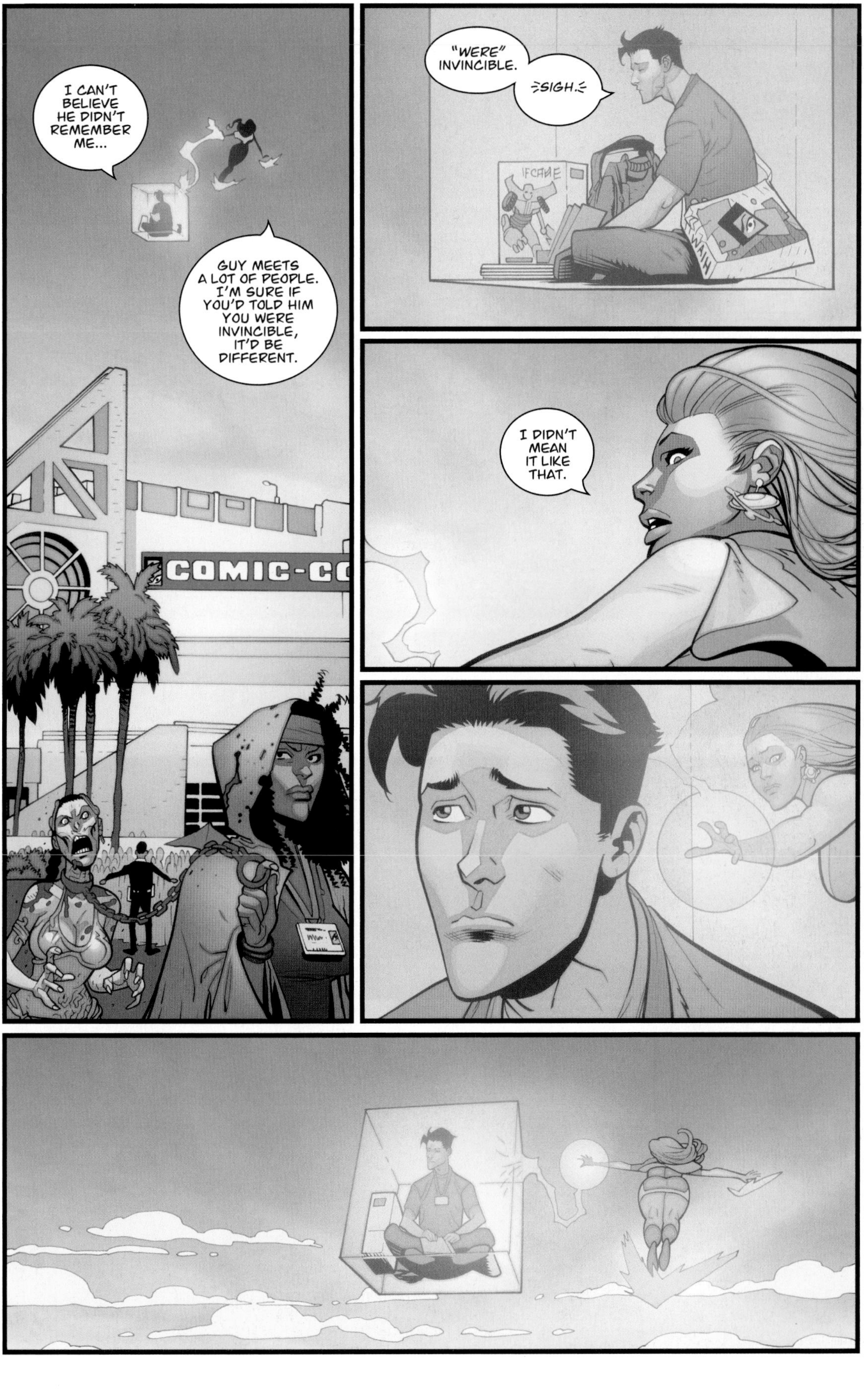

I CAN'T BELIEVE HE DIDN'T REMEMBER ME...
GUY MEETS A LOT OF PEOPLE. I'M SURE IF YOU'D TOLD HIM YOU WERE INVINCIBLE, IT'D BE DIFFERENT.
COMIC-CO
"WERE" INVINCIBLE.
SIGH.
I DIDN'T MEAN IT LIKE THAT.

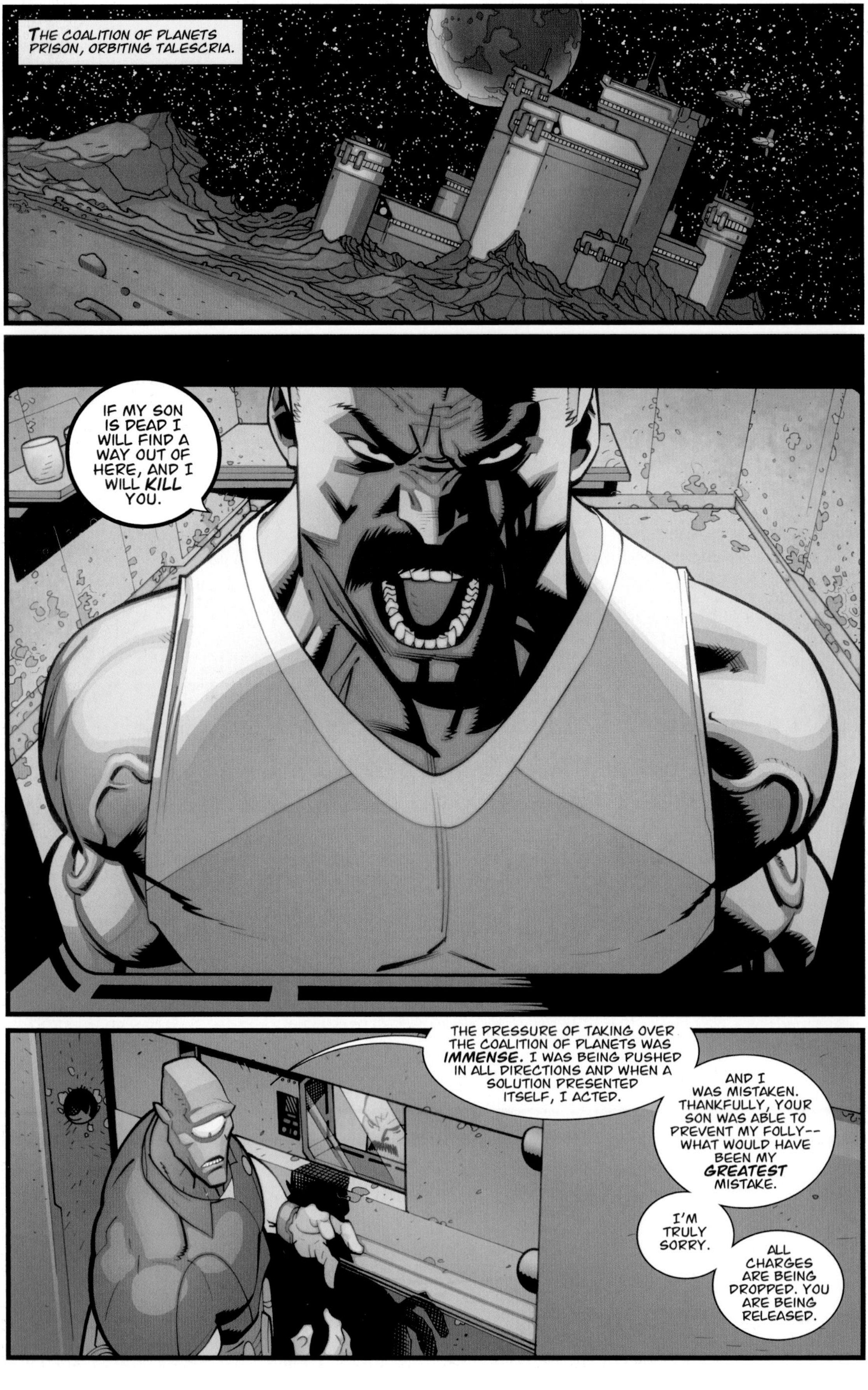
THE COALITION OF PLANETS PRISON, ORBITING TALESCRIA.
IF MY SON IS DEAD I WILL FIND A WAY OUT OF HERE, AND I WILL KILL YOU.
THE PRESSURE OF TAKING OVER THE COALITION OF PLANETS WAS IMMENSE. I WAS BEING PUSHED IN ALL DIRECTIONS AND WHEN A SOLUTION PRESENTED ITSELF, I ACTED.
AND I WAS MISTAKEN. THANKFULLY, YOUR SON WAS ABLE TO PREVENT MY FOLLY-- WHAT WOULD HAVE BEEN MY GREATEST MISTAKE.
I'M TRULY SORRY.
ALL CHARGES ARE BEING DROPPED. YOU ARE BEING RELEASED.

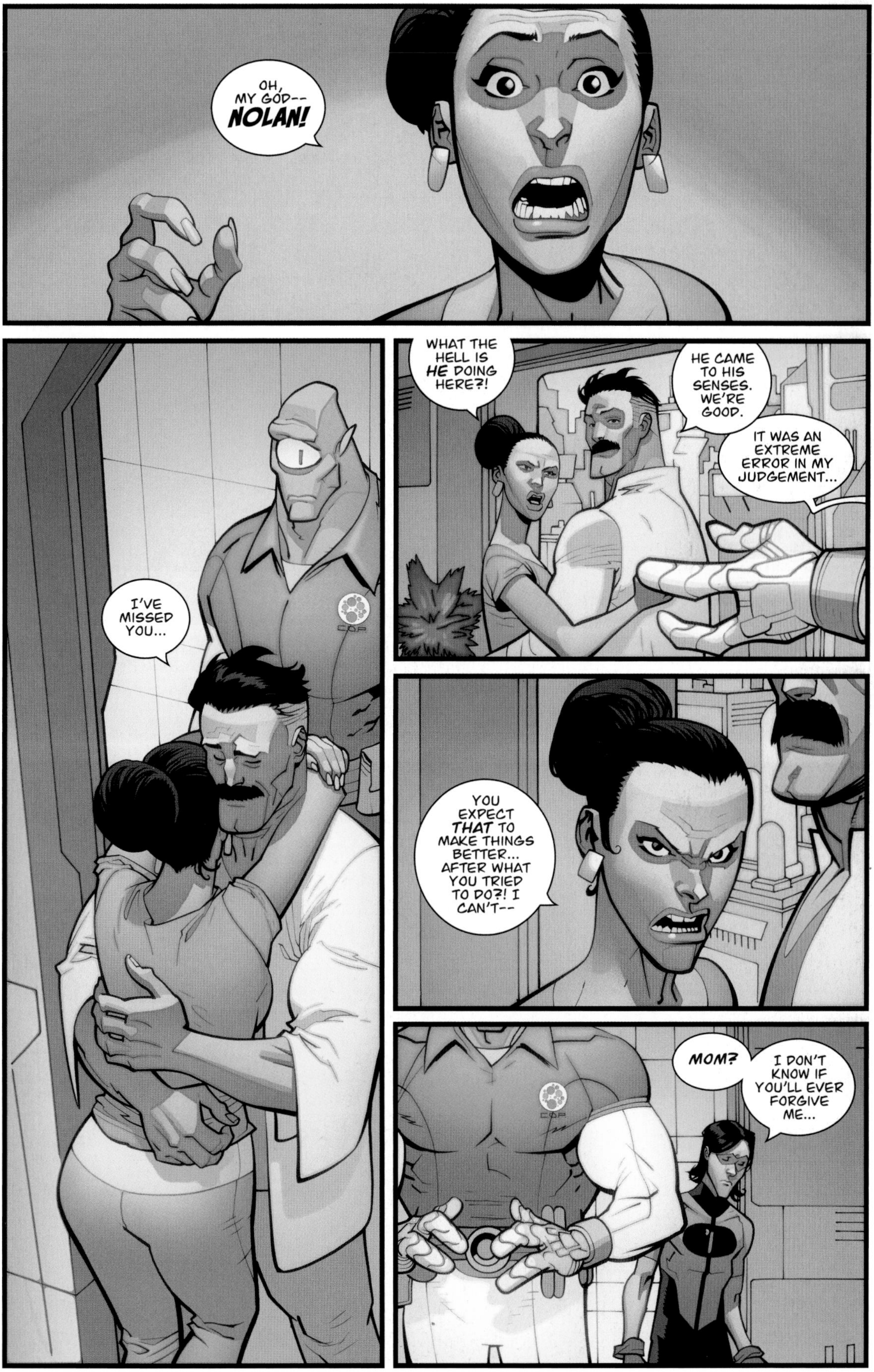
OH, MY GOD-- NOLAN!
I'VE MISSED YOU...
WHAT THE HELL IS HE DOING HERE?!
HE CAME TO HIS SENSES. WE'RE GOOD.
IT WAS AN EXTREME ERROR IN MY JUDGEMENT...
YOU EXPECT THAT TO MAKE THINGS BETTER... AFTER WHAT YOU TRIED TO DO?! I CAN'T--
MOM?
I DON'T KNOW IF YOU'LL EVER FORGIVE ME...
C.O.P.

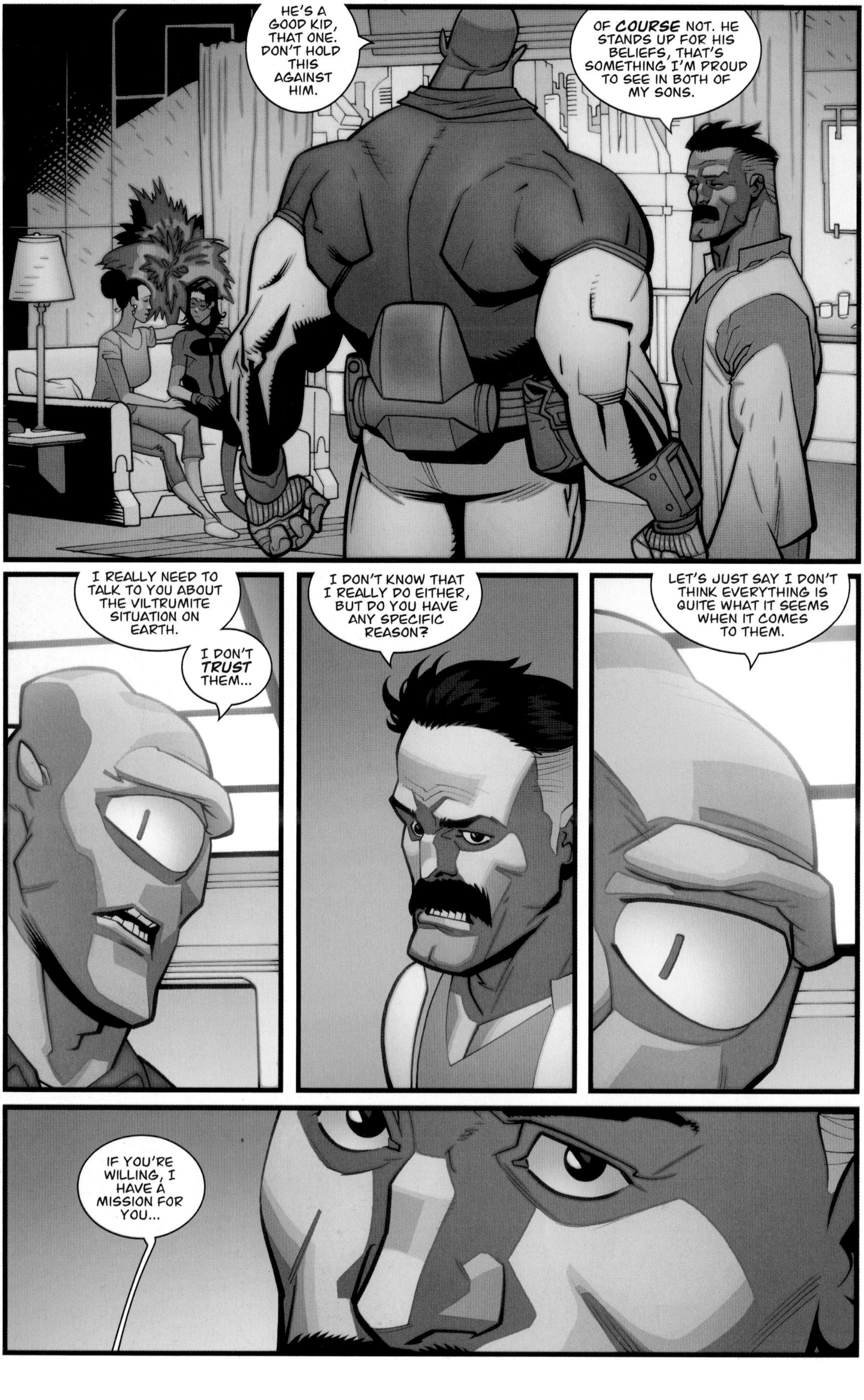
HE'S A GOOD KID, THAT ONE. DON'T HOLD THIS AGAINST HIM.
OF COURSE NOT. HE STANDS UP FOR HIS BELIEFS, THAT'S SOMETHING I'M PROUD TO SEE IN BOTH OF MY SONS.
I REALLY NEED TO TALK TO YOU ABOUT THE VILTRUMITE SITUATION ON EARTH.
I DON'T TRUST THEM...
I DON'T KNOW THAT I REALLY DO EITHER, BUT DO YOU HAVE ANY SPECIFIC REASON?
LET'S JUST SAY I DON'T THINK EVERYTHING IS QUITE WHAT IT SEEMS WHEN IT COMES TO THEM.
IF YOU'RE WILLING, I HAVE A MISSION FOR YOU...

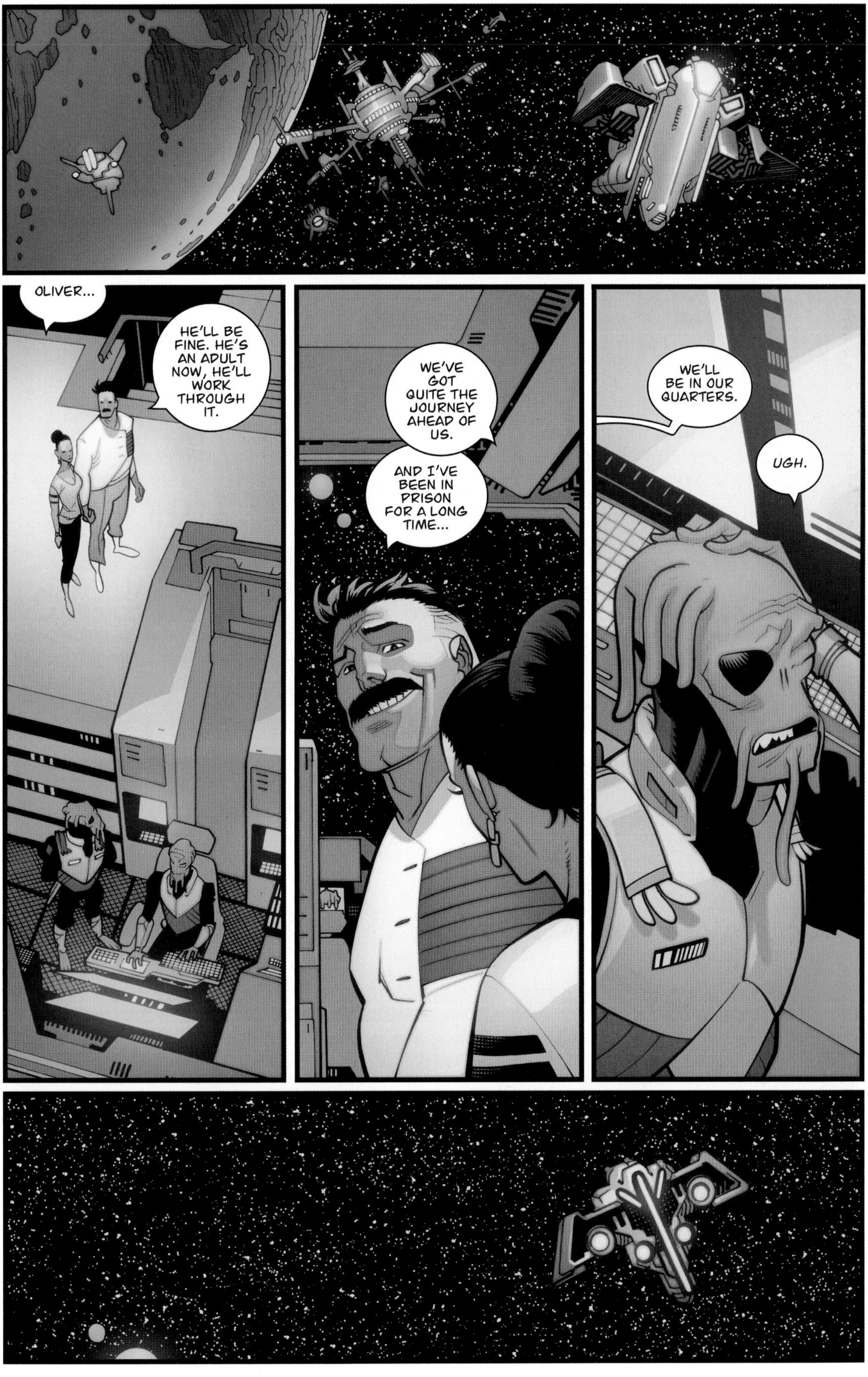
OLIVER...
HE'LL BE FINE. HE'S AN ADULT NOW, HE'LL WORK THROUGH IT.
WE'VE GOT QUITE THE JOURNEY AHEAD OF US.
AND I'VE BEEN IN PRISON FOR A LONG TIME...
WE'LL BE IN OUR QUARTERS.
UGH.

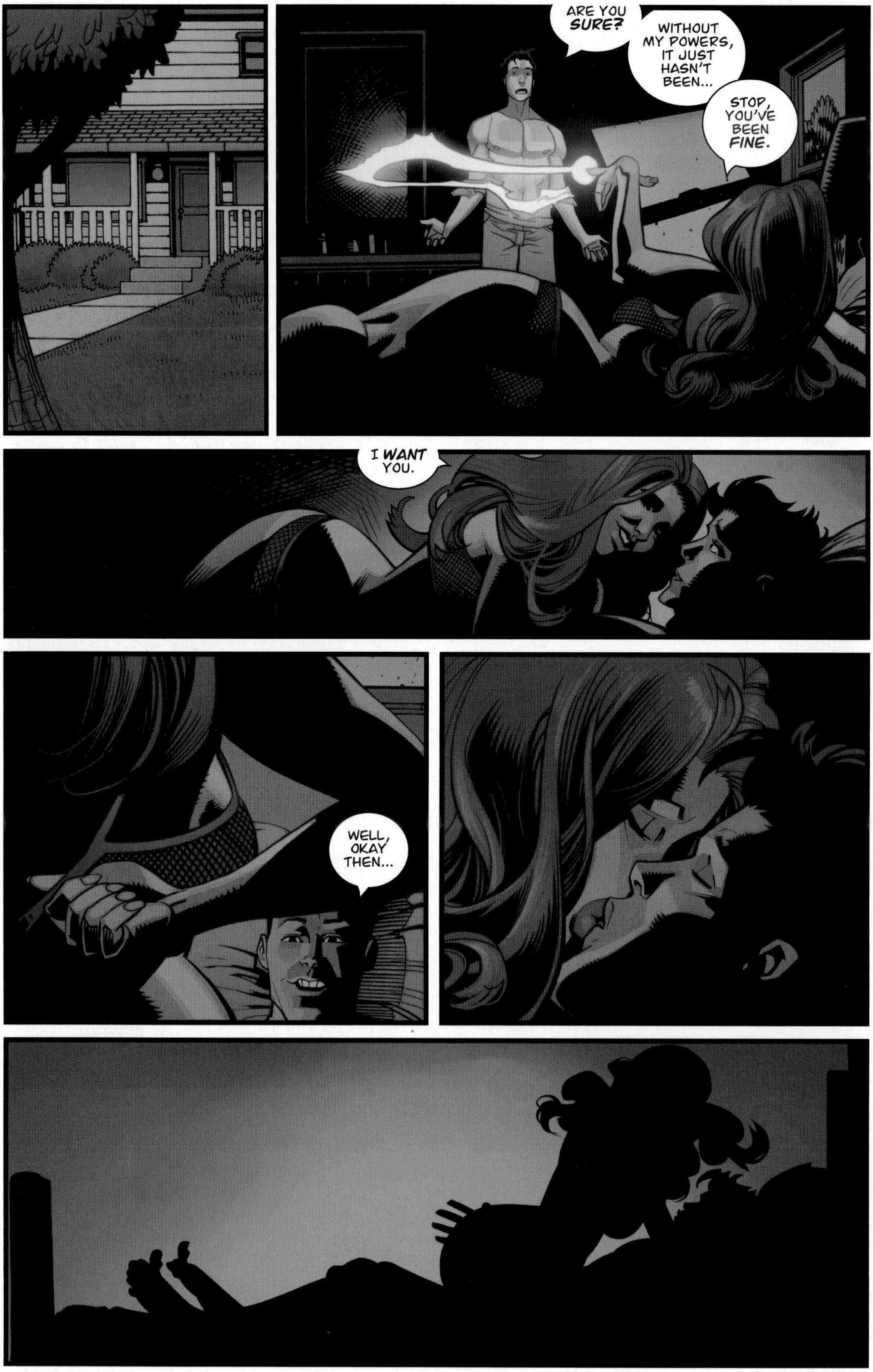
ARE YOU SURE?
WITHOUT MY POWERS, IT JUST HASN'T BEEN...
STOP, YOU'VE BEEN FINE.
I WANT YOU.
WELL, OKAY THEN...

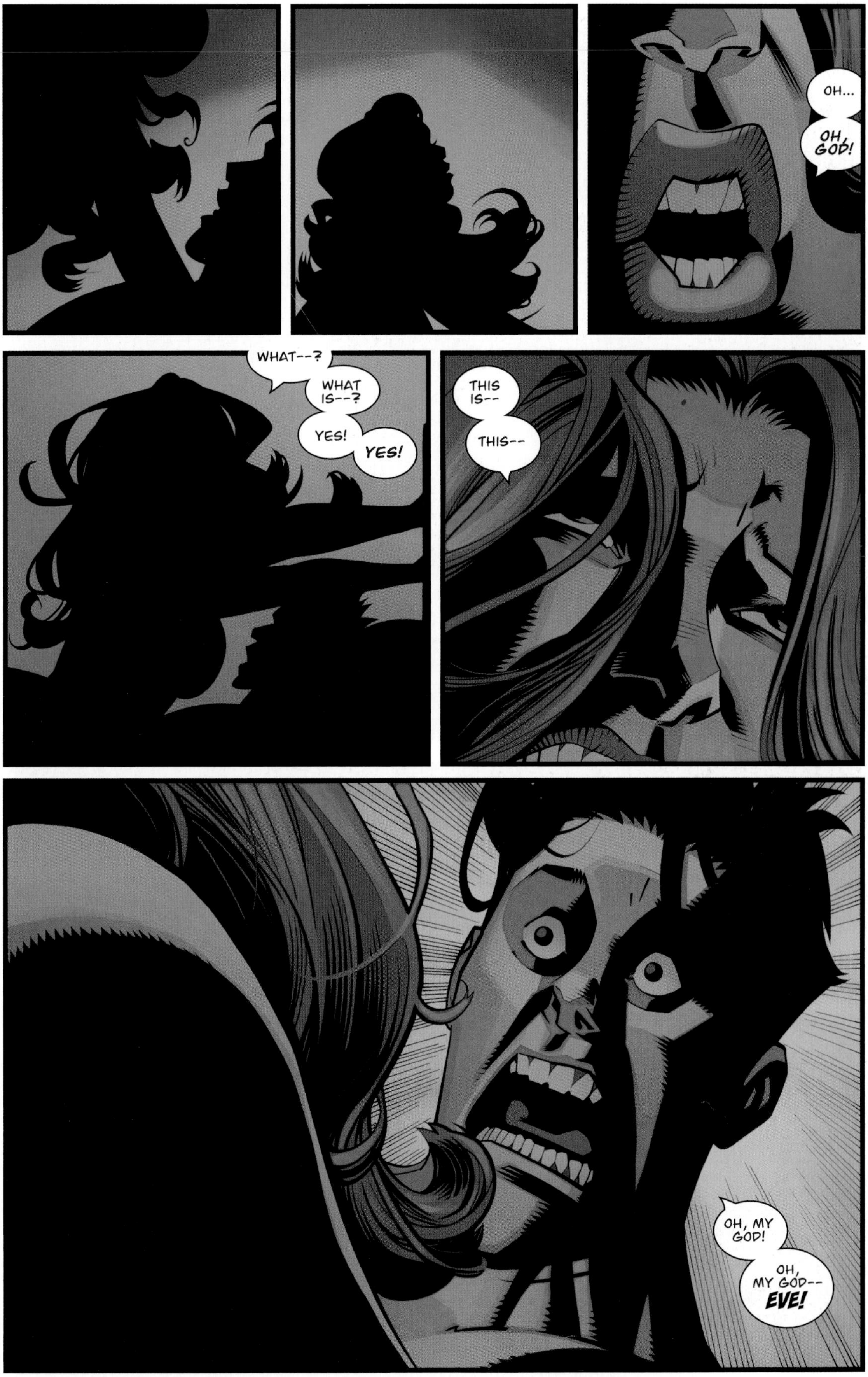
OH...
OH, GOD!
WHAT--?
WHAT IS--?
YES!
YES!
THIS IS--
THIS--
OH, MY GOD!
OH, MY GOD--
EVE!

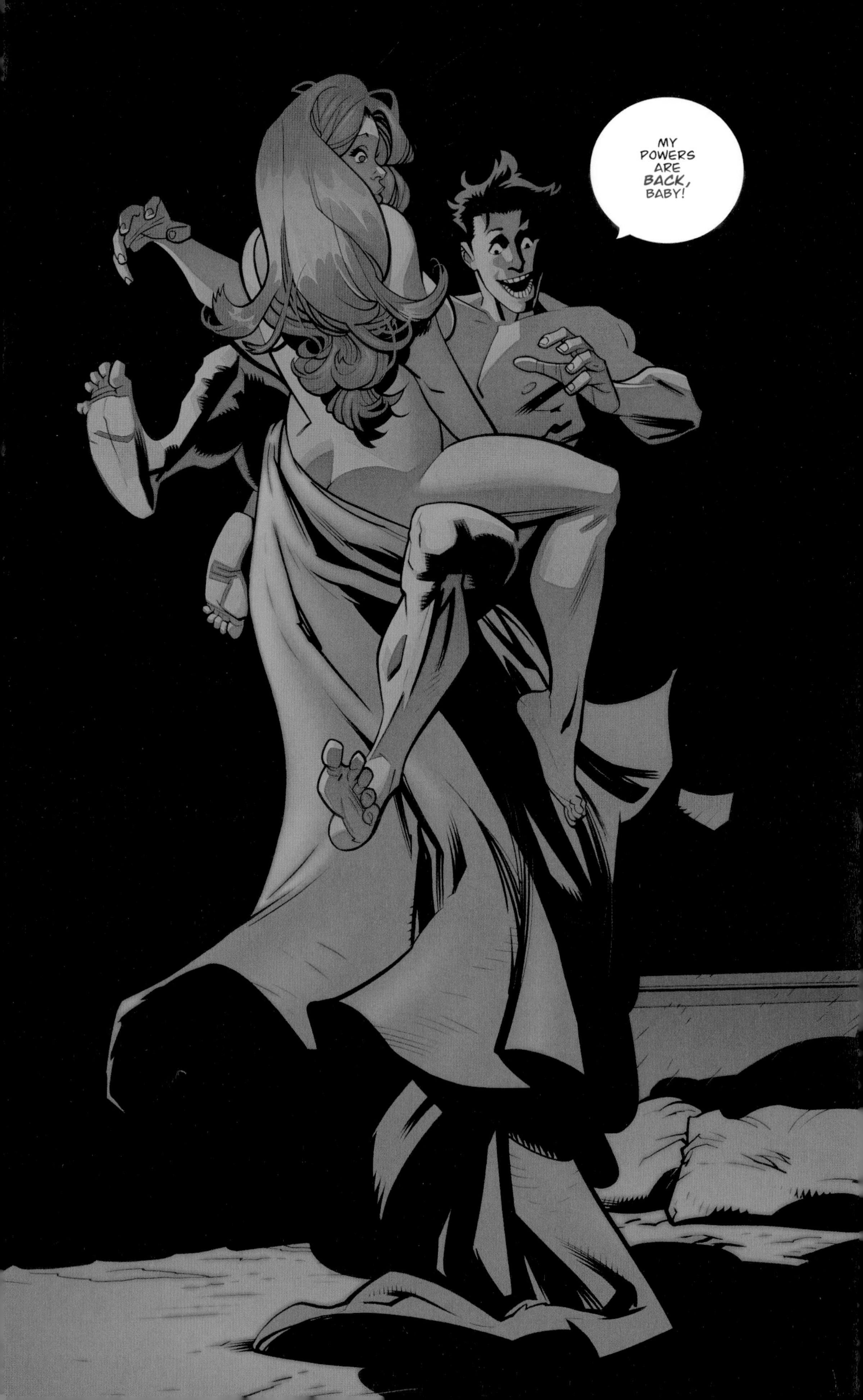
MY POWERS ARE BACK, BABY!

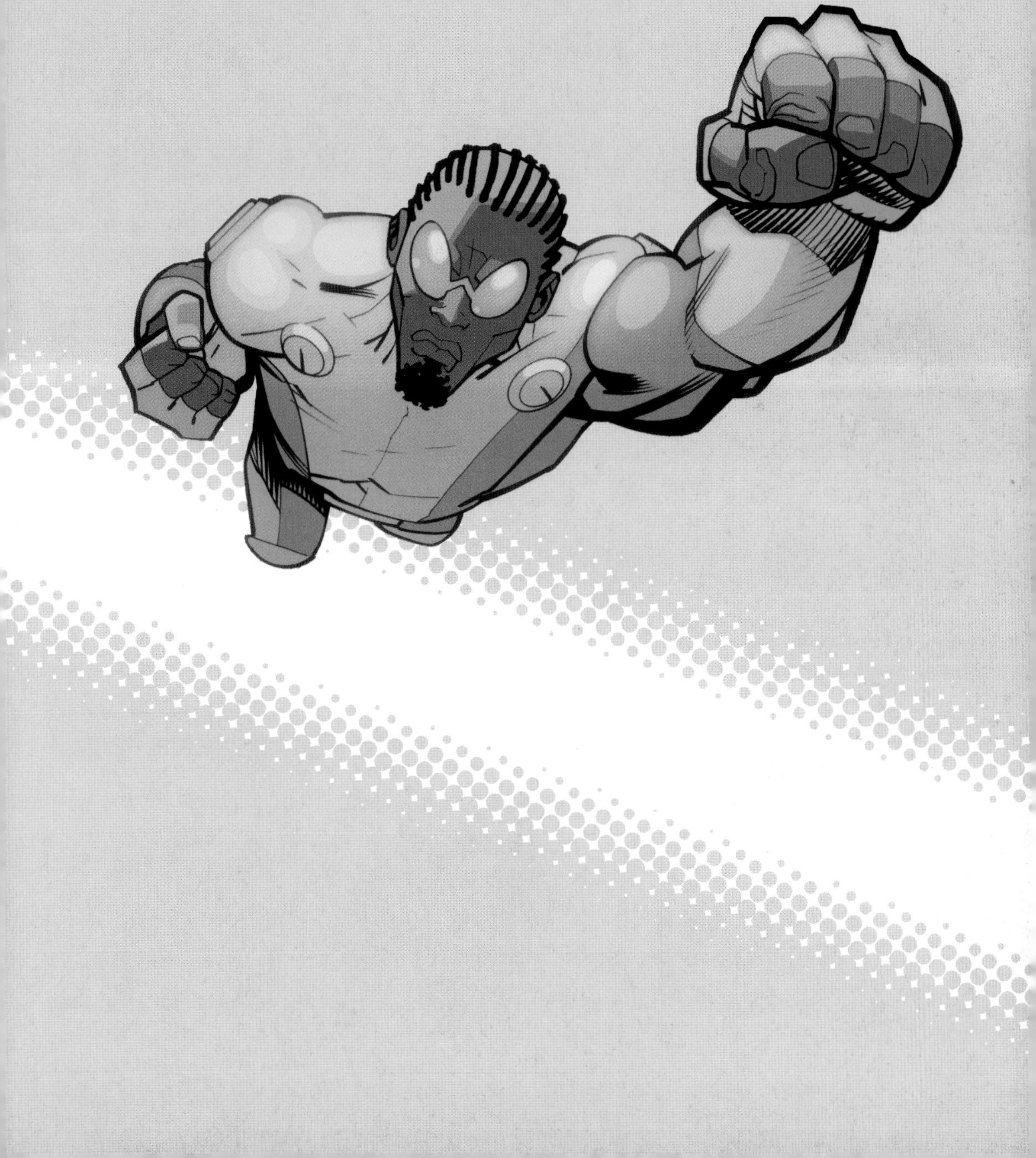

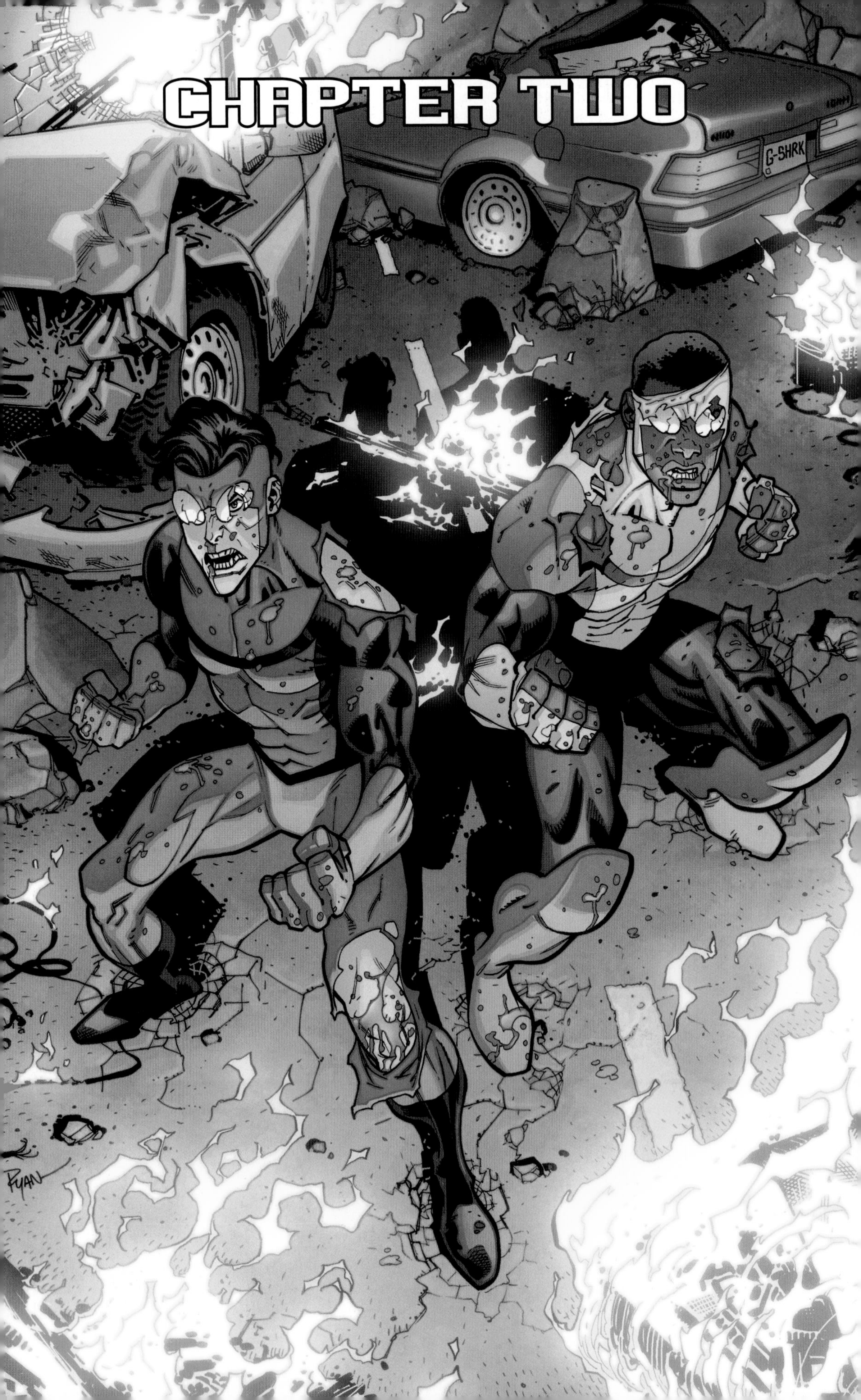
CHAPTER TWO
G-SHRK
RYAN

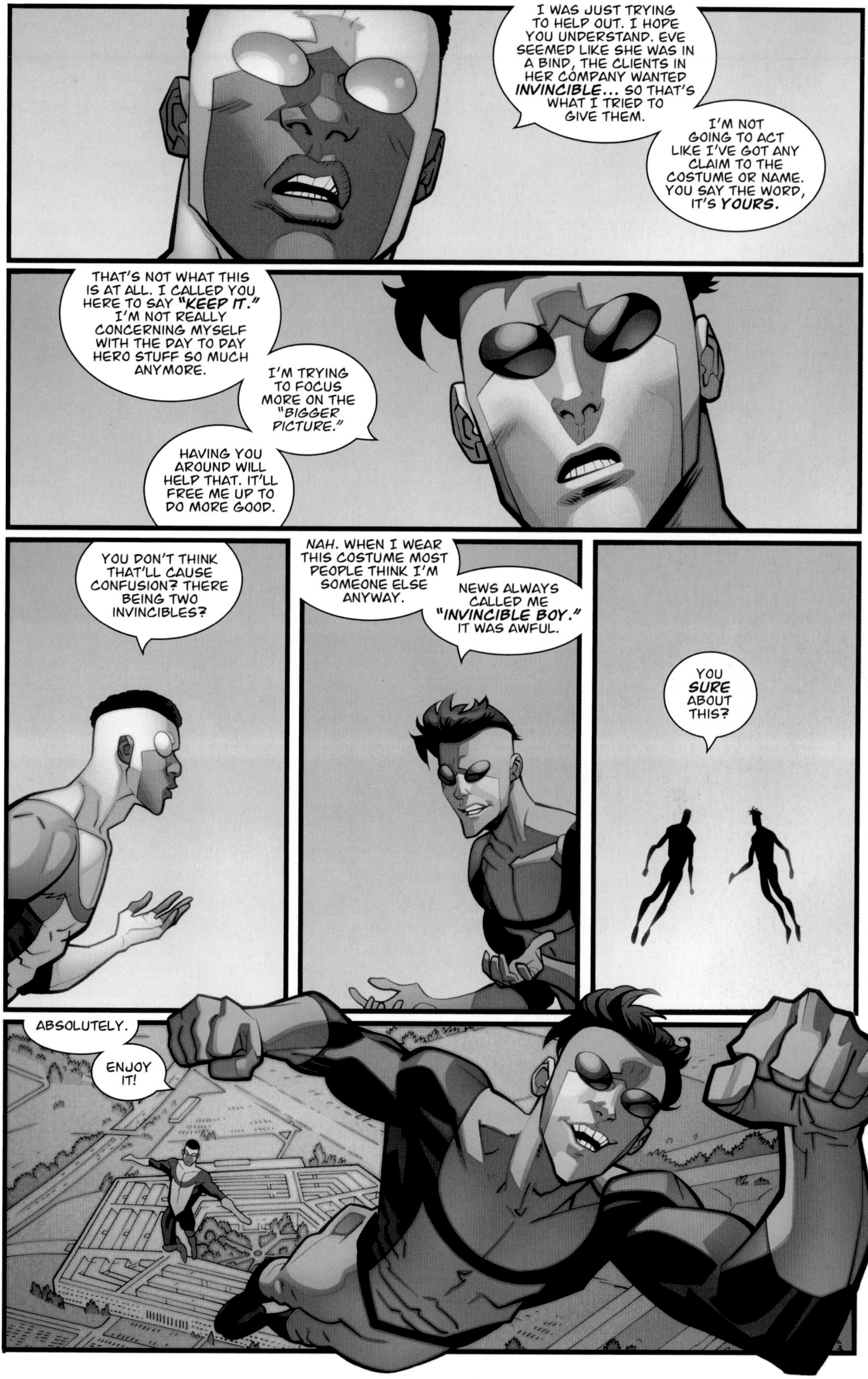

I WAS JUST TRYING TO HELP OUT. I HOPE YOU UNDERSTAND. EVE SEEMED LIKE SHE WAS IN A BIND, THE CLIENTS IN HER COMPANY WANTED INVINCIBLE... SO THAT'S WHAT I TRIED TO GIVE THEM.
I'M NOT GOING TO ACT LIKE I'VE GOT ANY CLAIM TO THE COSTUME OR NAME. YOU SAY THE WORD, IT'S YOURS.
THAT'S NOT WHAT THIS IS AT ALL. I CALLED YOU HERE TO SAY "KEEP IT." I'M NOT REALLY CONCERNING MYSELF WITH THE DAY TO DAY HERO STUFF SO MUCH ANYMORE.
I'M TRYING TO FOCUS MORE ON THE "BIGGER PICTURE."
HAVING YOU AROUND WILL HELP THAT. IT'LL FREE ME UP TO DO MORE GOOD.
YOU DON'T THINK THAT'LL CAUSE CONFUSION? THERE BEING TWO INVINCIBLES?
NAH. WHEN I WEAR THIS COSTUME MOST PEOPLE THINK I'M SOMEONE ELSE ANYWAY.
NEWS ALWAYS CALLED ME "INVINCIBLE BOY." IT WAS AWFUL.
YOU SURE ABOUT THIS?
ABSOLUTELY.
ENJOY IT!

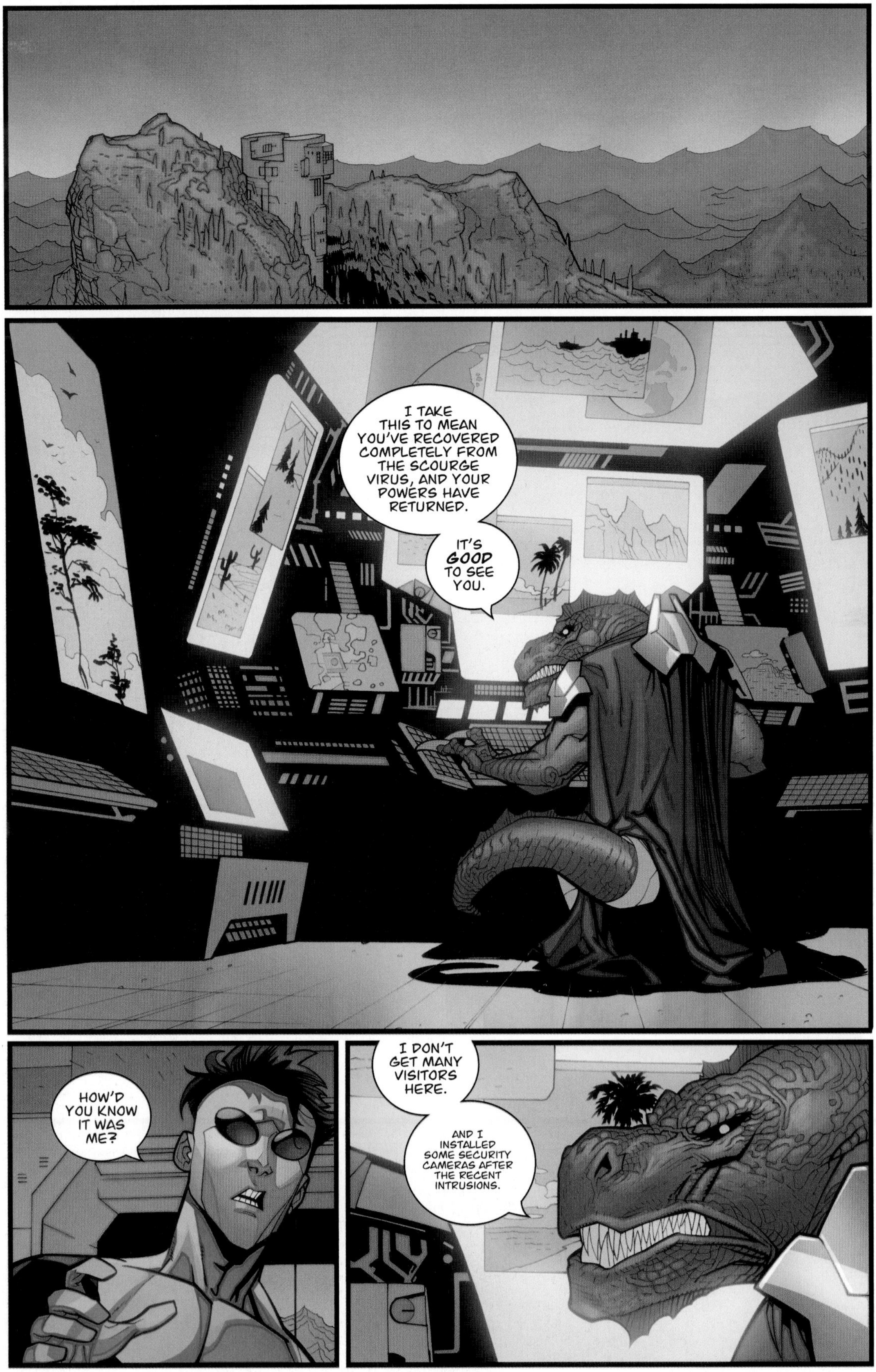
I TAKE THIS TO MEAN YOU'VE RECOVERED COMPLETELY FROM THE SCOURGE VIRUS, AND YOUR POWERS HAVE RETURNED.
IT'S GOOD TO SEE YOU.
HOW'D YOU KNOW IT WAS ME?
I DON'T GET MANY VISITORS HERE.
AND I INSTALLED SOME SECURITY CAMERAS AFTER THE RECENT INTRUSIONS.

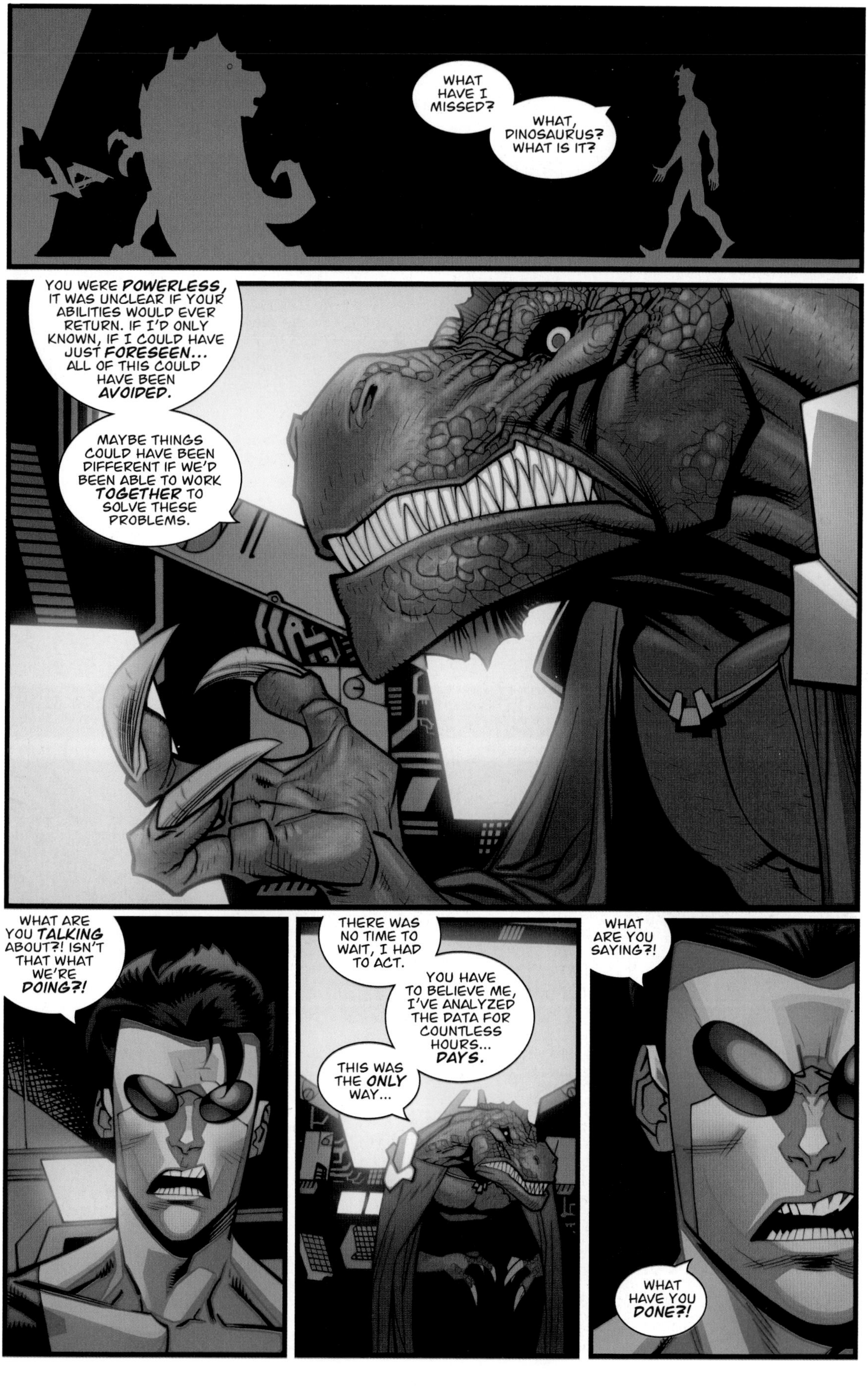
WHAT HAVE I MISSED?
WHAT, DINOSAURUS? WHAT IS IT?
YOU WERE POWERLESS, IT WAS UNCLEAR IF YOUR ABILITIES WOULD EVER RETURN. IF I'D ONLY KNOWN, IF I COULD HAVE JUST FORESEEN... ALL OF THIS COULD HAVE BEEN AVOIDED.
MAYBE THINGS COULD HAVE BEEN DIFFERENT IF WE'D BEEN ABLE TO WORK TOGETHER TO SOLVE THESE PROBLEMS.
WHAT ARE YOU TALKING ABOUT?! ISN'T THAT WHAT WE'RE DOING?!
THERE WAS NO TIME TO WAIT, I HAD TO ACT.
YOU HAVE TO BELIEVE ME, I'VE ANALYZED THE DATA FOR COUNTLESS HOURS... DAYS.
THIS WAS THE ONLY WAY...
WHAT ARE YOU SAYING?!
WHAT HAVE YOU DONE?!

WE REACHED A TIPPING POINT... I DON'T KNOW HOW I DIDN'T SEE IT COMING **SOONER.** I'VE DONE THE MATH AND I'VE GOTTEN IT DOWN TO THE MINUTE... WE ARE A MATTER OF **WEEKS** AWAY FROM THE DISASTROUS CHANGES IN OUR CLIMATE NOT ONLY BEING IRREVERSIBLE... BUT **ACCELERATING.**

THE WORLD POPULATION WOULD BE CUT BY **EIGHTY PERCENT** OVER THE NEXT CENTURY DUE TO WORLDWIDE FAMINE AND DROUGHT... OUR SPECIES WOULD FACE **EXTINCTION.**

THERE WAS NO TIME, I COULDN'T WAIT TO SPEAK TO YOU, I HAD TO ACT.

WHAT DID YOU DO?!

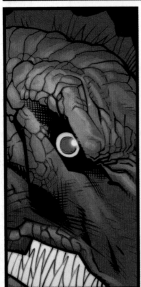

ONLY WHAT **HAD** TO BE DONE.

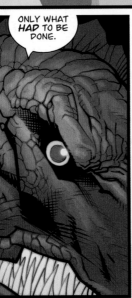

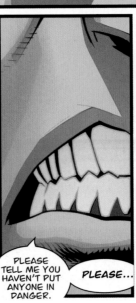

PLEASE TELL ME YOU HAVEN'T PUT ANYONE IN DANGER.

PLEASE...

MILLIONS MUST DIE IN ORDER FOR BILLIONS TO SURVIVE.

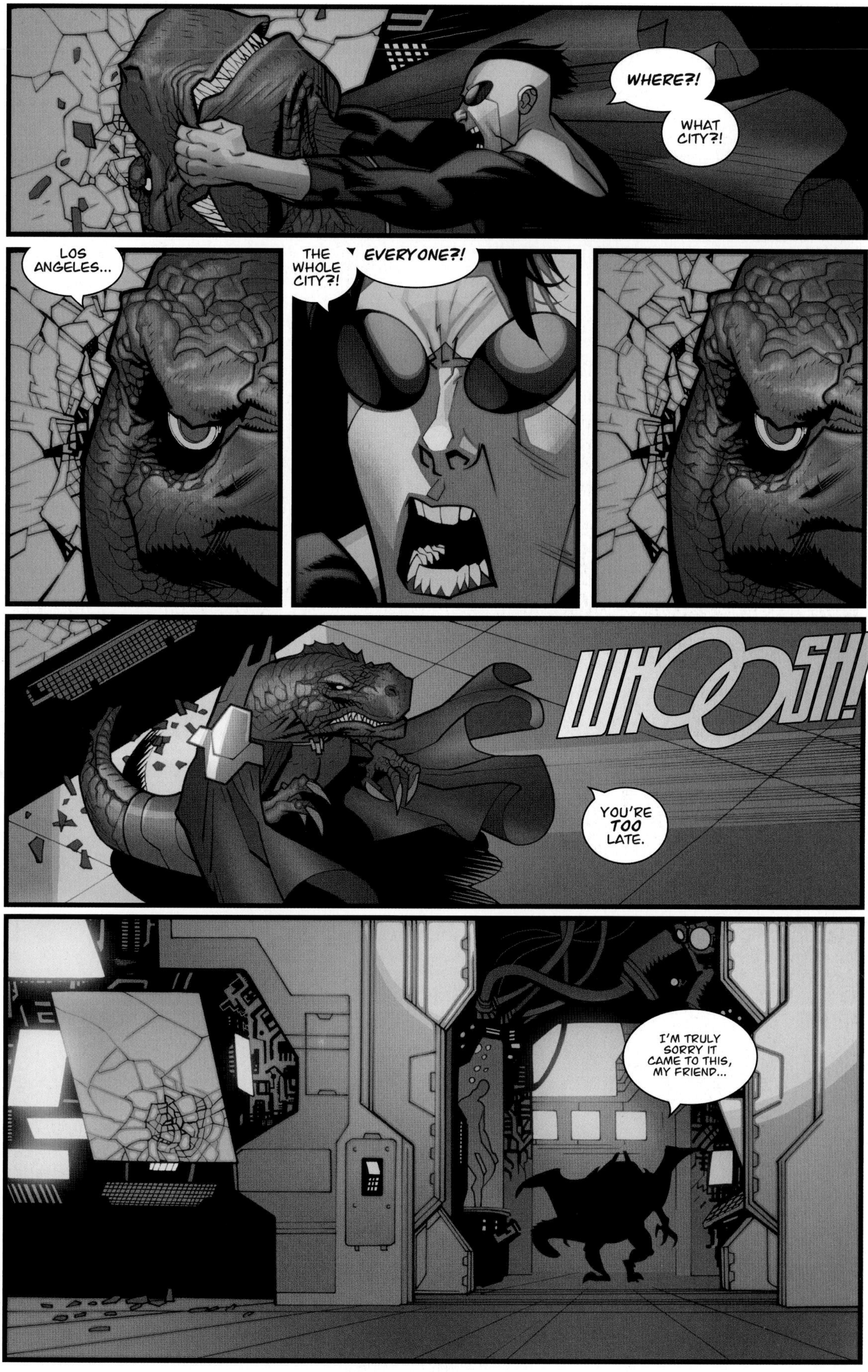
WHERE?!
WHAT CITY?!
LOS ANGELES...
THE WHOLE CITY?!
EVERYONE?!
WHOOSH!
YOU'RE TOO LATE.
I'M TRULY SORRY IT CAME TO THIS, MY FRIEND...

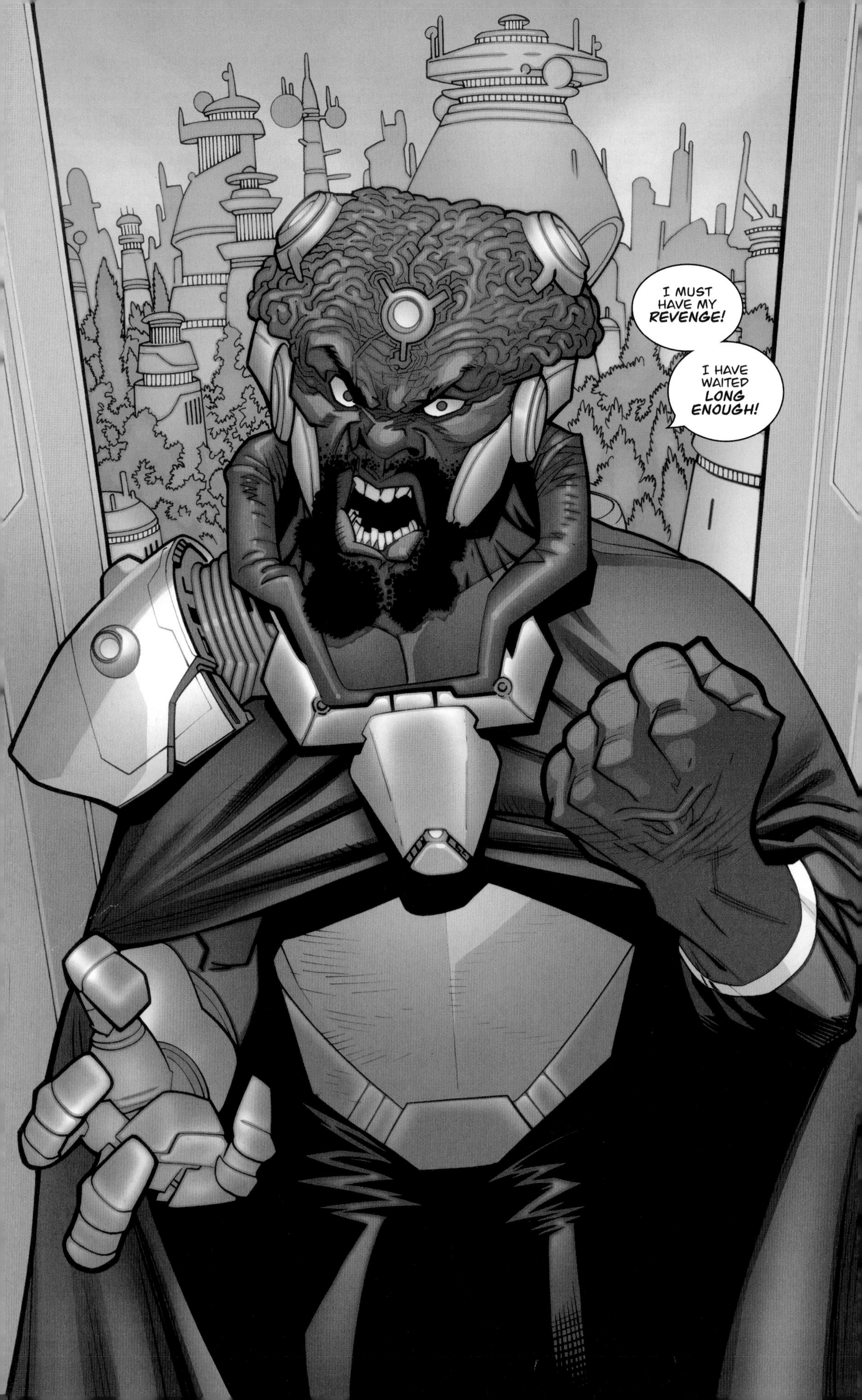
I MUST HAVE MY REVENGE!
I HAVE WAITED LONG ENOUGH!

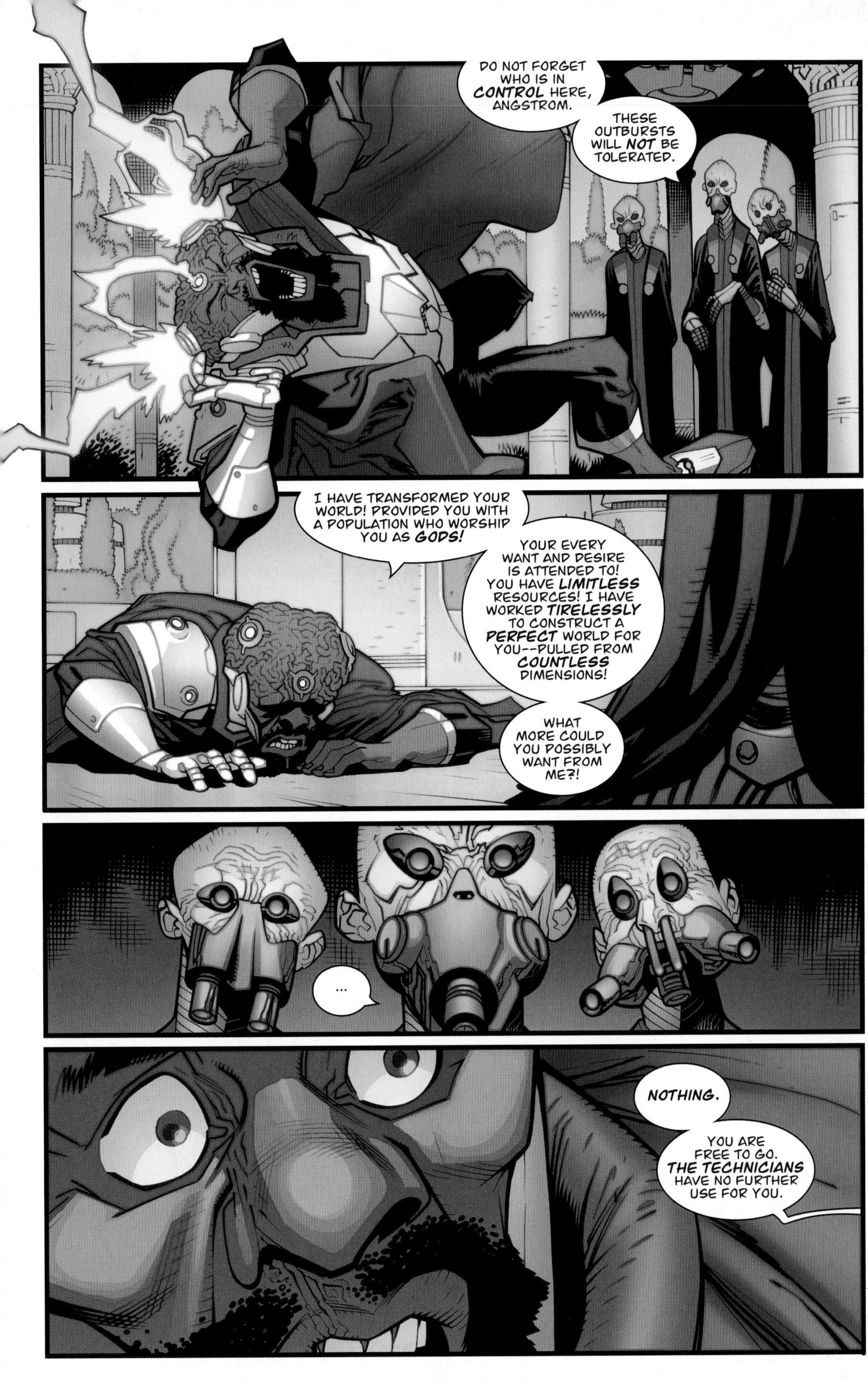
DO NOT FORGET WHO IS IN CONTROL HERE, ANGSTROM.
THESE OUTBURSTS WILL NOT BE TOLERATED.
I HAVE TRANSFORMED YOUR WORLD! PROVIDED YOU WITH A POPULATION WHO WORSHIP YOU AS GODS!
YOUR EVERY WANT AND DESIRE IS ATTENDED TO! YOU HAVE LIMITLESS RESOURCES! I HAVE WORKED TIRELESSLY TO CONSTRUCT A PERFECT WORLD FOR YOU--PULLED FROM COUNTLESS DIMENSIONS!
WHAT MORE COULD YOU POSSIBLY WANT FROM ME?!
...
NOTHING.
YOU ARE FREE TO GO. THE TECHNICIANS HAVE NO FURTHER USE FOR YOU.

MARK?! WHAT WAS THAT? I HEARD LOS ANGELES-- WE'RE MONITORING THE CITY AND WE DON'T SEE ANYTHING. I CAN'T UNDERSTAND YOU!

AND HOW DID YOU GET THIS NUMBER!

SORRY, I WAS FLYING REALLY FAST.

AND ROBOT PUT YOUR NUMBER IN THIS PHONE WHEN HE MADE IT FOR ME.

LOS ANGELES HAS NO CURRENT UNUSUAL ACTIVITY. IT'S QUIET.

WHAT'S REALLY GOING ON HERE, MARK?

IT'S LAS VEGAS ALL OVER AGAIN! WE HAVE TO FIND THE BOMBS BEFORE DINOSAURUS SETS THEM OFF-- WE DON'T HAVE ANY TIME!

I NEED YOU TO GET EVERYONE OUT HERE! NOW!

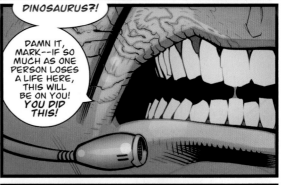

DINOSAURUS?!

DAMN IT, MARK--IF SO MUCH AS ONE PERSON LOSES A LIFE HERE, THIS WILL BE ON YOU! YOU DID THIS!

YOU CAN SCOLD ME LATER--THROW ME IN PRISON-- BUT FOR NOW--

JUST HELP ME MAKE IT RIGHT!

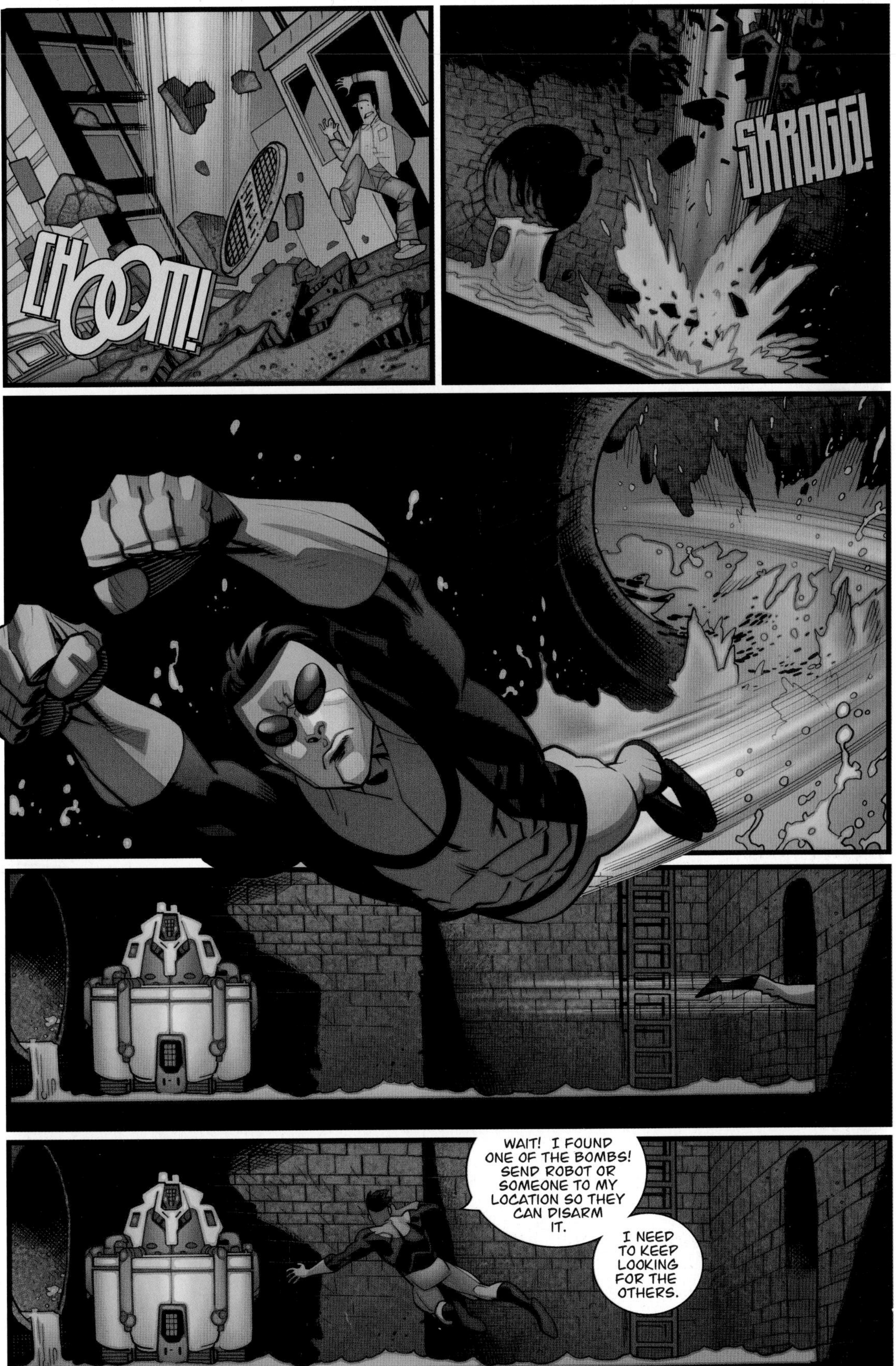
CHOOM!
SKRAGG!
WAIT! I FOUND ONE OF THE BOMBS! SEND ROBOT OR SOMEONE TO MY LOCATION SO THEY CAN DISARM IT.
I NEED TO KEEP LOOKING FOR THE OTHERS.

ANY KIND OF ETA FOR THE GUARDIANS?! THESE COULD ALL GO OFF AT ANY SECOND!

THEY'RE ARRIVING ON SITE RIGHT NOW. WE'RE SPACING THEM OUT INTO SEARCH GROUPS SO THEY CAN COVER MORE GROUND QUICKLY.

POP!

POP!

THANKS, MS. POPPER.

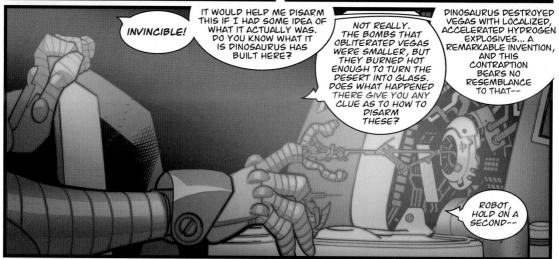

INVINCIBLE!

IT WOULD HELP ME DISARM THIS IF I HAD SOME IDEA OF WHAT IT ACTUALLY WAS. DO YOU KNOW WHAT IT IS DINOSAURUS HAS BUILT HERE?

NOT REALLY. THE BOMBS THAT OBLITERATED VEGAS WERE SMALLER, BUT THEY BURNED HOT ENOUGH TO TURN THE DESERT INTO GLASS. DOES WHAT HAPPENED THERE GIVE YOU ANY CLUE AS TO HOW TO DISARM THESE?

DINOSAURUS DESTROYED VEGAS WITH LOCALIZED, ACCELERATED HYDROGEN EXPLOSIVES... A REMARKABLE INVENTION, AND THIS CONTRAPTION BEARS NO RESEMBLANCE TO THAT--

ROBOT, HOLD ON A SECOND--

I FOUND ANOTHER ONE!

OKAY, INVINCIBLE'S FOUND ANOTHER BOMB.

ROBOT'S BUSY, WE NEED TO TELEPORT SOME TECH HEAD OVER THERE TO SHUT IT DOWN. IS THAT WEIRDO D.A. SINCLAIR REACHABLE?

OUTRUN, COME IN! I FIGURED YOU'D HAVE FOUND ABOUT SIX OF THESE SO FAR.

ONLY *THREE*, SIR. I'VE MARKED THEM ON THE GPS. STILL LOOKING.

ROBOT, WE'VE GOT FOUR OTHER DEVICES LOCATED. YOU'RE SURE THESE AREN'T BOMBS?

WE CAN'T JUST PLACE A SCIENTIST ON EACH ONE OF THESE THINGS AND HOPE FOR THE BEST. WHAT'S THE PLAN HERE? ANY IDEAS?

IF I HAD A DEFINITIVE PLAN WE COULD TELEPORT ALL MY OTHER ACTIVE DRONES HERE, AND I COULD DISARM THEM ALL REMOTELY. SADLY, I DON'T YET KNOW HOW THAT CAN BE DONE--HAVING ANOTHER PAIR OF EYES ON THESE WOULD HELP.

CECIL? GET SINCLAIR AND WHATEVER OTHER EGGHEADS YOU'VE GOT DOWN HERE TO HELP ROBOT.

ROBOT, ANY CLUES AS TO WHAT WE'RE DEALING WITH HERE? ANY INDICATION ON WHAT EXACTLY WILL HAPPEN IF THESE THINGS GO OFF ANYTIME SOON?

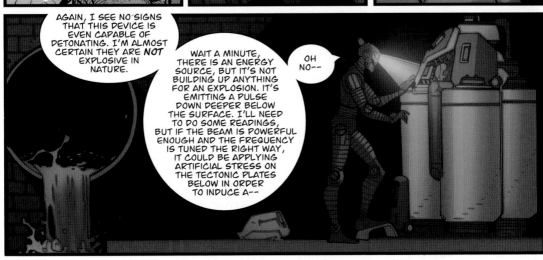

AGAIN, I SEE NO SIGNS THAT THIS DEVICE IS EVEN CAPABLE OF DETONATING. I'M ALMOST CERTAIN THEY ARE *NOT* EXPLOSIVE IN NATURE.

WAIT A MINUTE, THERE IS AN ENERGY SOURCE, BUT IT'S NOT BUILDING UP ANYTHING FOR AN EXPLOSION. IT'S EMITTING A PULSE DOWN DEEPER BELOW THE SURFACE. I'LL NEED TO DO SOME READINGS, BUT IF THE BEAM IS POWERFUL ENOUGH AND THE FREQUENCY IS TUNED THE RIGHT WAY, IT COULD BE APPLYING ARTIFICIAL STRESS ON THE TECTONIC PLATES BELOW IN ORDER TO INDUCE A--

OH NO--

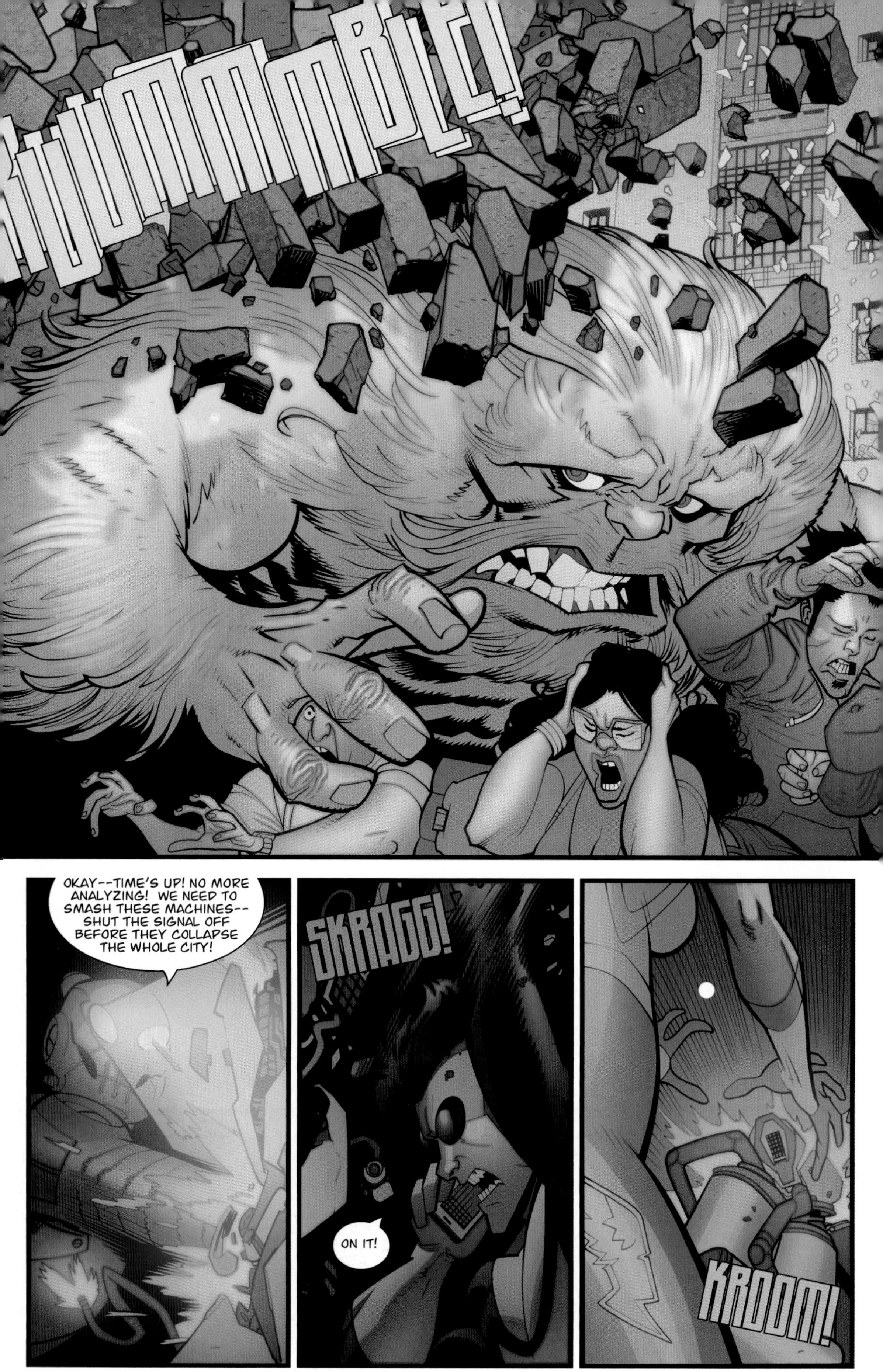
OKAY--TIME'S UP! NO MORE ANALYZING! WE NEED TO SMASH THESE MACHINES--SHUT THE SIGNAL OFF BEFORE THEY COLLAPSE THE WHOLE CITY!
SKRAGG!
ON IT!
KROOM!

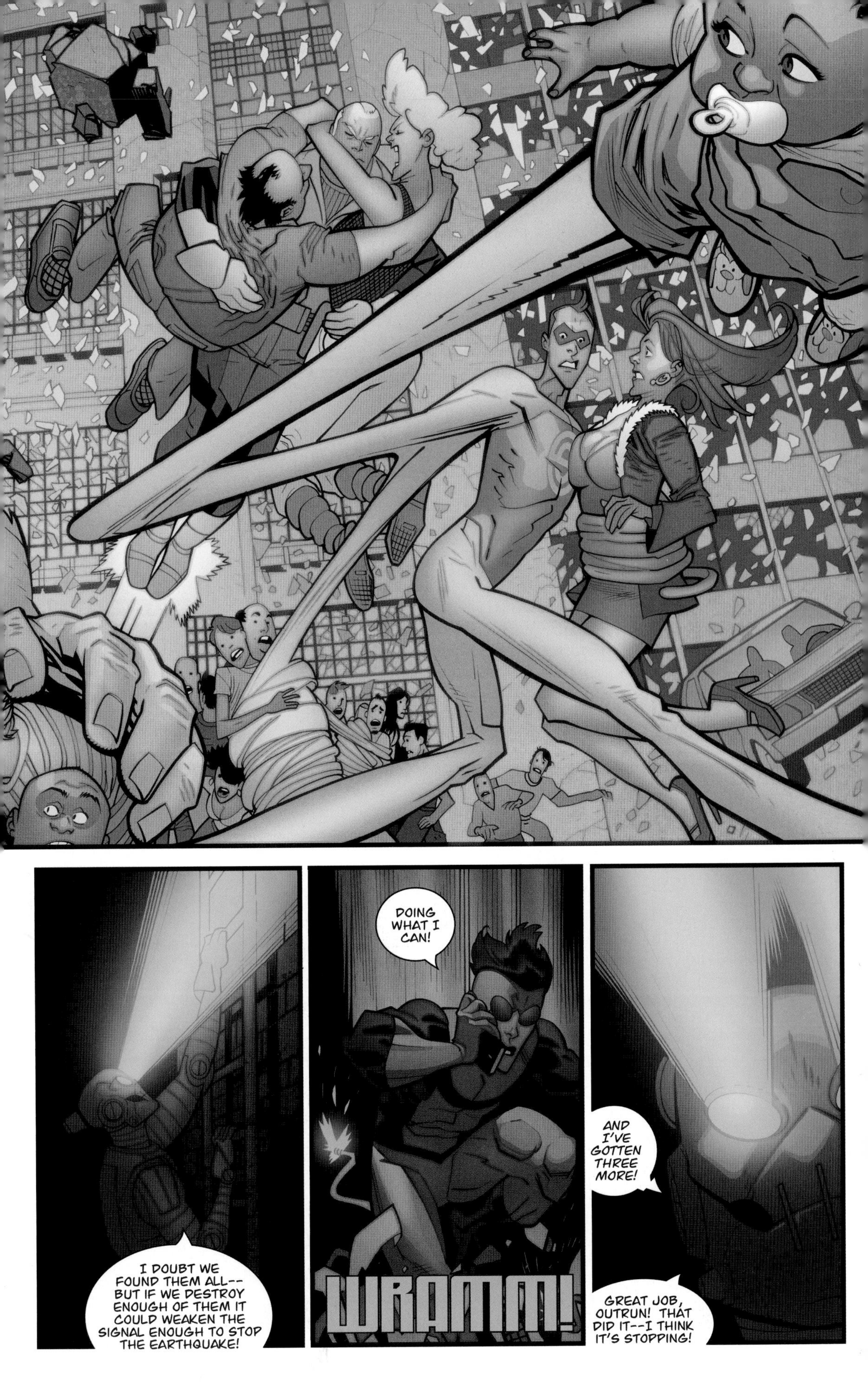
I DOUBT WE FOUND THEM ALL-- BUT IF WE DESTROY ENOUGH OF THEM IT COULD WEAKEN THE SIGNAL ENOUGH TO STOP THE EARTHQUAKE!
DOING WHAT I CAN!
WRAMM!
AND I'VE GOTTEN THREE MORE!
GREAT JOB, OUTRUN! THAT DID IT--I THINK IT'S STOPPING!

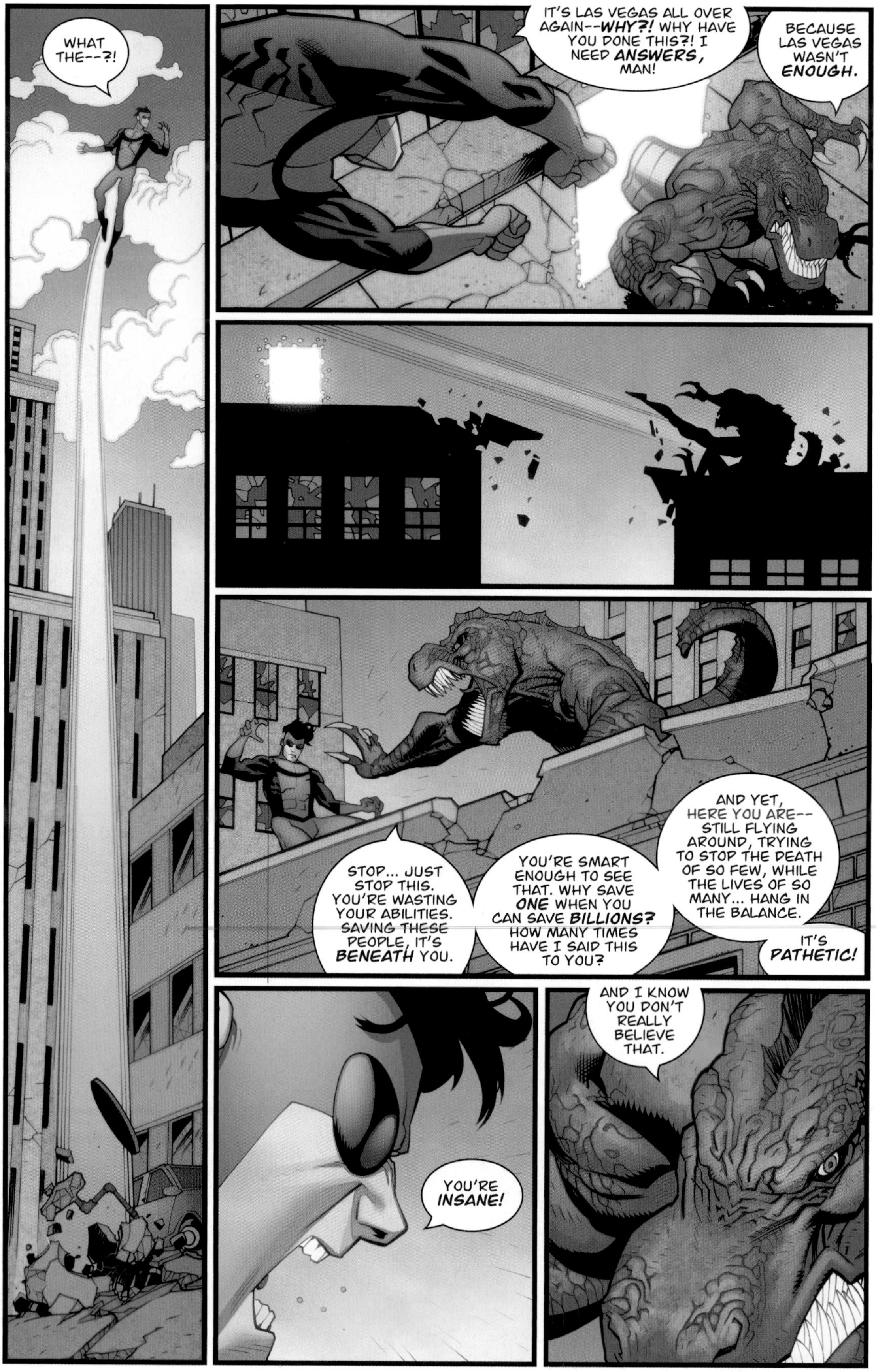
WHAT THE--?!
IT'S LAS VEGAS ALL OVER AGAIN--WHY?! WHY HAVE YOU DONE THIS?! I NEED ANSWERS, MAN!
BECAUSE LAS VEGAS WASN'T ENOUGH.
STOP... JUST STOP THIS. YOU'RE WASTING YOUR ABILITIES. SAVING THESE PEOPLE, IT'S BENEATH YOU.
YOU'RE SMART ENOUGH TO SEE THAT. WHY SAVE ONE WHEN YOU CAN SAVE BILLIONS? HOW MANY TIMES HAVE I SAID THIS TO YOU?
AND YET, HERE YOU ARE--STILL FLYING AROUND, TRYING TO STOP THE DEATH OF SO FEW, WHILE THE LIVES OF SO MANY... HANG IN THE BALANCE.
IT'S PATHETIC!
YOU'RE INSANE!
AND I KNOW YOU DON'T REALLY BELIEVE THAT.

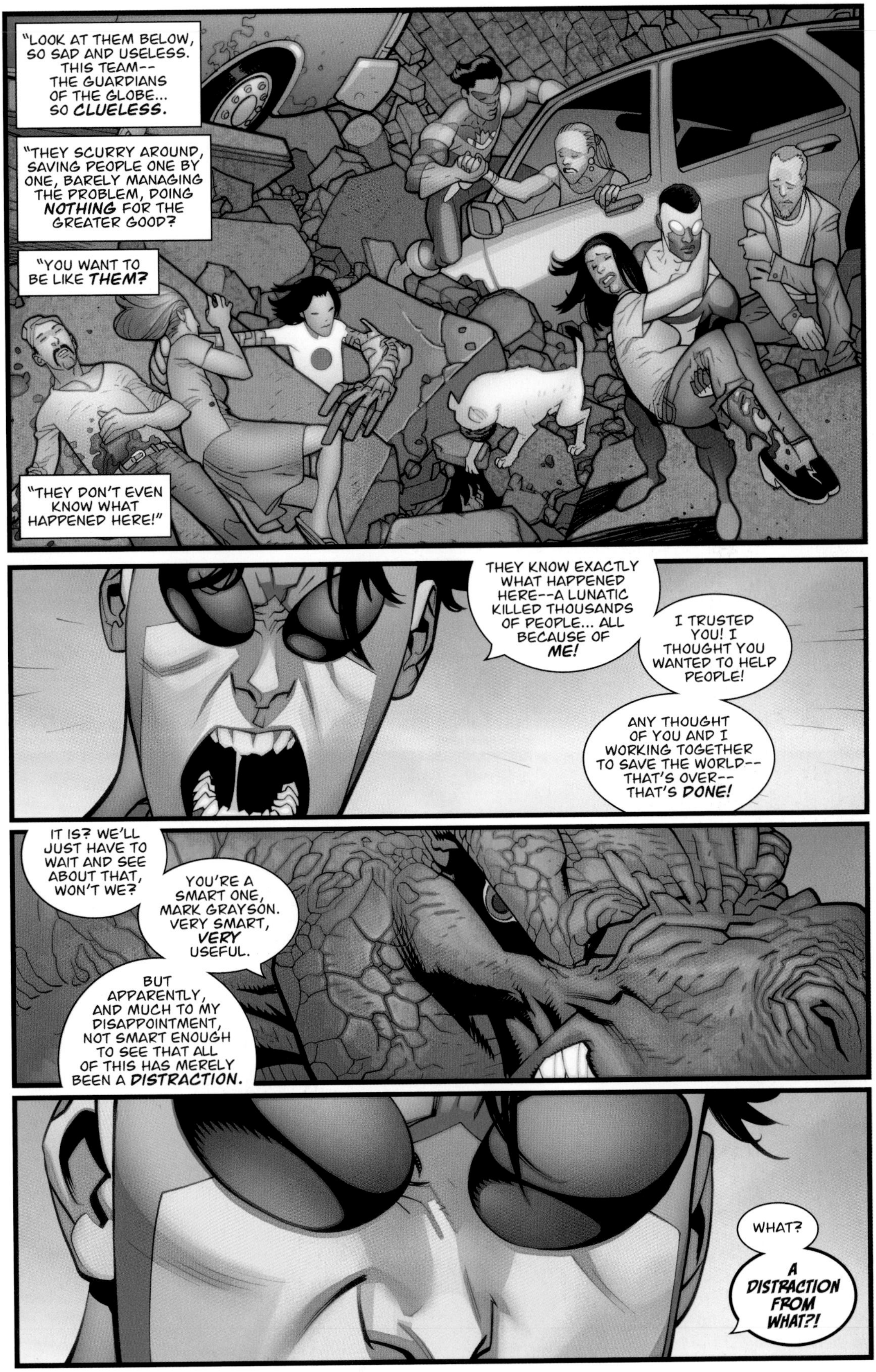
"LOOK AT THEM BELOW, SO SAD AND USELESS. THIS TEAM-- THE GUARDIANS OF THE GLOBE... SO CLUELESS.
"THEY SCURRY AROUND, SAVING PEOPLE ONE BY ONE, BARELY MANAGING THE PROBLEM, DOING NOTHING FOR THE GREATER GOOD?
"YOU WANT TO BE LIKE THEM?
"THEY DON'T EVEN KNOW WHAT HAPPENED HERE!"
THEY KNOW EXACTLY WHAT HAPPENED HERE--A LUNATIC KILLED THOUSANDS OF PEOPLE... ALL BECAUSE OF ME!
I TRUSTED YOU! I THOUGHT YOU WANTED TO HELP PEOPLE!
ANY THOUGHT OF YOU AND I WORKING TOGETHER TO SAVE THE WORLD-- THAT'S OVER-- THAT'S DONE!
IT IS? WE'LL JUST HAVE TO WAIT AND SEE ABOUT THAT, WON'T WE?
YOU'RE A SMART ONE, MARK GRAYSON. VERY SMART, VERY USEFUL.
BUT APPARENTLY, AND MUCH TO MY DISAPPOINTMENT, NOT SMART ENOUGH TO SEE THAT ALL OF THIS HAS MERELY BEEN A DISTRACTION.
WHAT?
A DISTRACTION FROM WHAT?!

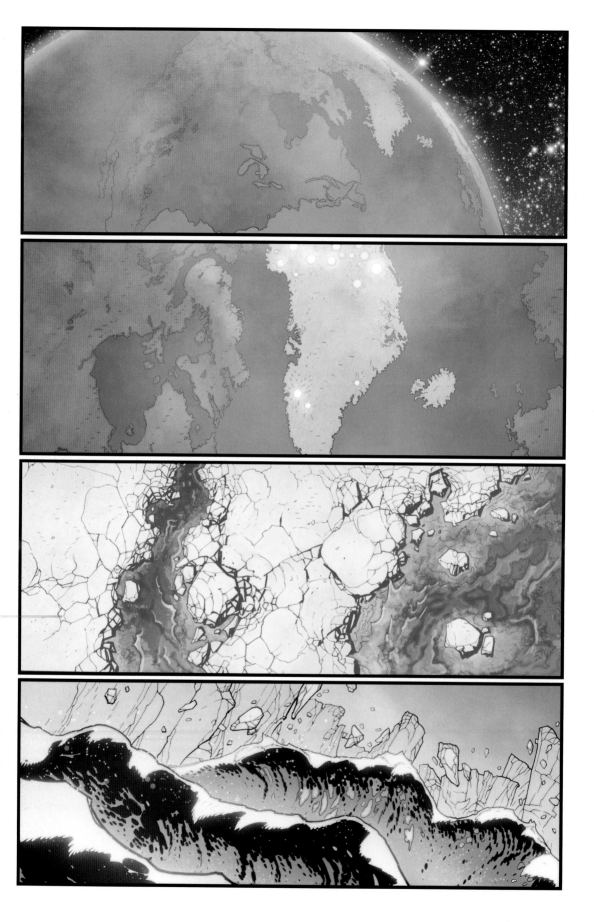

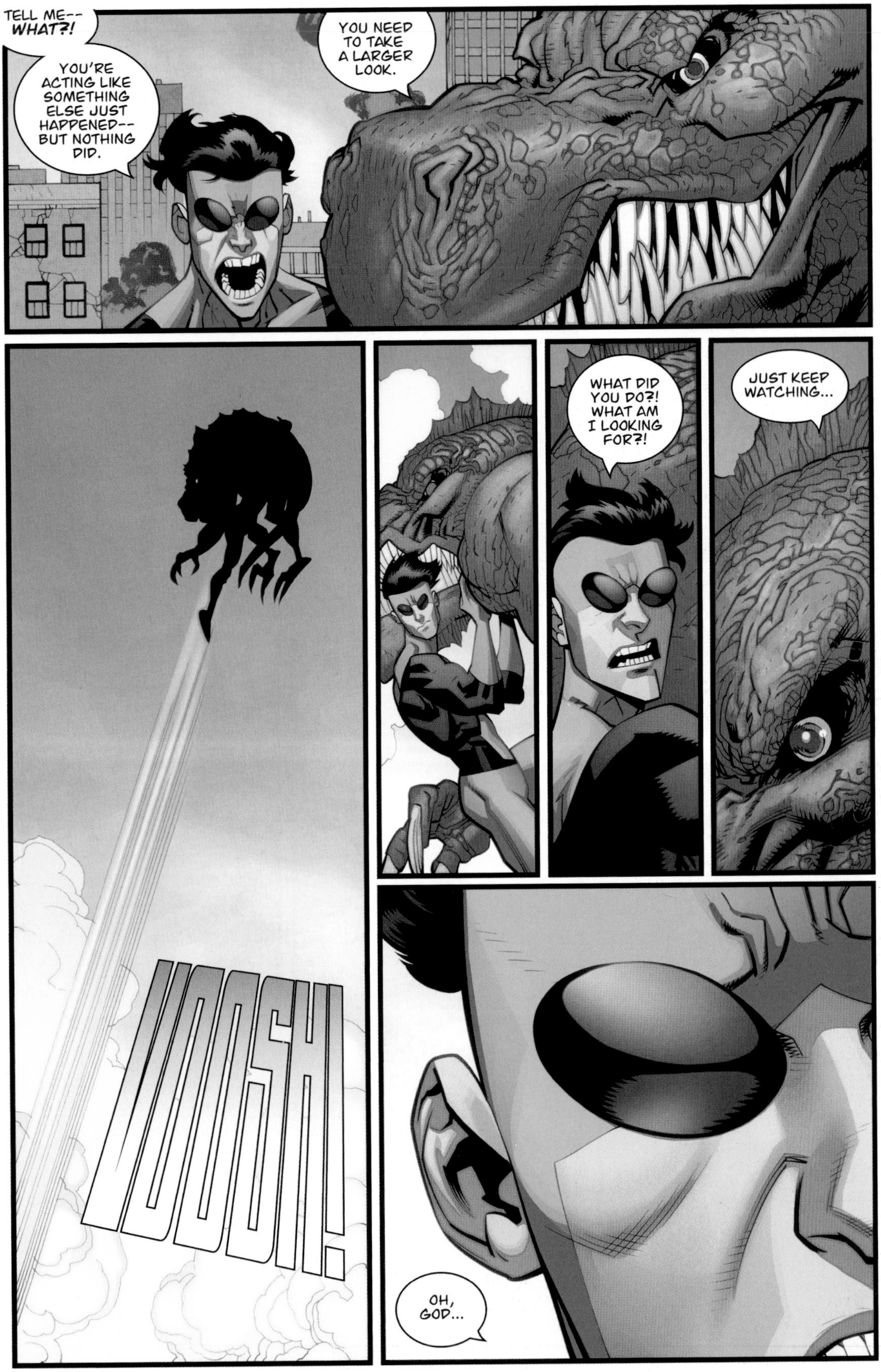
TELL ME-- WHAT?!
YOU'RE ACTING LIKE SOMETHING ELSE JUST HAPPENED-- BUT NOTHING DID.
YOU NEED TO TAKE A LARGER LOOK.
VOOSH!
WHAT DID YOU DO?! WHAT AM I LOOKING FOR?!
JUST KEEP WATCHING...
OH, GOD...

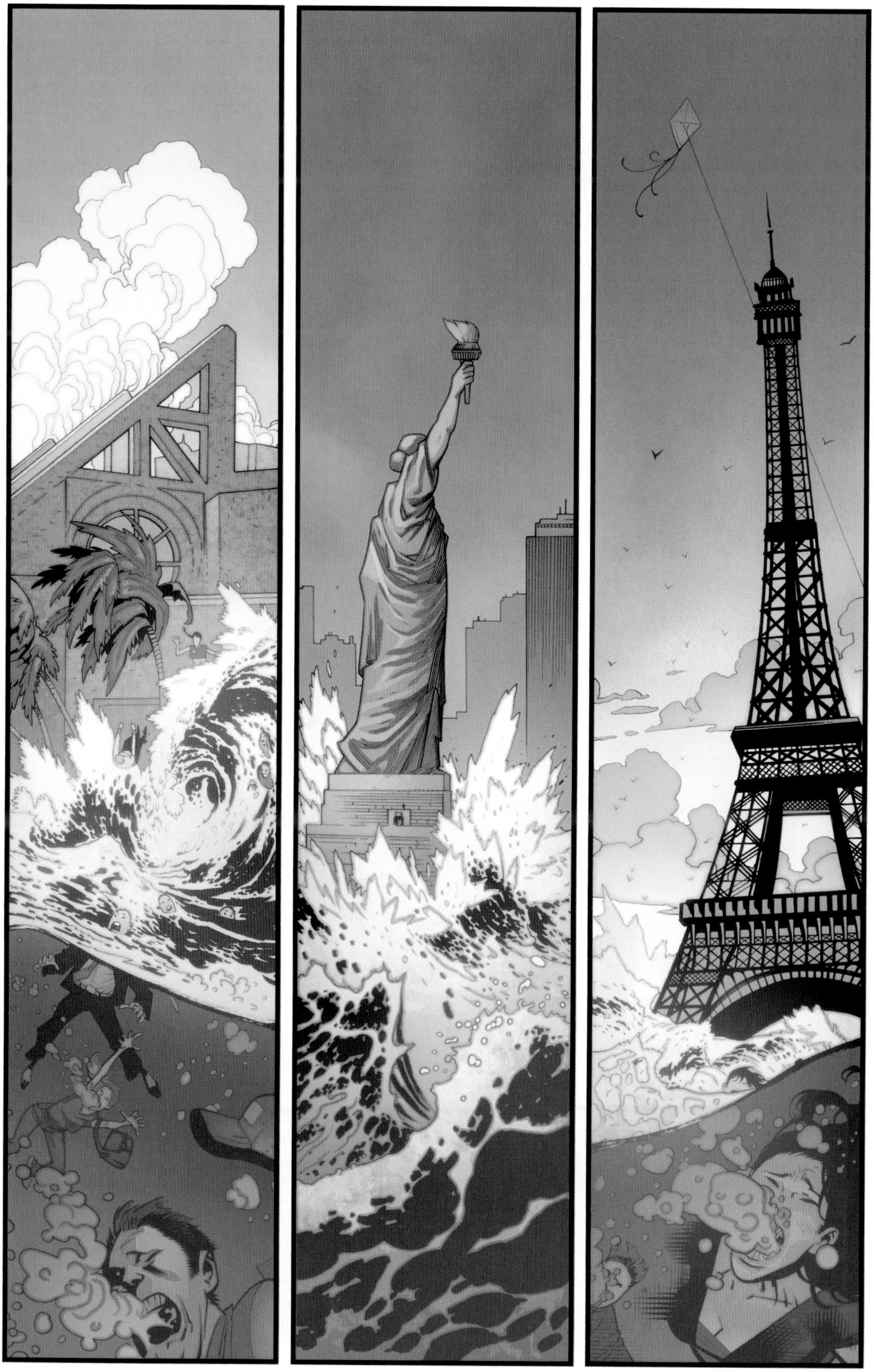

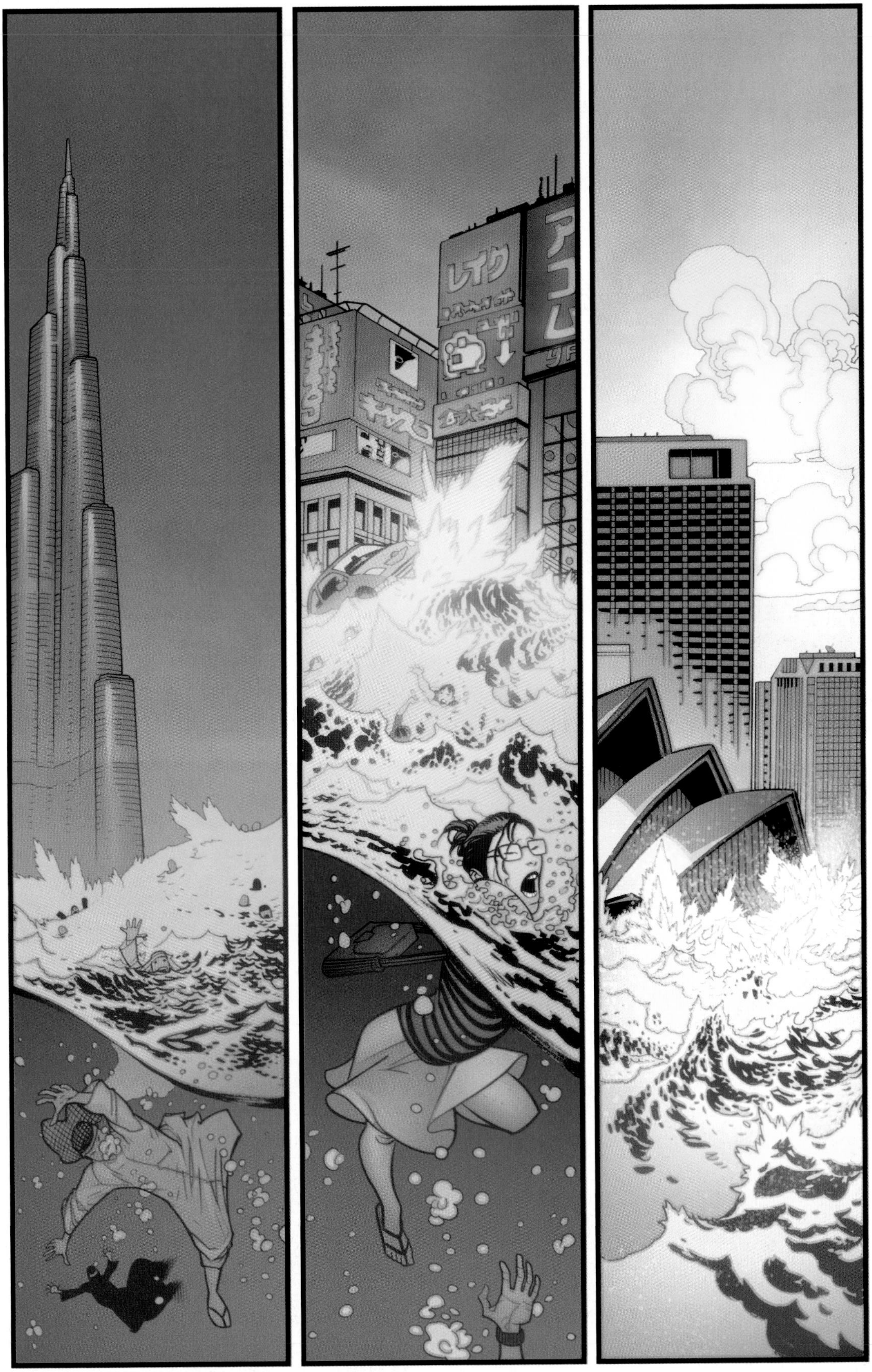
レイク
アコム

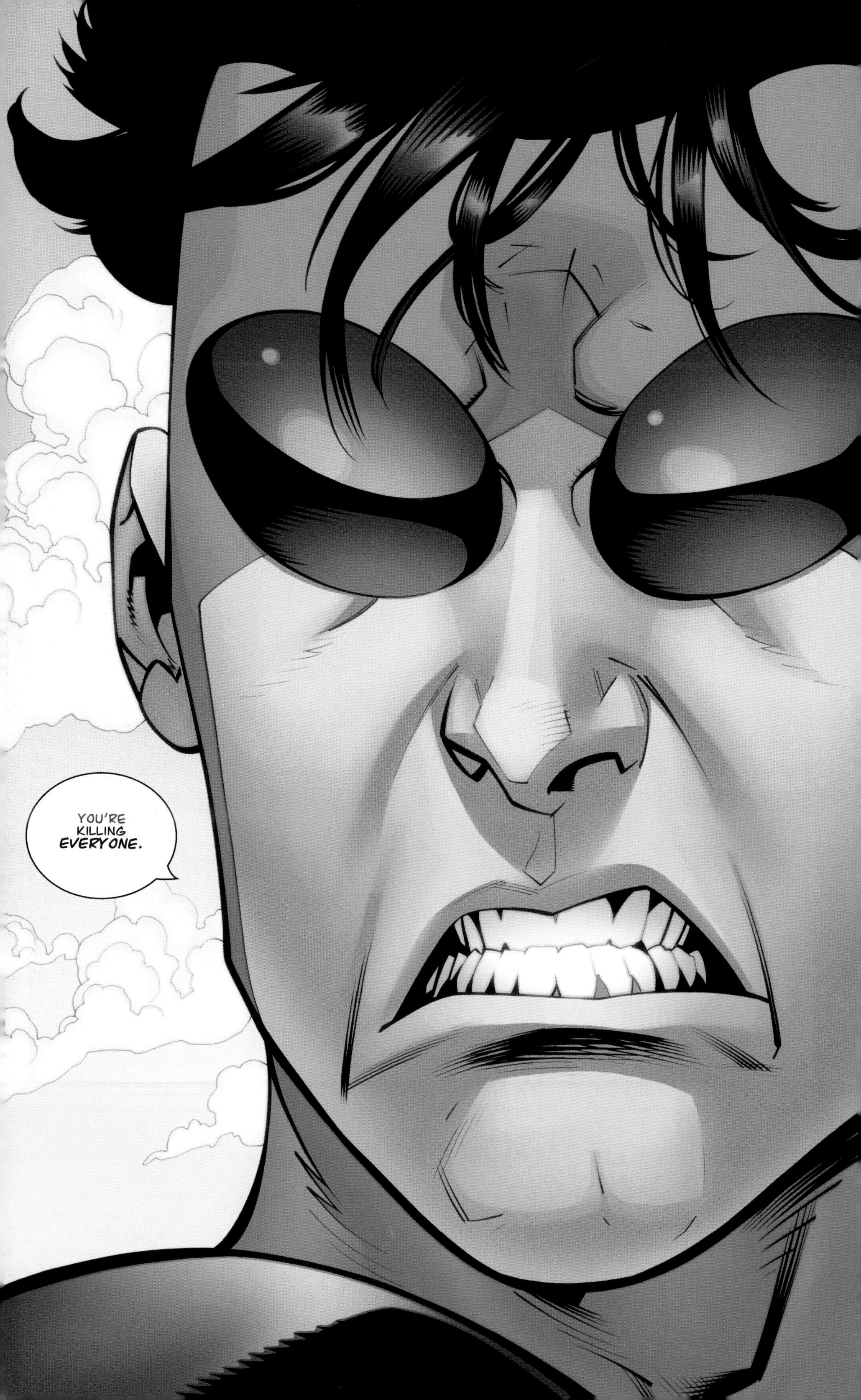
YOU'RE KILLING EVERYONE.

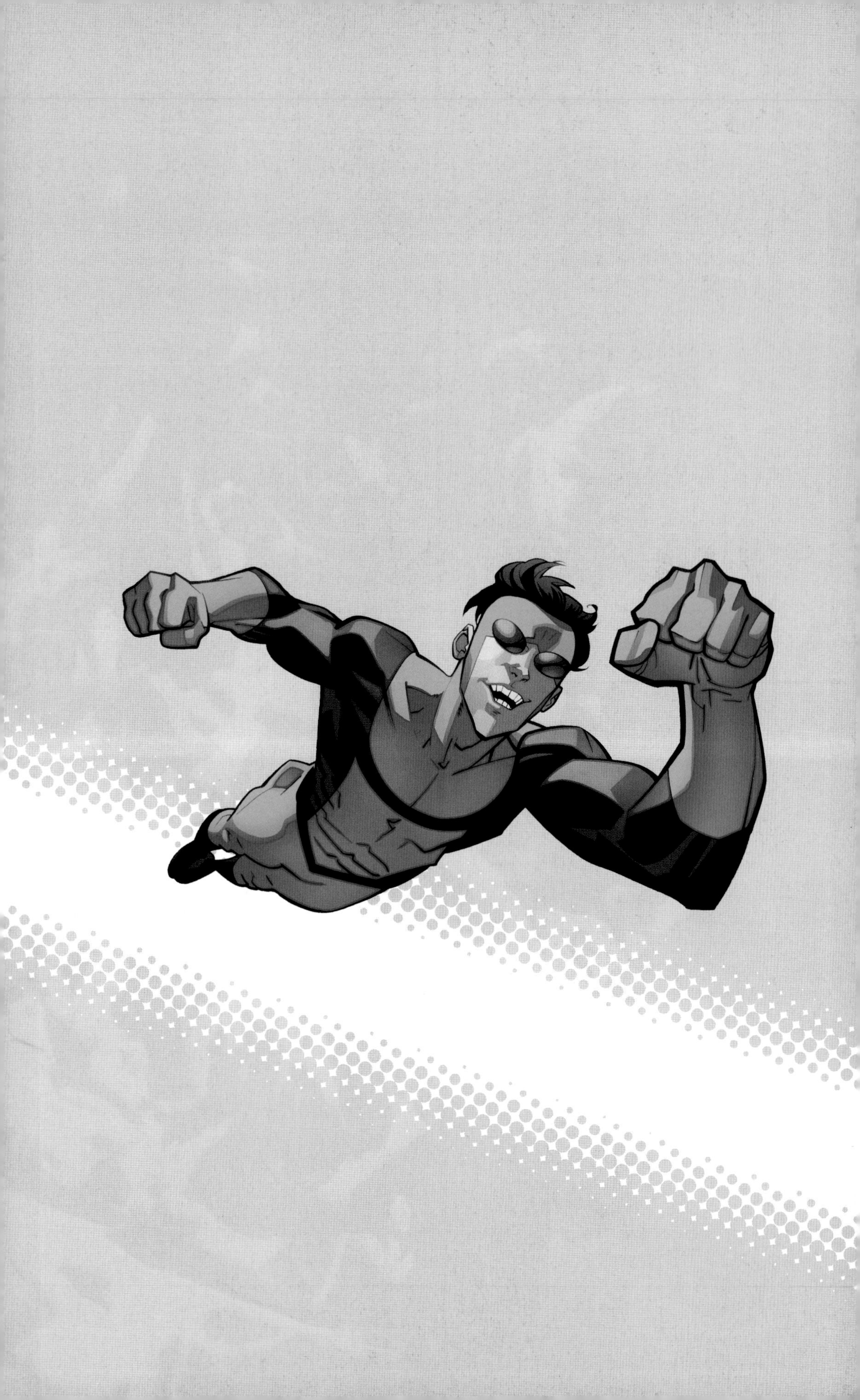

CHAPTER THREE

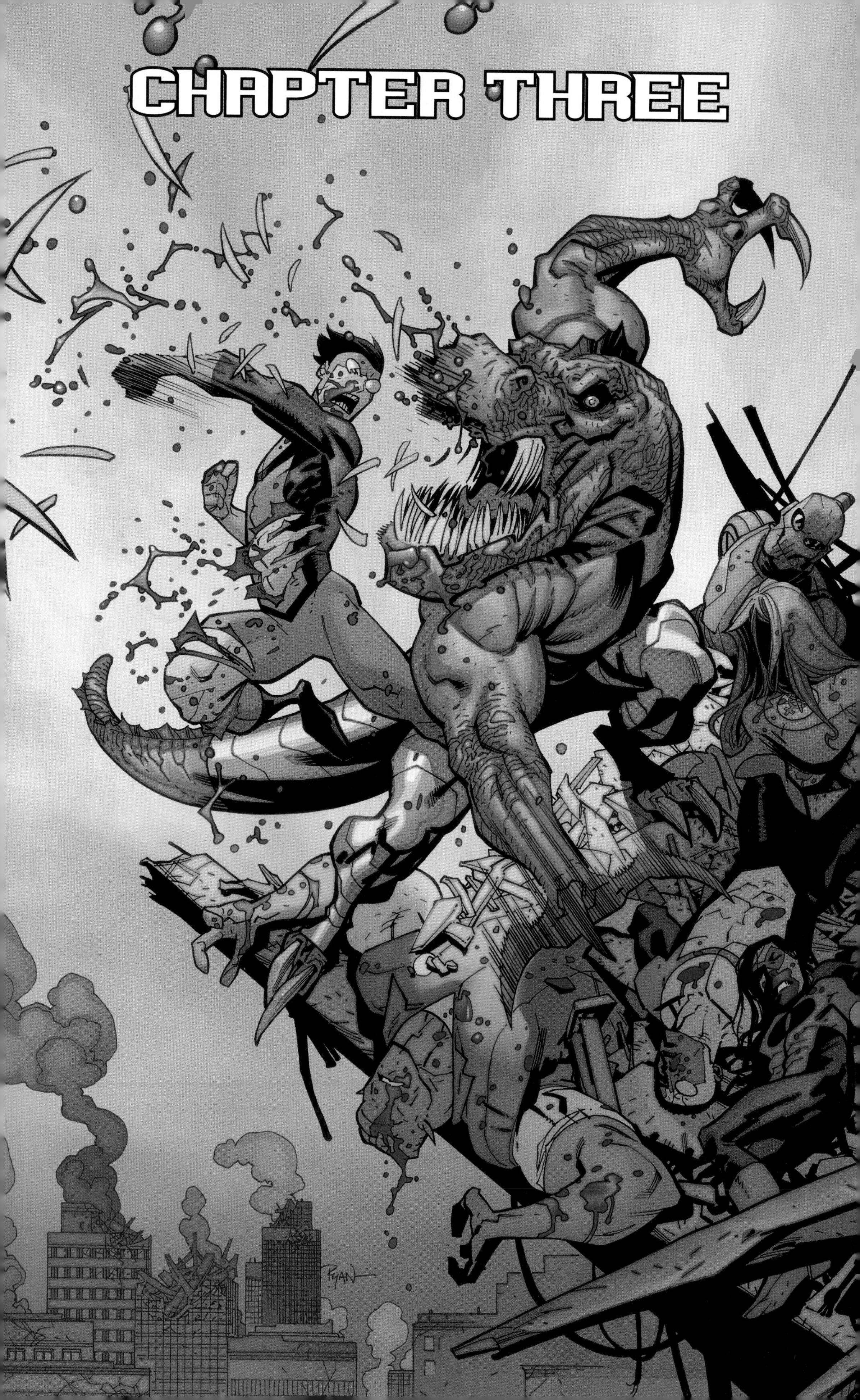

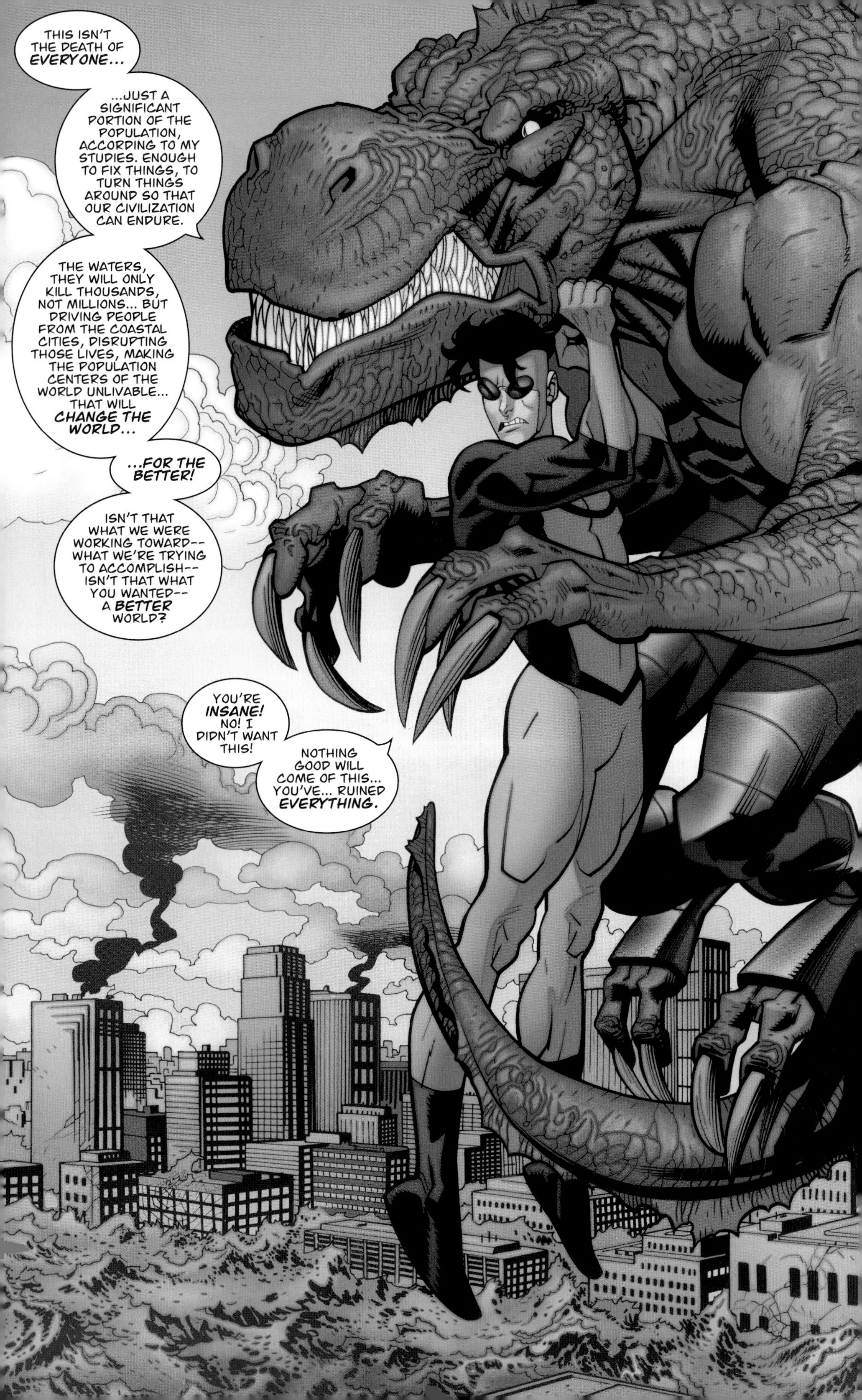
THIS ISN'T THE DEATH OF EVERYONE...
...JUST A SIGNIFICANT PORTION OF THE POPULATION, ACCORDING TO MY STUDIES. ENOUGH TO FIX THINGS, TO TURN THINGS AROUND SO THAT OUR CIVILIZATION CAN ENDURE.
THE WATERS, THEY WILL ONLY KILL THOUSANDS, NOT MILLIONS... BUT DRIVING PEOPLE FROM THE COASTAL CITIES, DISRUPTING THOSE LIVES, MAKING THE POPULATION CENTERS OF THE WORLD UNLIVABLE... THAT WILL CHANGE THE WORLD...
...FOR THE BETTER!
ISN'T THAT WHAT WE WERE WORKING TOWARD-- WHAT WE'RE TRYING TO ACCOMPLISH-- ISN'T THAT WHAT YOU WANTED-- A BETTER WORLD?
YOU'RE INSANE! NO! I DIDN'T WANT THIS!
NOTHING GOOD WILL COME OF THIS... YOU'VE... RUINED EVERYTHING.

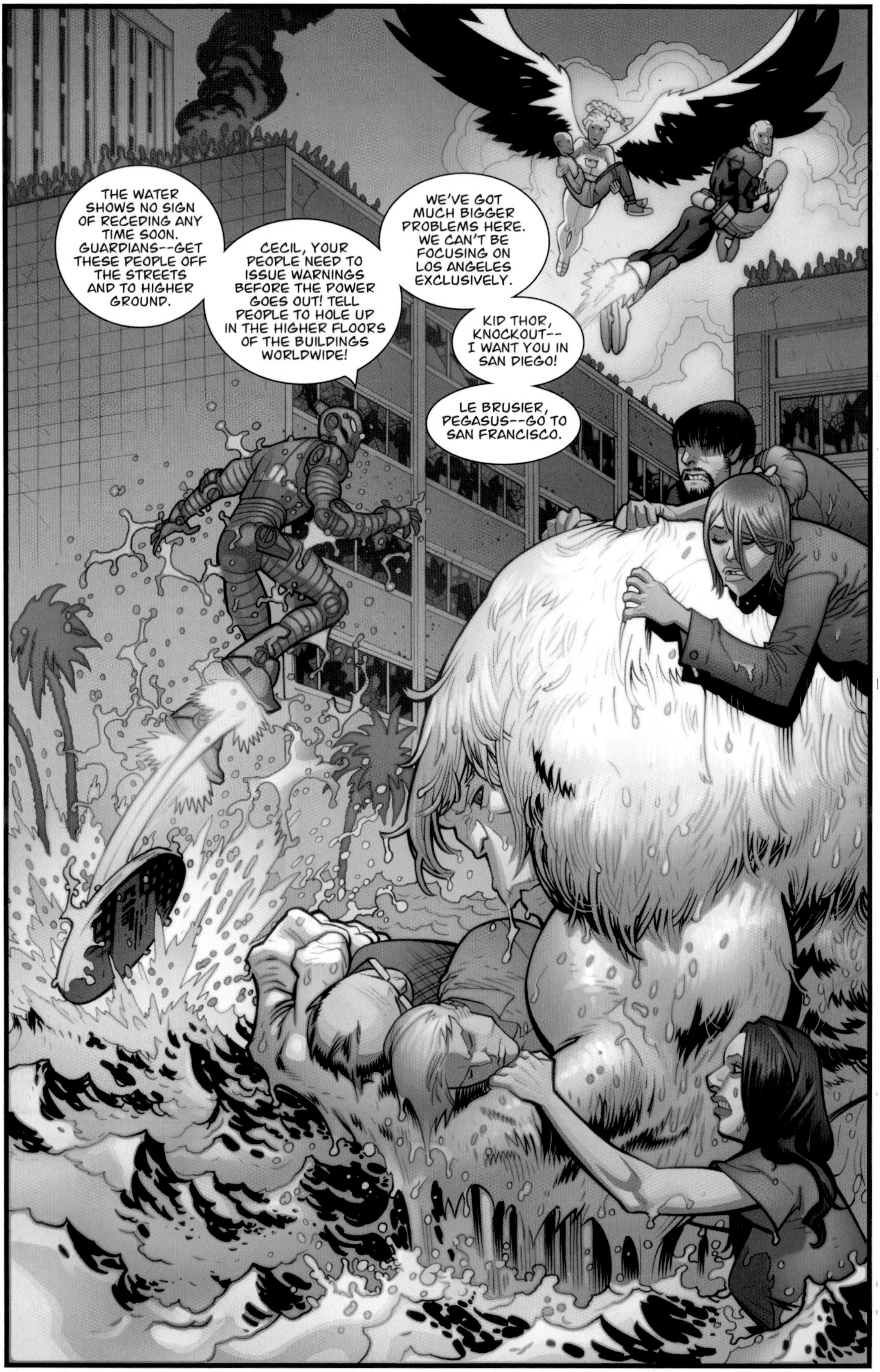
THE WATER SHOWS NO SIGN OF RECEDING ANY TIME SOON. GUARDIANS--GET THESE PEOPLE OFF THE STREETS AND TO HIGHER GROUND.
CECIL, YOUR PEOPLE NEED TO ISSUE WARNINGS BEFORE THE POWER GOES OUT! TELL PEOPLE TO HOLE UP IN THE HIGHER FLOORS OF THE BUILDINGS WORLDWIDE!
WE'VE GOT MUCH BIGGER PROBLEMS HERE. WE CAN'T BE FOCUSING ON LOS ANGELES EXCLUSIVELY.
KID THOR, KNOCKOUT--I WANT YOU IN SAN DIEGO!
LE BRUSIER, PEGASUS--GO TO SAN FRANCISCO.

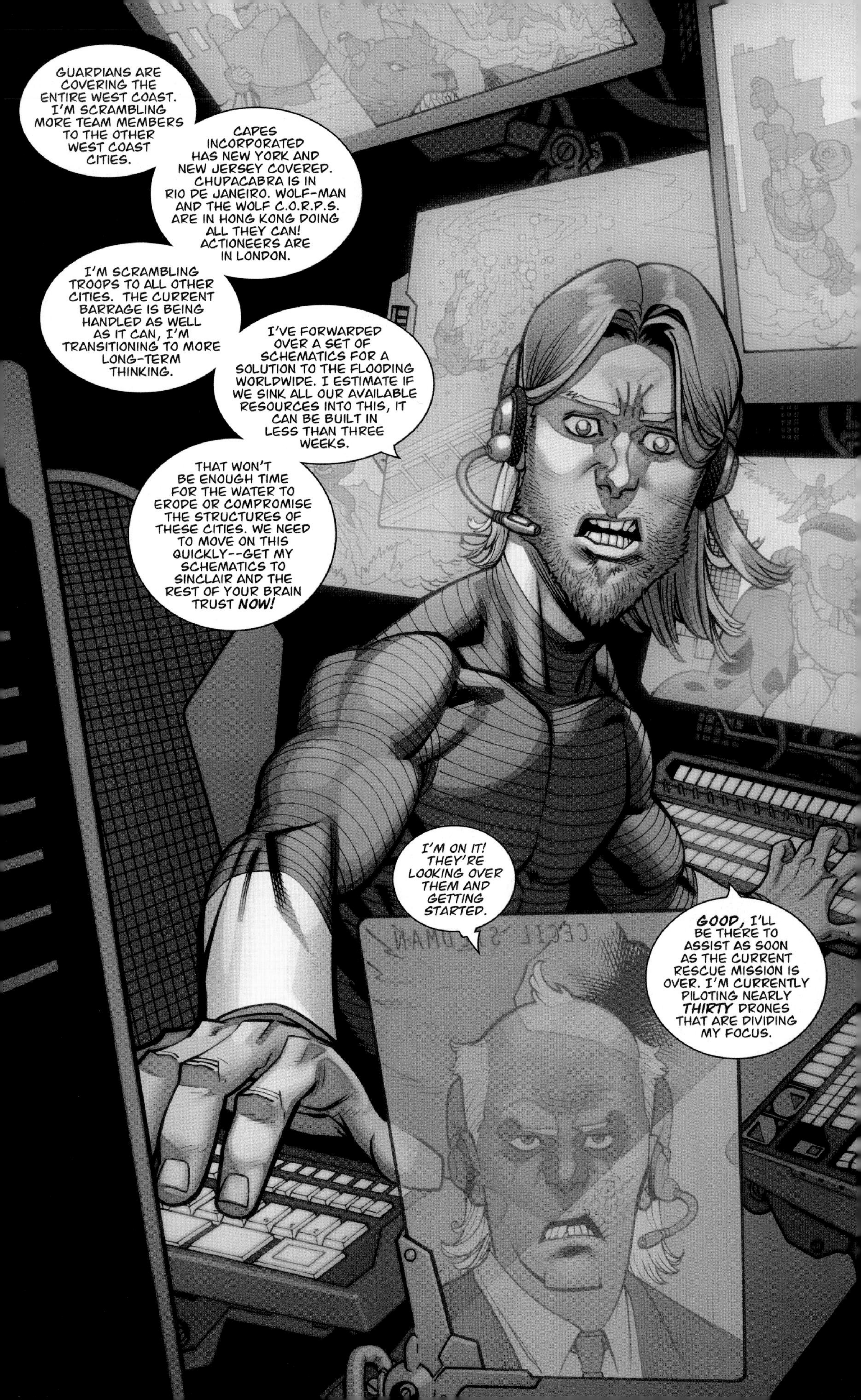
GUARDIANS ARE COVERING THE ENTIRE WEST COAST. I'M SCRAMBLING MORE TEAM MEMBERS TO THE OTHER WEST COAST CITIES.
CAPES INCORPORATED HAS NEW YORK AND NEW JERSEY COVERED. CHUPACABRA IS IN RIO DE JANEIRO. WOLF-MAN AND THE WOLF C.O.R.P.S. ARE IN HONG KONG DOING ALL THEY CAN! ACTIONEERS ARE IN LONDON.
I'M SCRAMBLING TROOPS TO ALL OTHER CITIES. THE CURRENT BARRAGE IS BEING HANDLED AS WELL AS IT CAN, I'M TRANSITIONING TO MORE LONG-TERM THINKING.
I'VE FORWARDED OVER A SET OF SCHEMATICS FOR A SOLUTION TO THE FLOODING WORLDWIDE. I ESTIMATE IF WE SINK ALL OUR AVAILABLE RESOURCES INTO THIS, IT CAN BE BUILT IN LESS THAN THREE WEEKS.
THAT WON'T BE ENOUGH TIME FOR THE WATER TO ERODE OR COMPROMISE THE STRUCTURES OF THESE CITIES. WE NEED TO MOVE ON THIS QUICKLY--GET MY SCHEMATICS TO SINCLAIR AND THE REST OF YOUR BRAIN TRUST *NOW!*
I'M ON IT! THEY'RE LOOKING OVER THEM AND GETTING STARTED.
GOOD, I'LL BE THERE TO ASSIST AS SOON AS THE CURRENT RESCUE MISSION IS OVER. I'M CURRENTLY PILOTING NEARLY ***THIRTY*** DRONES THAT ARE DIVIDING MY FOCUS.

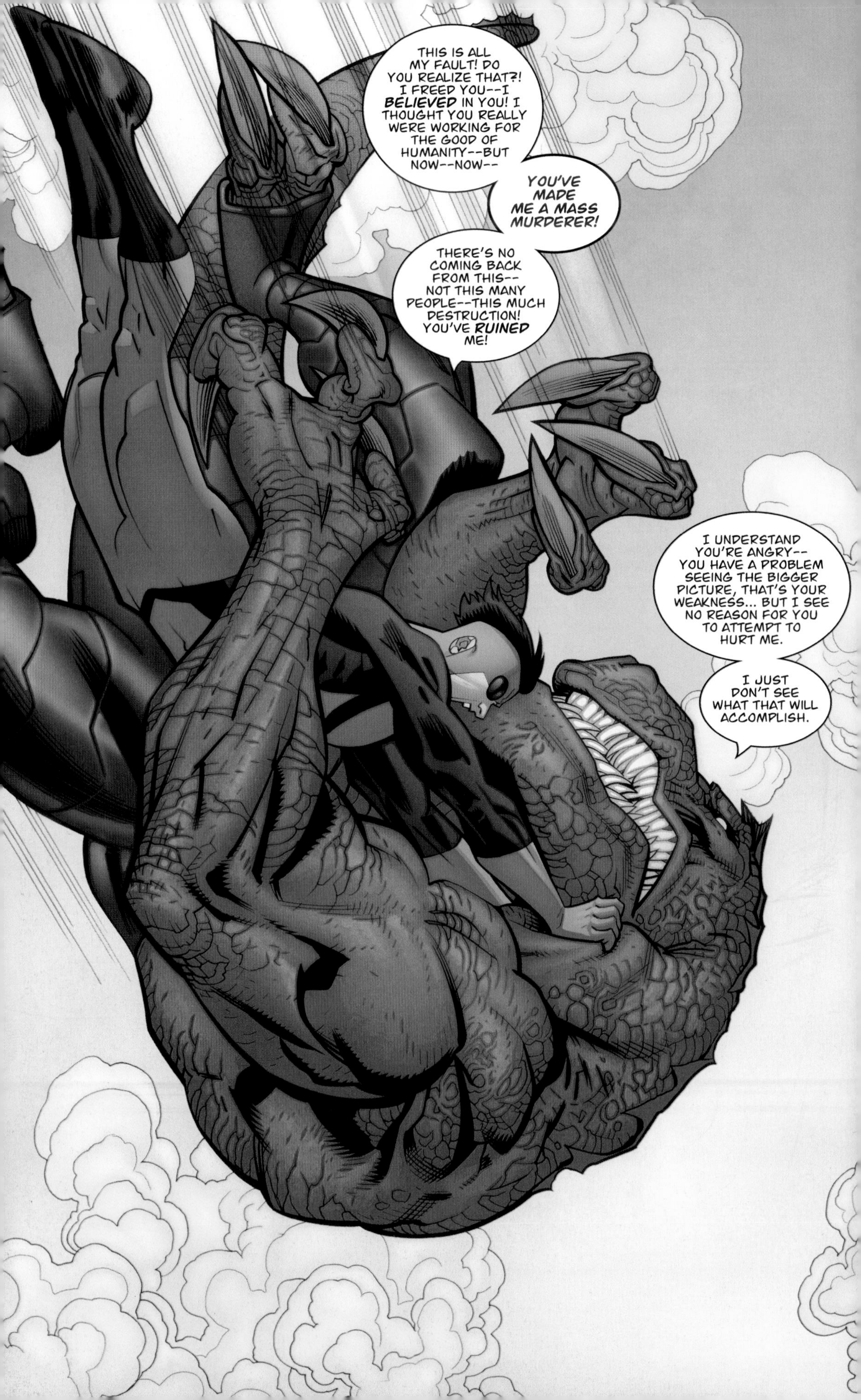
THIS IS ALL MY FAULT! DO YOU REALIZE THAT?! I FREED YOU--I BELIEVED IN YOU! I THOUGHT YOU REALLY WERE WORKING FOR THE GOOD OF HUMANITY--BUT NOW--NOW--
YOU'VE MADE ME A MASS MURDERER!
THERE'S NO COMING BACK FROM THIS--NOT THIS MANY PEOPLE--THIS MUCH DESTRUCTION! YOU'VE RUINED ME!
I UNDERSTAND YOU'RE ANGRY--YOU HAVE A PROBLEM SEEING THE BIGGER PICTURE, THAT'S YOUR WEAKNESS... BUT I SEE NO REASON FOR YOU TO ATTEMPT TO HURT ME.
I JUST DON'T SEE WHAT THAT WILL ACCOMPLISH.

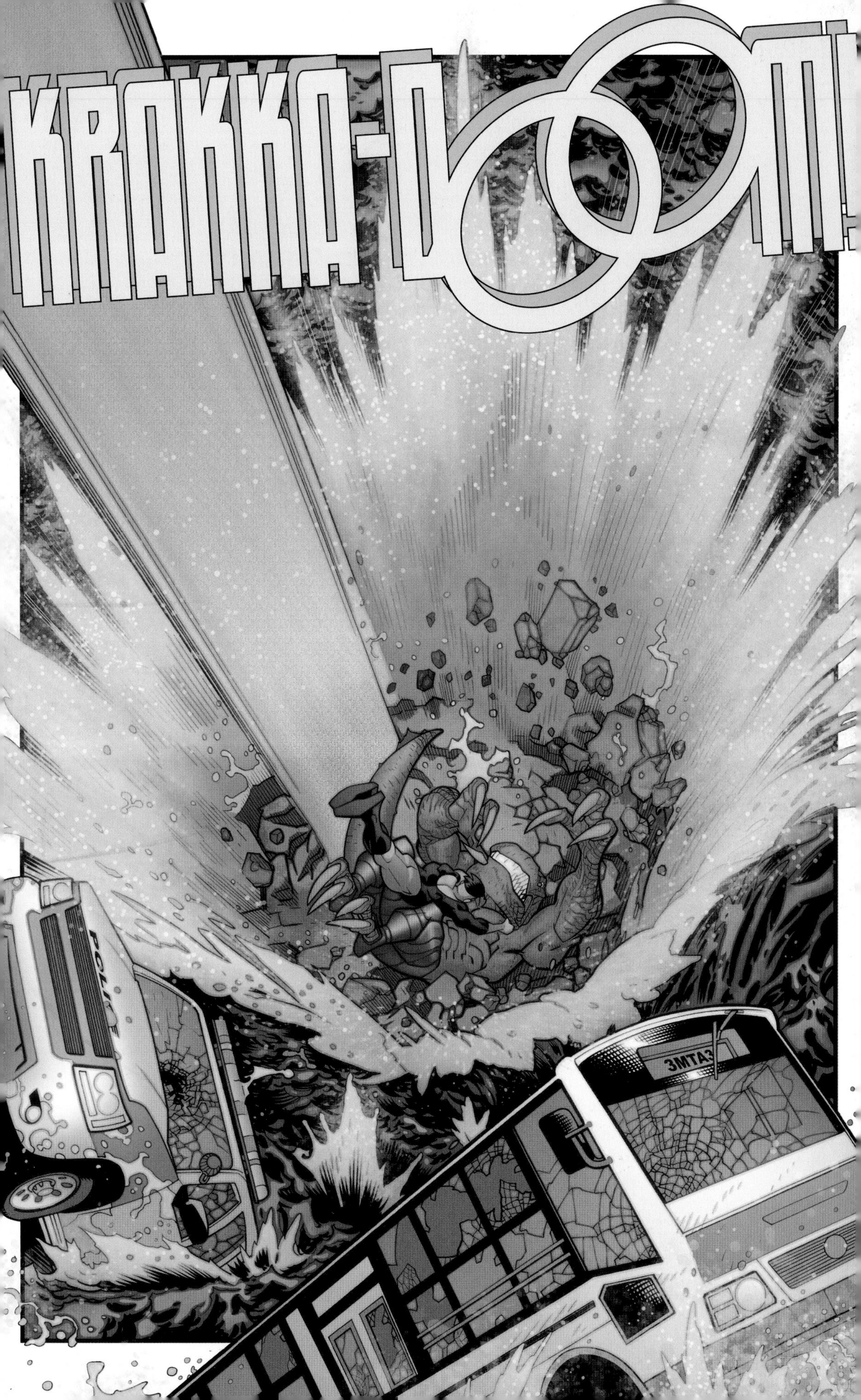
KRAKKA-DOOM!
POLICE
3MTA3

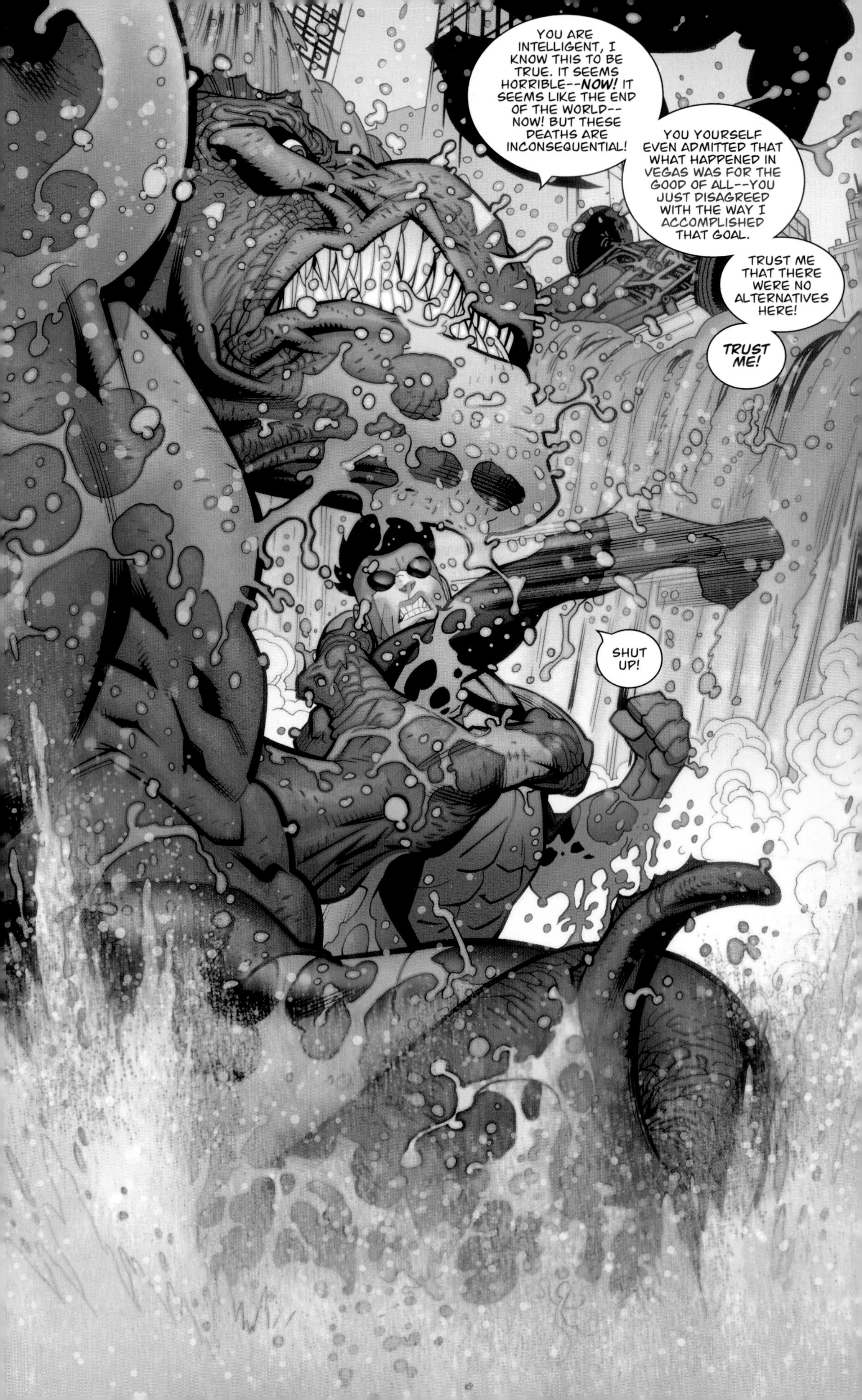
YOU ARE INTELLIGENT, I KNOW THIS TO BE TRUE. IT SEEMS HORRIBLE--*NOW!* IT SEEMS LIKE THE END OF THE WORLD-- NOW! BUT THESE DEATHS ARE INCONSEQUENTIAL!
YOU YOURSELF EVEN ADMITTED THAT WHAT HAPPENED IN VEGAS WAS FOR THE GOOD OF ALL--YOU JUST DISAGREED WITH THE WAY I ACCOMPLISHED THAT GOAL.
TRUST ME THAT THERE WERE NO ALTERNATIVES HERE!
TRUST ME!
SHUT UP!

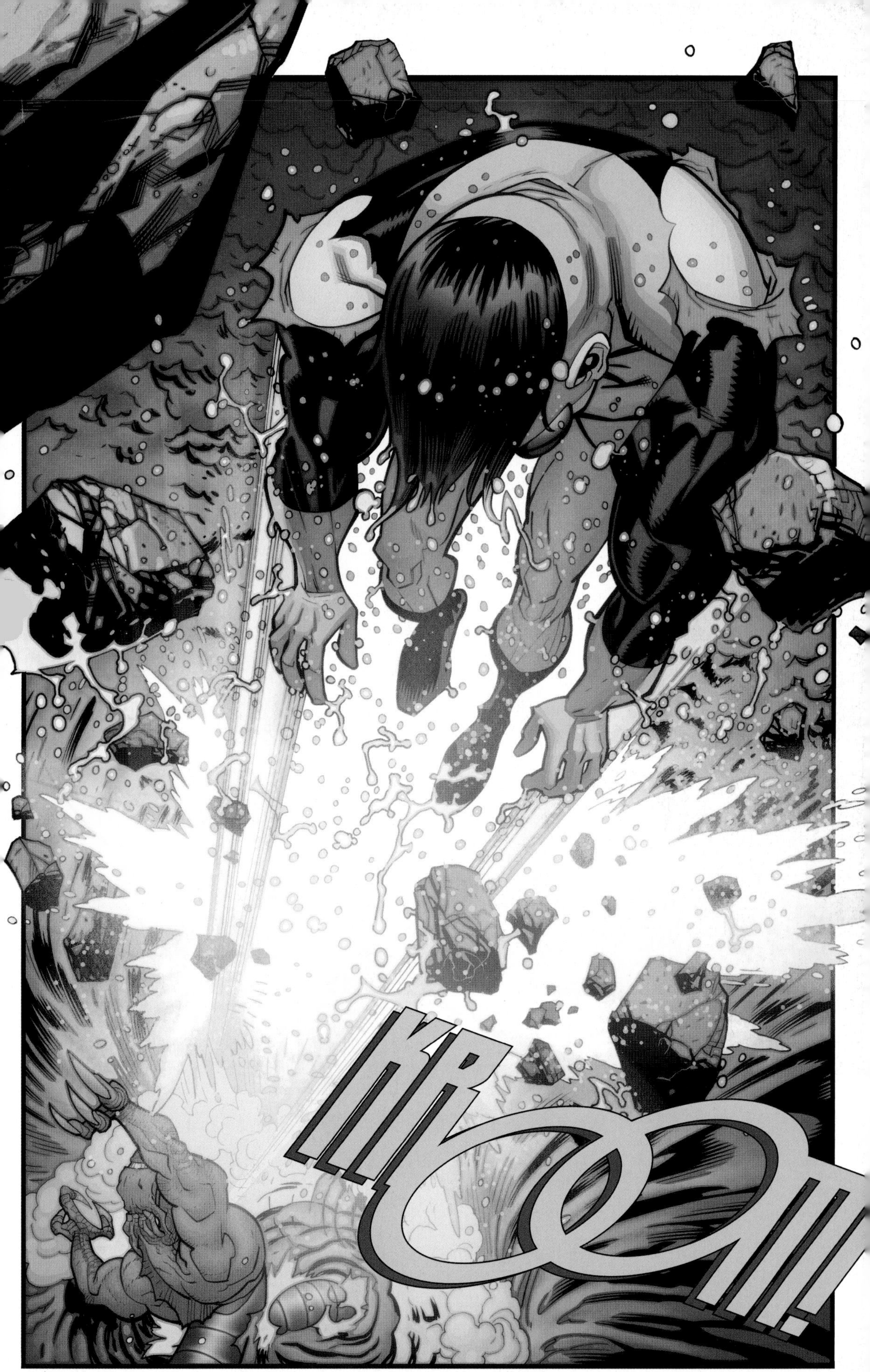
KRBOOM!!

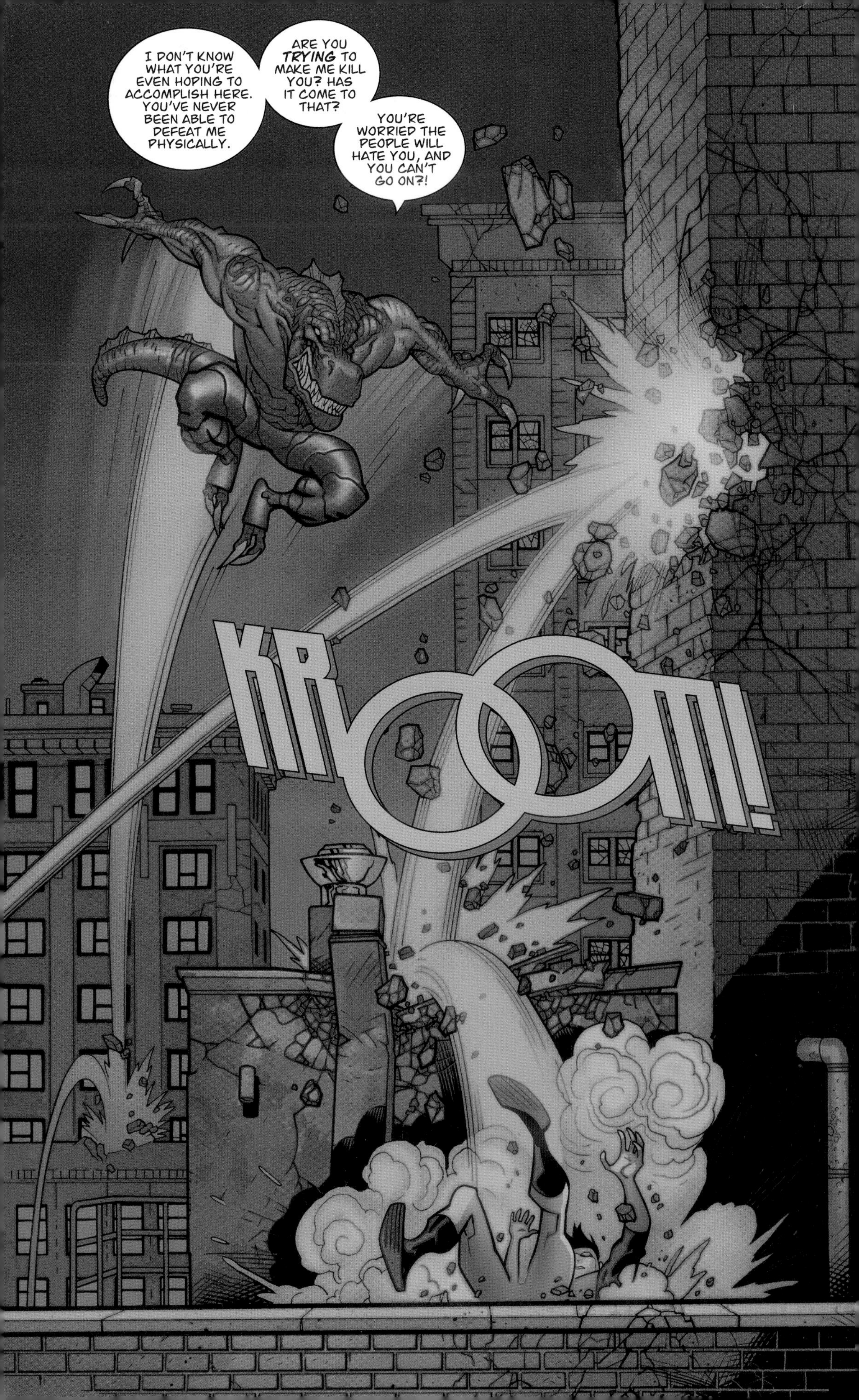
I DON'T KNOW WHAT YOU'RE EVEN HOPING TO ACCOMPLISH HERE. YOU'VE NEVER BEEN ABLE TO DEFEAT ME PHYSICALLY.
ARE YOU *TRYING* TO MAKE ME KILL YOU? HAS IT COME TO THAT?
YOU'RE WORRIED THE PEOPLE WILL HATE YOU, AND YOU CAN'T GO ON?!
KROOM!!

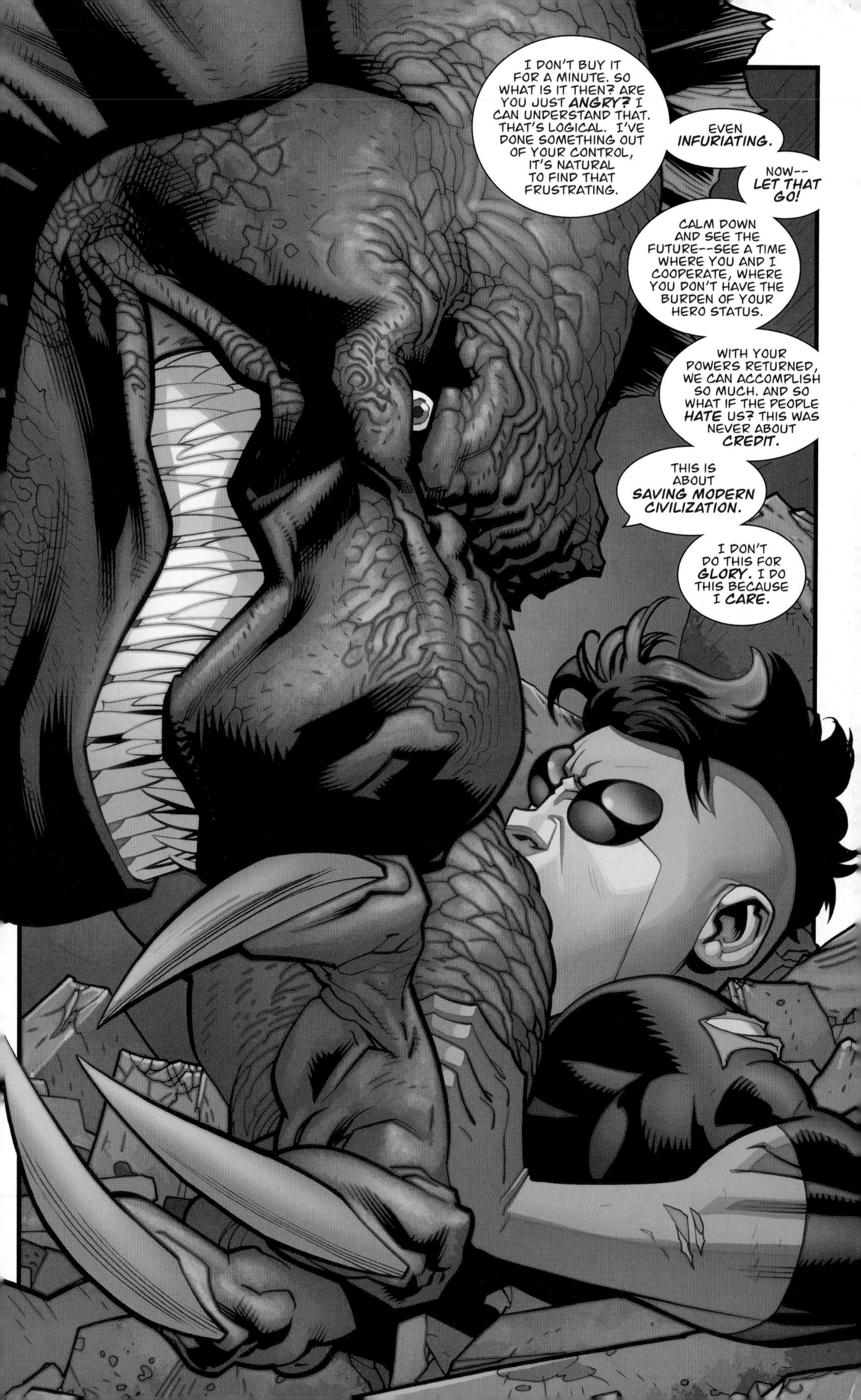
I DON'T BUY IT FOR A MINUTE. SO WHAT IS IT THEN? ARE YOU JUST ANGRY? I CAN UNDERSTAND THAT. THAT'S LOGICAL. I'VE DONE SOMETHING OUT OF YOUR CONTROL, IT'S NATURAL TO FIND THAT FRUSTRATING.
EVEN INFURIATING.
NOW-- LET THAT GO!
CALM DOWN AND SEE THE FUTURE--SEE A TIME WHERE YOU AND I COOPERATE, WHERE YOU DON'T HAVE THE BURDEN OF YOUR HERO STATUS.
WITH YOUR POWERS RETURNED, WE CAN ACCOMPLISH SO MUCH. AND SO WHAT IF THE PEOPLE HATE US? THIS WAS NEVER ABOUT CREDIT.
THIS IS ABOUT SAVING MODERN CIVILIZATION.
I DON'T DO THIS FOR GLORY. I DO THIS BECAUSE I CARE.

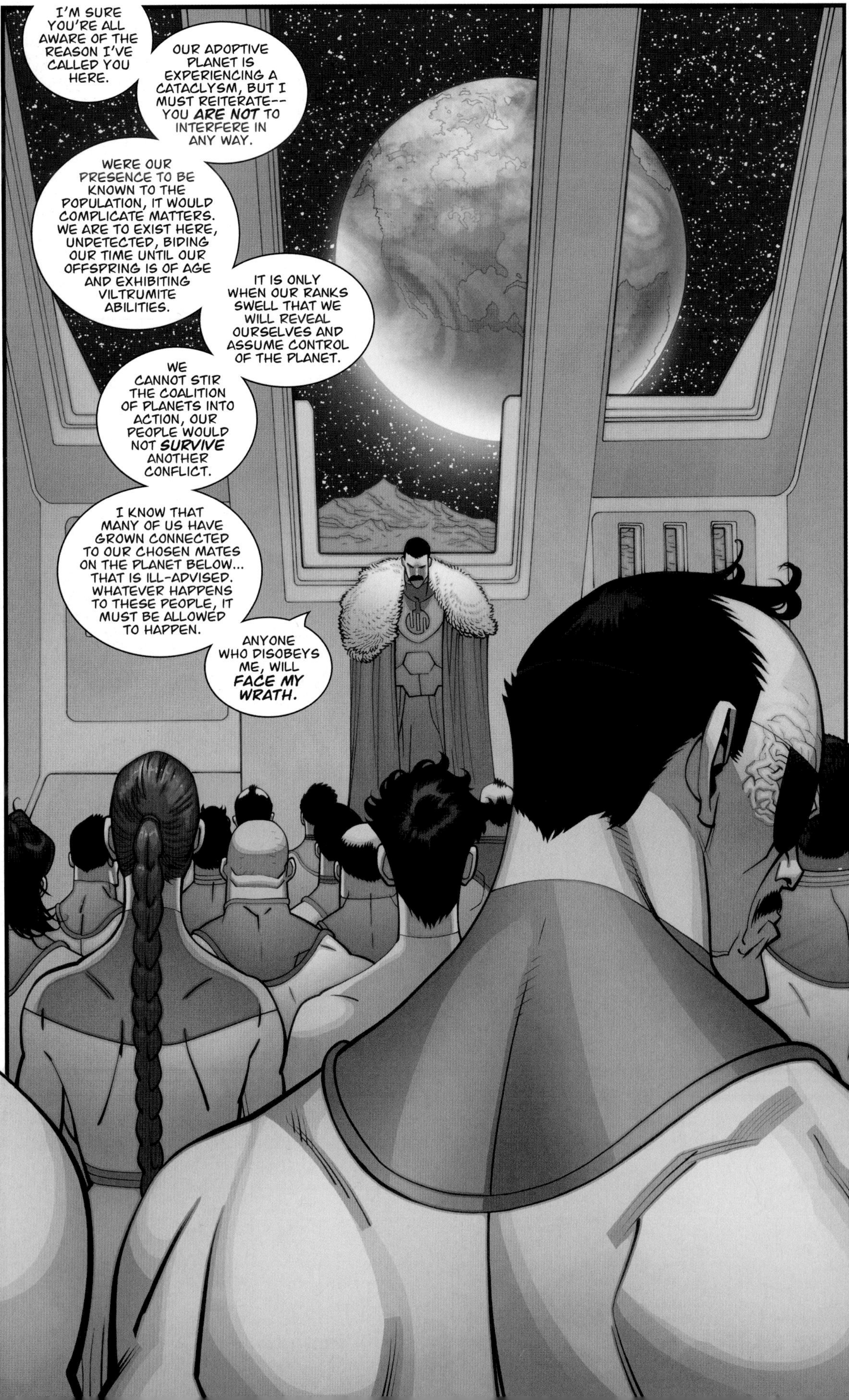
I'M SURE YOU'RE ALL AWARE OF THE REASON I'VE CALLED YOU HERE.
OUR ADOPTIVE PLANET IS EXPERIENCING A CATACLYSM, BUT I MUST REITERATE-- YOU ARE NOT TO INTERFERE IN ANY WAY.
WERE OUR PRESENCE TO BE KNOWN TO THE POPULATION, IT WOULD COMPLICATE MATTERS. WE ARE TO EXIST HERE, UNDETECTED, BIDING OUR TIME UNTIL OUR OFFSPRING IS OF AGE AND EXHIBITING VILTRUMITE ABILITIES.
IT IS ONLY WHEN OUR RANKS SWELL THAT WE WILL REVEAL OURSELVES AND ASSUME CONTROL OF THE PLANET.
WE CANNOT STIR THE COALITION OF PLANETS INTO ACTION, OUR PEOPLE WOULD NOT SURVIVE ANOTHER CONFLICT.
I KNOW THAT MANY OF US HAVE GROWN CONNECTED TO OUR CHOSEN MATES ON THE PLANET BELOW... THAT IS ILL-ADVISED. WHATEVER HAPPENS TO THESE PEOPLE, IT MUST BE ALLOWED TO HAPPEN.
ANYONE WHO DISOBEYS ME, WILL FACE MY WRATH.

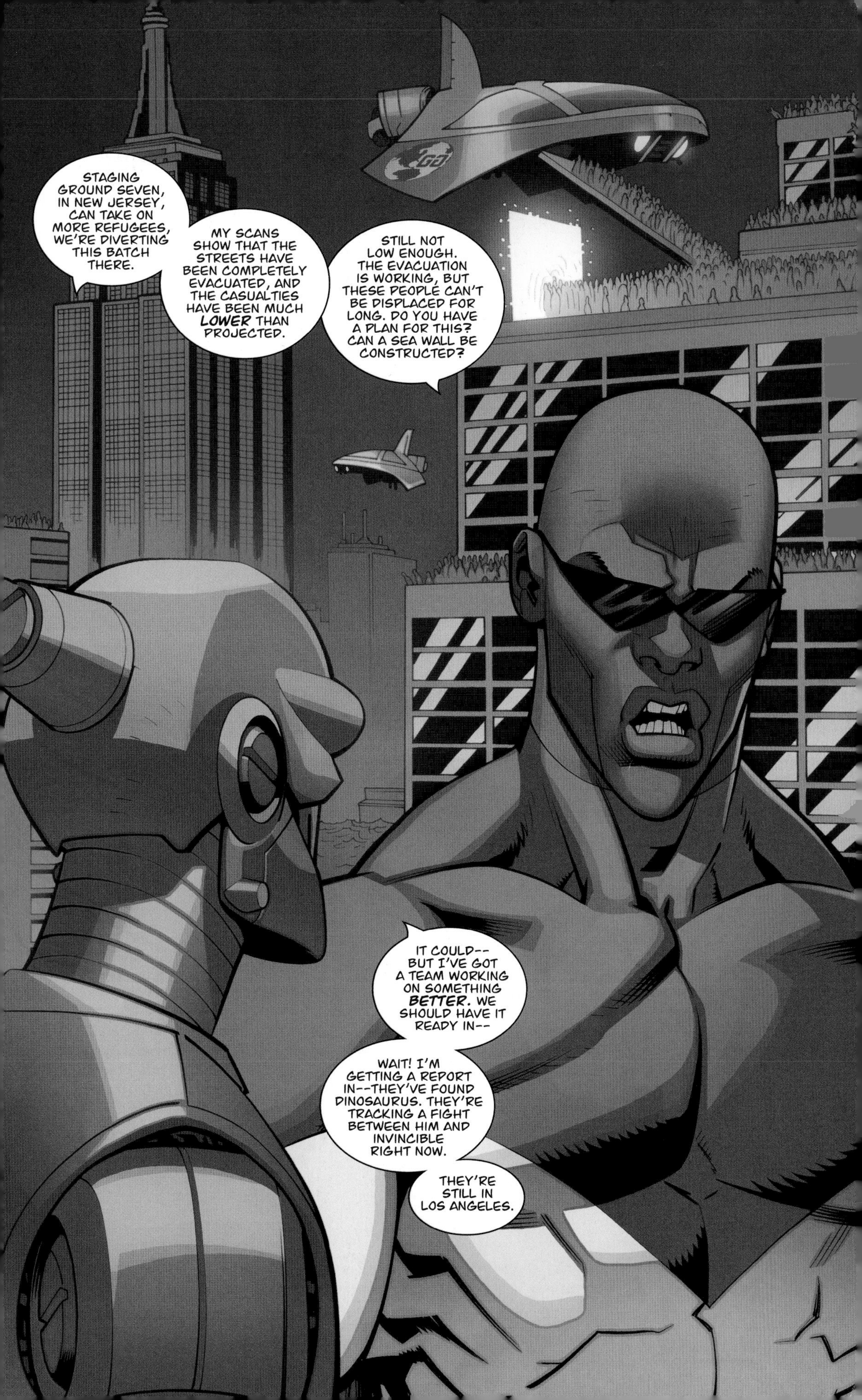
STAGING GROUND SEVEN, IN NEW JERSEY, CAN TAKE ON MORE REFUGEES, WE'RE DIVERTING THIS BATCH THERE.
MY SCANS SHOW THAT THE STREETS HAVE BEEN COMPLETELY EVACUATED, AND THE CASUALTIES HAVE BEEN MUCH LOWER THAN PROJECTED.
STILL NOT LOW ENOUGH. THE EVACUATION IS WORKING, BUT THESE PEOPLE CAN'T BE DISPLACED FOR LONG. DO YOU HAVE A PLAN FOR THIS? CAN A SEA WALL BE CONSTRUCTED?
IT COULD-- BUT I'VE GOT A TEAM WORKING ON SOMETHING BETTER. WE SHOULD HAVE IT READY IN--
WAIT! I'M GETTING A REPORT IN--THEY'VE FOUND DINOSAURUS. THEY'RE TRACKING A FIGHT BETWEEN HIM AND INVINCIBLE RIGHT NOW.
THEY'RE STILL IN LOS ANGELES.

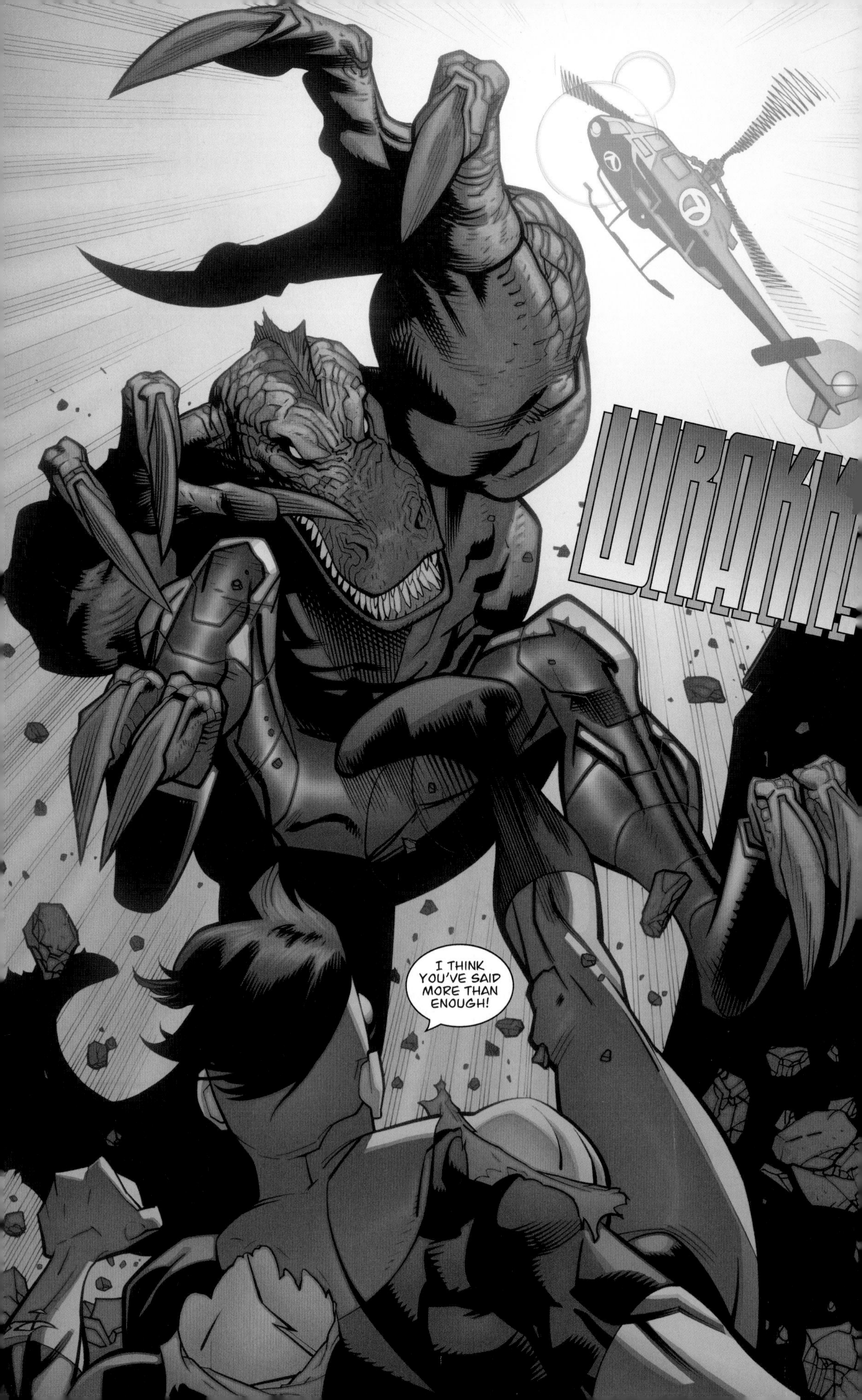
WRAKK!
I THINK YOU'VE SAID MORE THAN ENOUGH!

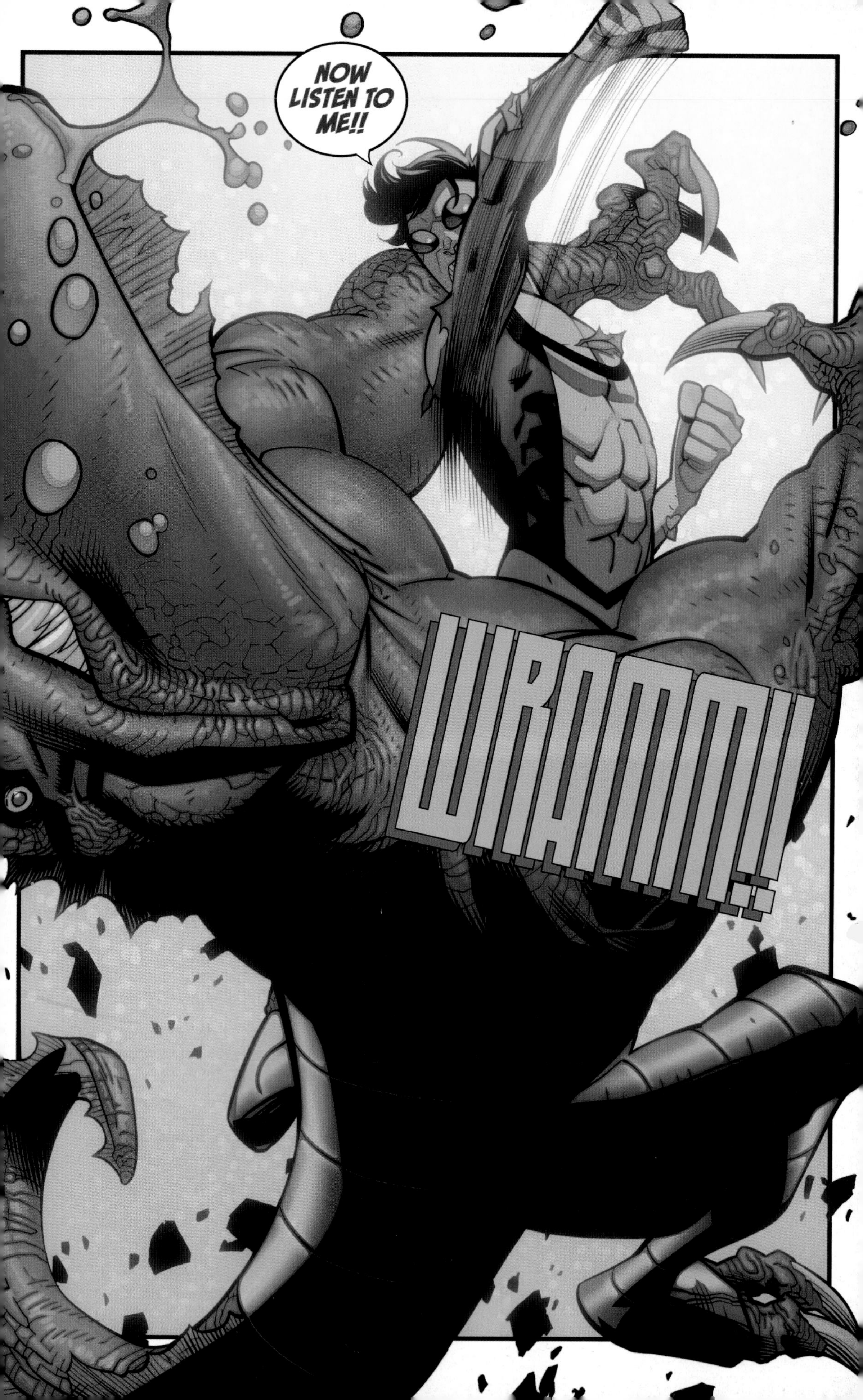
NOW LISTEN TO ME!!
WHAMM!!

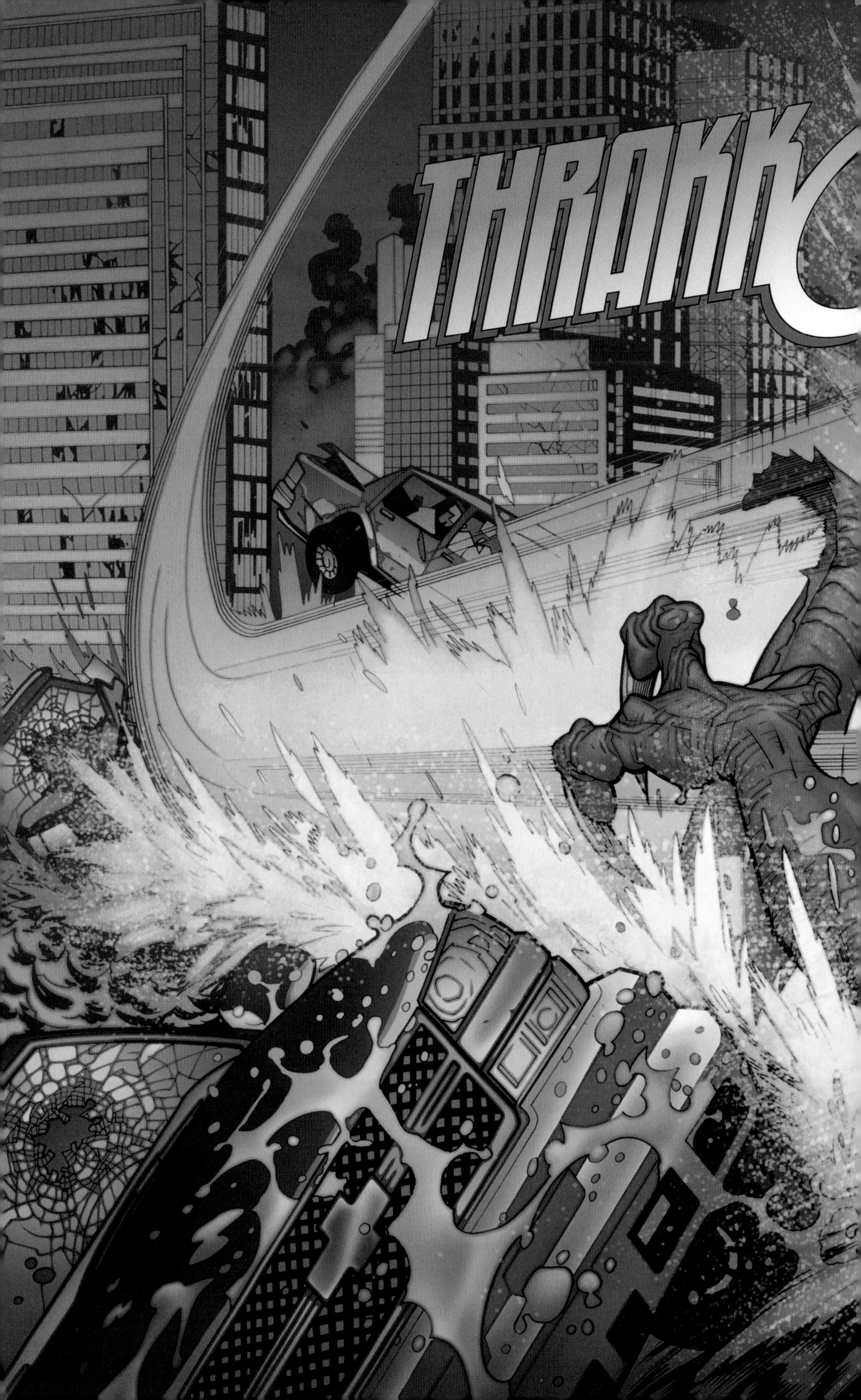
THRAKK

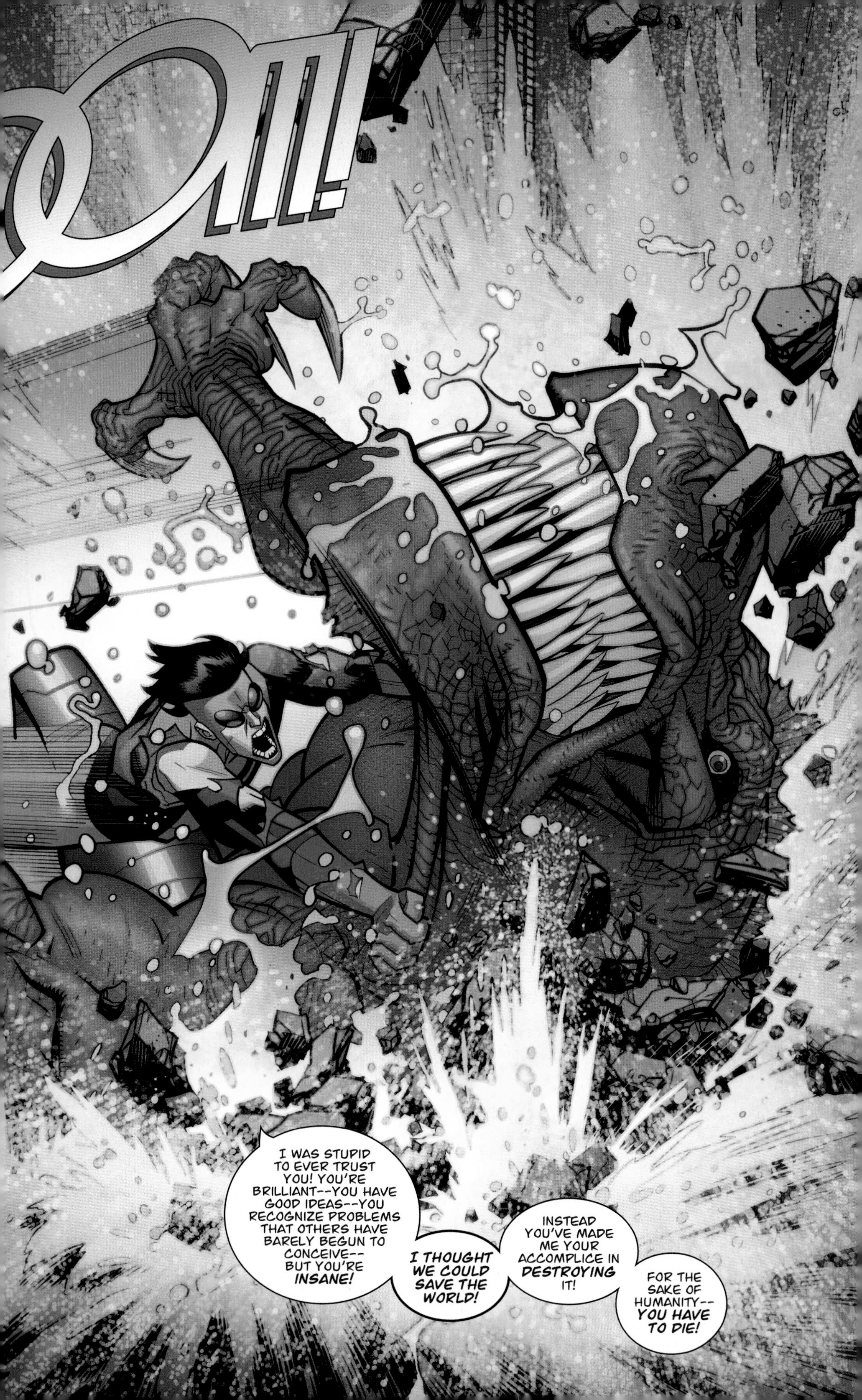
I WAS STUPID TO EVER TRUST YOU! YOU'RE BRILLIANT--YOU HAVE GOOD IDEAS--YOU RECOGNIZE PROBLEMS THAT OTHERS HAVE BARELY BEGUN TO CONCEIVE-- BUT YOU'RE INSANE!
I THOUGHT WE COULD SAVE THE WORLD!
INSTEAD YOU'VE MADE ME YOUR ACCOMPLICE IN DESTROYING IT!
FOR THE SAKE OF HUMANITY-- YOU HAVE TO DIE!

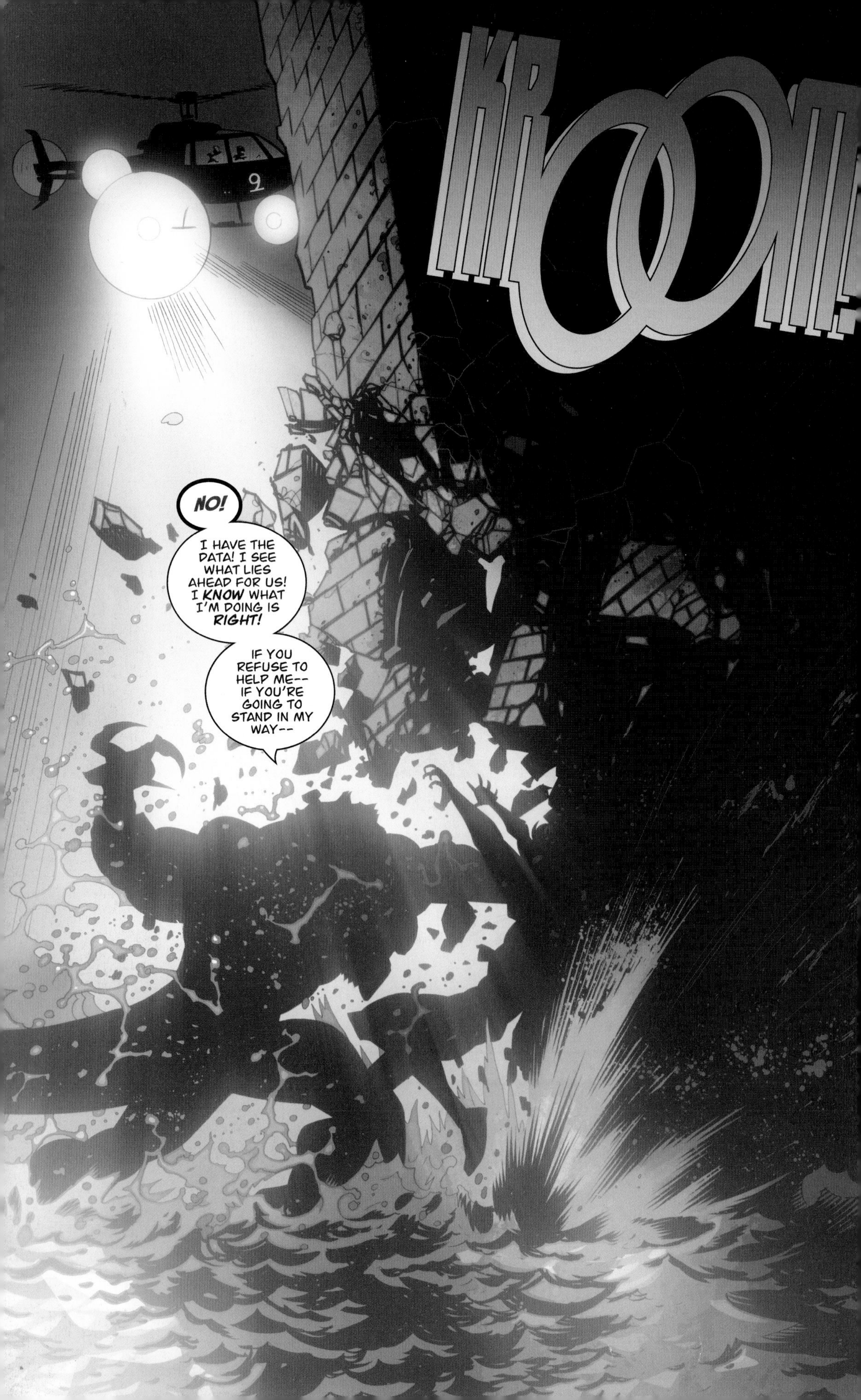
KROOM!
NO!
I HAVE THE DATA! I SEE WHAT LIES AHEAD FOR US! I KNOW WHAT I'M DOING IS RIGHT!
IF YOU REFUSE TO HELP ME-- IF YOU'RE GOING TO STAND IN MY WAY--

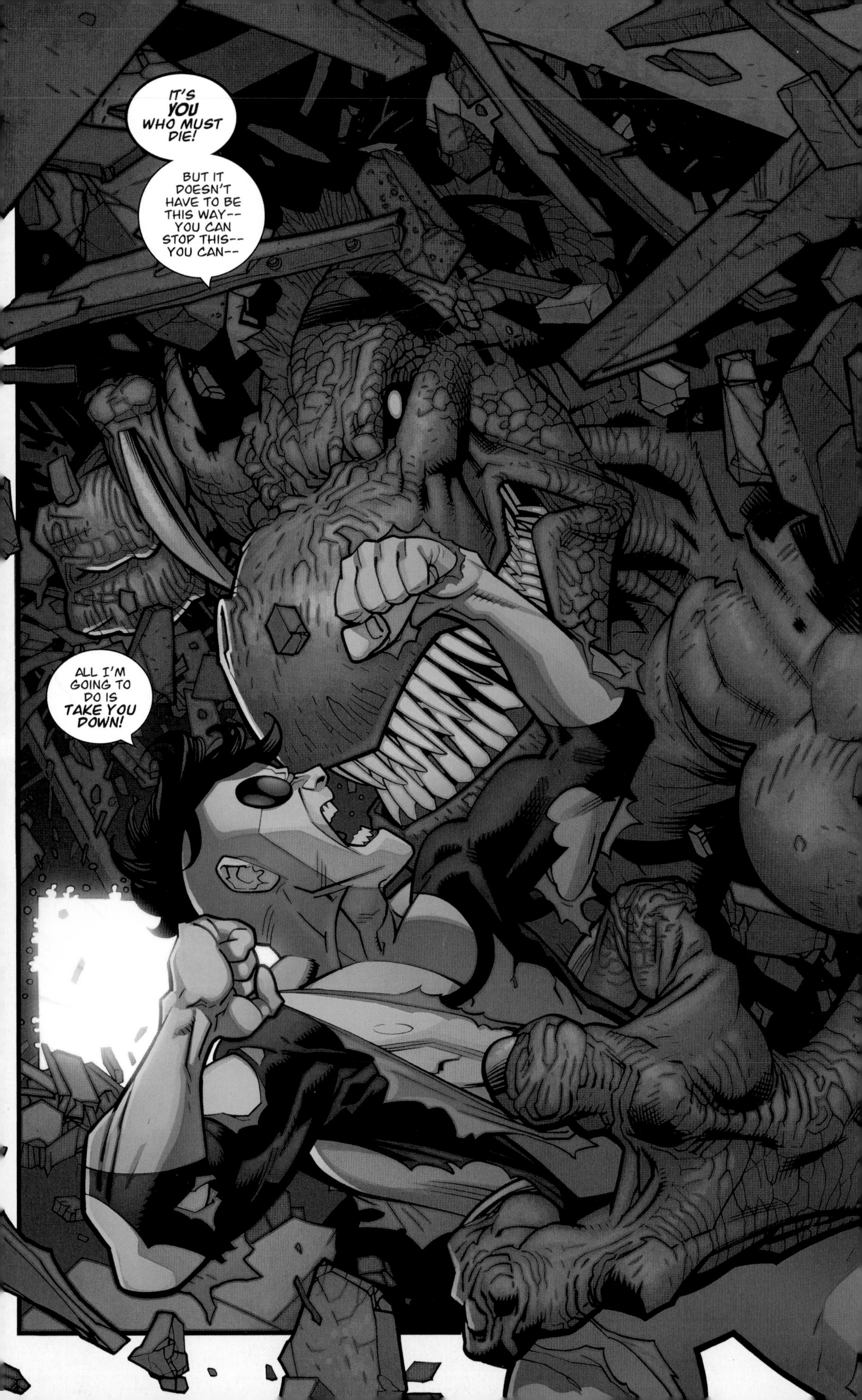
IT'S YOU WHO MUST DIE!
BUT IT DOESN'T HAVE TO BE THIS WAY-- YOU CAN STOP THIS-- YOU CAN--
ALL I'M GOING TO DO IS TAKE YOU DOWN!

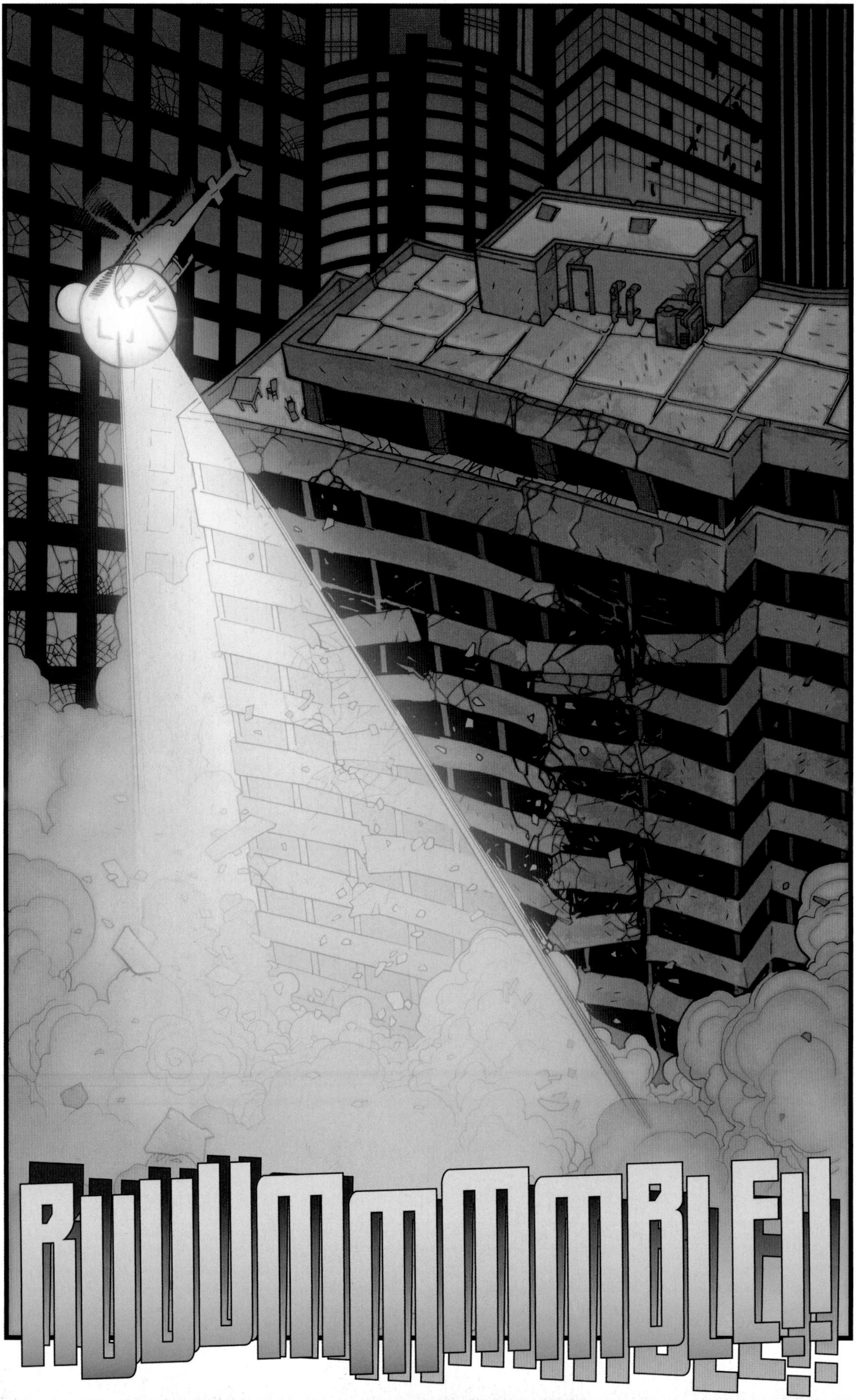
RUUUMMMMBLE!!

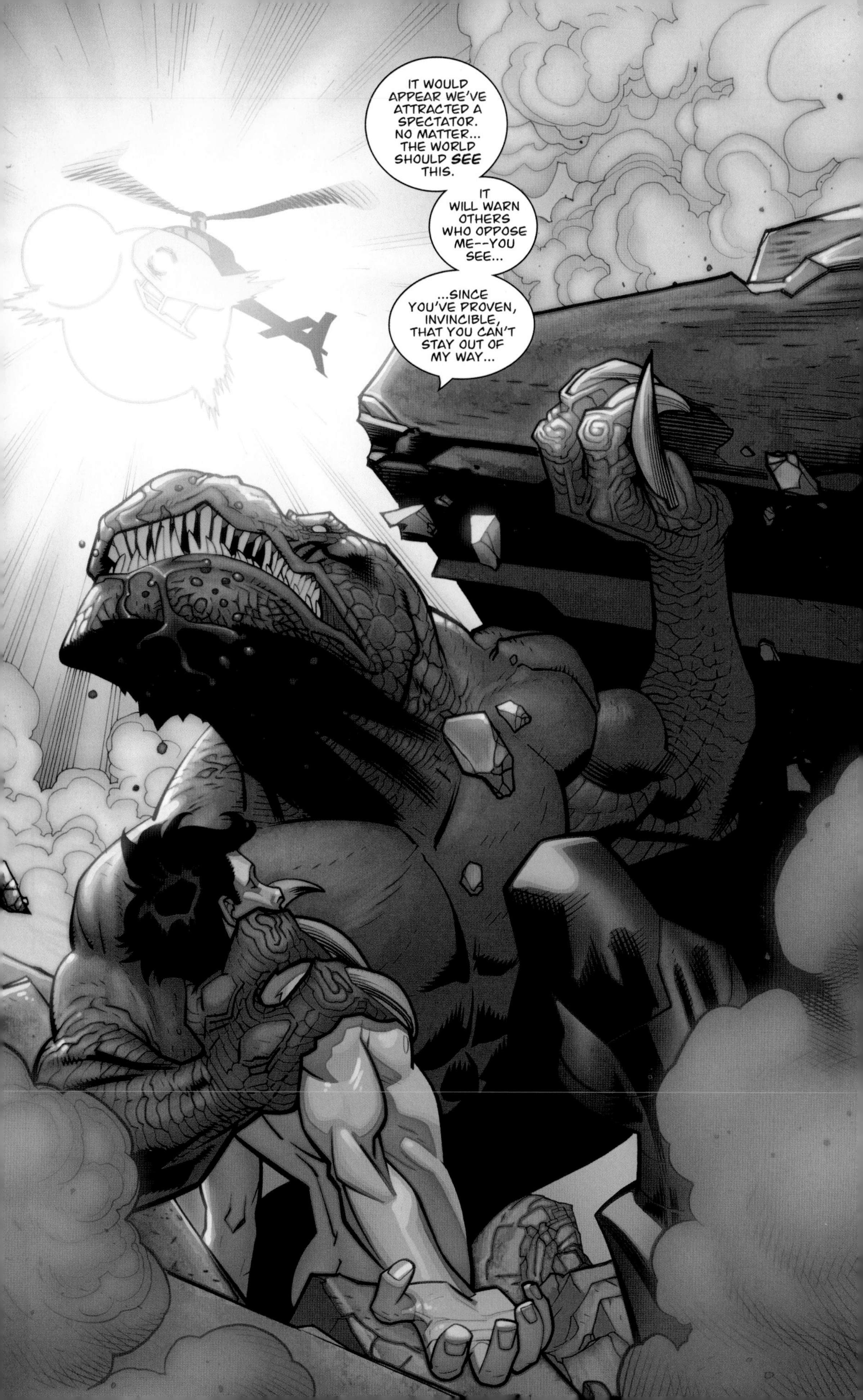
IT WOULD APPEAR WE'VE ATTRACTED A SPECTATOR. NO MATTER... THE WORLD SHOULD **SEE** THIS.
IT WILL WARN OTHERS WHO OPPOSE ME--YOU SEE...
...SINCE YOU'VE PROVEN, INVINCIBLE, THAT YOU CAN'T STAY OUT OF MY WAY...

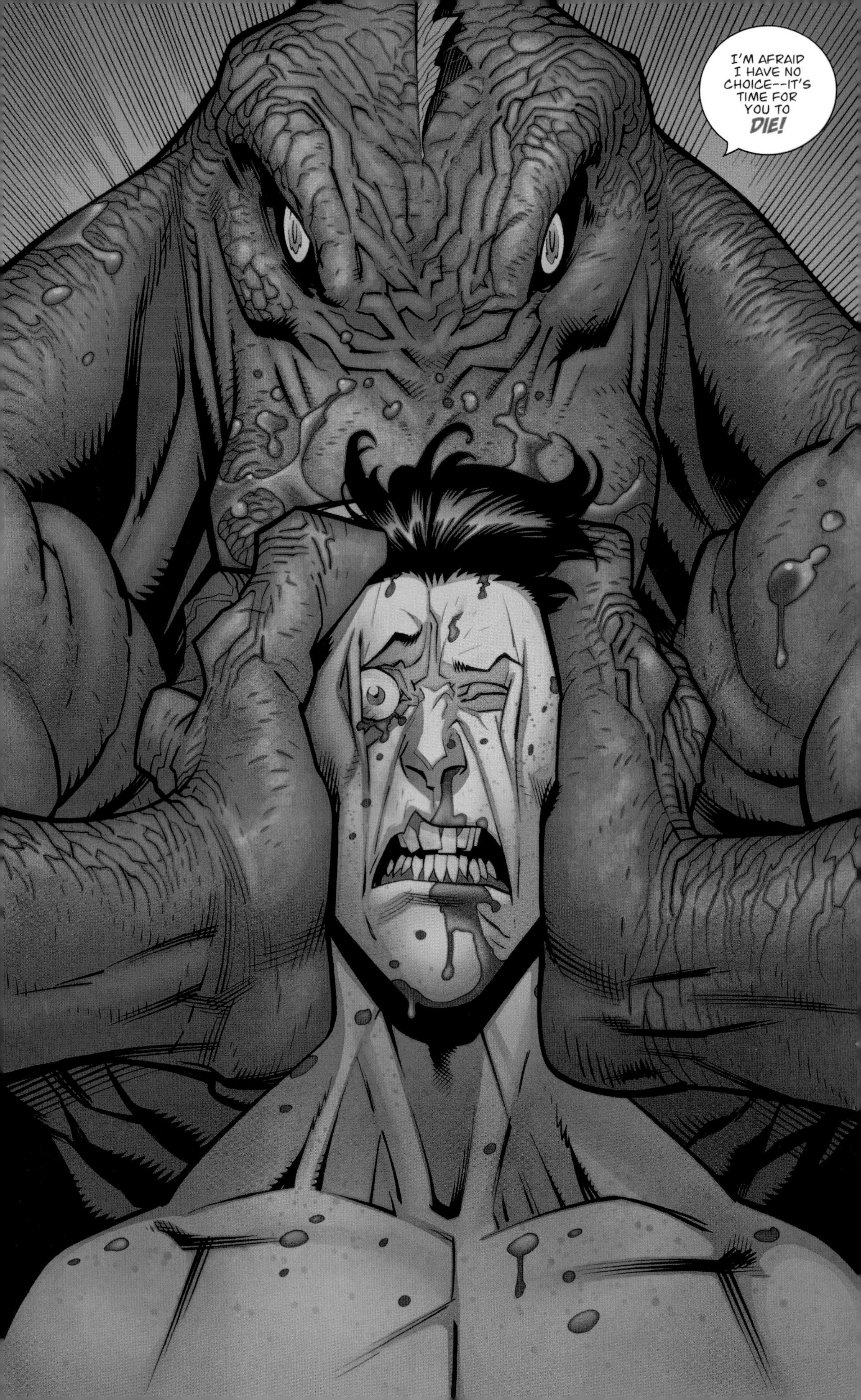
I'M AFRAID I HAVE NO CHOICE--IT'S TIME FOR YOU TO DIE!

CHAPTER FOUR

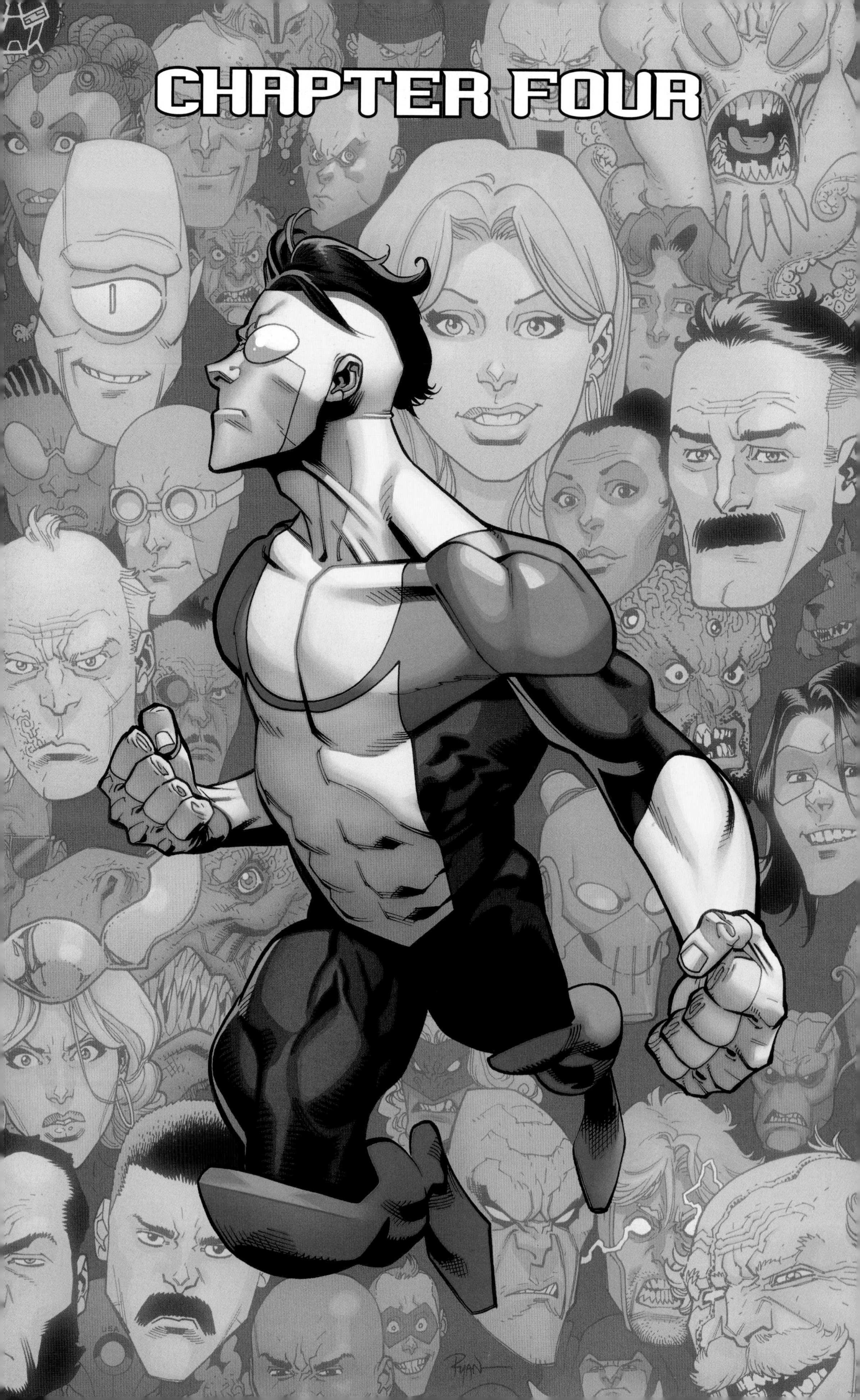

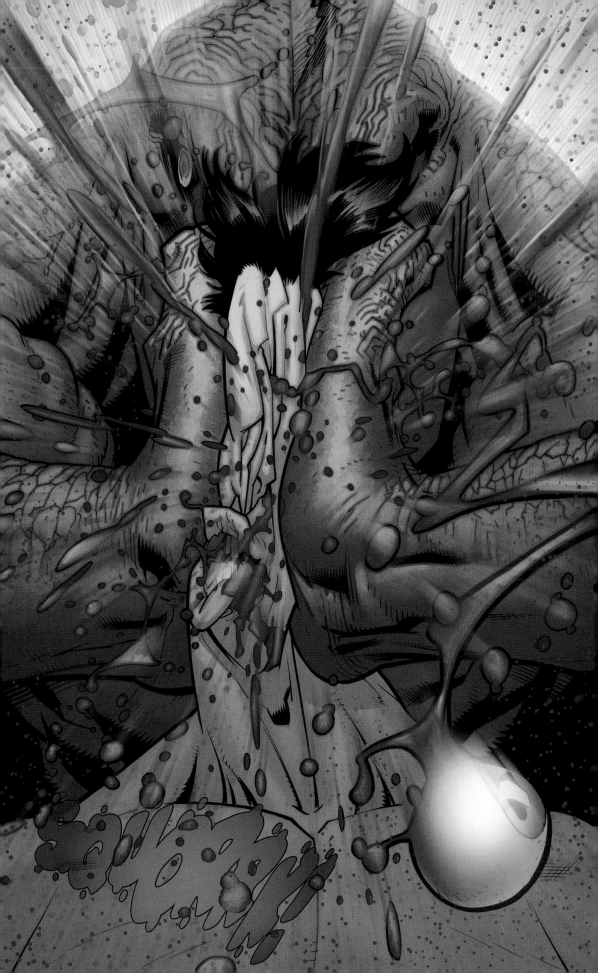

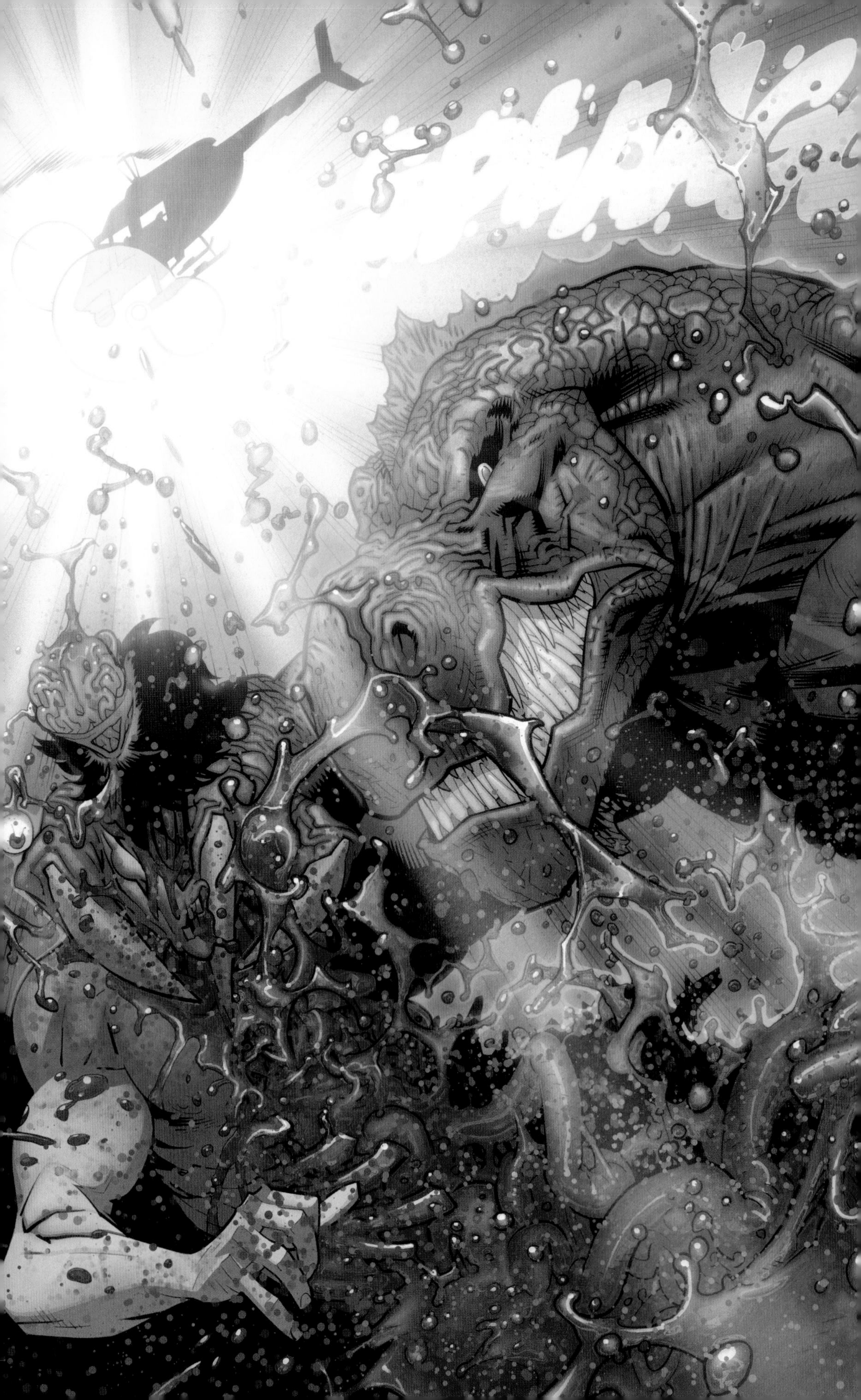

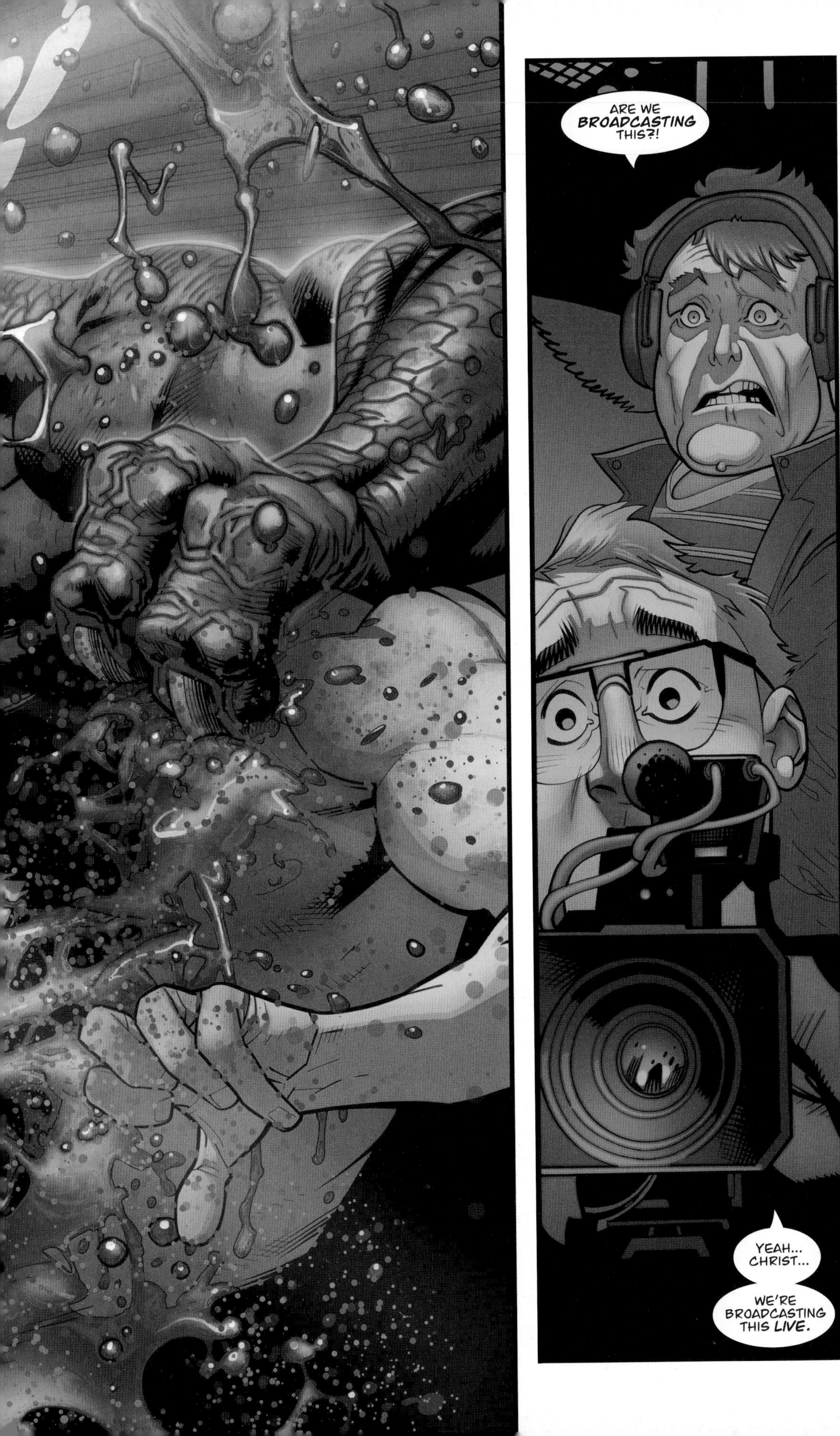
ARE WE BROADCASTING THIS?!
YEAH... CHRIST...
WE'RE BROADCASTING THIS LIVE.

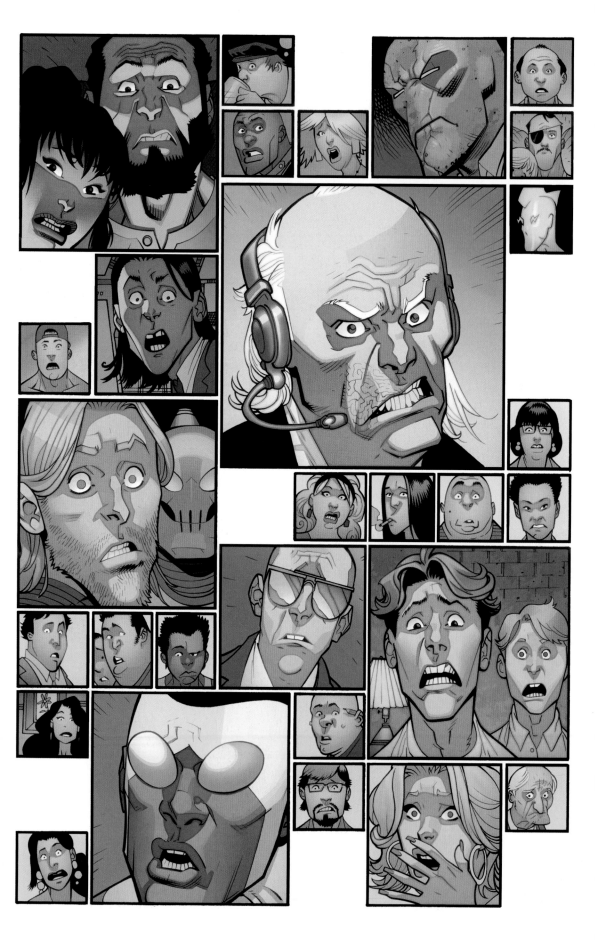

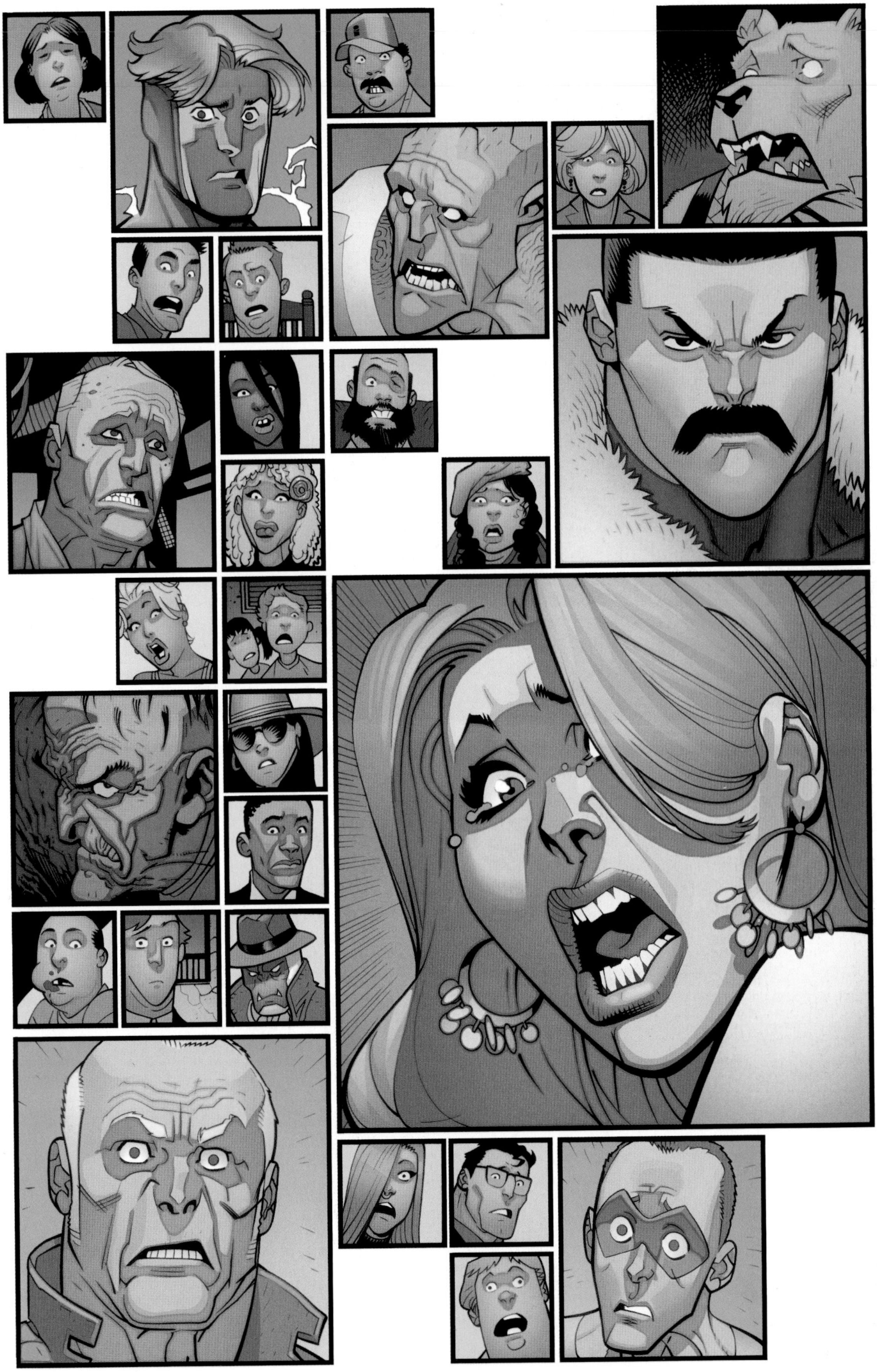

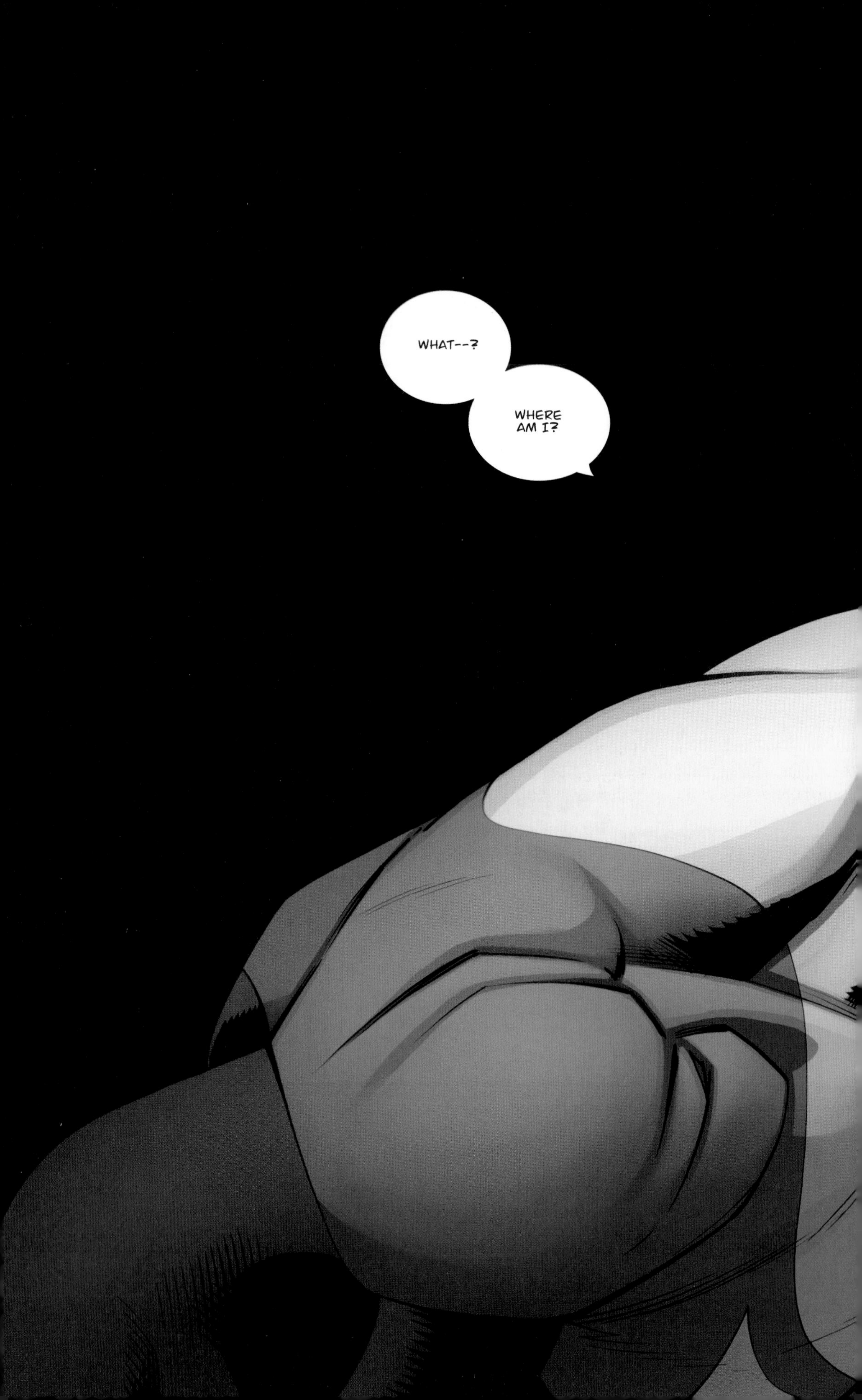
WHAT--?
WHERE AM I?

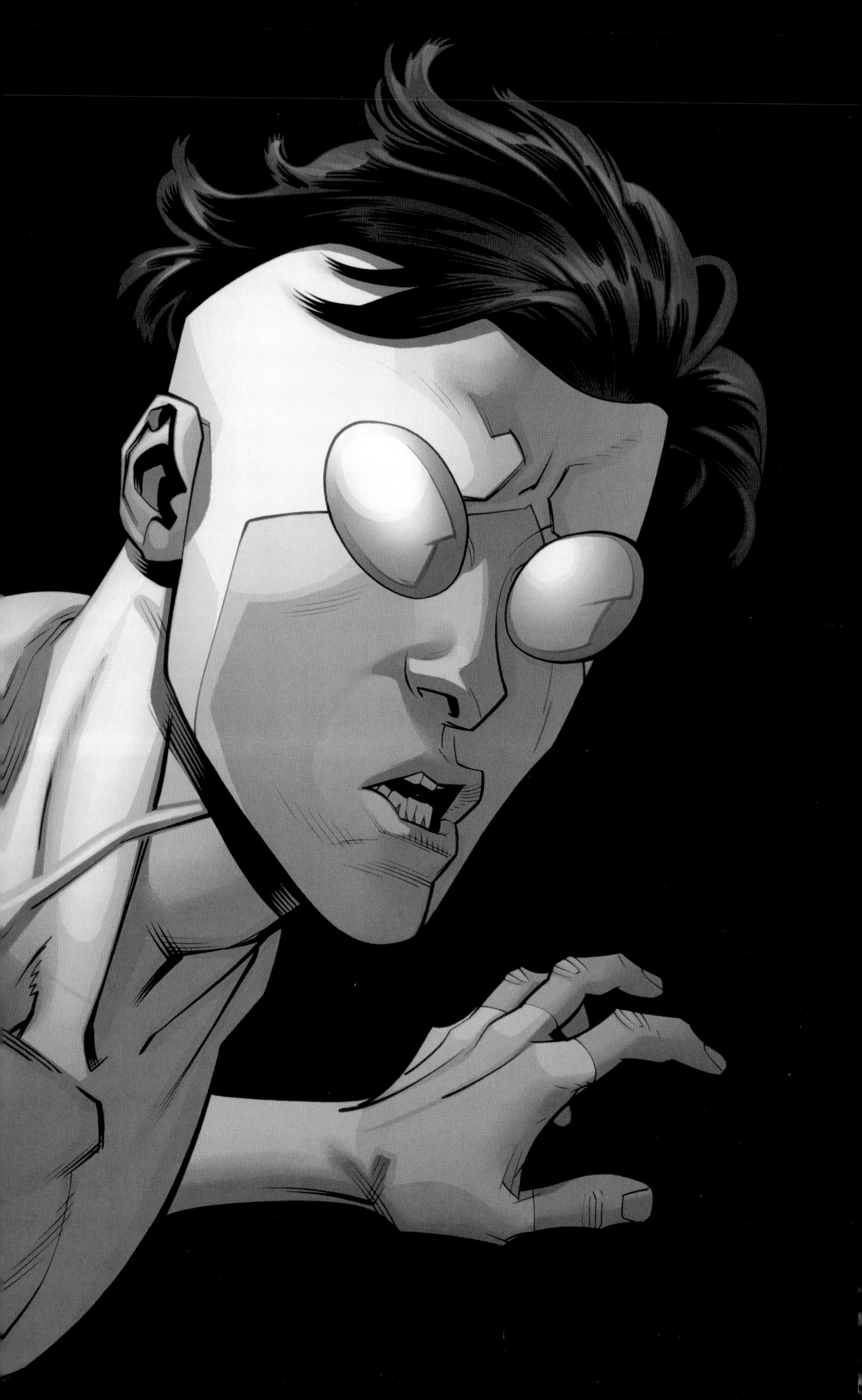

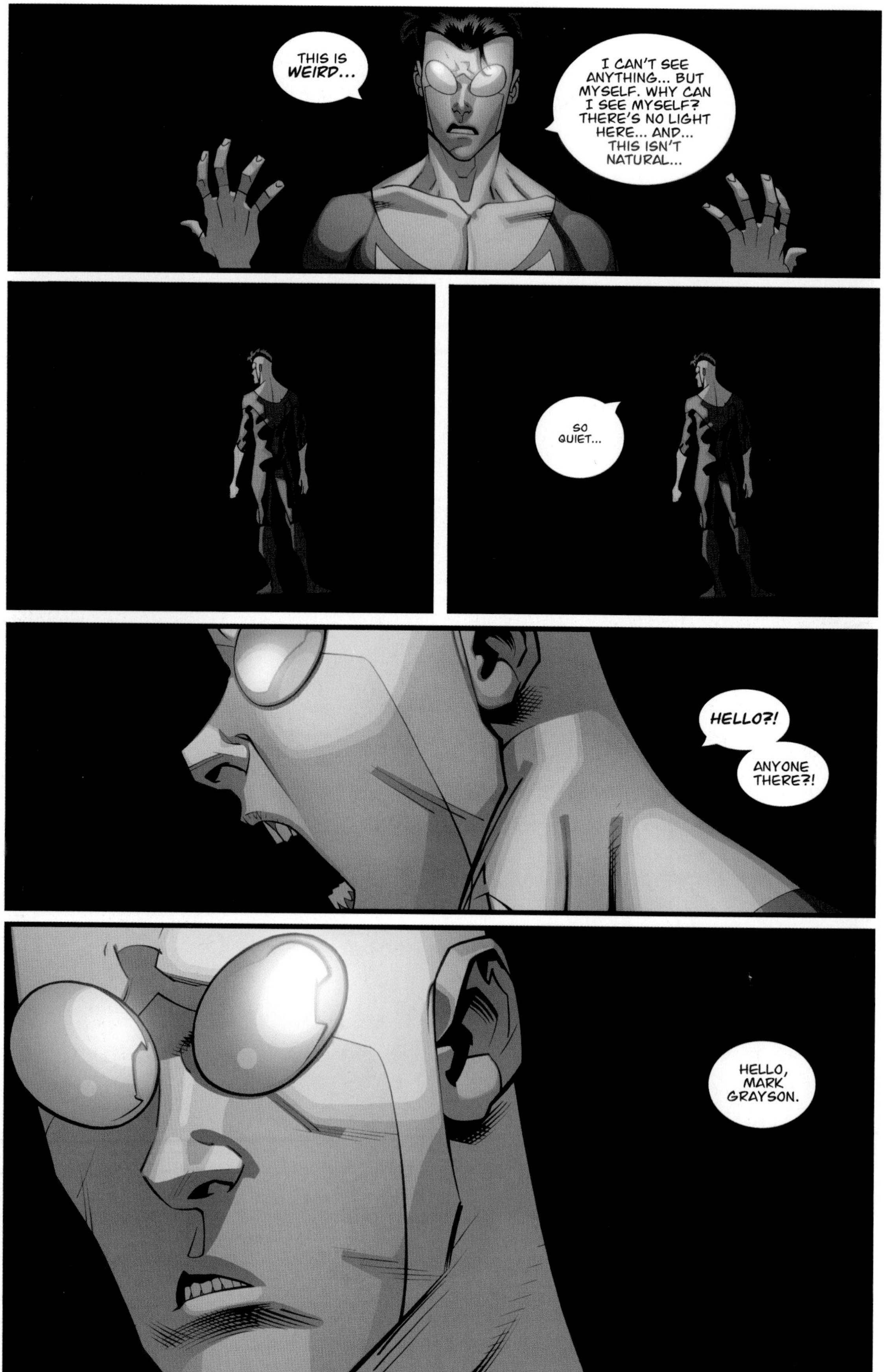
THIS IS WEIRD...
I CAN'T SEE ANYTHING... BUT MYSELF. WHY CAN I SEE MYSELF? THERE'S NO LIGHT HERE... AND... THIS ISN'T NATURAL...
SO QUIET...
HELLO?!
ANYONE THERE?!
HELLO, MARK GRAYSON.

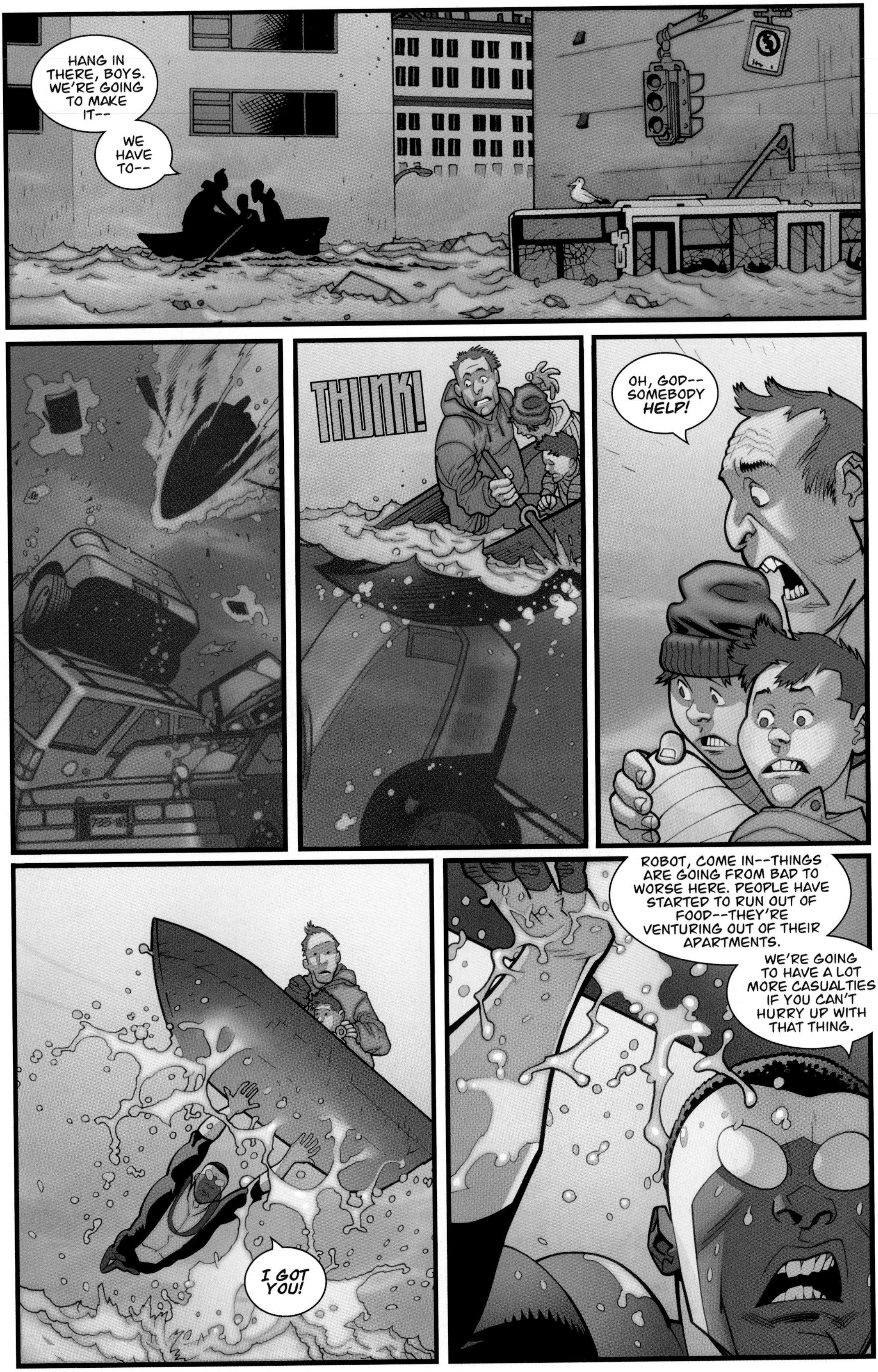
HANG IN THERE, BOYS. WE'RE GOING TO MAKE IT--
WE HAVE TO--
THUNK!
OH, GOD-- SOMEBODY HELP!
I GOT YOU!
ROBOT, COME IN--THINGS ARE GOING FROM BAD TO WORSE HERE. PEOPLE HAVE STARTED TO RUN OUT OF FOOD--THEY'RE VENTURING OUT OF THEIR APARTMENTS.
WE'RE GOING TO HAVE A LOT MORE CASUALTIES IF YOU CAN'T HURRY UP WITH THAT THING.

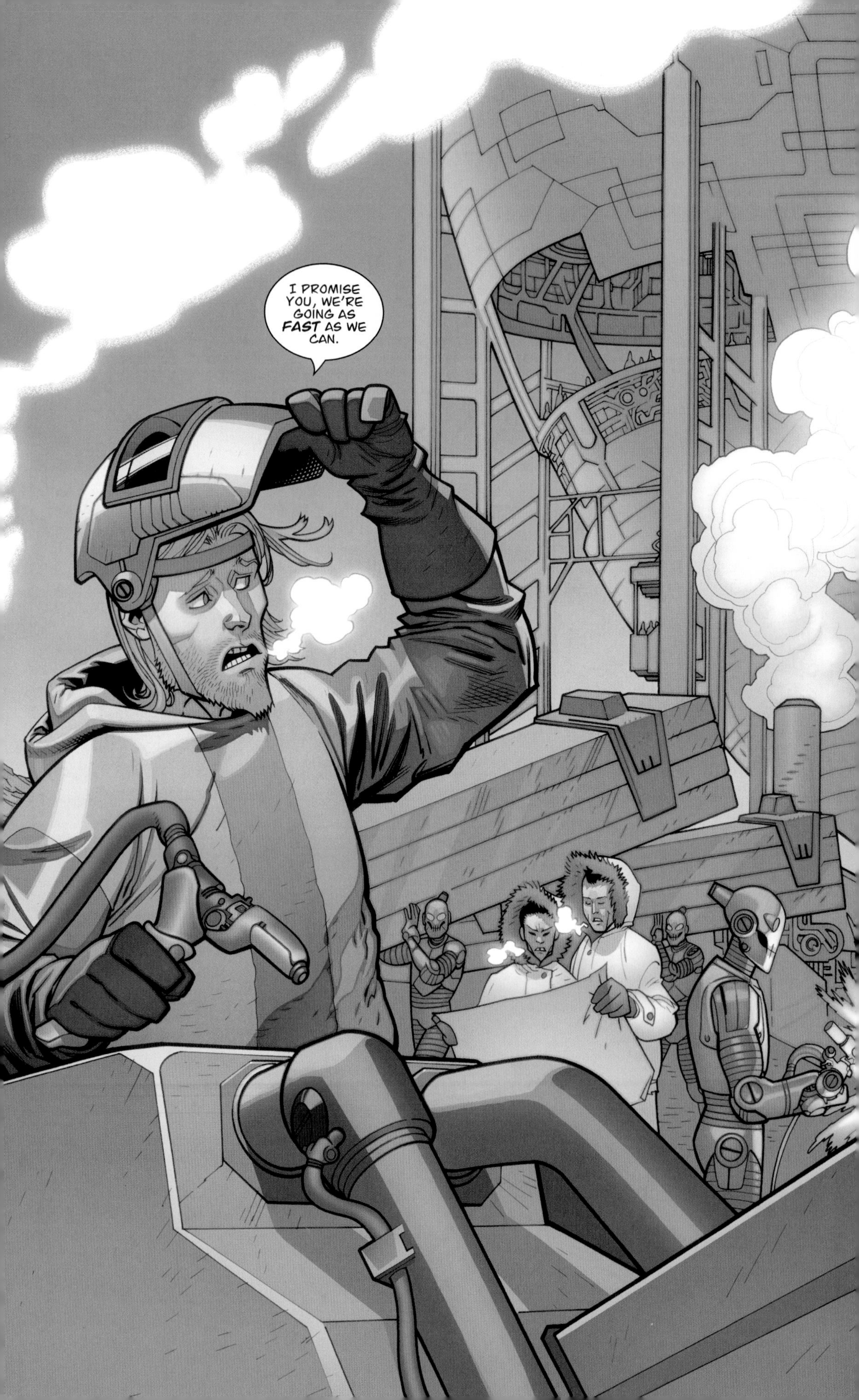
I PROMISE YOU, WE'RE GOING AS FAST AS WE CAN.

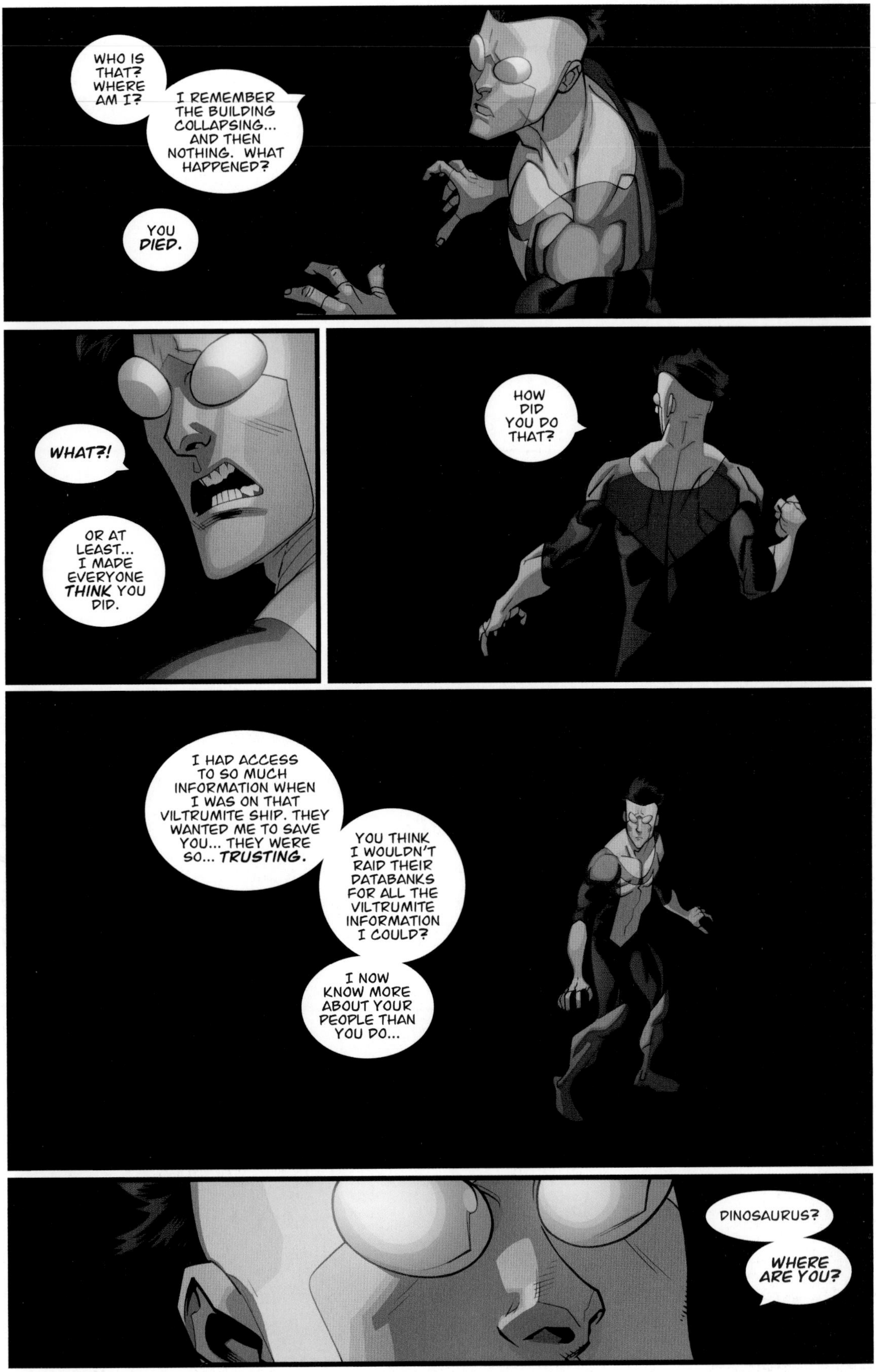
WHO IS THAT? WHERE AM I?
I REMEMBER THE BUILDING COLLAPSING... AND THEN NOTHING. WHAT HAPPENED?
YOU *DIED*.
WHAT?!
OR AT LEAST... I MADE EVERYONE *THINK* YOU DID.
HOW DID YOU DO THAT?
I HAD ACCESS TO SO MUCH INFORMATION WHEN I WAS ON THAT VILTRUMITE SHIP. THEY WANTED ME TO SAVE YOU... THEY WERE SO... *TRUSTING*.
YOU THINK I WOULDN'T RAID THEIR DATABANKS FOR ALL THE VILTRUMITE INFORMATION I COULD?
I NOW KNOW MORE ABOUT YOUR PEOPLE THAN YOU DO...
DINOSAURUS?
WHERE ARE YOU?

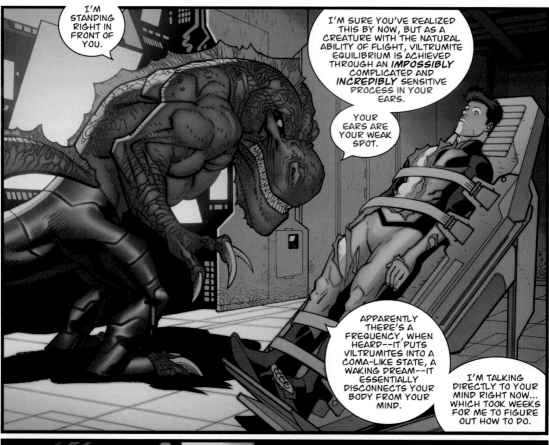

I'M STANDING RIGHT IN FRONT OF YOU.

I'M SURE YOU'VE REALIZED THIS BY NOW, BUT AS A CREATURE WITH THE NATURAL ABILITY OF FLIGHT, VILTRUMITE EQUILIBRIUM IS ACHIEVED THROUGH AN *IMPOSSIBLY* COMPLICATED AND *INCREDIBLY* SENSITIVE PROCESS IN YOUR EARS.

YOUR EARS ARE YOUR WEAK SPOT.

APPARENTLY THERE'S A FREQUENCY, WHEN HEARD--IT PUTS VILTRUMITES INTO A COMA-LIKE STATE, A WAKING DREAM--IT ESSENTIALLY DISCONNECTS YOUR BODY FROM YOUR MIND.

I'M TALKING DIRECTLY TO YOUR MIND RIGHT NOW... WHICH TOOK WEEKS FOR ME TO FIGURE OUT HOW TO DO.

OKAY... THAT MAKES MAYBE A *LITTLE* SENSE.

WHY DOES EVERYONE THINK I'M DEAD?

OH, *THAT*...

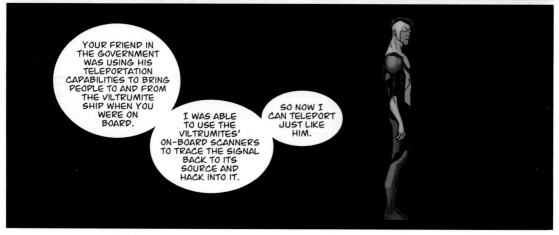

YOUR FRIEND IN THE GOVERNMENT WAS USING HIS TELEPORTATION CAPABILITIES TO BRING PEOPLE TO AND FROM THE VILTRUMITE SHIP WHEN YOU WERE ON BOARD.

I WAS ABLE TO USE THE VILTRUMITES' ON-BOARD SCANNERS TO TRACE THE SIGNAL BACK TO ITS SOURCE AND HACK INTO IT.

SO NOW I CAN TELEPORT JUST LIKE HIM.

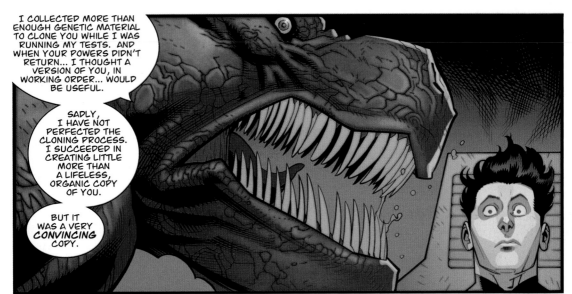

I COLLECTED MORE THAN ENOUGH GENETIC MATERIAL TO CLONE YOU WHILE I WAS RUNNING MY TESTS. AND WHEN YOUR POWERS DIDN'T RETURN... I THOUGHT A VERSION OF YOU, IN WORKING ORDER... WOULD BE USEFUL.

SADLY, I HAVE NOT PERFECTED THE CLONING PROCESS. I SUCCEEDED IN CREATING LITTLE MORE THAN A LIFELESS, ORGANIC COPY OF YOU.

BUT IT WAS A VERY *CONVINCING* COPY.

"I USED A DOORWAY TO SWITCH BODIES WHILE THE BUILDING COLLAPSED.

"YOU WERE SENT HERE, WHERE THE FREQUENCY WAS ALREADY BEING BROADCAST TO PUT YOU IN THIS STATE.

"THEN I EVISCERATED YOUR VERY CONVINCING CLONE IN FRONT OF A WORLDWIDE AUDIENCE."*

*IT HAPPENED IN THIS VERY ISSUE!

DON'T YOU GET WHAT I'VE DONE? I'VE FREED YOU FROM ALL OBLIGATIONS. YOU HAVE NO DISTRACTIONS NOW.

YOU DON'T HAVE TO ANSWER TO ANYONE. YOU DON'T HAVE TO BE THERE FOR ANYONE. YOU'RE NO LONGER THE VILLAIN-- YOU DIDN'T CAUSE THIS, YOU DIED TRYING TO DEFEAT THE ONE WHO DID... YOU'RE A *MARTYR.*

NO ONE WILL COME AFTER YOU. YOU'RE *FREE.* FREE TO WORK WITH ME... FREE TO CONTINUE OUR PLANS...

...FREE TO SAVE THE WORLD.

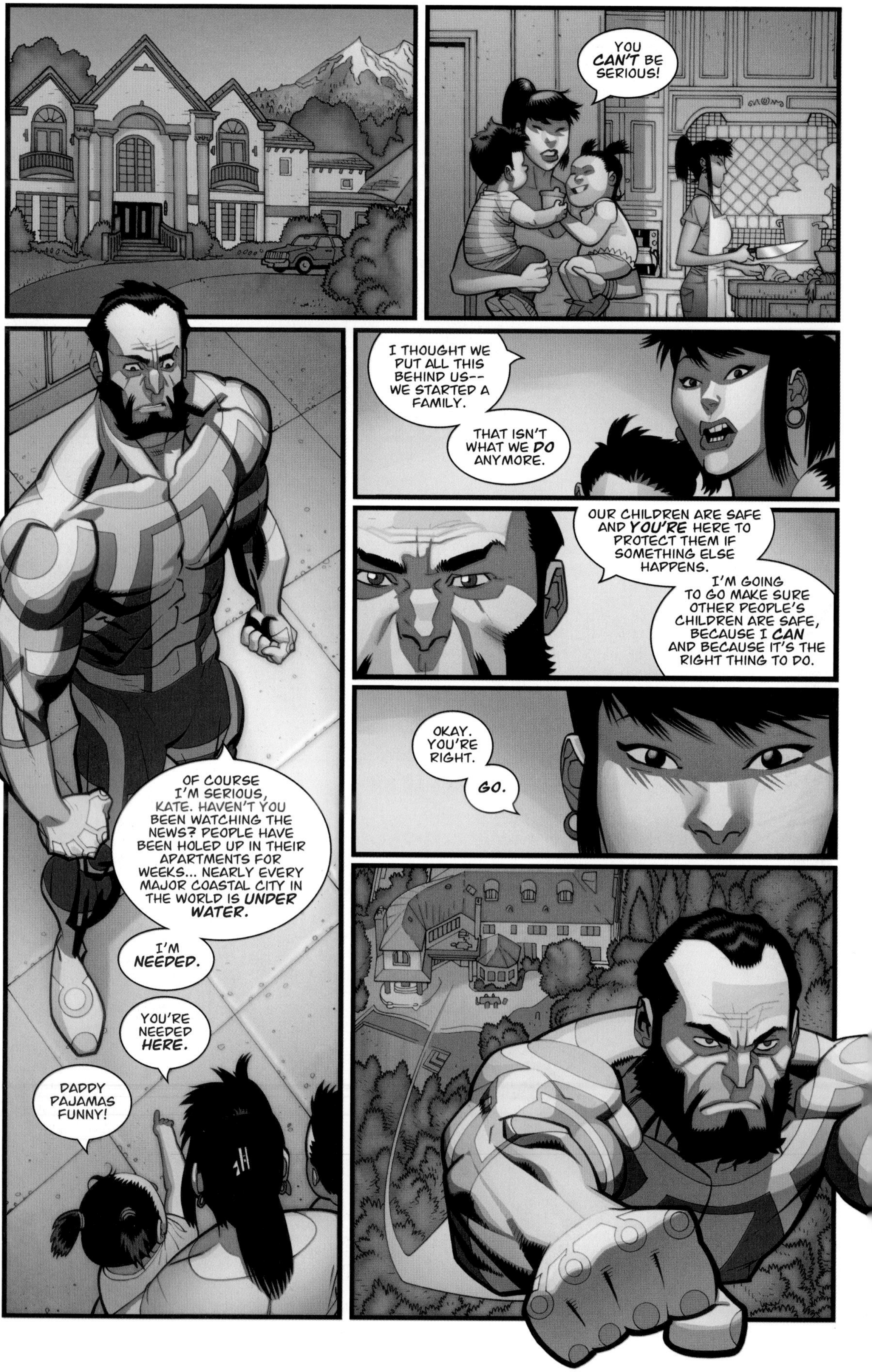
YOU CAN'T BE SERIOUS!
OF COURSE I'M SERIOUS, KATE. HAVEN'T YOU BEEN WATCHING THE NEWS? PEOPLE HAVE BEEN HOLED UP IN THEIR APARTMENTS FOR WEEKS... NEARLY EVERY MAJOR COASTAL CITY IN THE WORLD IS UNDER WATER.
I'M NEEDED.
YOU'RE NEEDED HERE.
DADDY PAJAMAS FUNNY!
I THOUGHT WE PUT ALL THIS BEHIND US-- WE STARTED A FAMILY.
THAT ISN'T WHAT WE DO ANYMORE.
OUR CHILDREN ARE SAFE AND YOU'RE HERE TO PROTECT THEM IF SOMETHING ELSE HAPPENS.
I'M GOING TO GO MAKE SURE OTHER PEOPLE'S CHILDREN ARE SAFE, BECAUSE I CAN AND BECAUSE IT'S THE RIGHT THING TO DO.
OKAY. YOU'RE RIGHT.
GO.

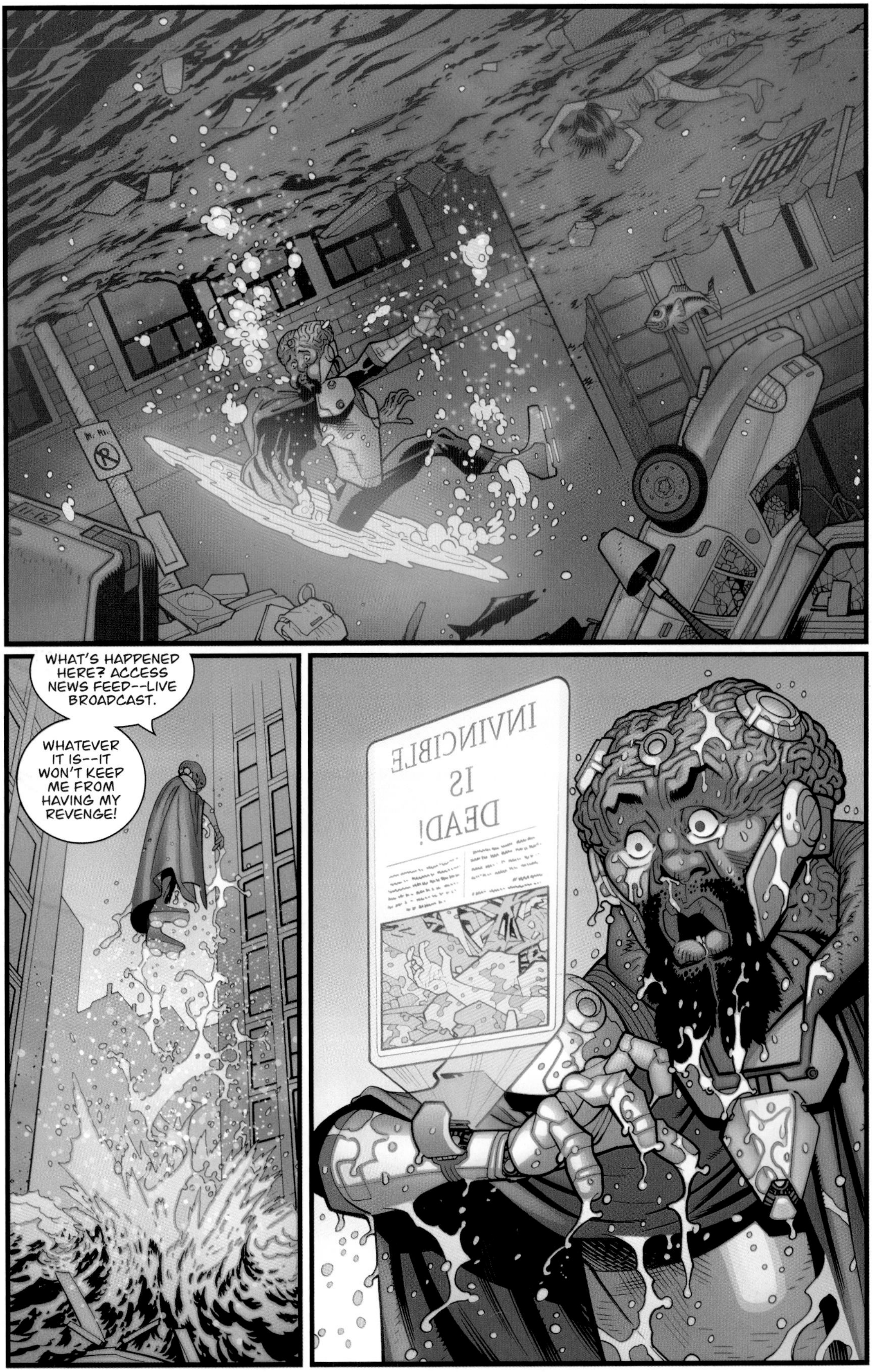
WHAT'S HAPPENED HERE? ACCESS NEWS FEED--LIVE BROADCAST.
WHATEVER IT IS--IT WON'T KEEP ME FROM HAVING MY REVENGE!
INVINCIBLE IS DEAD!

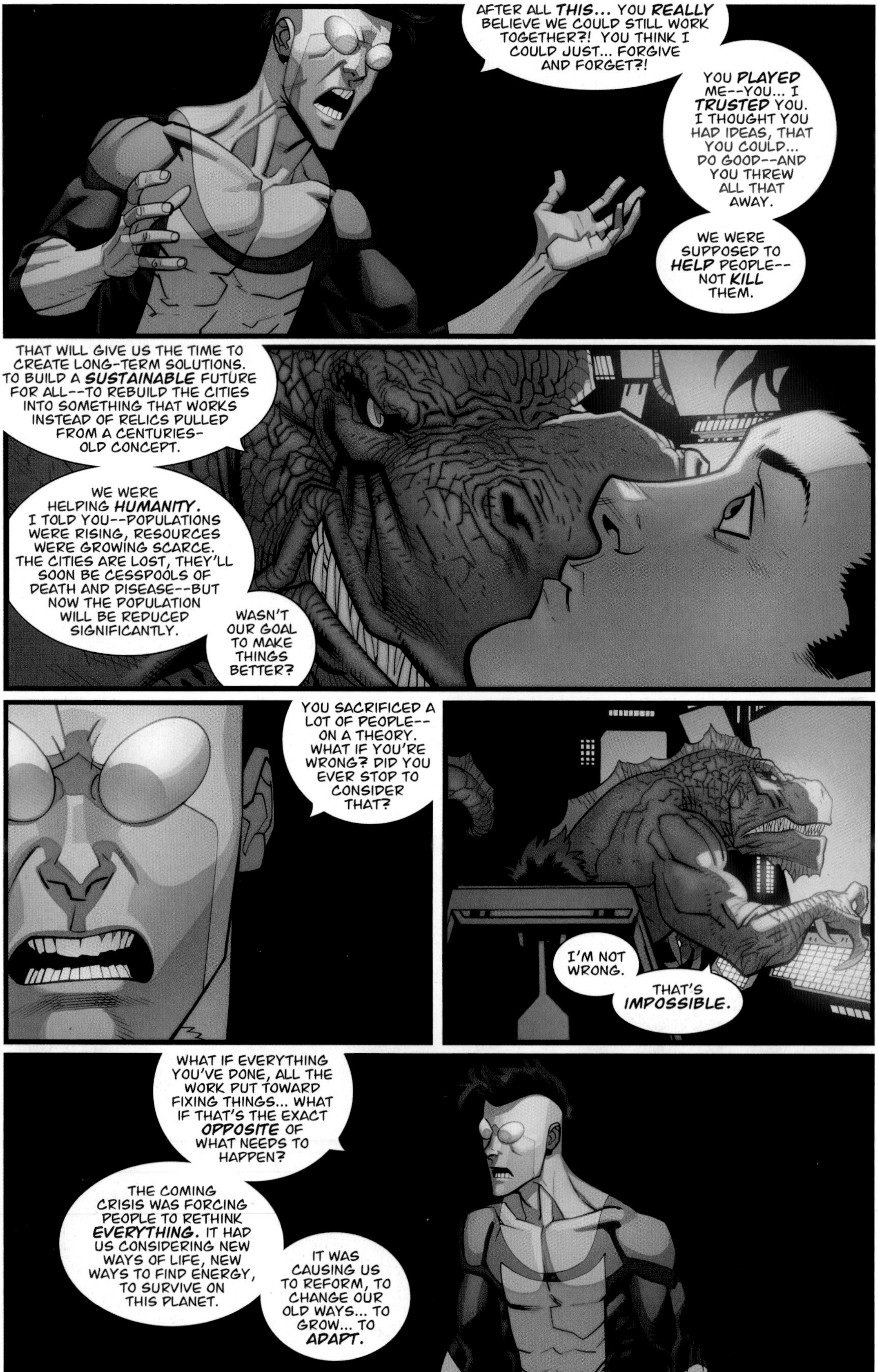
AFTER ALL THIS... YOU REALLY BELIEVE WE COULD STILL WORK TOGETHER?! YOU THINK I COULD JUST... FORGIVE AND FORGET?!
YOU PLAYED ME--YOU... I TRUSTED YOU. I THOUGHT YOU HAD IDEAS, THAT YOU COULD... DO GOOD--AND YOU THREW ALL THAT AWAY.
WE WERE SUPPOSED TO HELP PEOPLE--NOT KILL THEM.
THAT WILL GIVE US THE TIME TO CREATE LONG-TERM SOLUTIONS. TO BUILD A SUSTAINABLE FUTURE FOR ALL--TO REBUILD THE CITIES INTO SOMETHING THAT WORKS INSTEAD OF RELICS PULLED FROM A CENTURIES-OLD CONCEPT.
WE WERE HELPING HUMANITY. I TOLD YOU--POPULATIONS WERE RISING, RESOURCES WERE GROWING SCARCE. THE CITIES ARE LOST, THEY'LL SOON BE CESSPOOLS OF DEATH AND DISEASE--BUT NOW THE POPULATION WILL BE REDUCED SIGNIFICANTLY.
WASN'T OUR GOAL TO MAKE THINGS BETTER?
YOU SACRIFICED A LOT OF PEOPLE--ON A THEORY. WHAT IF YOU'RE WRONG? DID YOU EVER STOP TO CONSIDER THAT?
I'M NOT WRONG.
THAT'S IMPOSSIBLE.
WHAT IF EVERYTHING YOU'VE DONE, ALL THE WORK PUT TOWARD FIXING THINGS... WHAT IF THAT'S THE EXACT OPPOSITE OF WHAT NEEDS TO HAPPEN?
THE COMING CRISIS WAS FORCING PEOPLE TO RETHINK EVERYTHING. IT HAD US CONSIDERING NEW WAYS OF LIFE, NEW WAYS TO FIND ENERGY, TO SURVIVE ON THIS PLANET.
IT WAS CAUSING US TO REFORM, TO CHANGE OUR OLD WAYS... TO GROW... TO ADAPT.

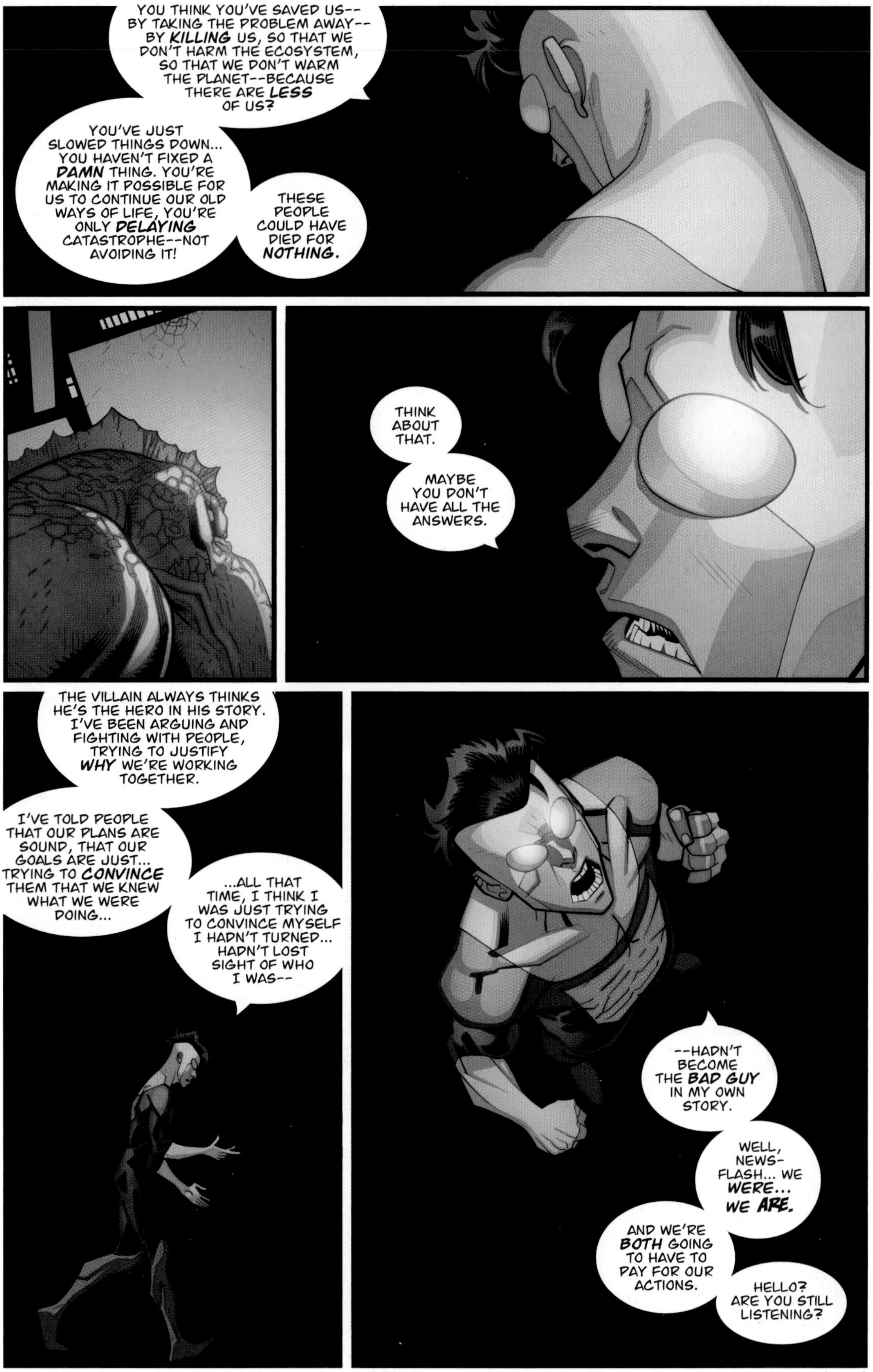
YOU THINK YOU'VE SAVED US-- BY TAKING THE PROBLEM AWAY-- BY KILLING US, SO THAT WE DON'T HARM THE ECOSYSTEM, SO THAT WE DON'T WARM THE PLANET--BECAUSE THERE ARE LESS OF US?
YOU'VE JUST SLOWED THINGS DOWN... YOU HAVEN'T FIXED A DAMN THING. YOU'RE MAKING IT POSSIBLE FOR US TO CONTINUE OUR OLD WAYS OF LIFE, YOU'RE ONLY DELAYING CATASTROPHE--NOT AVOIDING IT!
THESE PEOPLE COULD HAVE DIED FOR NOTHING.
THINK ABOUT THAT.
MAYBE YOU DON'T HAVE ALL THE ANSWERS.
THE VILLAIN ALWAYS THINKS HE'S THE HERO IN HIS STORY. I'VE BEEN ARGUING AND FIGHTING WITH PEOPLE, TRYING TO JUSTIFY WHY WE'RE WORKING TOGETHER.
I'VE TOLD PEOPLE THAT OUR PLANS ARE SOUND, THAT OUR GOALS ARE JUST... TRYING TO CONVINCE THEM THAT WE KNEW WHAT WE WERE DOING...
...ALL THAT TIME, I THINK I WAS JUST TRYING TO CONVINCE MYSELF I HADN'T TURNED... HADN'T LOST SIGHT OF WHO I WAS--
--HADN'T BECOME THE BAD GUY IN MY OWN STORY.
WELL, NEWS-FLASH... WE WERE... WE ARE.
AND WE'RE BOTH GOING TO HAVE TO PAY FOR OUR ACTIONS.
HELLO? ARE YOU STILL LISTENING?

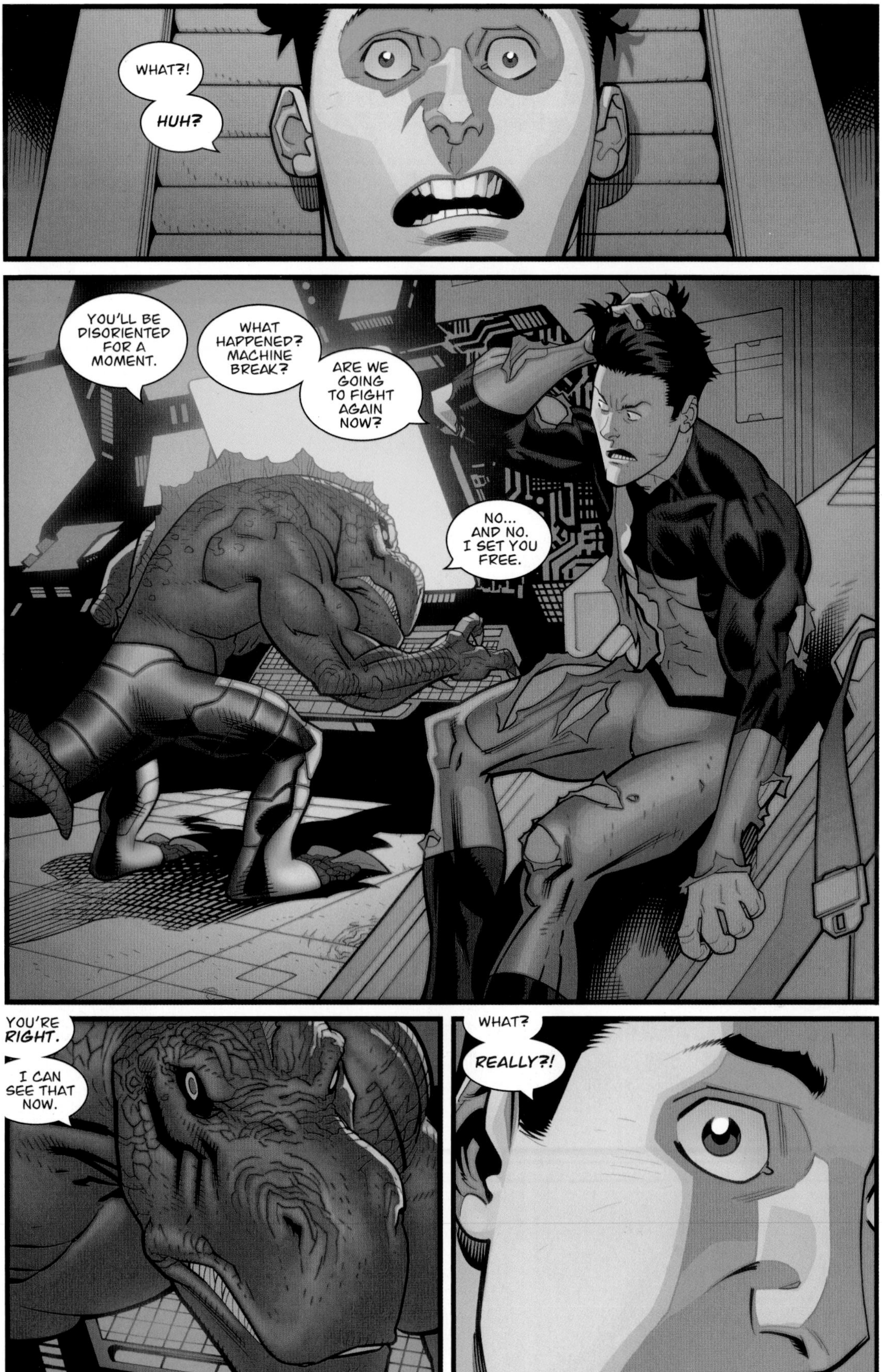
WHAT?!
HUH?
YOU'LL BE DISORIENTED FOR A MOMENT.
WHAT HAPPENED? MACHINE BREAK?
ARE WE GOING TO FIGHT AGAIN NOW?
NO... AND NO. I SET YOU FREE.
YOU'RE RIGHT.
I CAN SEE THAT NOW.
WHAT?
REALLY?!

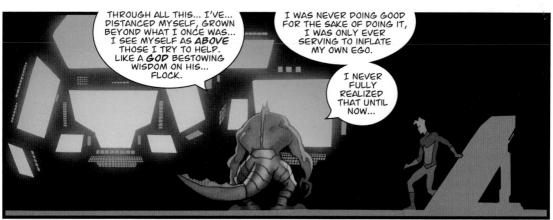

THROUGH ALL THIS... I'VE... DISTANCED MYSELF, GROWN BEYOND WHAT I ONCE WAS... I SEE MYSELF AS *ABOVE* THOSE I TRY TO HELP. LIKE A *GOD* BESTOWING WISDOM ON HIS... FLOCK.

I WAS NEVER DOING GOOD FOR THE SAKE OF DOING IT, I WAS ONLY EVER SERVING TO INFLATE MY OWN EGO.

I NEVER FULLY REALIZED THAT UNTIL NOW...

SO, OKAY THEN... HELP ME FIX THIS. YOU'VE GOT TO KNOW SOME WAY TO GET THE OCEAN WATER OUT OF THOSE CITIES. SOME KIND OF SEA WALL, OR--

NO.

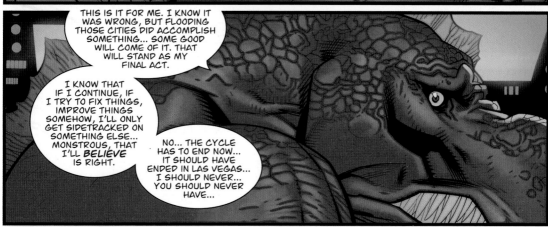

THIS IS IT FOR ME. I KNOW IT WAS WRONG, BUT FLOODING THOSE CITIES DID ACCOMPLISH SOMETHING... SOME GOOD WILL COME OF IT. THAT WILL STAND AS MY FINAL ACT.

I KNOW THAT IF I CONTINUE, IF I TRY TO FIX THINGS, IMPROVE THINGS SOMEHOW, I'LL ONLY GET SIDETRACKED ON SOMETHING ELSE... MONSTROUS, THAT I'LL *BELIEVE* IS RIGHT.

NO... THE CYCLE HAS TO END NOW... IT SHOULD HAVE ENDED IN LAS VEGAS... I SHOULD NEVER... YOU SHOULD NEVER HAVE...

SO... WHAT ARE YOU SAYING?

YOU HAVE TO *KILL* ME.

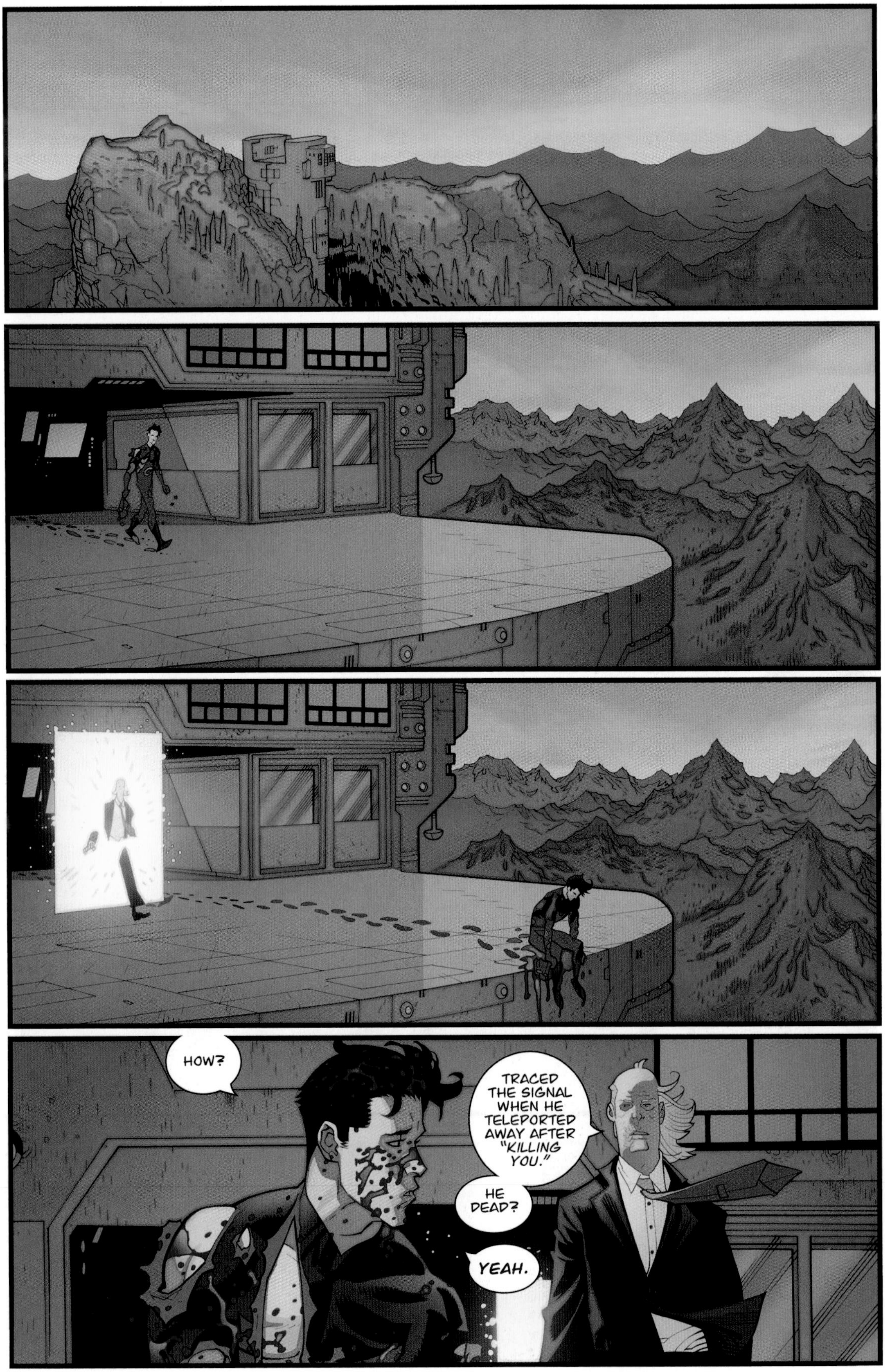
HOW?
TRACED THE SIGNAL WHEN HE TELEPORTED AWAY AFTER "KILLING YOU."
HE DEAD?
YEAH.

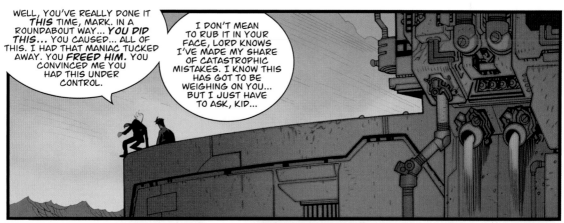

WELL, YOU'VE REALLY DONE IT *THIS* TIME, MARK. IN A ROUNDABOUT WAY... *YOU DID THIS*... YOU CAUSED... ALL OF THIS. I HAD THAT MANIAC TUCKED AWAY. YOU *FREED HIM.* YOU CONVINCED ME YOU HAD THIS UNDER CONTROL.

I DON'T MEAN TO RUB IT IN YOUR FACE, LORD KNOWS I'VE MADE MY SHARE OF CATASTROPHIC MISTAKES. I KNOW THIS HAS GOT TO BE WEIGHING ON YOU... BUT I JUST HAVE TO ASK, KID...

STILL FEEL LIKE YOU KNOW WHAT'S BEST?

STILL FEEL LIKE A MORAL AUTHORITY-- THAT YOU KNOW WHAT'S *RIGHT* FOR THE WORLD?

NO.

WELL... THAT'S A START.

WHAT COMES NEXT... THAT'S UP TO *YOU.*

I ASSUME I'LL GO TO JAIL... I DON'T EXPECT TO BE ABLE TO SKATE PAST THIS ONE. A LOT OF PEOPLE DIED HERE... AND I FEEL LIKE I *SHOULD* PAY FOR MY CRIMES.

I'D HOPE, OF COURSE... THAT YOU'D LET ME HELP IN WHATEVER WAY I CAN IN THE EFFORT TO UNDO THIS. THERE HAS TO BE SOME WAY TO GET SEA LEVEL BACK TO WHERE IT SHOULD BE--TRY AND RESTORE THE CITIES...

OH, THAT...

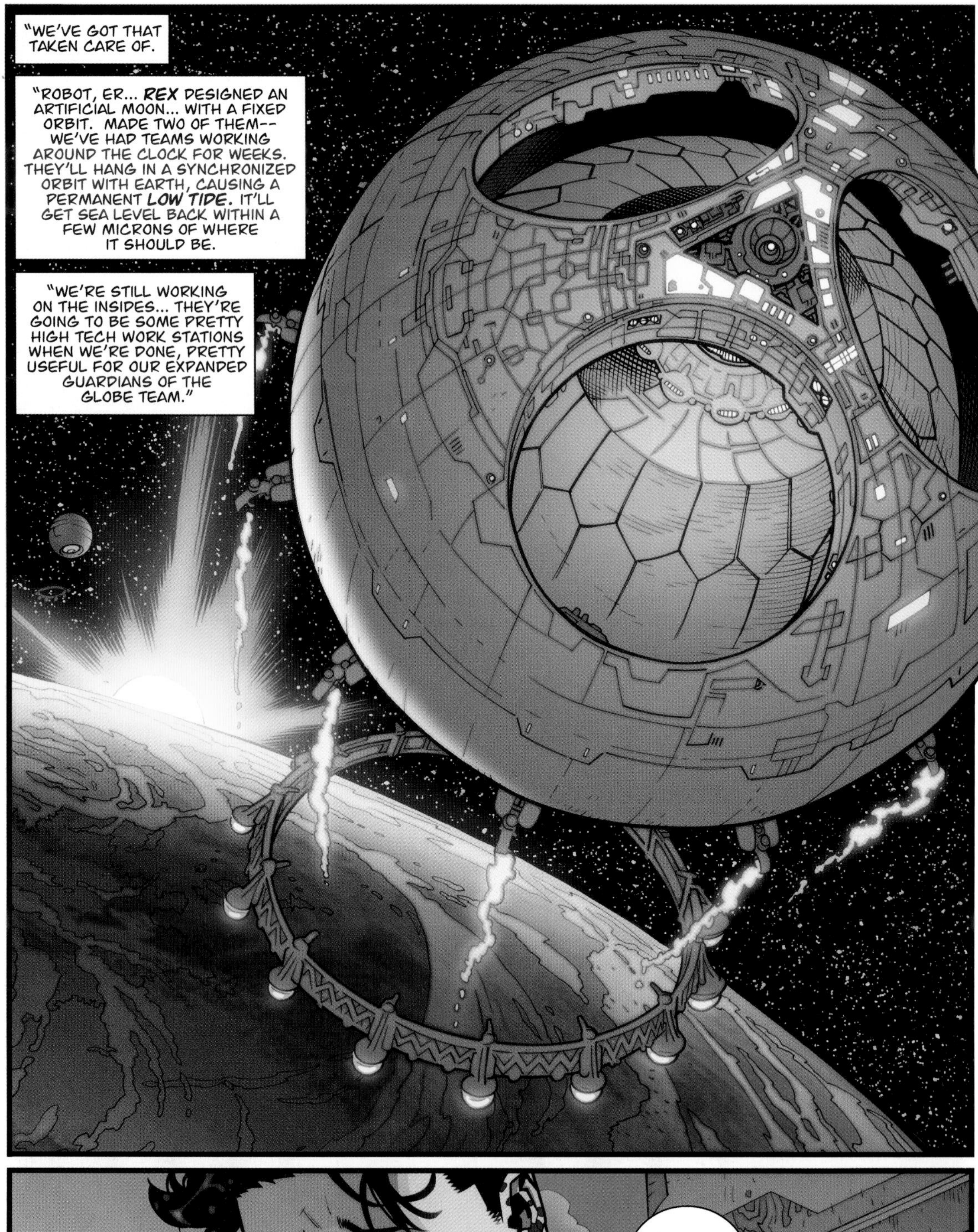
"WE'VE GOT THAT TAKEN CARE OF.
"ROBOT, ER... REX DESIGNED AN ARTIFICIAL MOON... WITH A FIXED ORBIT. MADE TWO OF THEM-- WE'VE HAD TEAMS WORKING AROUND THE CLOCK FOR WEEKS. THEY'LL HANG IN A SYNCHRONIZED ORBIT WITH EARTH, CAUSING A PERMANENT LOW TIDE. IT'LL GET SEA LEVEL BACK WITHIN A FEW MICRONS OF WHERE IT SHOULD BE.
"WE'RE STILL WORKING ON THE INSIDES... THEY'RE GOING TO BE SOME PRETTY HIGH TECH WORK STATIONS WHEN WE'RE DONE, PRETTY USEFUL FOR OUR EXPANDED GUARDIANS OF THE GLOBE TEAM."
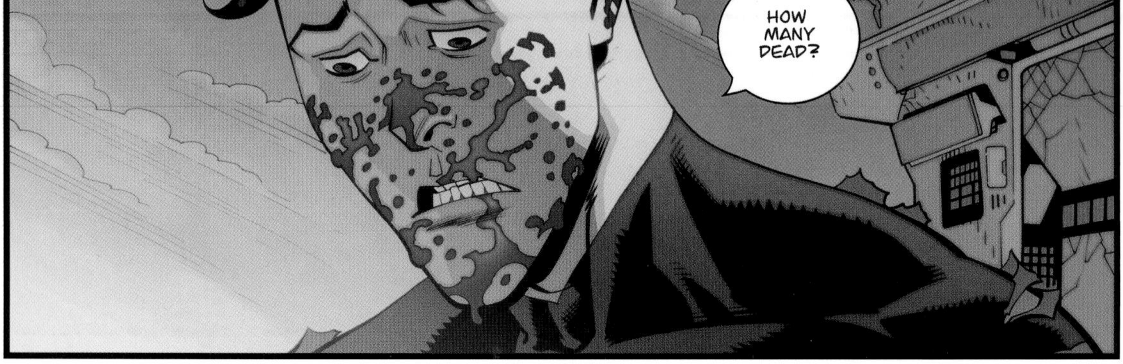
HOW MANY DEAD?

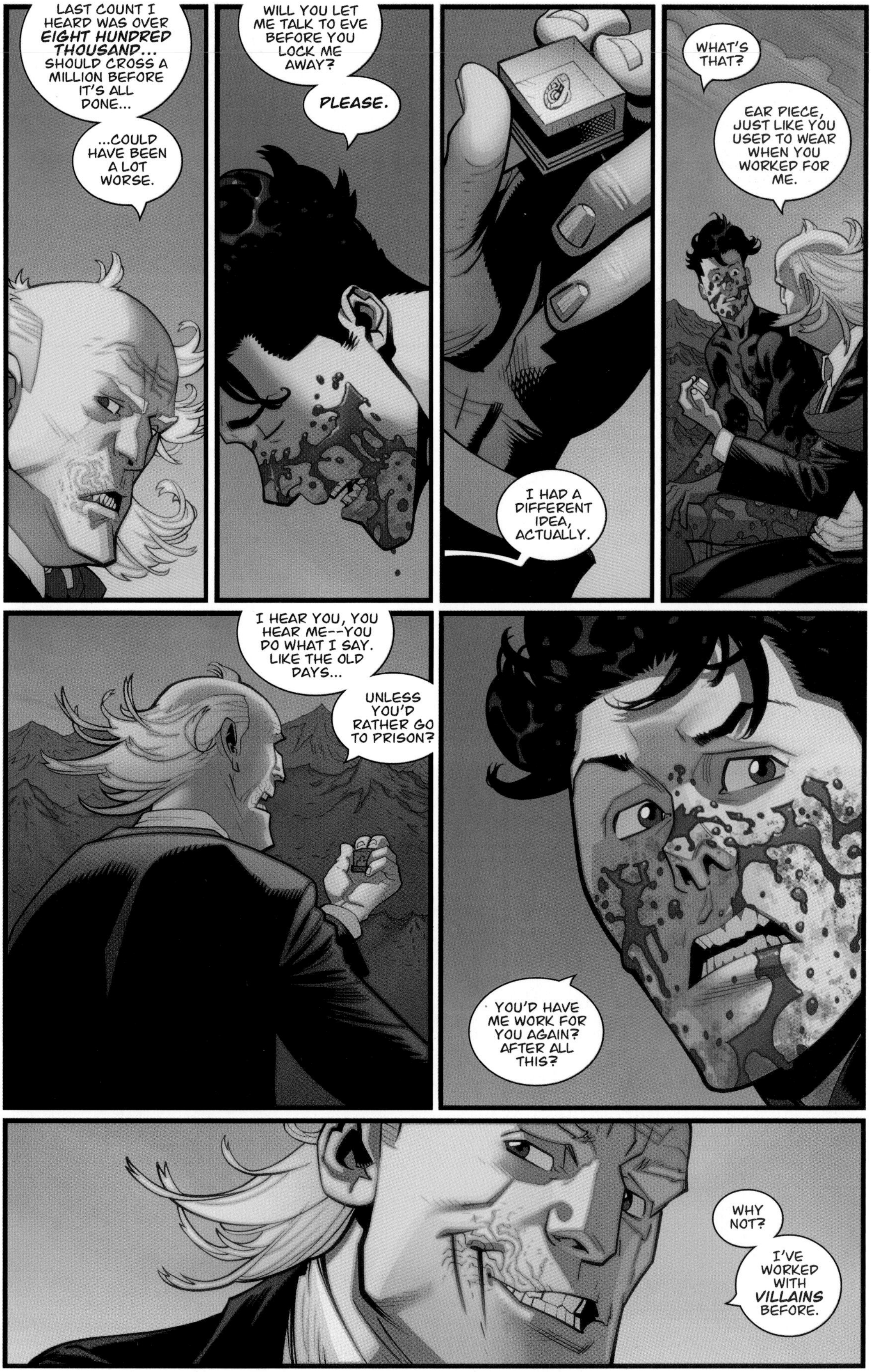
LAST COUNT I HEARD WAS OVER **EIGHT HUNDRED THOUSAND...** SHOULD CROSS A MILLION BEFORE IT'S ALL DONE...
...COULD HAVE BEEN A LOT WORSE.
WILL YOU LET ME TALK TO EVE BEFORE YOU LOCK ME AWAY?
PLEASE.
I HAD A DIFFERENT IDEA, ACTUALLY.
WHAT'S THAT?
EAR PIECE, JUST LIKE YOU USED TO WEAR WHEN YOU WORKED FOR ME.
I HEAR YOU, YOU HEAR ME--YOU DO WHAT I SAY. LIKE THE OLD DAYS...
UNLESS YOU'D RATHER GO TO PRISON?
YOU'D HAVE ME WORK FOR YOU AGAIN? AFTER ALL THIS?
WHY NOT?
I'VE WORKED WITH **VILLAINS** BEFORE.

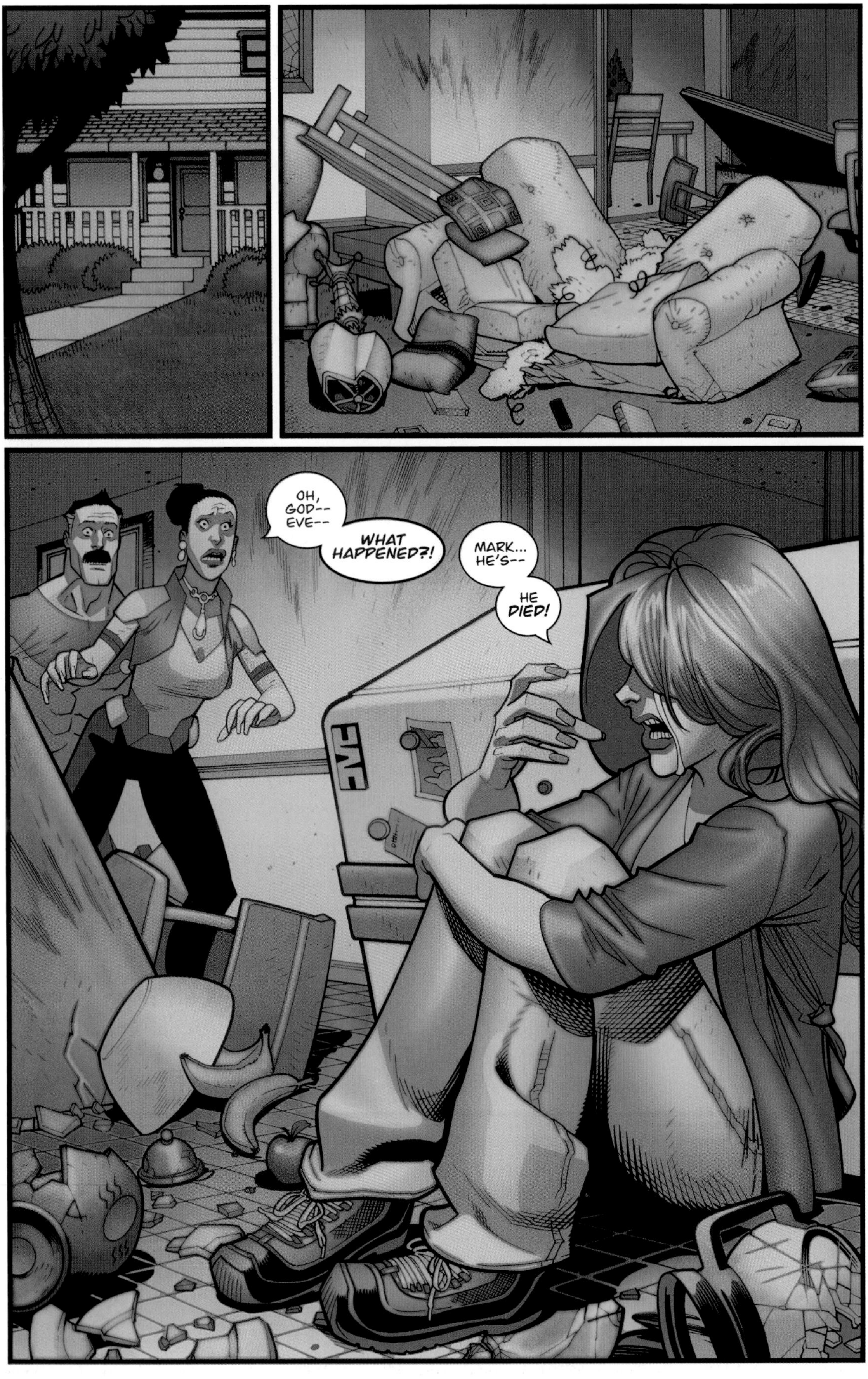

OH, GOD-- EVE--
WHAT HAPPENED?!
MARK... HE'S--
HE DIED!

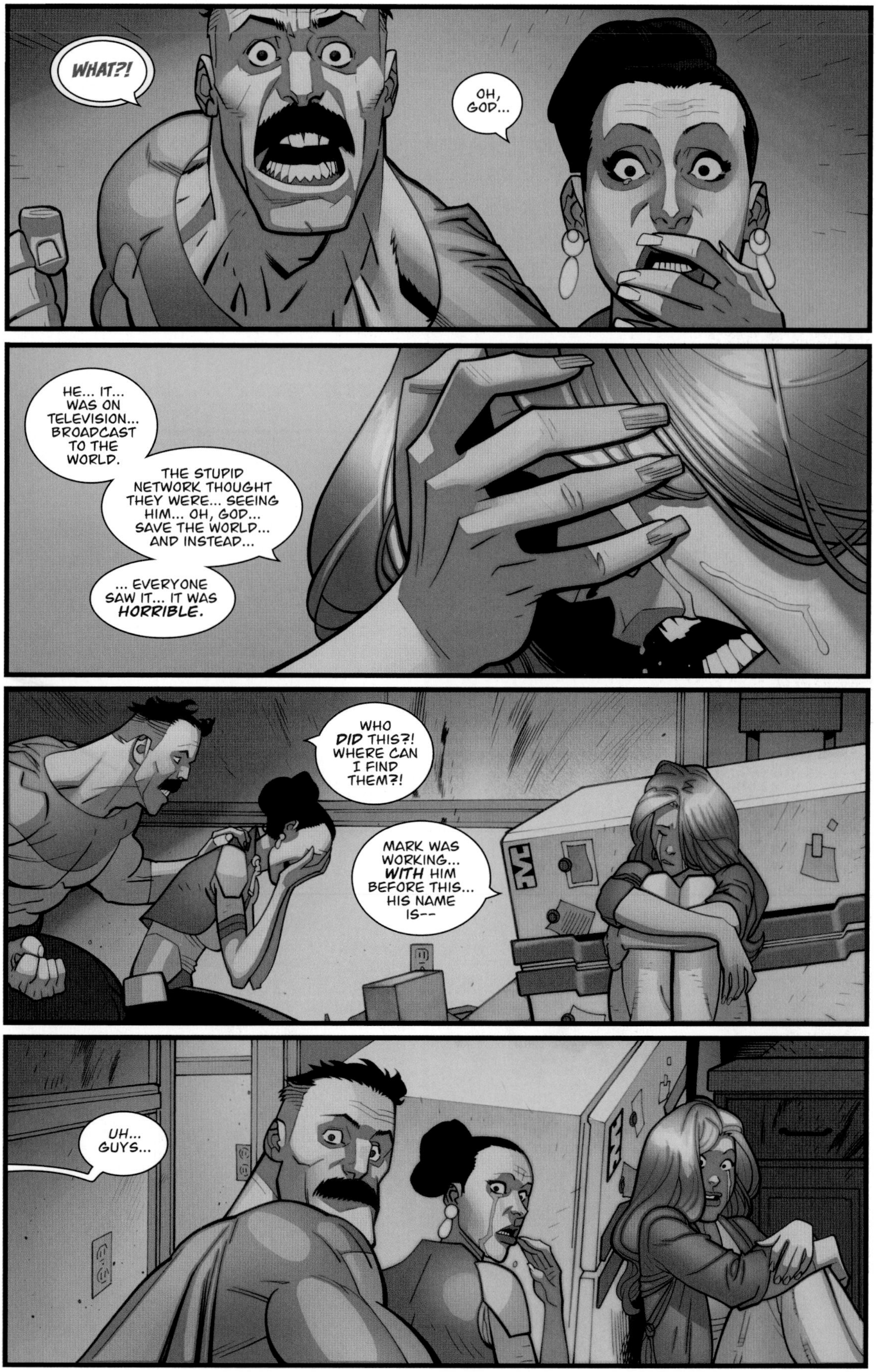
WHAT?!
OH, GOD...
HE... IT... WAS ON TELEVISION... BROADCAST TO THE WORLD.
THE STUPID NETWORK THOUGHT THEY WERE... SEEING HIM... OH, GOD... SAVE THE WORLD... AND INSTEAD...
... EVERYONE SAW IT... IT WAS HORRIBLE.
WHO DID THIS?! WHERE CAN I FIND THEM?!
MARK WAS WORKING... WITH HIM BEFORE THIS... HIS NAME IS--
UH... GUYS...

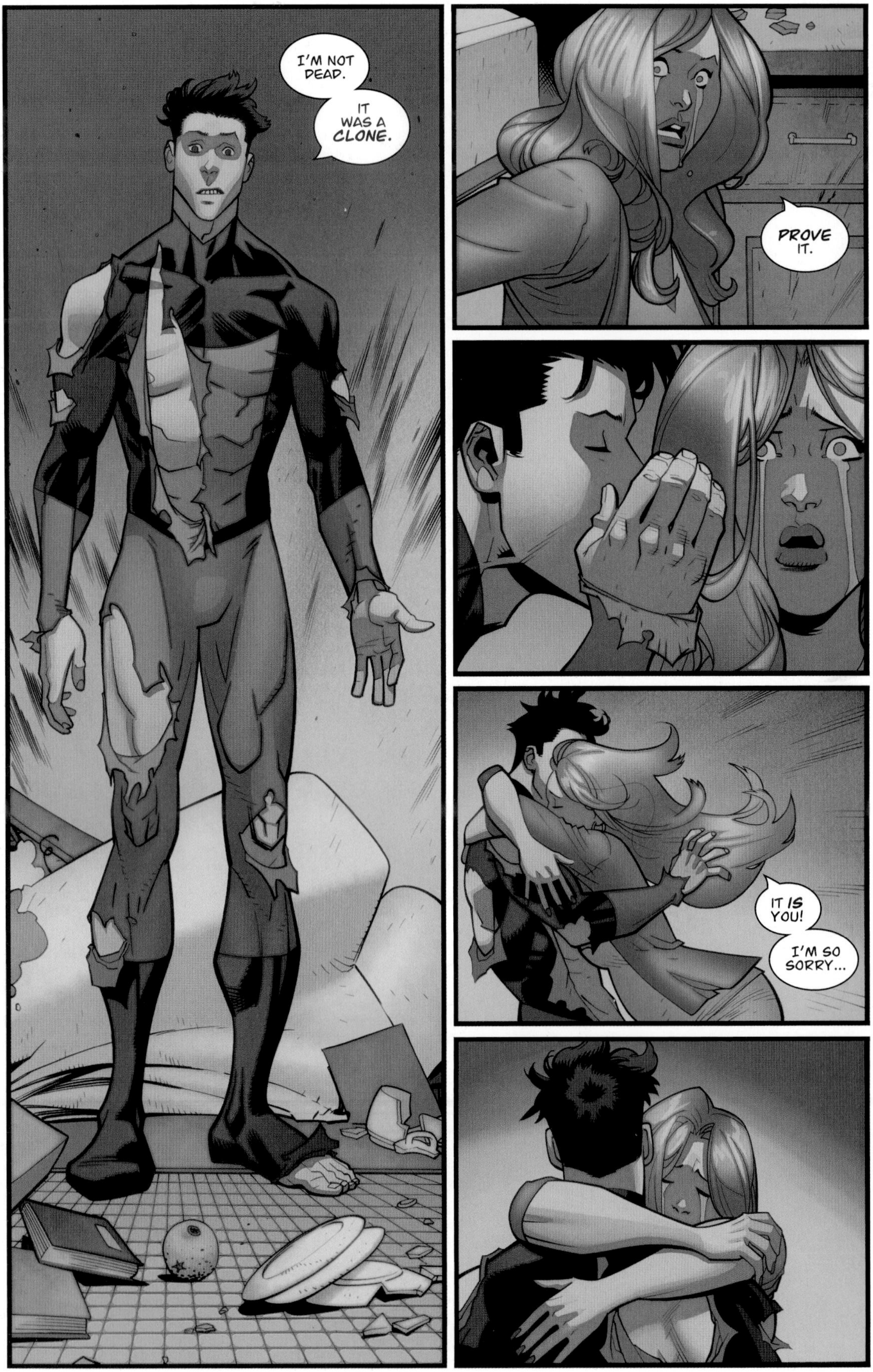
I'M NOT DEAD.
IT WAS A CLONE.
PROVE IT.
IT IS YOU!
I'M SO SORRY...

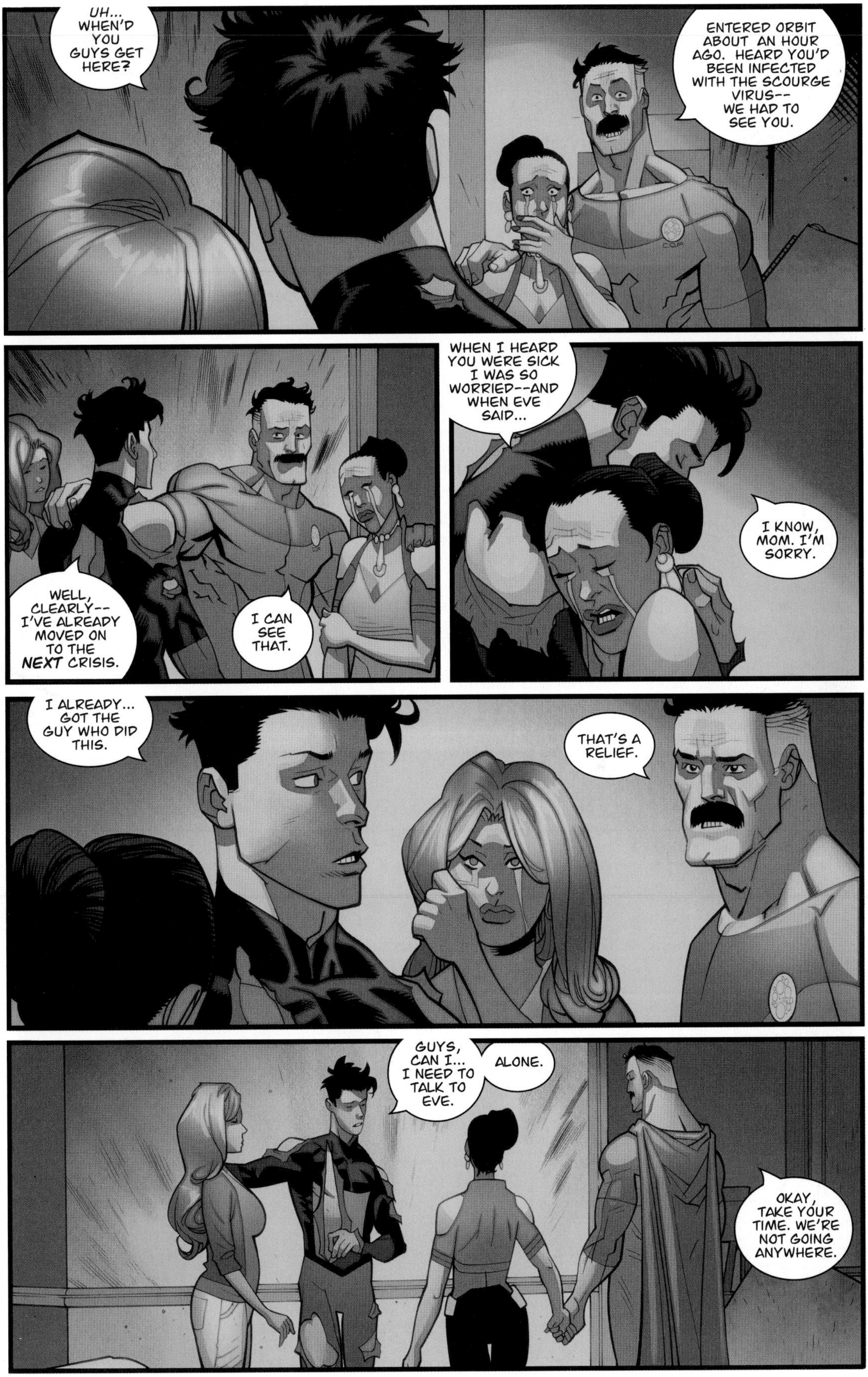
UH... WHEN'D YOU GUYS GET HERE?
ENTERED ORBIT ABOUT AN HOUR AGO. HEARD YOU'D BEEN INFECTED WITH THE SCOURGE VIRUS-- WE HAD TO SEE YOU.
WELL, CLEARLY-- I'VE ALREADY MOVED ON TO THE NEXT CRISIS.
I CAN SEE THAT.
WHEN I HEARD YOU WERE SICK I WAS SO WORRIED--AND WHEN EVE SAID...
I KNOW, MOM. I'M SORRY.
I ALREADY... GOT THE GUY WHO DID THIS.
THAT'S A RELIEF.
GUYS, CAN I... I NEED TO TALK TO EVE.
ALONE.
OKAY, TAKE YOUR TIME. WE'RE NOT GOING ANYWHERE.

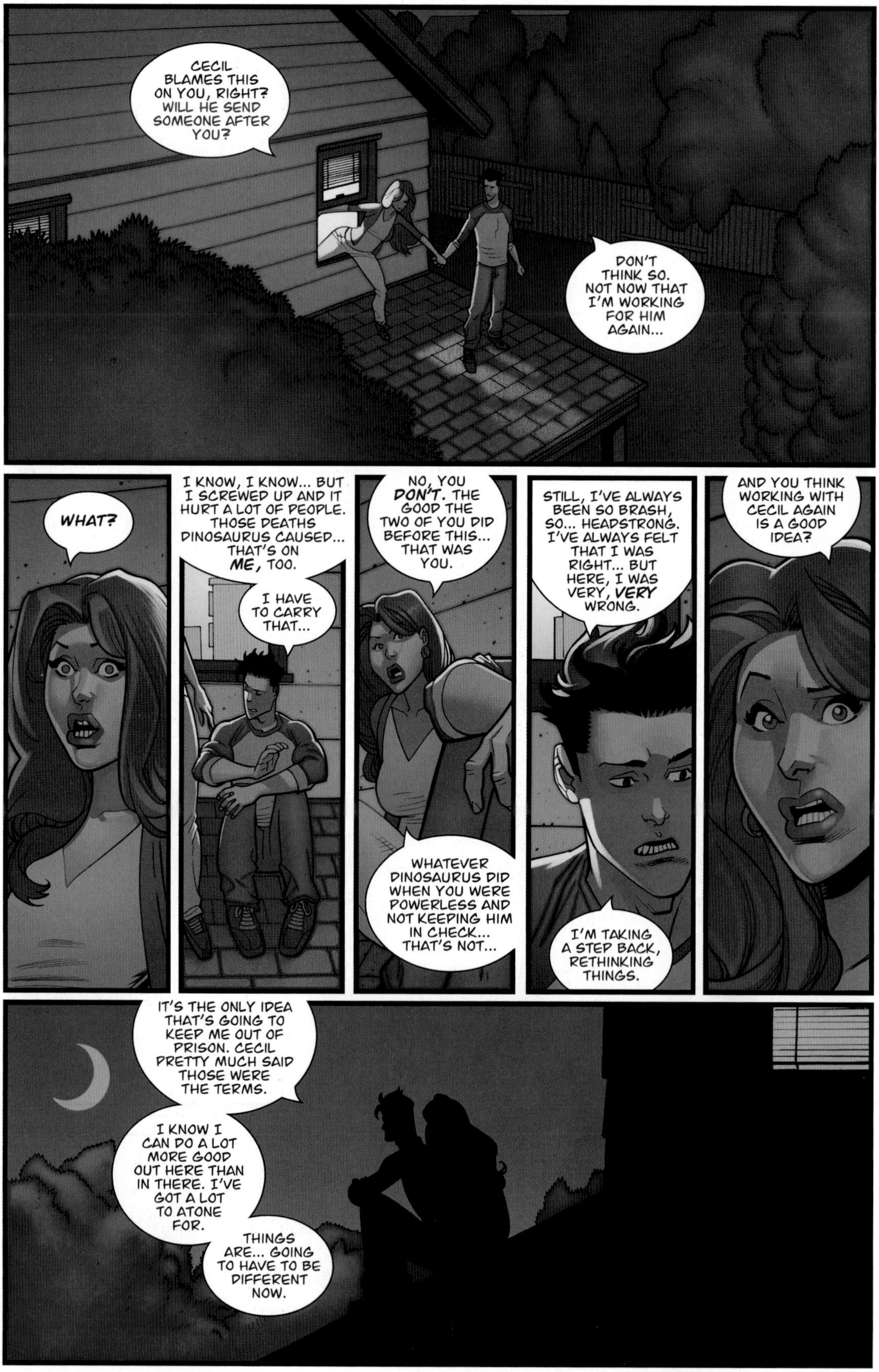
CECIL BLAMES THIS ON YOU, RIGHT? WILL HE SEND SOMEONE AFTER YOU?
DON'T THINK SO. NOT NOW THAT I'M WORKING FOR HIM AGAIN...
WHAT?
I KNOW, I KNOW... BUT I SCREWED UP AND IT HURT A LOT OF PEOPLE. THOSE DEATHS DINOSAURUS CAUSED... THAT'S ON ME, TOO.
I HAVE TO CARRY THAT...
NO, YOU DON'T. THE GOOD THE TWO OF YOU DID BEFORE THIS... THAT WAS YOU.
WHATEVER DINOSAURUS DID WHEN YOU WERE POWERLESS AND NOT KEEPING HIM IN CHECK... THAT'S NOT...
STILL, I'VE ALWAYS BEEN SO BRASH, SO... HEADSTRONG. I'VE ALWAYS FELT THAT I WAS RIGHT... BUT HERE, I WAS VERY, VERY WRONG.
I'M TAKING A STEP BACK, RETHINKING THINGS.
AND YOU THINK WORKING WITH CECIL AGAIN IS A GOOD IDEA?
IT'S THE ONLY IDEA THAT'S GOING TO KEEP ME OUT OF PRISON. CECIL PRETTY MUCH SAID THOSE WERE THE TERMS.
I KNOW I CAN DO A LOT MORE GOOD OUT HERE THAN IN THERE. I'VE GOT A LOT TO ATONE FOR.
THINGS ARE... GOING TO HAVE TO BE DIFFERENT NOW.

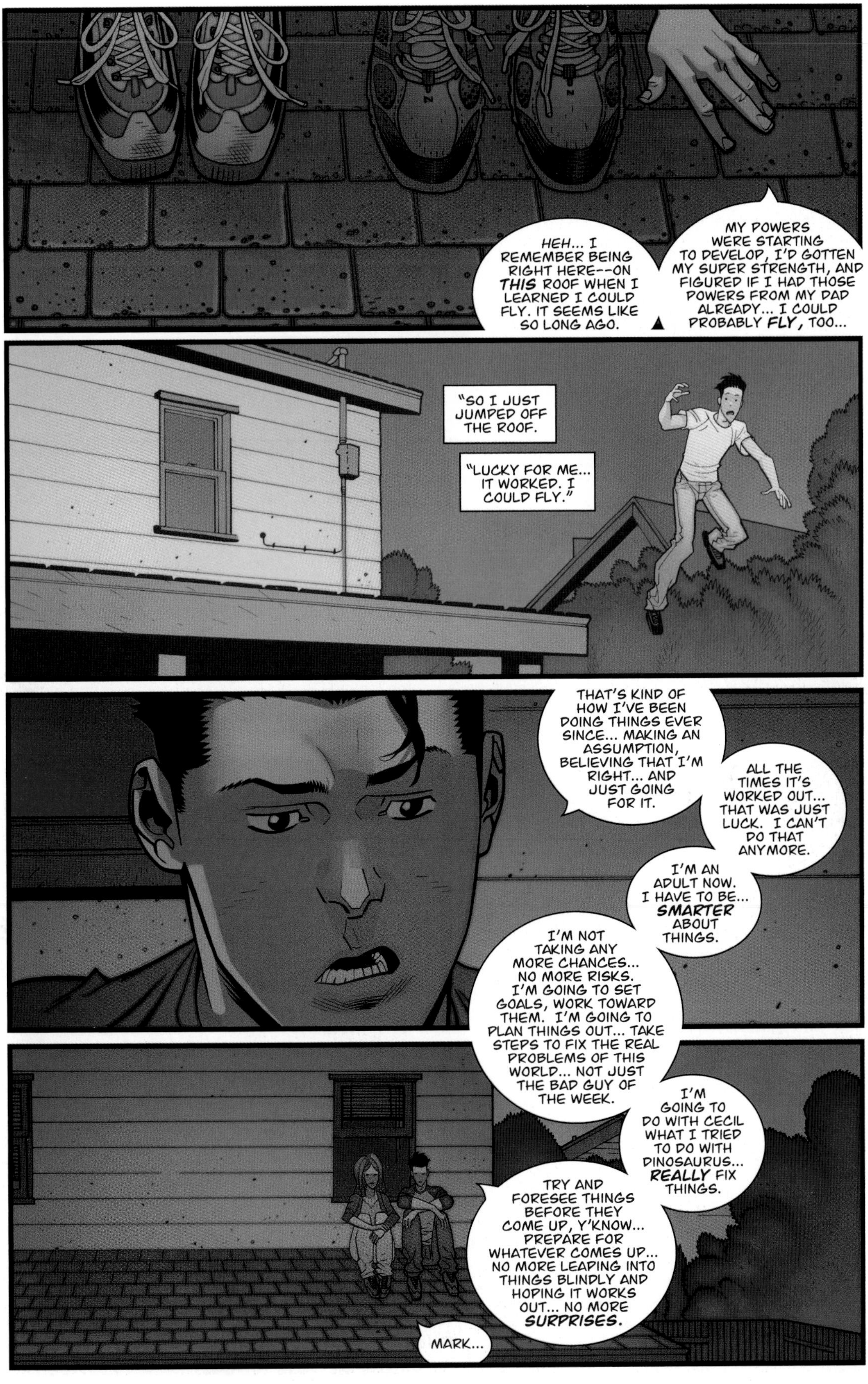
HEH... I REMEMBER BEING RIGHT HERE--ON THIS ROOF WHEN I LEARNED I COULD FLY. IT SEEMS LIKE SO LONG AGO.
MY POWERS WERE STARTING TO DEVELOP, I'D GOTTEN MY SUPER STRENGTH, AND FIGURED IF I HAD THOSE POWERS FROM MY DAD ALREADY... I COULD PROBABLY FLY, TOO...
"SO I JUST JUMPED OFF THE ROOF.
"LUCKY FOR ME... IT WORKED. I COULD FLY."
THAT'S KIND OF HOW I'VE BEEN DOING THINGS EVER SINCE... MAKING AN ASSUMPTION, BELIEVING THAT I'M RIGHT... AND JUST GOING FOR IT.
ALL THE TIMES IT'S WORKED OUT... THAT WAS JUST LUCK. I CAN'T DO THAT ANYMORE.
I'M AN ADULT NOW. I HAVE TO BE... SMARTER ABOUT THINGS.
I'M NOT TAKING ANY MORE CHANCES... NO MORE RISKS. I'M GOING TO SET GOALS, WORK TOWARD THEM. I'M GOING TO PLAN THINGS OUT... TAKE STEPS TO FIX THE REAL PROBLEMS OF THIS WORLD... NOT JUST THE BAD GUY OF THE WEEK.
I'M GOING TO DO WITH CECIL WHAT I TRIED TO DO WITH DINOSAURUS... REALLY FIX THINGS.
TRY AND FORESEE THINGS BEFORE THEY COME UP, Y'KNOW... PREPARE FOR WHATEVER COMES UP... NO MORE LEAPING INTO THINGS BLINDLY AND HOPING IT WORKS OUT... NO MORE SURPRISES.
MARK...

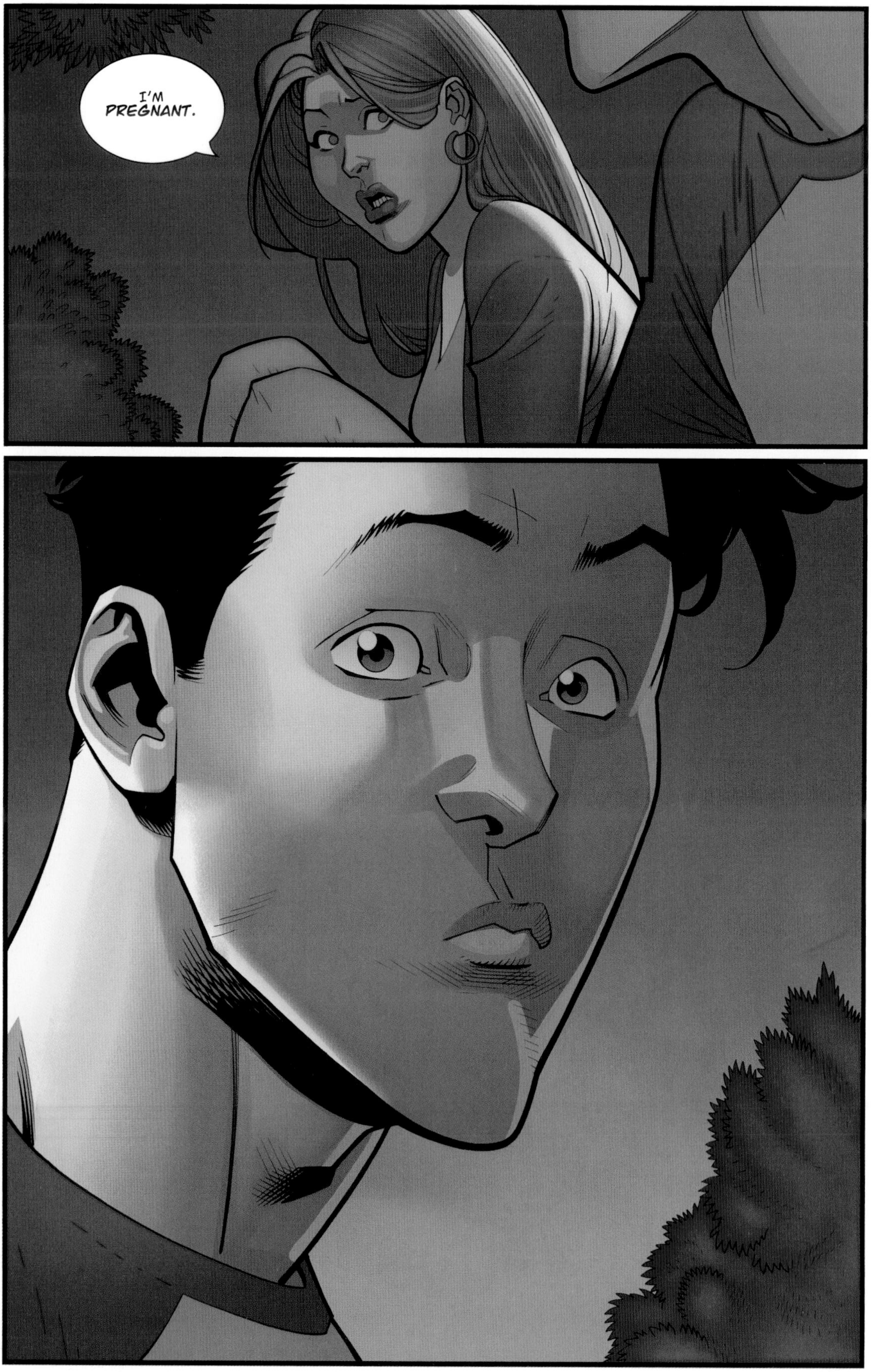
I'M PREGNANT.

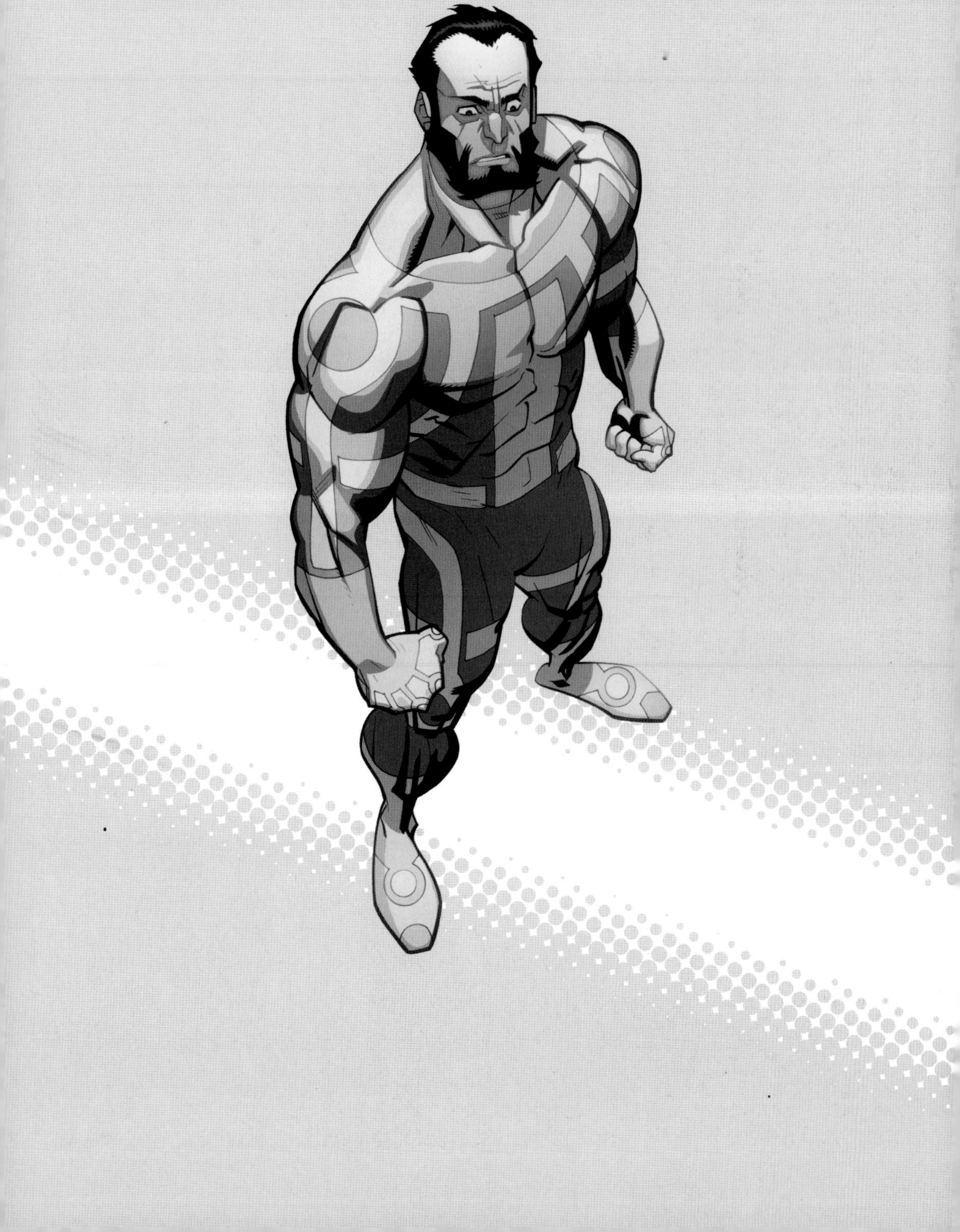

CHAPTER FIVE

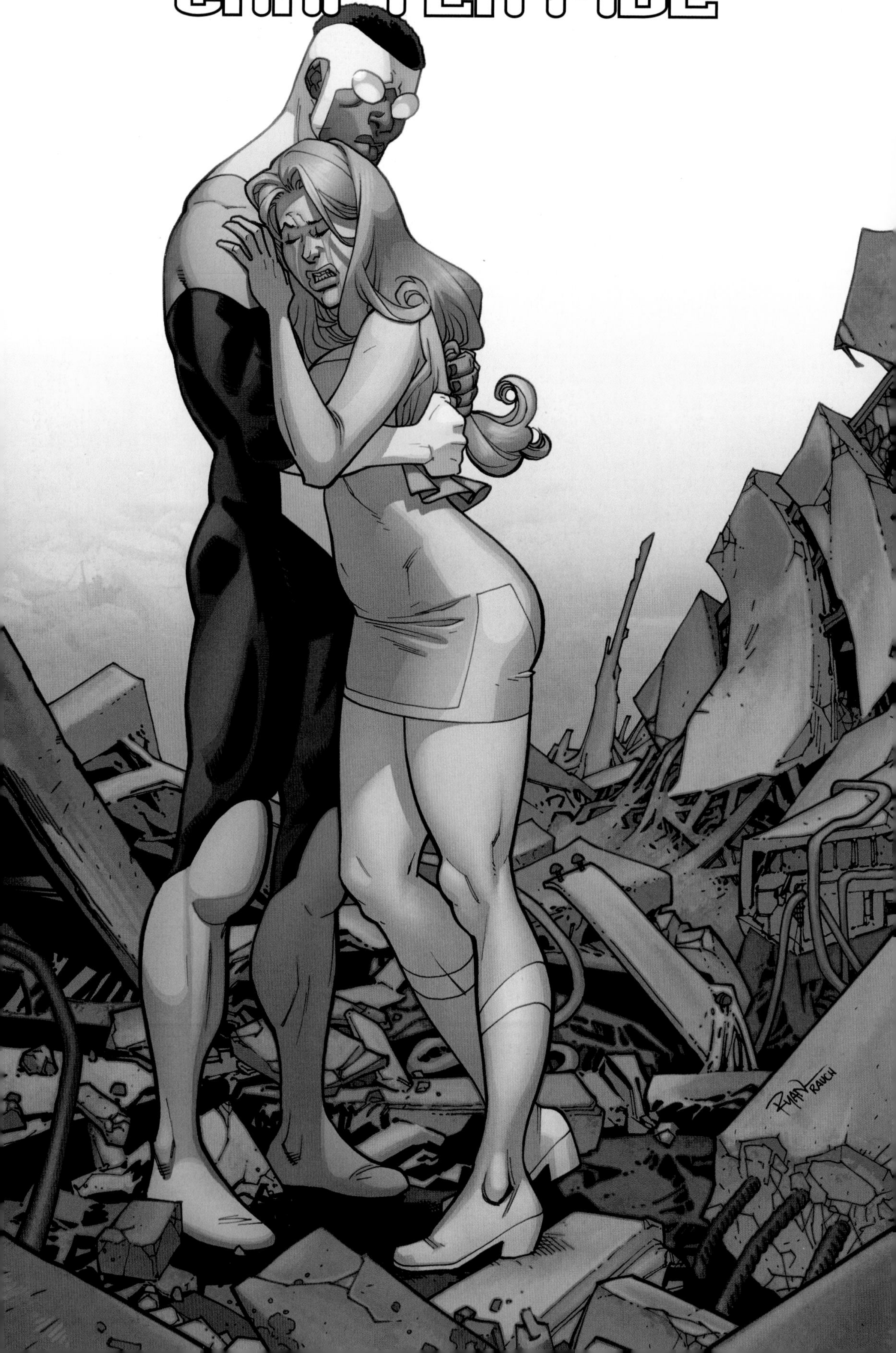

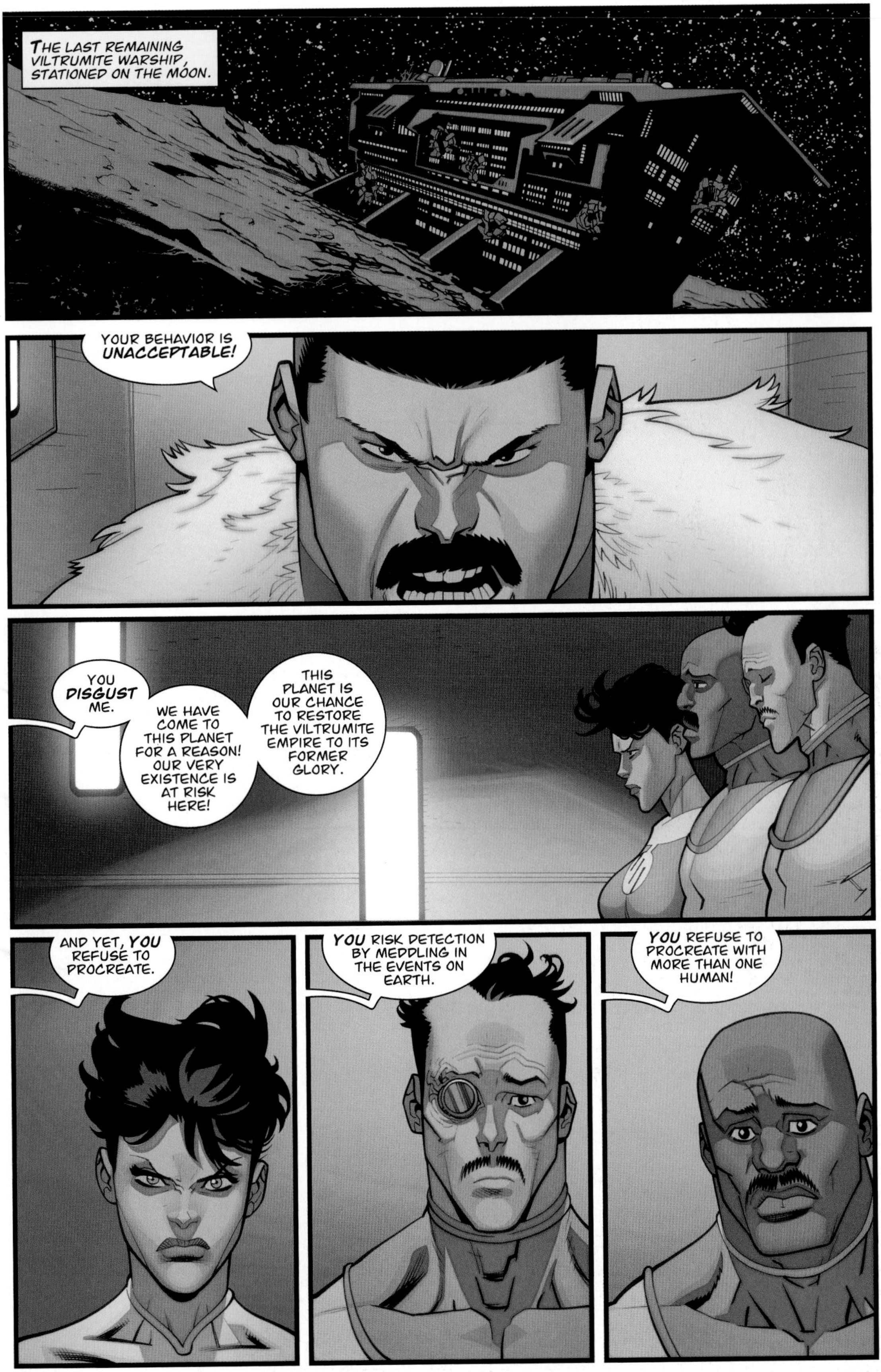
THE LAST REMAINING VILTRUMITE WARSHIP, STATIONED ON THE MOON.
YOUR BEHAVIOR IS UNACCEPTABLE!
YOU DISGUST ME.
WE HAVE COME TO THIS PLANET FOR A REASON! OUR VERY EXISTENCE IS AT RISK HERE!
THIS PLANET IS OUR CHANCE TO RESTORE THE VILTRUMITE EMPIRE TO ITS FORMER GLORY.
AND YET, YOU REFUSE TO PROCREATE.
YOU RISK DETECTION BY MEDDLING IN THE EVENTS ON EARTH.
YOU REFUSE TO PROCREATE WITH MORE THAN ONE HUMAN!

I HAVE **NEVER** WANTED TO PRODUCE OFFSPRING. I'M AWARE OF MY RESPONSIBILI-TIES... BUT I EXPECT YOU TO RECOGNIZE THE DIFFERENCE IN WHAT YOU'RE ASKING **ME** TO DO, AND WHAT MY MALE COUNTERPARTS ARE DOING.

MY MATE WAS IN DANGER... MANY OF THEM WERE. I COULDN'T BRING MYSELF TO SACRIFICE ANY OF THEM.

BESIDES-- ISN'T THE IDEA TO PRODUCE AS MANY OFFSPRING AS POSSIBLE?

MY MATE, SHE HAS BEEN... HURT IN THE PAST BY A COMPANION WHO WAS **DISLOYAL.** SHE DOESN'T APPROVE OF MY PROCREATING WITH OTHER WOMEN.

WERE I TO DO SO... SHE WOULD BECOME UPSET. I DON'T WISH TO DO THAT TO HER.

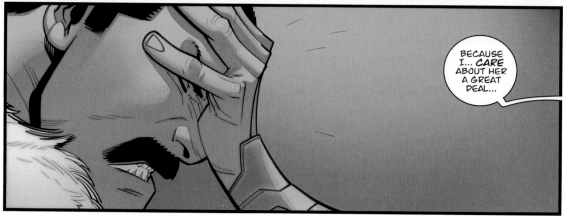

BECAUSE I... **CARE** ABOUT HER A GREAT DEAL...

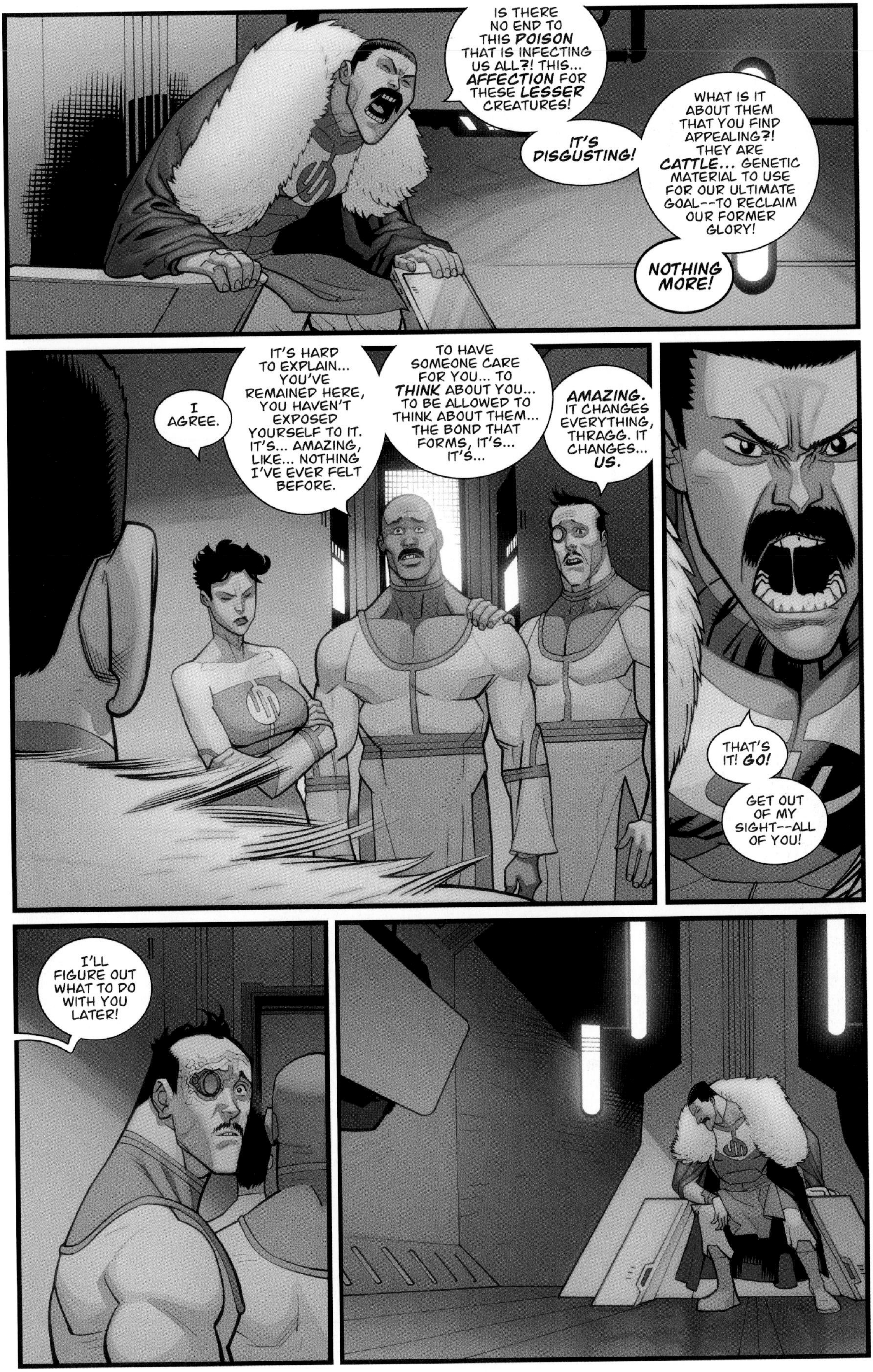
IS THERE NO END TO THIS POISON THAT IS INFECTING US ALL?! THIS... AFFECTION FOR THESE LESSER CREATURES!
IT'S DISGUSTING!
WHAT IS IT ABOUT THEM THAT YOU FIND APPEALING?! THEY ARE CATTLE... GENETIC MATERIAL TO USE FOR OUR ULTIMATE GOAL--TO RECLAIM OUR FORMER GLORY!
NOTHING MORE!
I AGREE.
IT'S HARD TO EXPLAIN... YOU'VE REMAINED HERE, YOU HAVEN'T EXPOSED YOURSELF TO IT. IT'S... AMAZING, LIKE... NOTHING I'VE EVER FELT BEFORE.
TO HAVE SOMEONE CARE FOR YOU... TO THINK ABOUT YOU... TO BE ALLOWED TO THINK ABOUT THEM... THE BOND THAT FORMS, IT'S... IT'S...
AMAZING. IT CHANGES EVERYTHING, THRAGG. IT CHANGES... US.
THAT'S IT! GO!
GET OUT OF MY SIGHT--ALL OF YOU!
I'LL FIGURE OUT WHAT TO DO WITH YOU LATER!

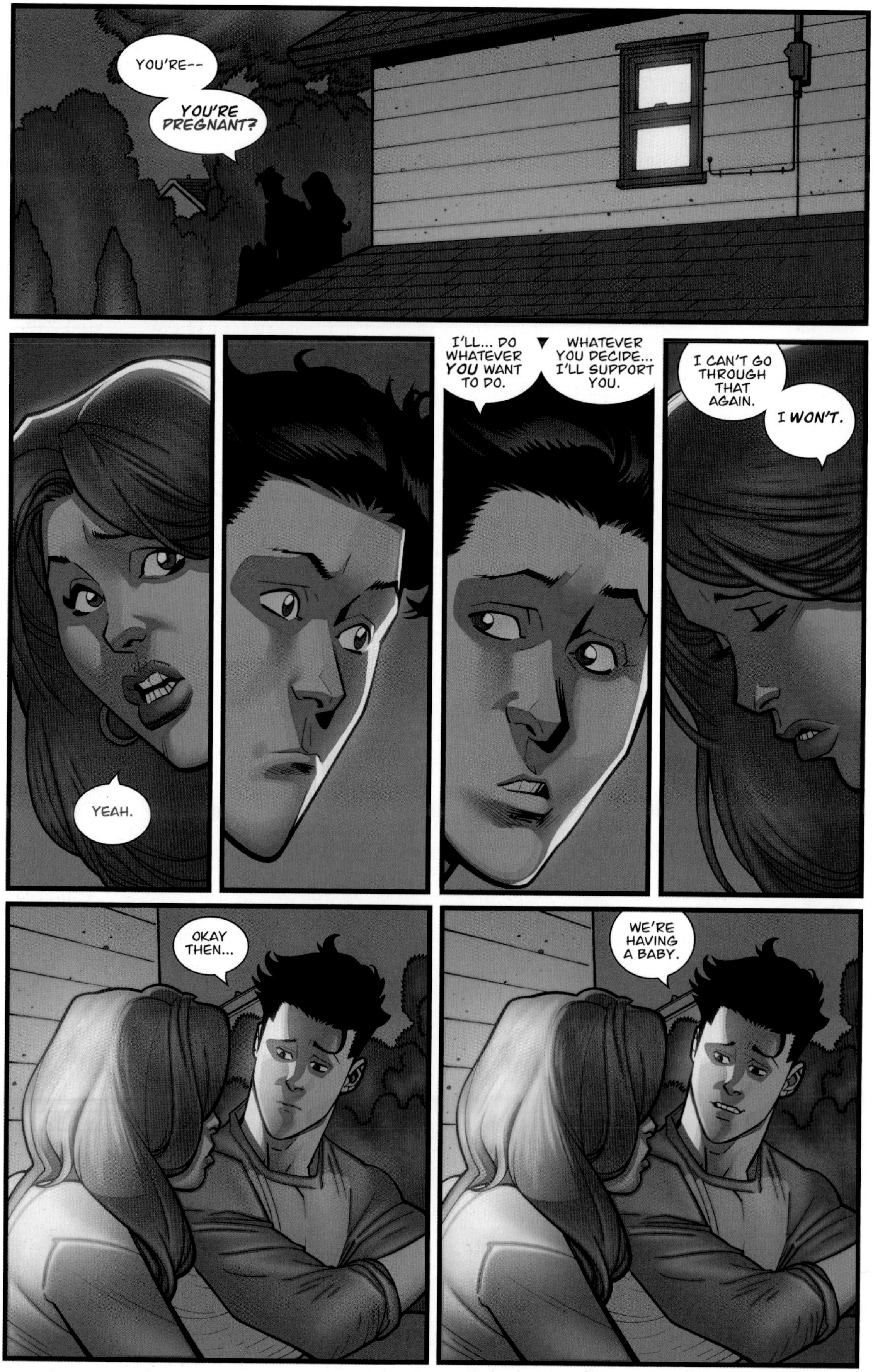
YOU'RE--
YOU'RE PREGNANT?
YEAH.
I'LL... DO WHATEVER YOU WANT TO DO.
WHATEVER YOU DECIDE... I'LL SUPPORT YOU.
I CAN'T GO THROUGH THAT AGAIN.
I WON'T.
OKAY THEN...
WE'RE HAVING A BABY.

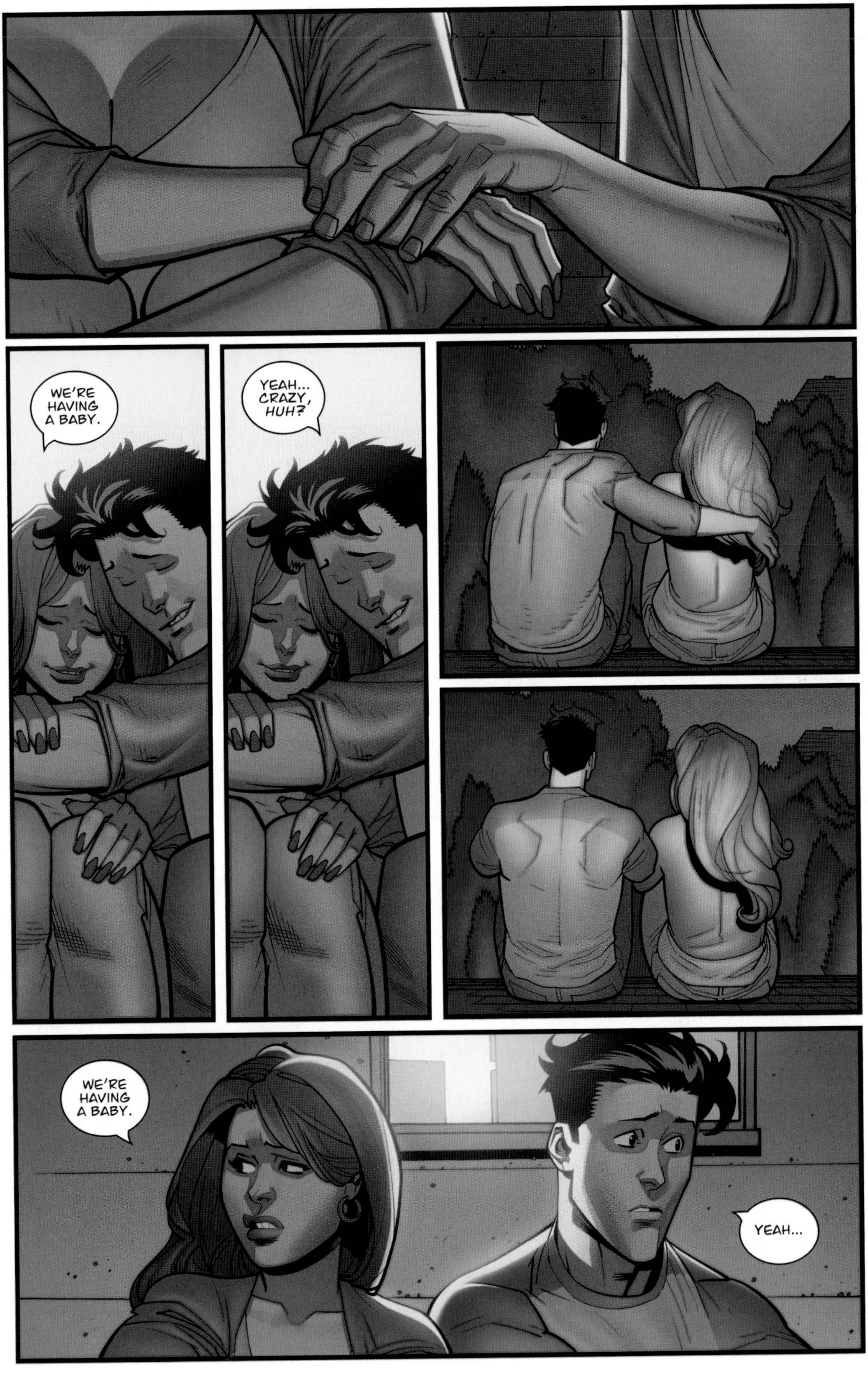
WE'RE HAVING A BABY.
YEAH... CRAZY, HUH?
WE'RE HAVING A BABY.
YEAH...

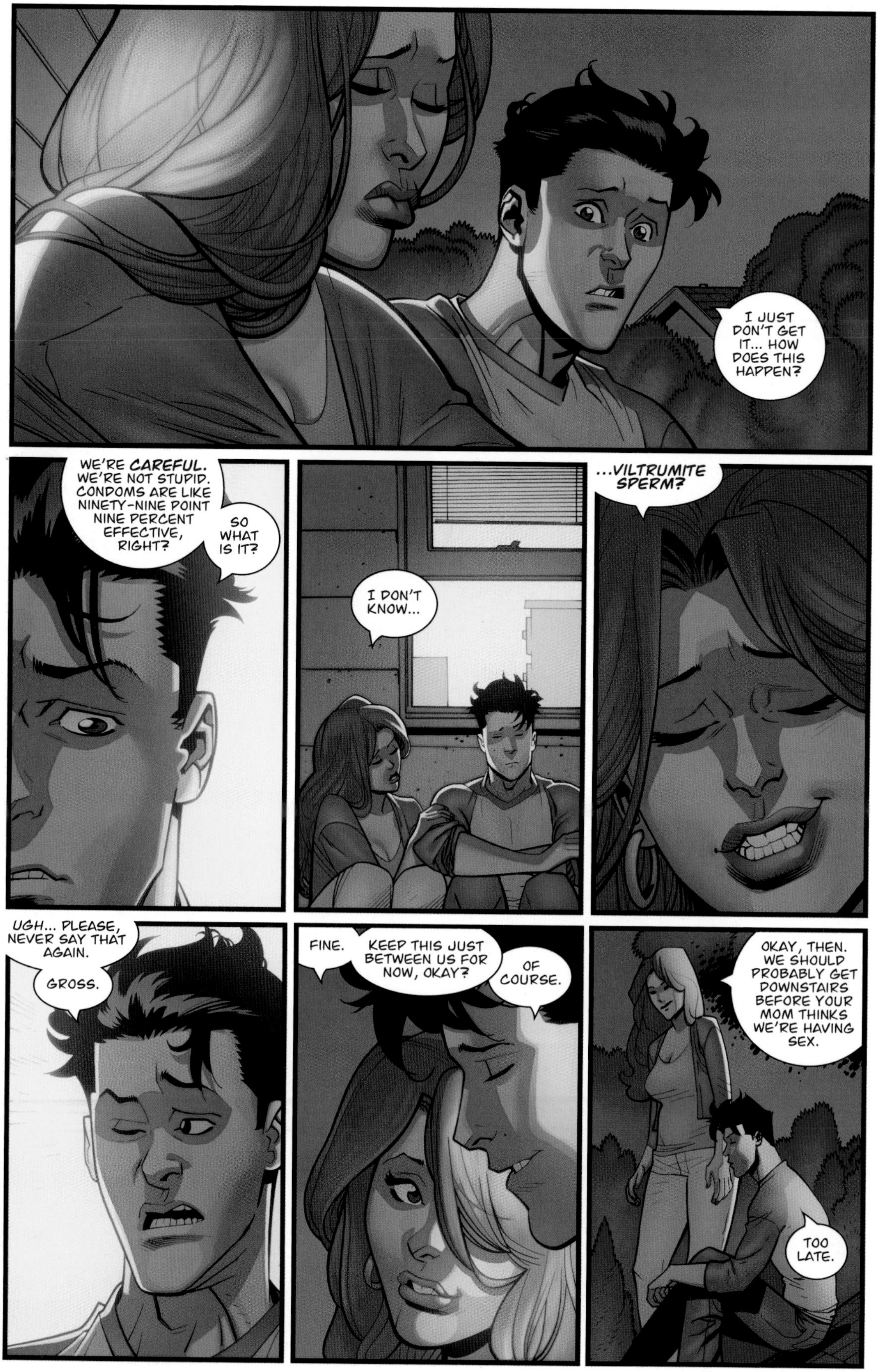
I JUST DON'T GET IT... HOW DOES THIS HAPPEN?
WE'RE **CAREFUL**. WE'RE NOT STUPID. CONDOMS ARE LIKE NINETY-NINE POINT NINE PERCENT EFFECTIVE, RIGHT?
SO WHAT IS IT?
I DON'T KNOW...
...VILTRUMITE SPERM?
UGH... PLEASE, NEVER SAY THAT AGAIN.
GROSS.
FINE.
KEEP THIS JUST BETWEEN US FOR NOW, OKAY?
OF COURSE.
OKAY, THEN. WE SHOULD PROBABLY GET DOWNSTAIRS BEFORE YOUR MOM THINKS WE'RE HAVING SEX.
TOO LATE.

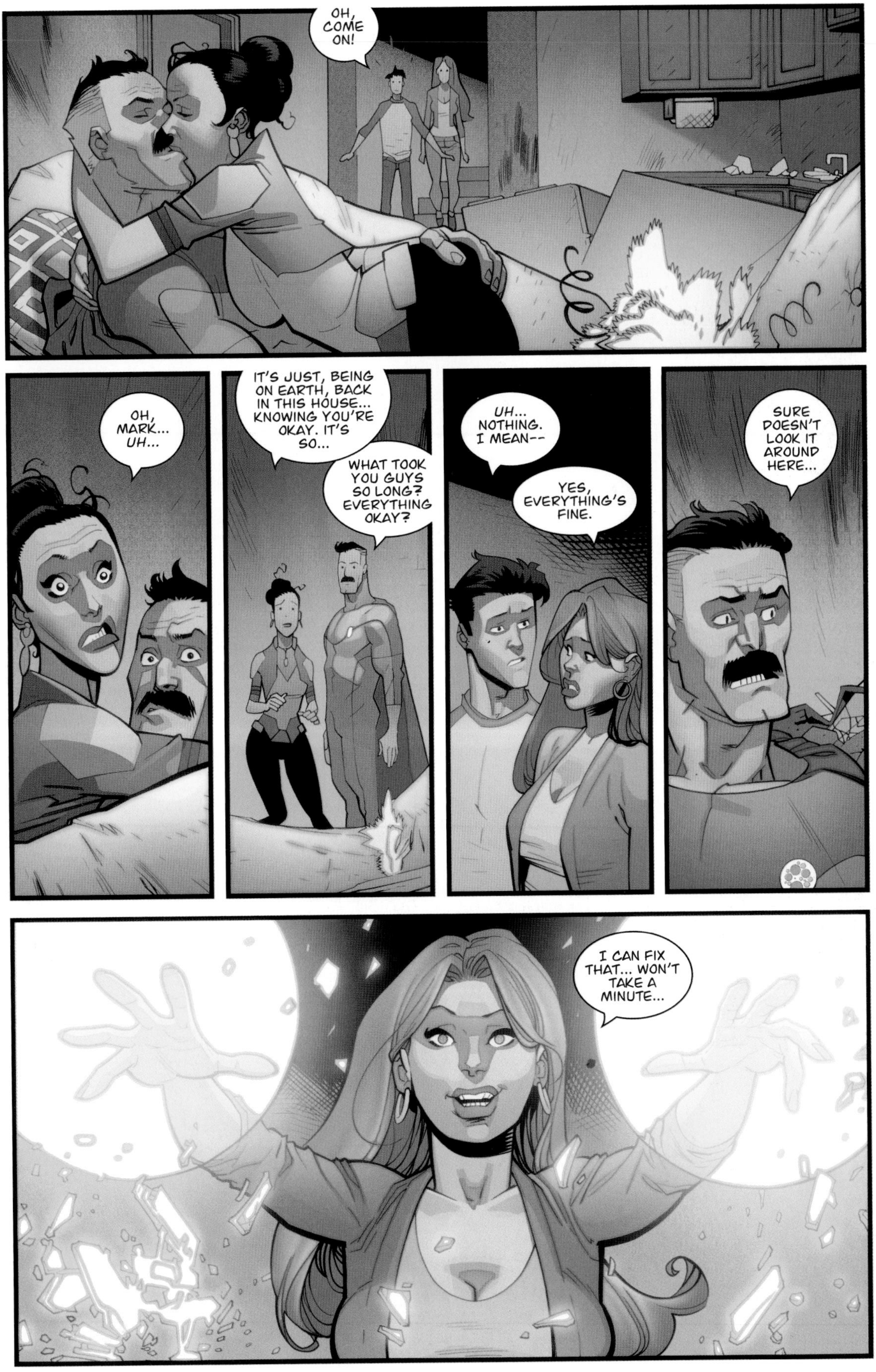
OH, COME ON!
OH, MARK... UH...
IT'S JUST, BEING ON EARTH, BACK IN THIS HOUSE... KNOWING YOU'RE OKAY. IT'S SO...
WHAT TOOK YOU GUYS SO LONG? EVERYTHING OKAY?
UH... NOTHING. I MEAN--
YES, EVERYTHING'S FINE.
SURE DOESN'T LOOK IT AROUND HERE...
I CAN FIX THAT... WON'T TAKE A MINUTE...

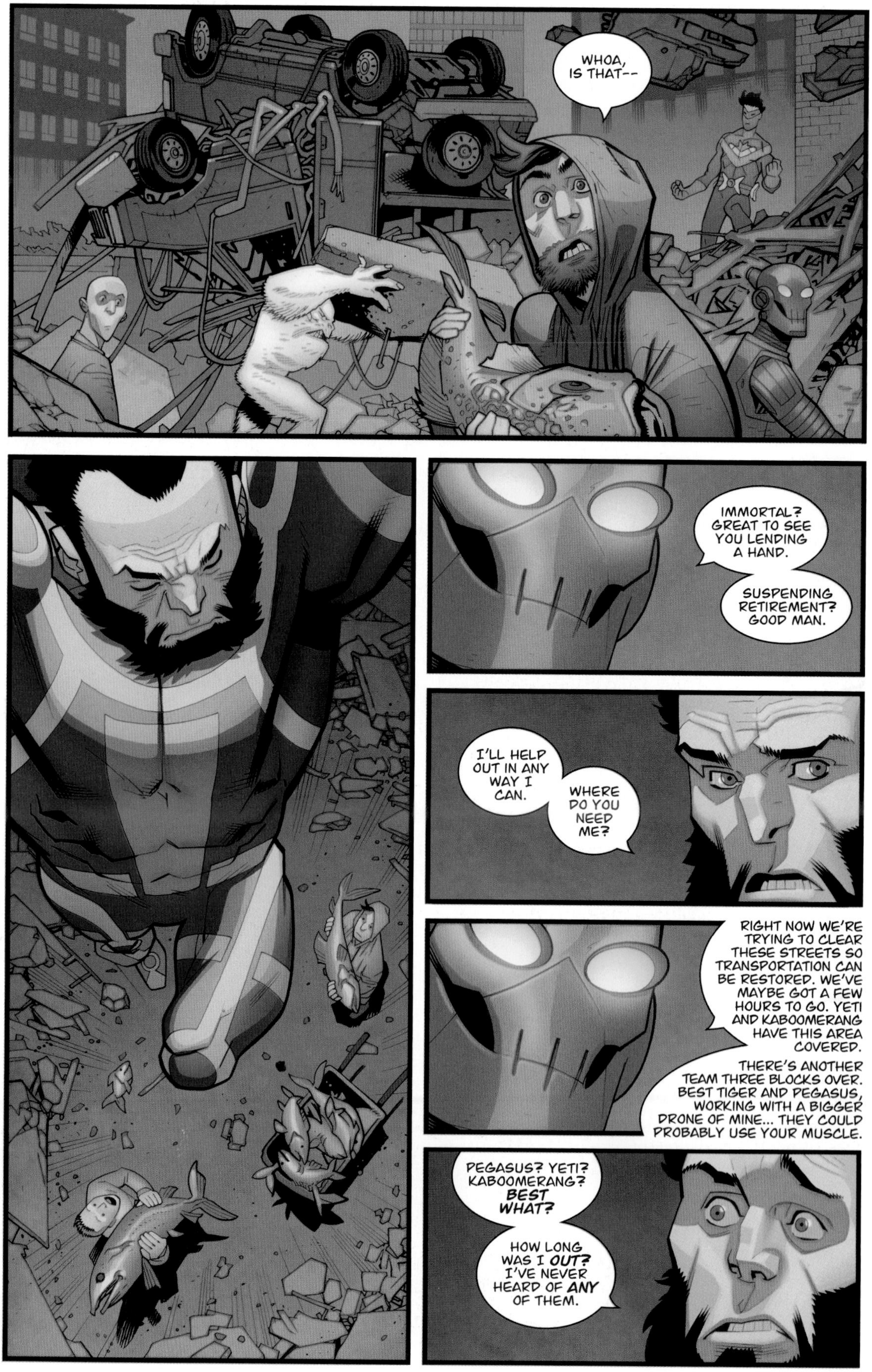
WHOA, IS THAT--
IMMORTAL? GREAT TO SEE YOU LENDING A HAND.
SUSPENDING RETIREMENT? GOOD MAN.
I'LL HELP OUT IN ANY WAY I CAN.
WHERE DO YOU NEED ME?
RIGHT NOW WE'RE TRYING TO CLEAR THESE STREETS SO TRANSPORTATION CAN BE RESTORED. WE'VE MAYBE GOT A FEW HOURS TO GO. YETI AND KABOOMERANG HAVE THIS AREA COVERED.
THERE'S ANOTHER TEAM THREE BLOCKS OVER. BEST TIGER AND PEGASUS, WORKING WITH A BIGGER DRONE OF MINE... THEY COULD PROBABLY USE YOUR MUSCLE.
PEGASUS? YETI? KABOOMERANG? BEST WHAT?
HOW LONG WAS I OUT? I'VE NEVER HEARD OF ANY OF THEM.

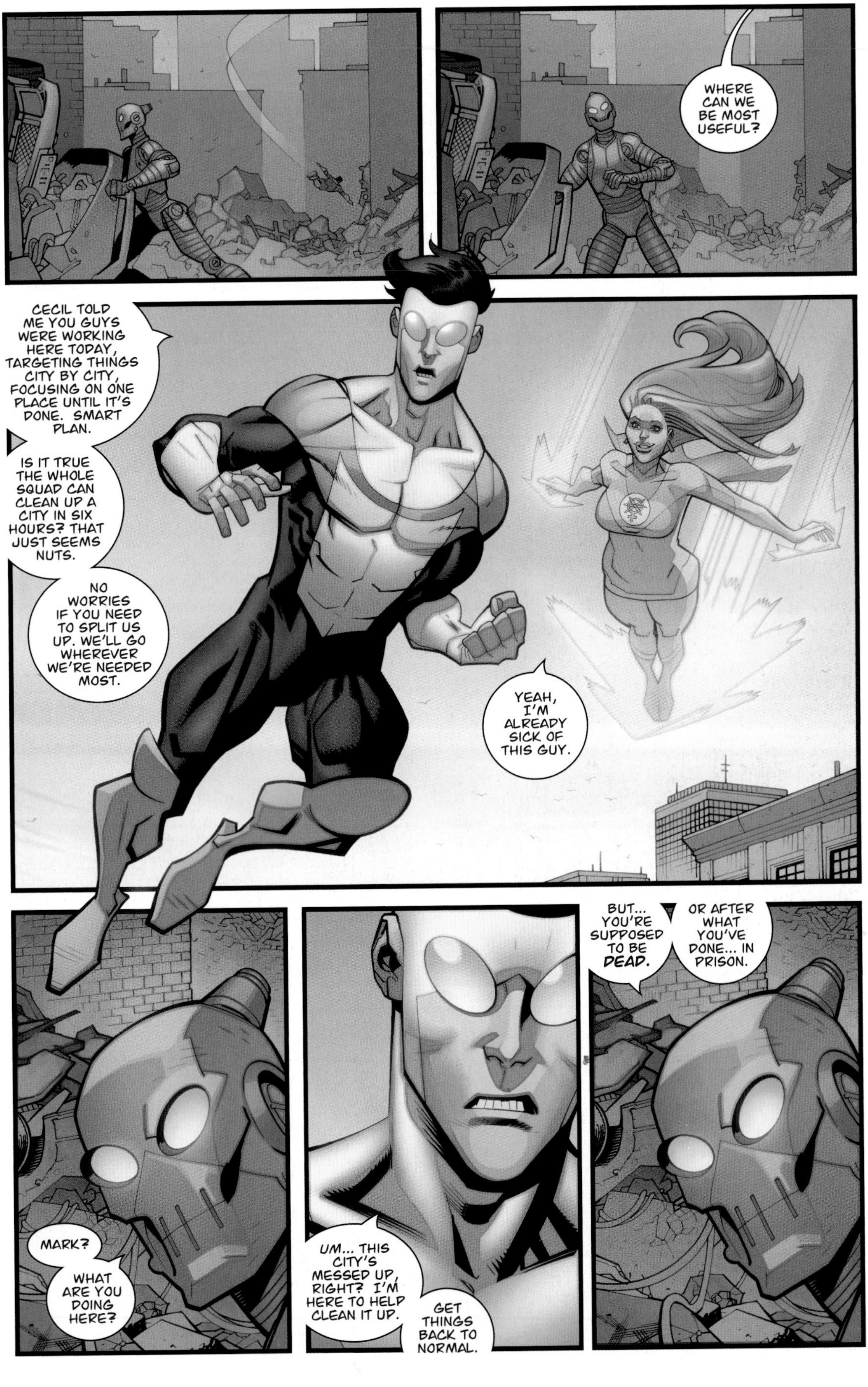
WHERE CAN WE BE MOST USEFUL?
CECIL TOLD ME YOU GUYS WERE WORKING HERE TODAY, TARGETING THINGS CITY BY CITY, FOCUSING ON ONE PLACE UNTIL IT'S DONE. SMART PLAN.
IS IT TRUE THE WHOLE SQUAD CAN CLEAN UP A CITY IN SIX HOURS? THAT JUST SEEMS NUTS.
NO WORRIES IF YOU NEED TO SPLIT US UP. WE'LL GO WHEREVER WE'RE NEEDED MOST.
YEAH, I'M ALREADY SICK OF THIS GUY.
MARK?
WHAT ARE YOU DOING HERE?
UM... THIS CITY'S MESSED UP, RIGHT? I'M HERE TO HELP CLEAN IT UP.
GET THINGS BACK TO NORMAL.
BUT... YOU'RE SUPPOSED TO BE **DEAD.**
OR AFTER WHAT YOU'VE DONE... IN PRISON.

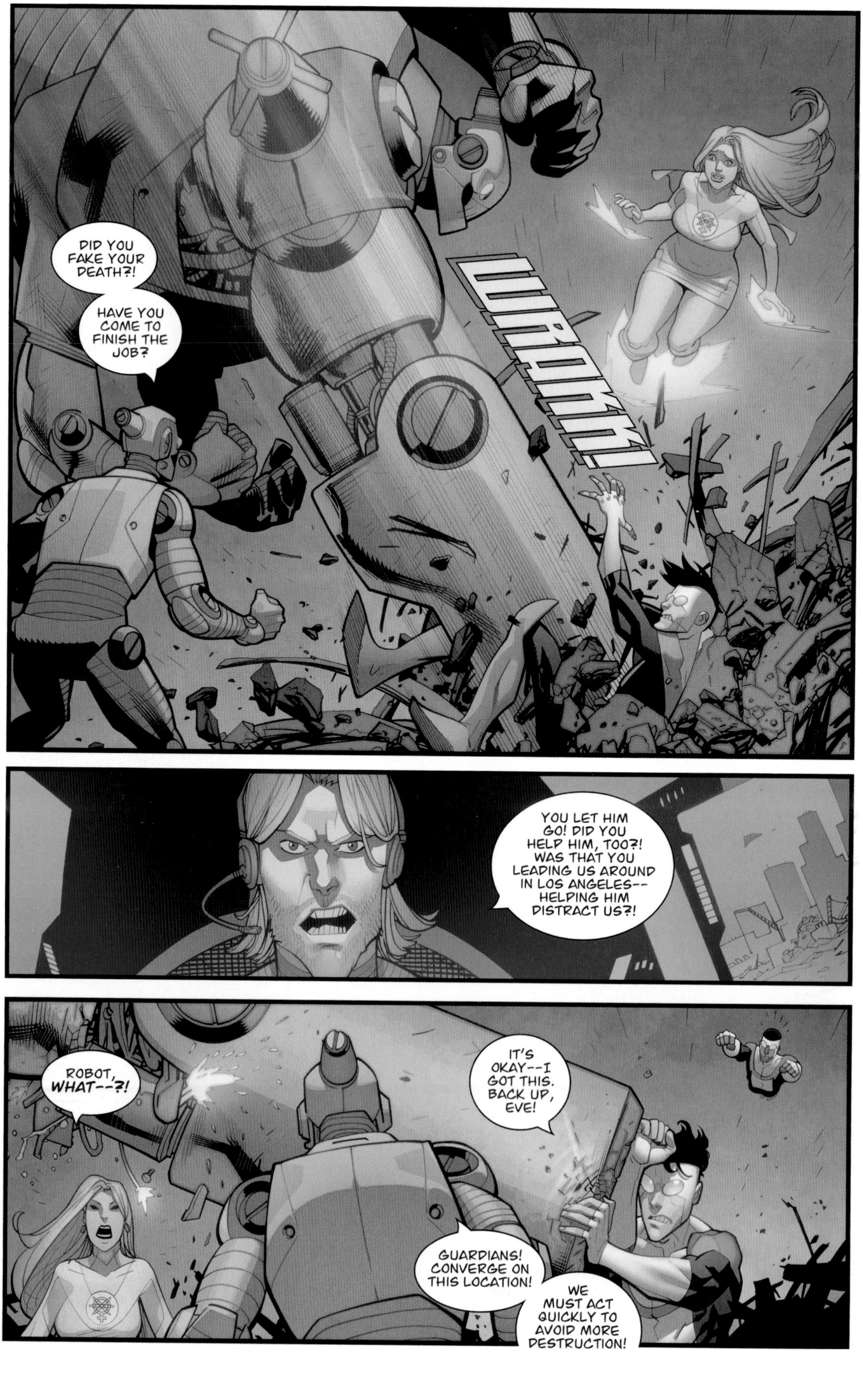
DID YOU FAKE YOUR DEATH?!
HAVE YOU COME TO FINISH THE JOB?
WRAKK!
YOU LET HIM GO! DID YOU HELP HIM, TOO?! WAS THAT YOU LEADING US AROUND IN LOS ANGELES-- HELPING HIM DISTRACT US?!
ROBOT, WHAT--?!
IT'S OKAY--I GOT THIS. BACK UP, EVE!
GUARDIANS! CONVERGE ON THIS LOCATION!
WE MUST ACT QUICKLY TO AVOID MORE DESTRUCTION!

DAMN IT, REX!

EVERYBODY STAND DOWN!

GET BACK TO YOUR POSITIONS AND RESUME CLEAN-UP-- THAT'S AN ORDER!

GUYS, I'M REALLY SORRY TO--

BROOM!!

I TAKE IT BACK!

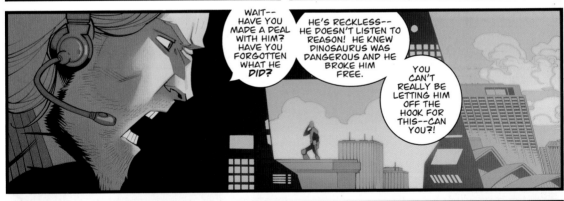

WAIT-- HAVE YOU MADE A DEAL WITH HIM? HAVE YOU FORGOTTEN WHAT HE DID?

HE'S RECKLESS-- HE DOESN'T LISTEN TO REASON! HE KNEW DINOSAURUS WAS DANGEROUS AND HE BROKE HIM FREE.

YOU CAN'T REALLY BE LETTING HIM OFF THE HOOK FOR THIS--CAN YOU?!

COME WITH ME. WE'LL SORT THIS OUT LATER.

ARE YOU GOING TO BE OKAY?

I'LL BE FINE. GO.

THAT'S IT?! YOU'RE JUST LETTING HIM WALK AWAY?!

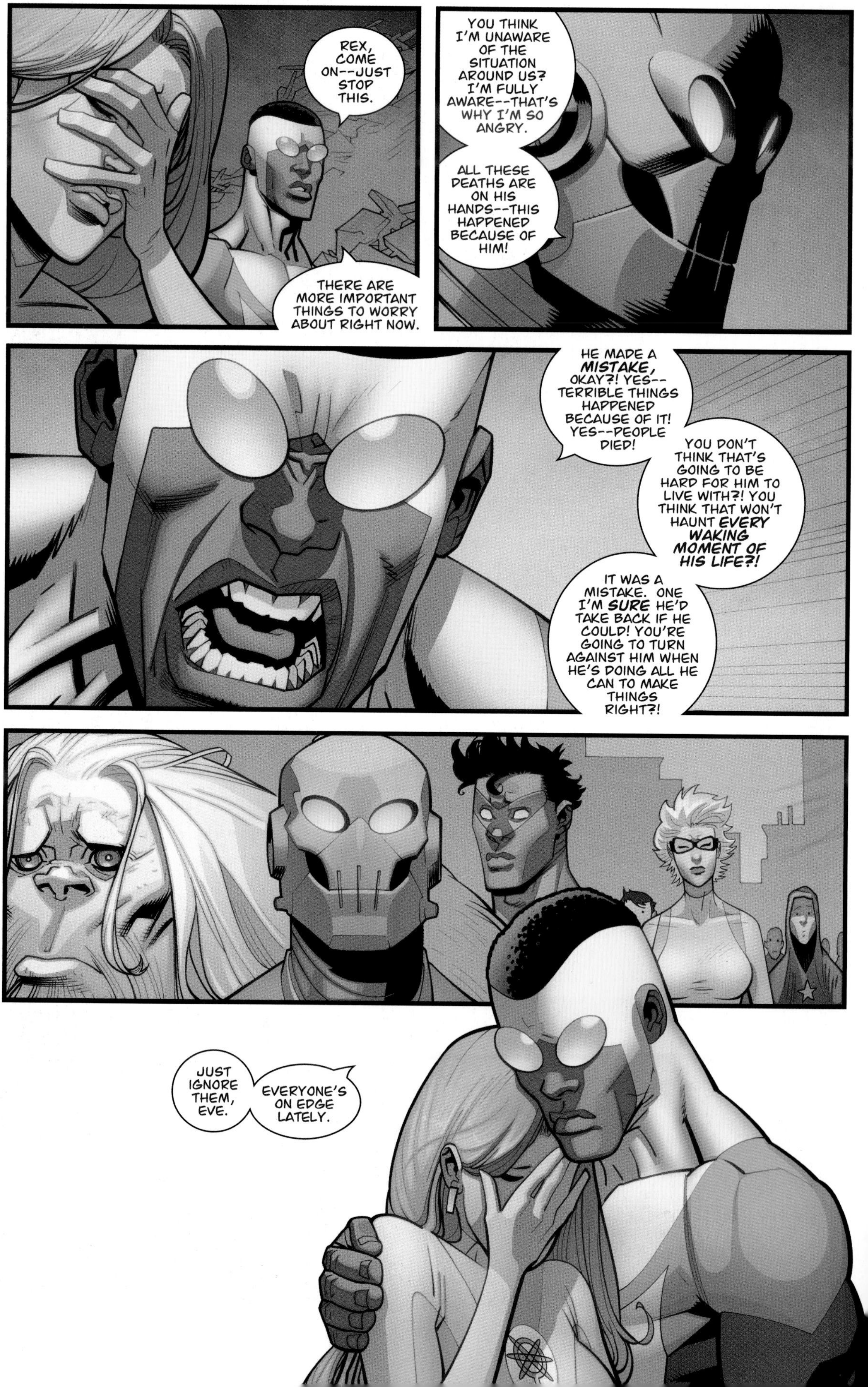
REX, COME ON--JUST STOP THIS.
THERE ARE MORE IMPORTANT THINGS TO WORRY ABOUT RIGHT NOW.
YOU THINK I'M UNAWARE OF THE SITUATION AROUND US? I'M FULLY AWARE--THAT'S WHY I'M SO ANGRY.
ALL THESE DEATHS ARE ON HIS HANDS--THIS HAPPENED BECAUSE OF HIM!
HE MADE A MISTAKE, OKAY?! YES--TERRIBLE THINGS HAPPENED BECAUSE OF IT! YES--PEOPLE DIED!
YOU DON'T THINK THAT'S GOING TO BE HARD FOR HIM TO LIVE WITH?! YOU THINK THAT WON'T HAUNT EVERY WAKING MOMENT OF HIS LIFE?!
IT WAS A MISTAKE. ONE I'M SURE HE'D TAKE BACK IF HE COULD! YOU'RE GOING TO TURN AGAINST HIM WHEN HE'S DOING ALL HE CAN TO MAKE THINGS RIGHT?!
JUST IGNORE THEM, EVE.
EVERYONE'S ON EDGE LATELY.

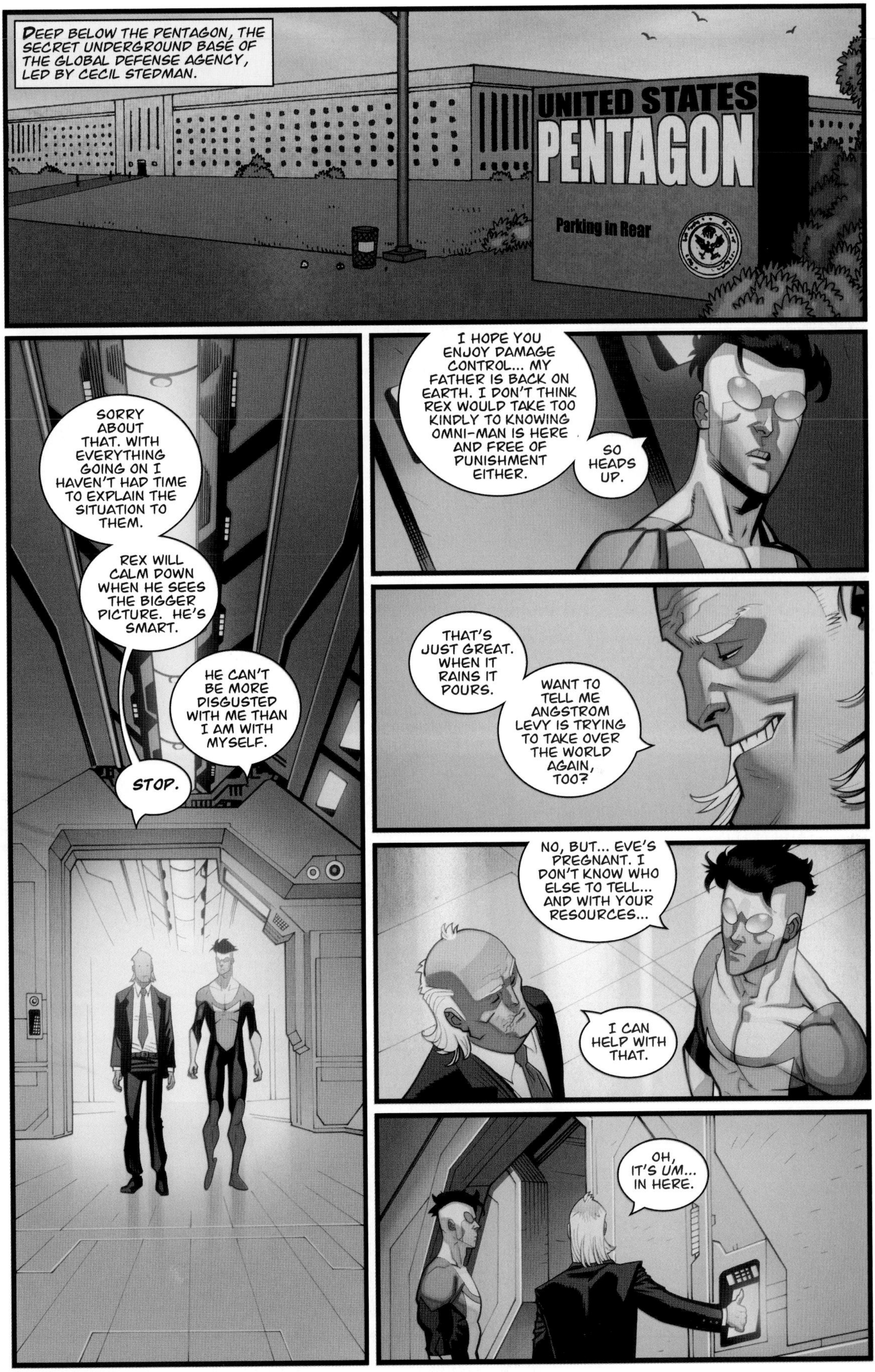
DEEP BELOW THE PENTAGON, THE SECRET UNDERGROUND BASE OF THE GLOBAL DEFENSE AGENCY, LED BY CECIL STEDMAN.
UNITED STATES PENTAGON
Parking in Rear
SORRY ABOUT THAT. WITH EVERYTHING GOING ON I HAVEN'T HAD TIME TO EXPLAIN THE SITUATION TO THEM.
REX WILL CALM DOWN WHEN HE SEES THE BIGGER PICTURE. HE'S SMART.
HE CAN'T BE MORE DISGUSTED WITH ME THAN I AM WITH MYSELF.
STOP.
I HOPE YOU ENJOY DAMAGE CONTROL... MY FATHER IS BACK ON EARTH. I DON'T THINK REX WOULD TAKE TOO KINDLY TO KNOWING OMNI-MAN IS HERE AND FREE OF PUNISHMENT EITHER.
SO HEADS UP.
THAT'S JUST GREAT. WHEN IT RAINS IT POURS.
WANT TO TELL ME ANGSTROM LEVY IS TRYING TO TAKE OVER THE WORLD AGAIN, TOO?
NO, BUT... EVE'S PREGNANT. I DON'T KNOW WHO ELSE TO TELL... AND WITH YOUR RESOURCES...
I CAN HELP WITH THAT.
OH, IT'S UM... IN HERE.

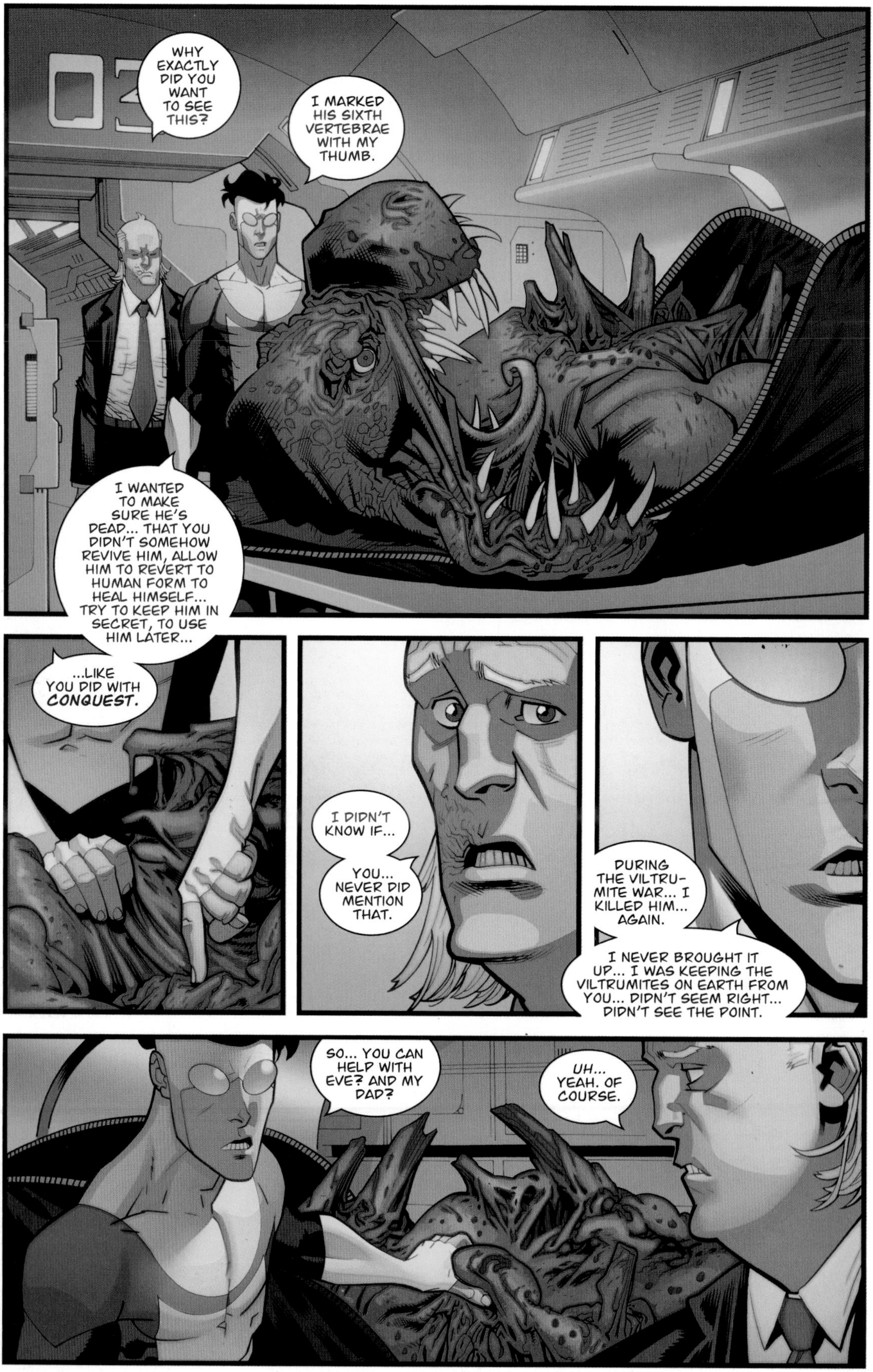
WHY EXACTLY DID YOU WANT TO SEE THIS?
I MARKED HIS SIXTH VERTEBRAE WITH MY THUMB.
I WANTED TO MAKE SURE HE'S DEAD... THAT YOU DIDN'T SOMEHOW REVIVE HIM, ALLOW HIM TO REVERT TO HUMAN FORM TO HEAL HIMSELF... TRY TO KEEP HIM IN SECRET, TO USE HIM LATER...
...LIKE YOU DID WITH CONQUEST.
I DIDN'T KNOW IF...
YOU... NEVER DID MENTION THAT.
DURING THE VILTRUMITE WAR... I KILLED HIM... AGAIN.
I NEVER BROUGHT IT UP... I WAS KEEPING THE VILTRUMITES ON EARTH FROM YOU... DIDN'T SEEM RIGHT... DIDN'T SEE THE POINT.
SO... YOU CAN HELP WITH EVE? AND MY DAD?
UH... YEAH. OF COURSE.

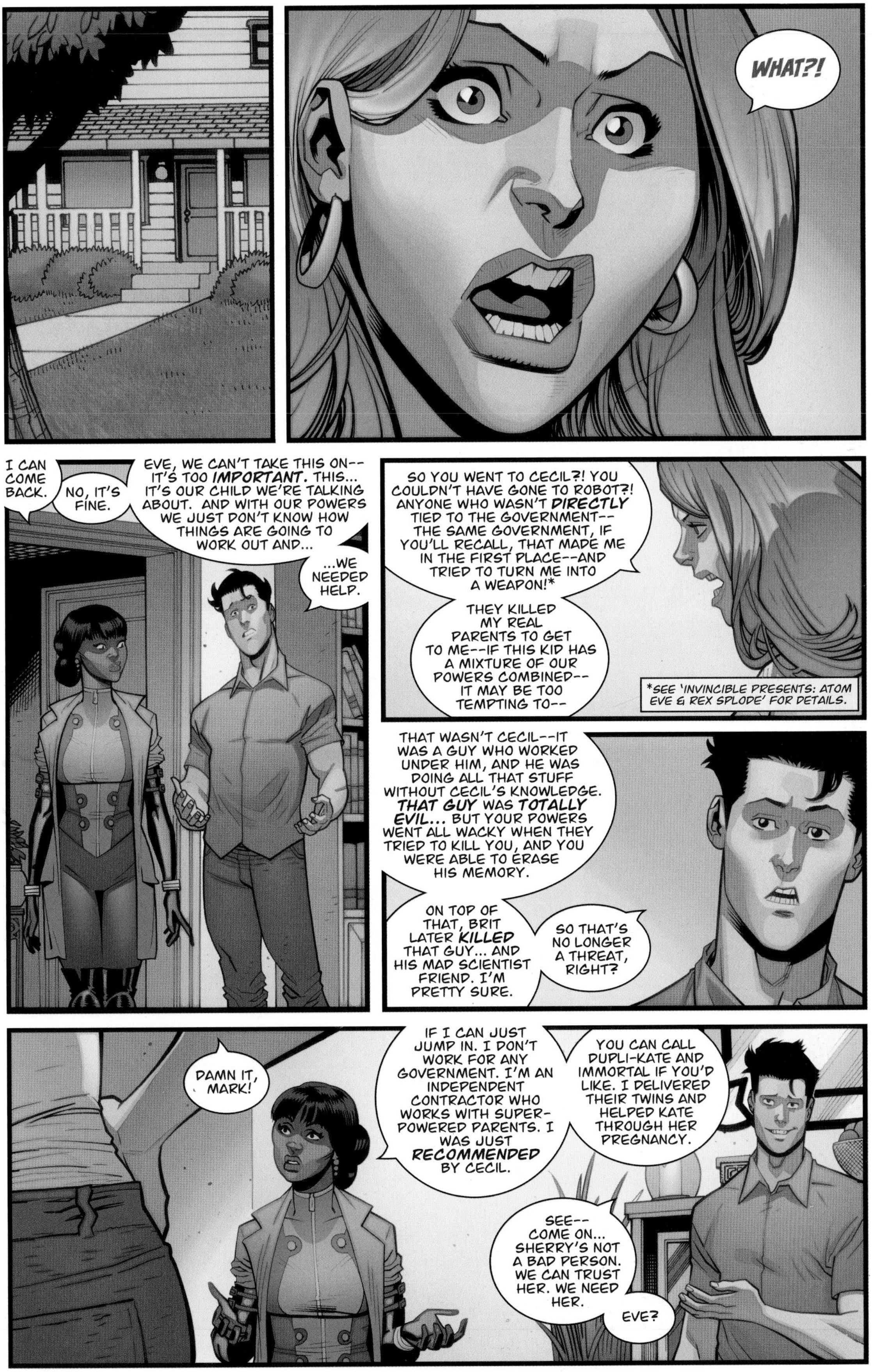
WHAT?!
I CAN COME BACK.
NO, IT'S FINE.
EVE, WE CAN'T TAKE THIS ON-- IT'S TOO IMPORTANT. THIS... IT'S OUR CHILD WE'RE TALKING ABOUT. AND WITH OUR POWERS WE JUST DON'T KNOW HOW THINGS ARE GOING TO WORK OUT AND...
...WE NEEDED HELP.
SO YOU WENT TO CECIL?! YOU COULDN'T HAVE GONE TO ROBOT?! ANYONE WHO WASN'T DIRECTLY TIED TO THE GOVERNMENT-- THE SAME GOVERNMENT, IF YOU'LL RECALL, THAT MADE ME IN THE FIRST PLACE--AND TRIED TO TURN ME INTO A WEAPON!*
THEY KILLED MY REAL PARENTS TO GET TO ME--IF THIS KID HAS A MIXTURE OF OUR POWERS COMBINED-- IT MAY BE TOO TEMPTING TO--
*SEE 'INVINCIBLE PRESENTS: ATOM EVE & REX SPLODE' FOR DETAILS.
THAT WASN'T CECIL--IT WAS A GUY WHO WORKED UNDER HIM, AND HE WAS DOING ALL THAT STUFF WITHOUT CECIL'S KNOWLEDGE. THAT GUY WAS TOTALLY EVIL... BUT YOUR POWERS WENT ALL WACKY WHEN THEY TRIED TO KILL YOU, AND YOU WERE ABLE TO ERASE HIS MEMORY.
ON TOP OF THAT, BRIT LATER KILLED THAT GUY... AND HIS MAD SCIENTIST FRIEND. I'M PRETTY SURE.
SO THAT'S NO LONGER A THREAT, RIGHT?
DAMN IT, MARK!
IF I CAN JUST JUMP IN. I DON'T WORK FOR ANY GOVERNMENT. I'M AN INDEPENDENT CONTRACTOR WHO WORKS WITH SUPER-POWERED PARENTS. I WAS JUST RECOMMENDED BY CECIL.
YOU CAN CALL DUPLI-KATE AND IMMORTAL IF YOU'D LIKE. I DELIVERED THEIR TWINS AND HELPED KATE THROUGH HER PREGNANCY.
SEE-- COME ON... SHERRY'S NOT A BAD PERSON. WE CAN TRUST HER. WE NEED HER.
EVE?

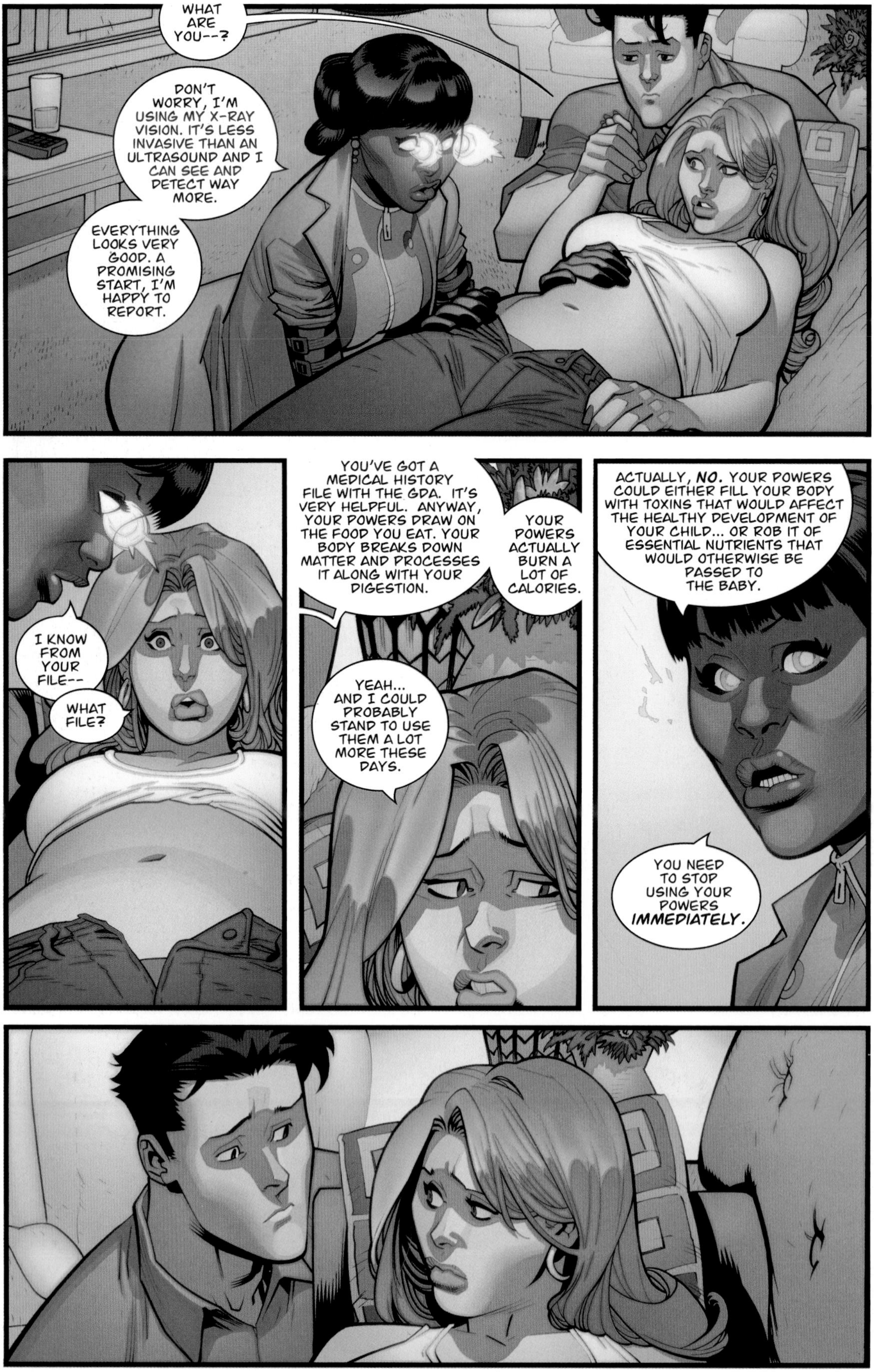
WHAT ARE YOU--?
DON'T WORRY, I'M USING MY X-RAY VISION. IT'S LESS INVASIVE THAN AN ULTRASOUND AND I CAN SEE AND DETECT WAY MORE.
EVERYTHING LOOKS VERY GOOD. A PROMISING START, I'M HAPPY TO REPORT.
I KNOW FROM YOUR FILE--
WHAT FILE?
YOU'VE GOT A MEDICAL HISTORY FILE WITH THE GDA. IT'S VERY HELPFUL. ANYWAY, YOUR POWERS DRAW ON THE FOOD YOU EAT. YOUR BODY BREAKS DOWN MATTER AND PROCESSES IT ALONG WITH YOUR DIGESTION.
YOUR POWERS ACTUALLY BURN A LOT OF CALORIES.
YEAH... AND I COULD PROBABLY STAND TO USE THEM A LOT MORE THESE DAYS.
ACTUALLY, **NO.** YOUR POWERS COULD EITHER FILL YOUR BODY WITH TOXINS THAT WOULD AFFECT THE HEALTHY DEVELOPMENT OF YOUR CHILD... OR ROB IT OF ESSENTIAL NUTRIENTS THAT WOULD OTHERWISE BE PASSED TO THE BABY.
YOU NEED TO STOP USING YOUR POWERS ***IMMEDIATELY.***

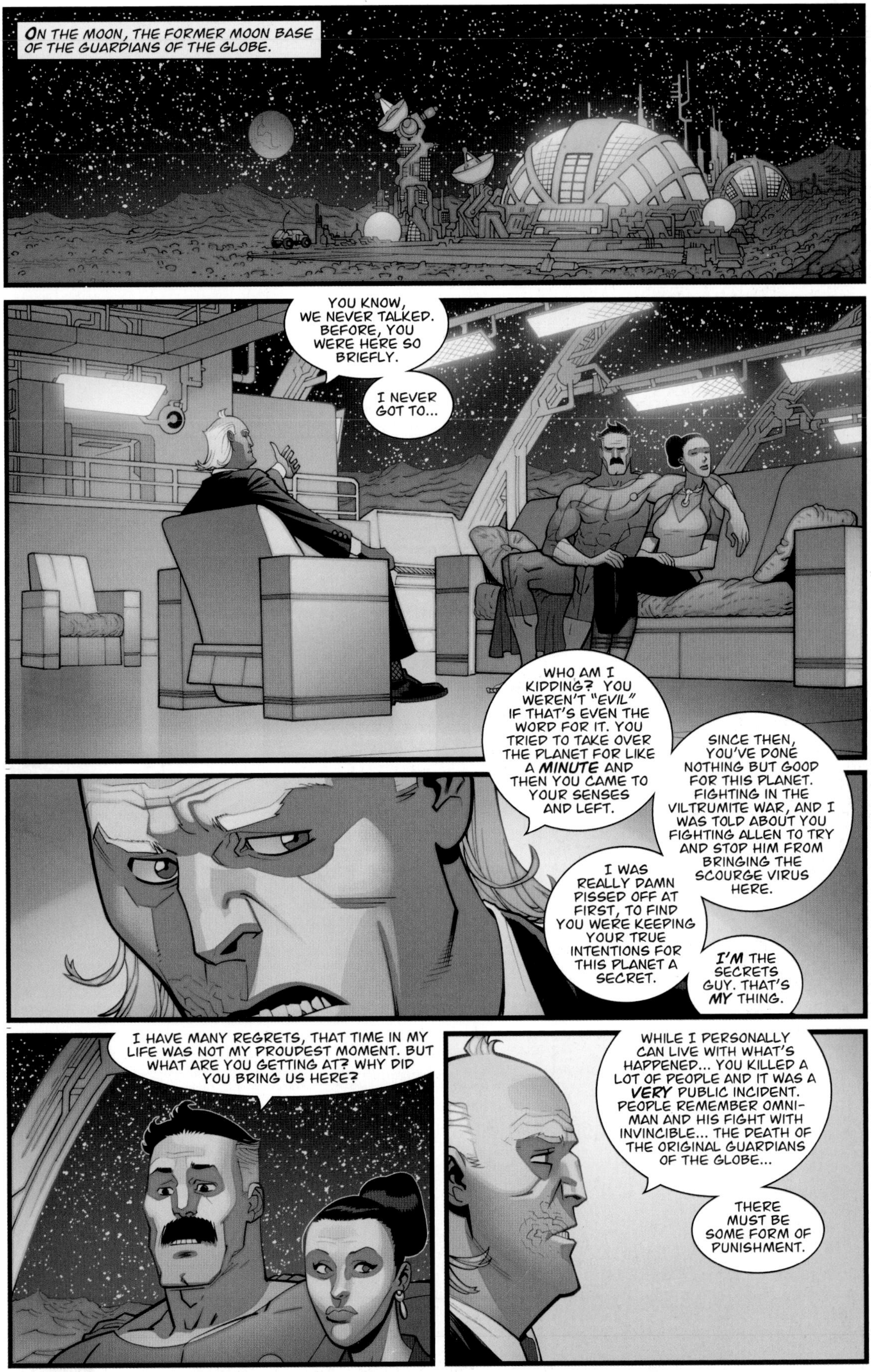
ON THE MOON, THE FORMER MOON BASE OF THE GUARDIANS OF THE GLOBE.
YOU KNOW, WE NEVER TALKED. BEFORE, YOU WERE HERE SO BRIEFLY.
I NEVER GOT TO...
WHO AM I KIDDING? YOU WEREN'T "EVIL" IF THAT'S EVEN THE WORD FOR IT. YOU TRIED TO TAKE OVER THE PLANET FOR LIKE A MINUTE AND THEN YOU CAME TO YOUR SENSES AND LEFT.
SINCE THEN, YOU'VE DONE NOTHING BUT GOOD FOR THIS PLANET. FIGHTING IN THE VILTRUMITE WAR, AND I WAS TOLD ABOUT YOU FIGHTING ALLEN TO TRY AND STOP HIM FROM BRINGING THE SCOURGE VIRUS HERE.
I WAS REALLY DAMN PISSED OFF AT FIRST, TO FIND YOU WERE KEEPING YOUR TRUE INTENTIONS FOR THIS PLANET A SECRET.
I'M THE SECRETS GUY. THAT'S MY THING.
I HAVE MANY REGRETS, THAT TIME IN MY LIFE WAS NOT MY PROUDEST MOMENT. BUT WHAT ARE YOU GETTING AT? WHY DID YOU BRING US HERE?
WHILE I PERSONALLY CAN LIVE WITH WHAT'S HAPPENED... YOU KILLED A LOT OF PEOPLE AND IT WAS A VERY PUBLIC INCIDENT. PEOPLE REMEMBER OMNI-MAN AND HIS FIGHT WITH INVINCIBLE... THE DEATH OF THE ORIGINAL GUARDIANS OF THE GLOBE...
THERE MUST BE SOME FORM OF PUNISHMENT.

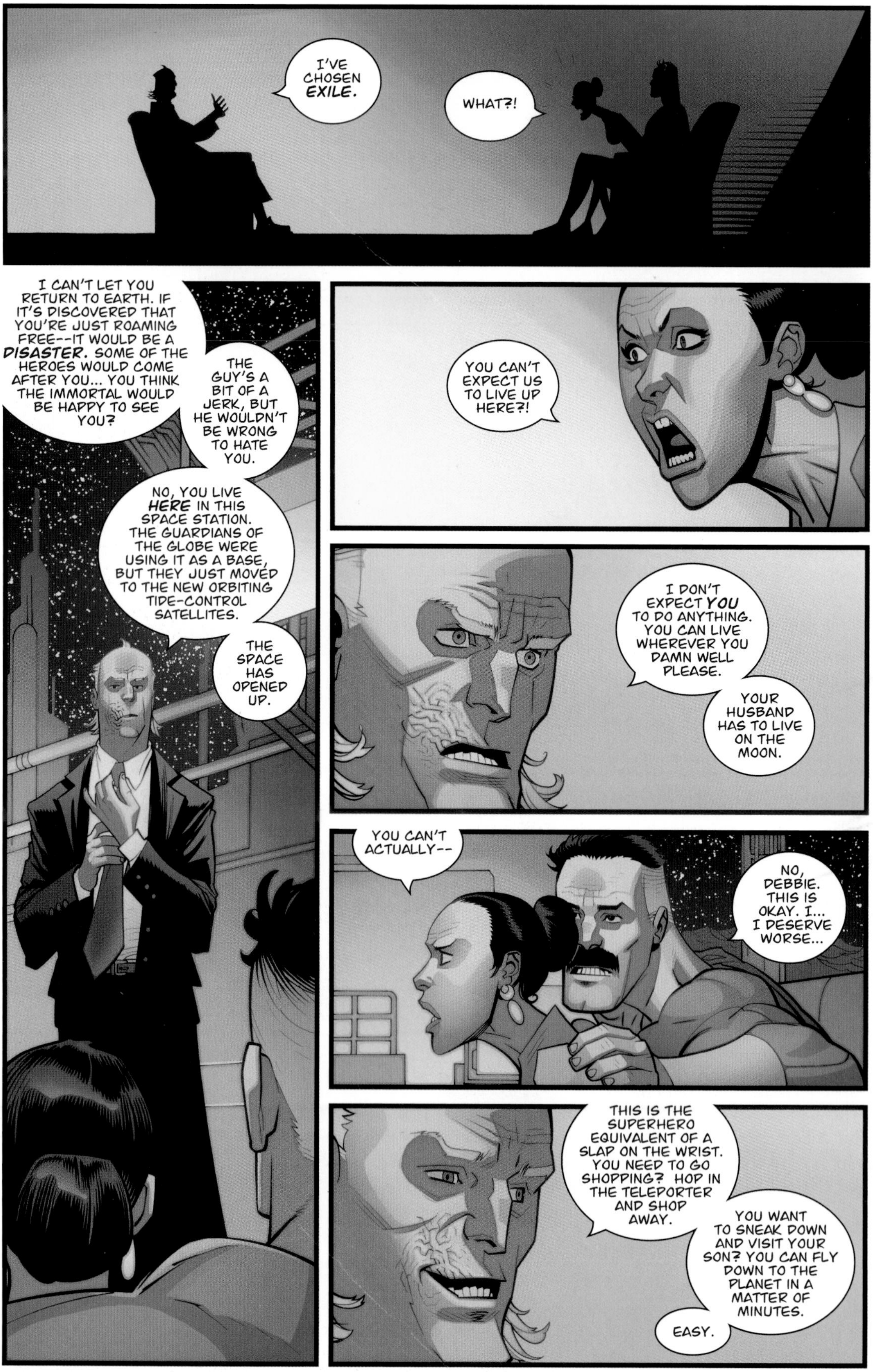

I'VE CHOSEN EXILE.
WHAT?!
I CAN'T LET YOU RETURN TO EARTH. IF IT'S DISCOVERED THAT YOU'RE JUST ROAMING FREE--IT WOULD BE A DISASTER. SOME OF THE HEROES WOULD COME AFTER YOU... YOU THINK THE IMMORTAL WOULD BE HAPPY TO SEE YOU?
THE GUY'S A BIT OF A JERK, BUT HE WOULDN'T BE WRONG TO HATE YOU.
NO, YOU LIVE HERE IN THIS SPACE STATION. THE GUARDIANS OF THE GLOBE WERE USING IT AS A BASE, BUT THEY JUST MOVED TO THE NEW ORBITING TIDE-CONTROL SATELLITES.
THE SPACE HAS OPENED UP.
YOU CAN'T EXPECT US TO LIVE UP HERE?!
I DON'T EXPECT YOU TO DO ANYTHING. YOU CAN LIVE WHEREVER YOU DAMN WELL PLEASE.
YOUR HUSBAND HAS TO LIVE ON THE MOON.
YOU CAN'T ACTUALLY--
NO, DEBBIE. THIS IS OKAY. I... I DESERVE WORSE...
THIS IS THE SUPERHERO EQUIVALENT OF A SLAP ON THE WRIST. YOU NEED TO GO SHOPPING? HOP IN THE TELEPORTER AND SHOP AWAY.
YOU WANT TO SNEAK DOWN AND VISIT YOUR SON? YOU CAN FLY DOWN TO THE PLANET IN A MATTER OF MINUTES.
EASY.

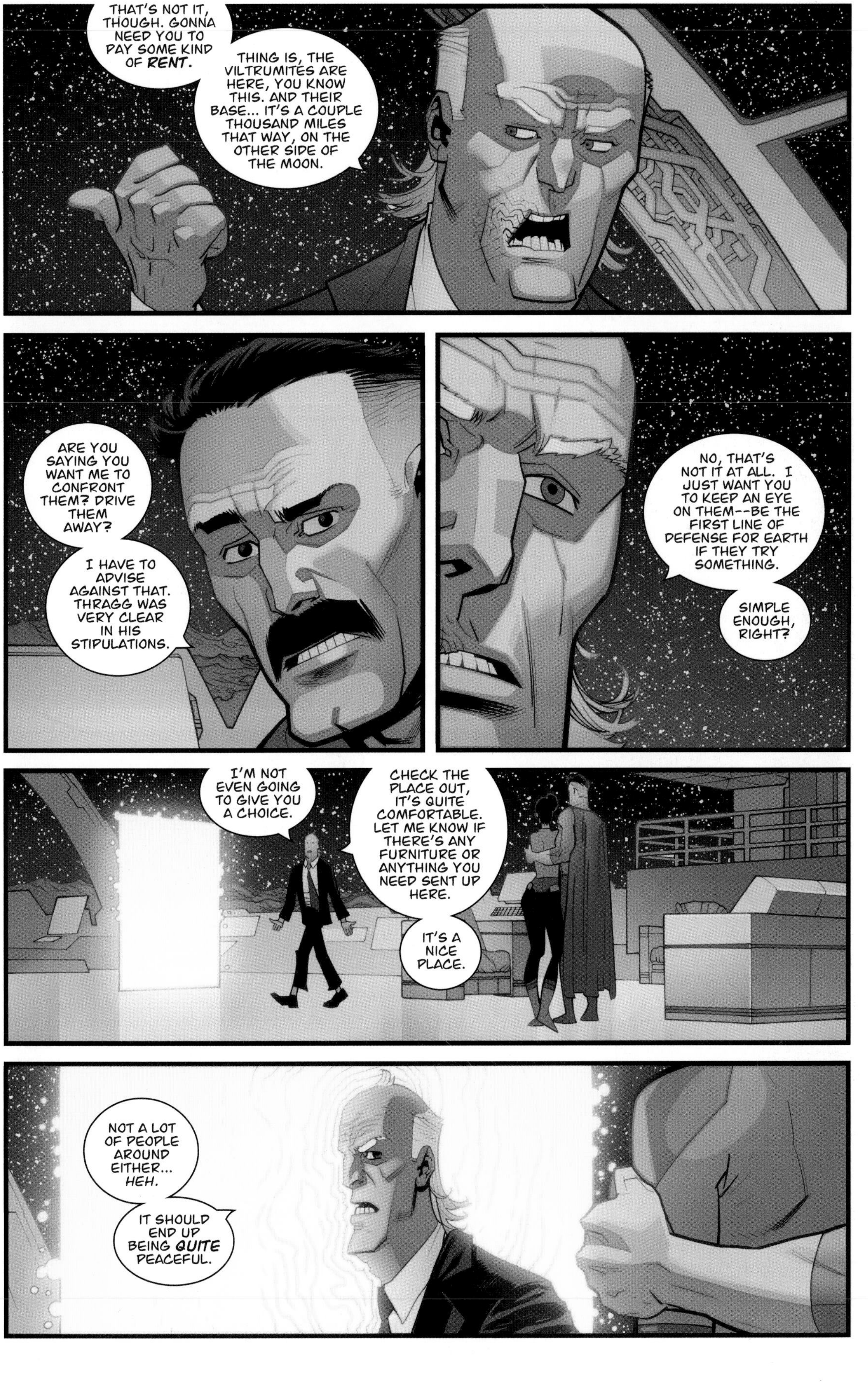
THAT'S NOT IT, THOUGH. GONNA NEED YOU TO PAY SOME KIND OF **RENT**.
THING IS, THE VILTRUMITES ARE HERE, YOU KNOW THIS. AND THEIR BASE... IT'S A COUPLE THOUSAND MILES THAT WAY, ON THE OTHER SIDE OF THE MOON.
ARE YOU SAYING YOU WANT ME TO CONFRONT THEM? DRIVE THEM AWAY?
I HAVE TO ADVISE AGAINST THAT. THRAGG WAS VERY CLEAR IN HIS STIPULATIONS.
NO, THAT'S NOT IT AT ALL. I JUST WANT YOU TO KEEP AN EYE ON THEM--BE THE FIRST LINE OF DEFENSE FOR EARTH IF THEY TRY SOMETHING.
SIMPLE ENOUGH, RIGHT?
I'M NOT EVEN GOING TO GIVE YOU A CHOICE.
CHECK THE PLACE OUT, IT'S QUITE COMFORTABLE. LET ME KNOW IF THERE'S ANY FURNITURE OR ANYTHING YOU NEED SENT UP HERE.
IT'S A NICE PLACE.
NOT A LOT OF PEOPLE AROUND EITHER... HEH.
IT SHOULD END UP BEING **QUITE** PEACEFUL.

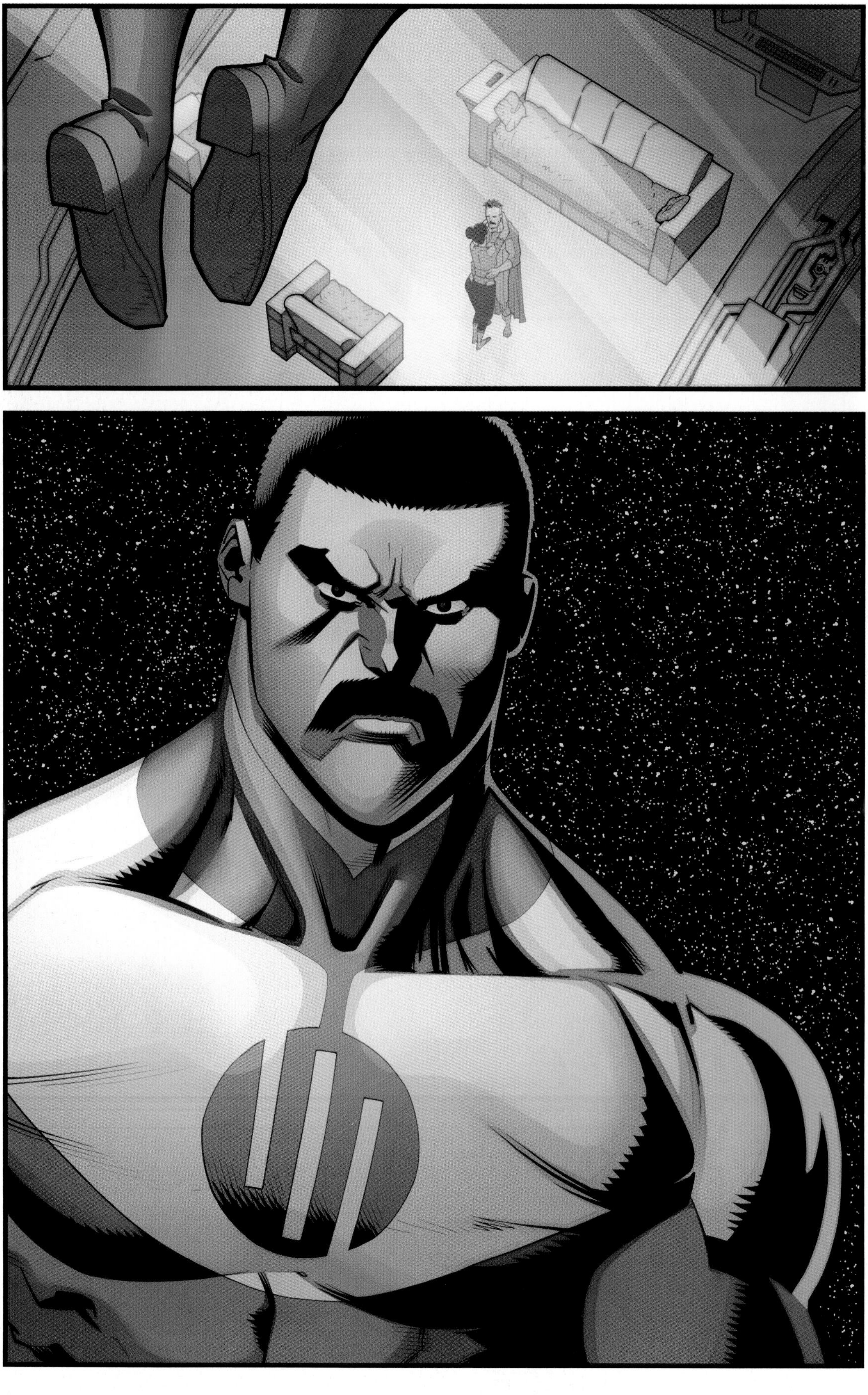

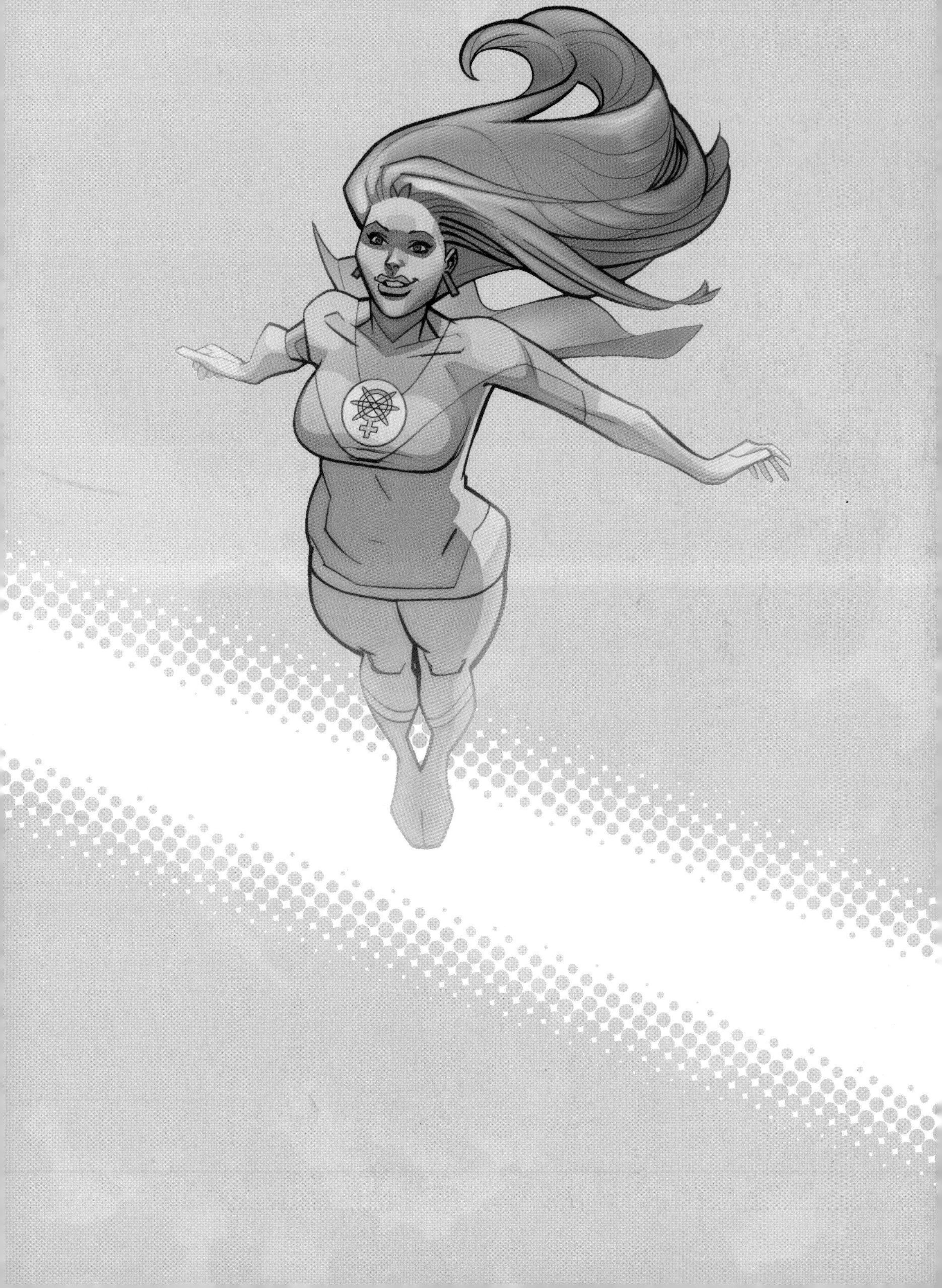

CHAPTER SIX

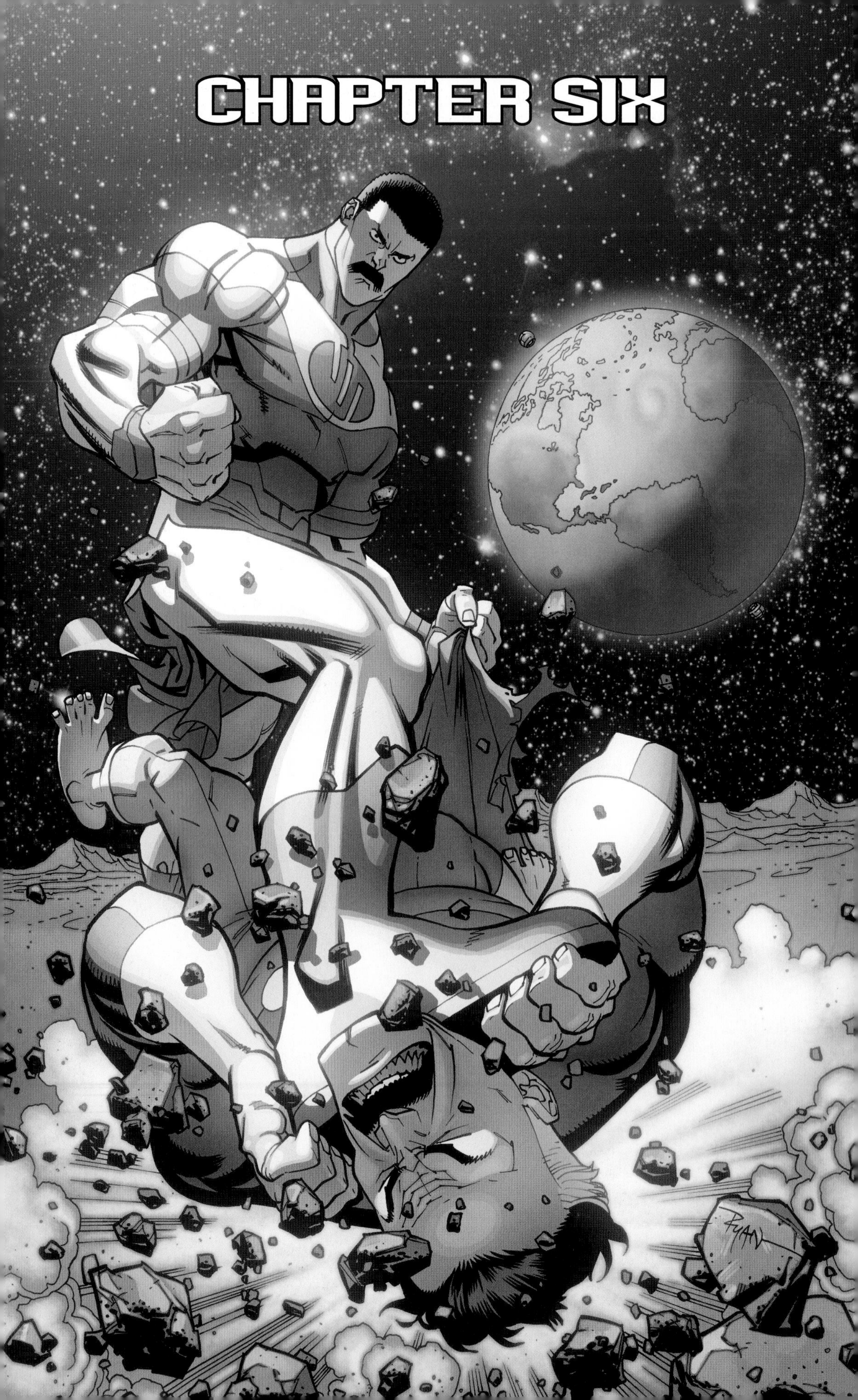

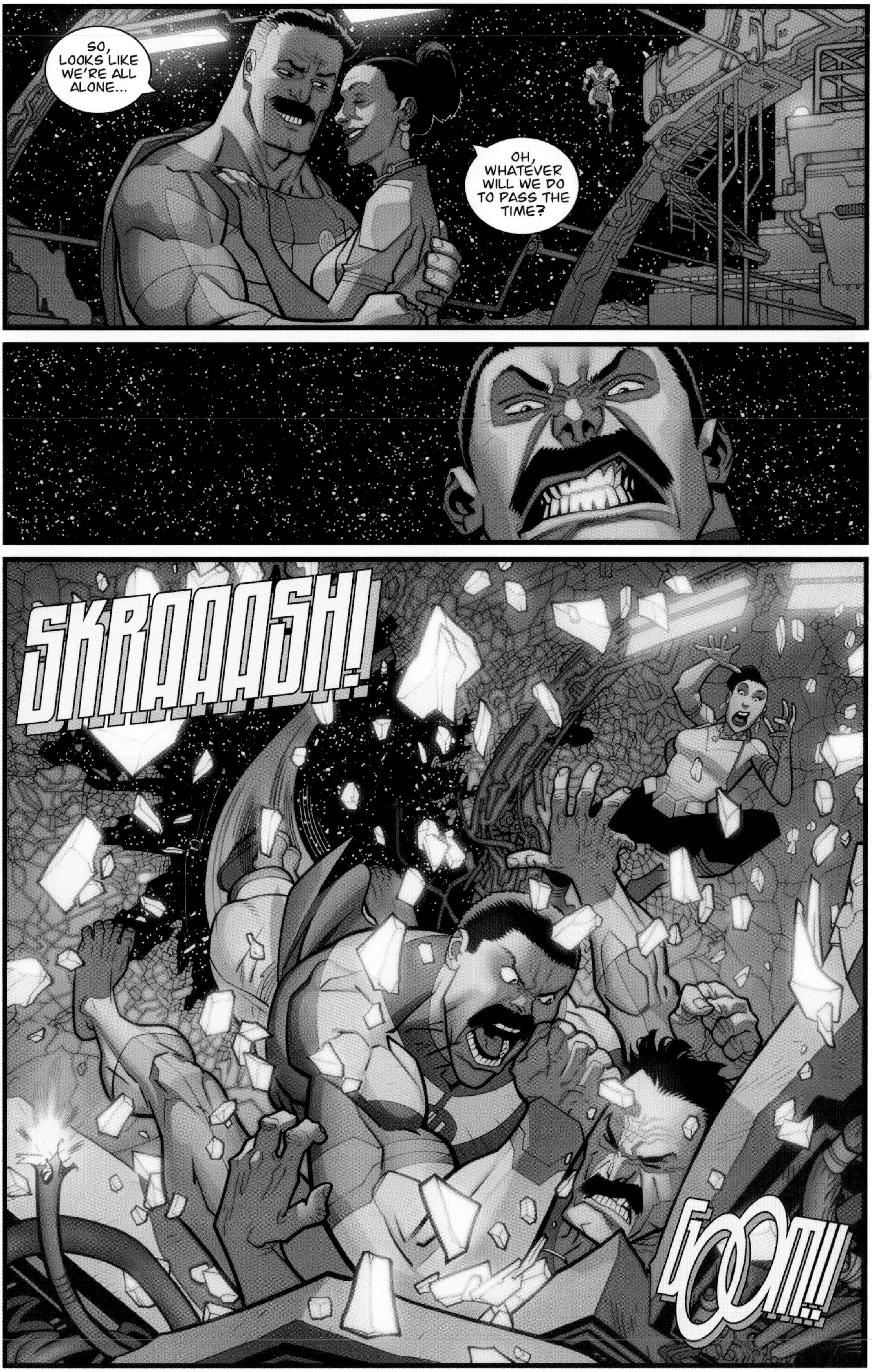
SO, LOOKS LIKE WE'RE ALL ALONE...
OH, WHATEVER WILL WE DO TO PASS THE TIME?
SKRAAASH!
GOOM!!

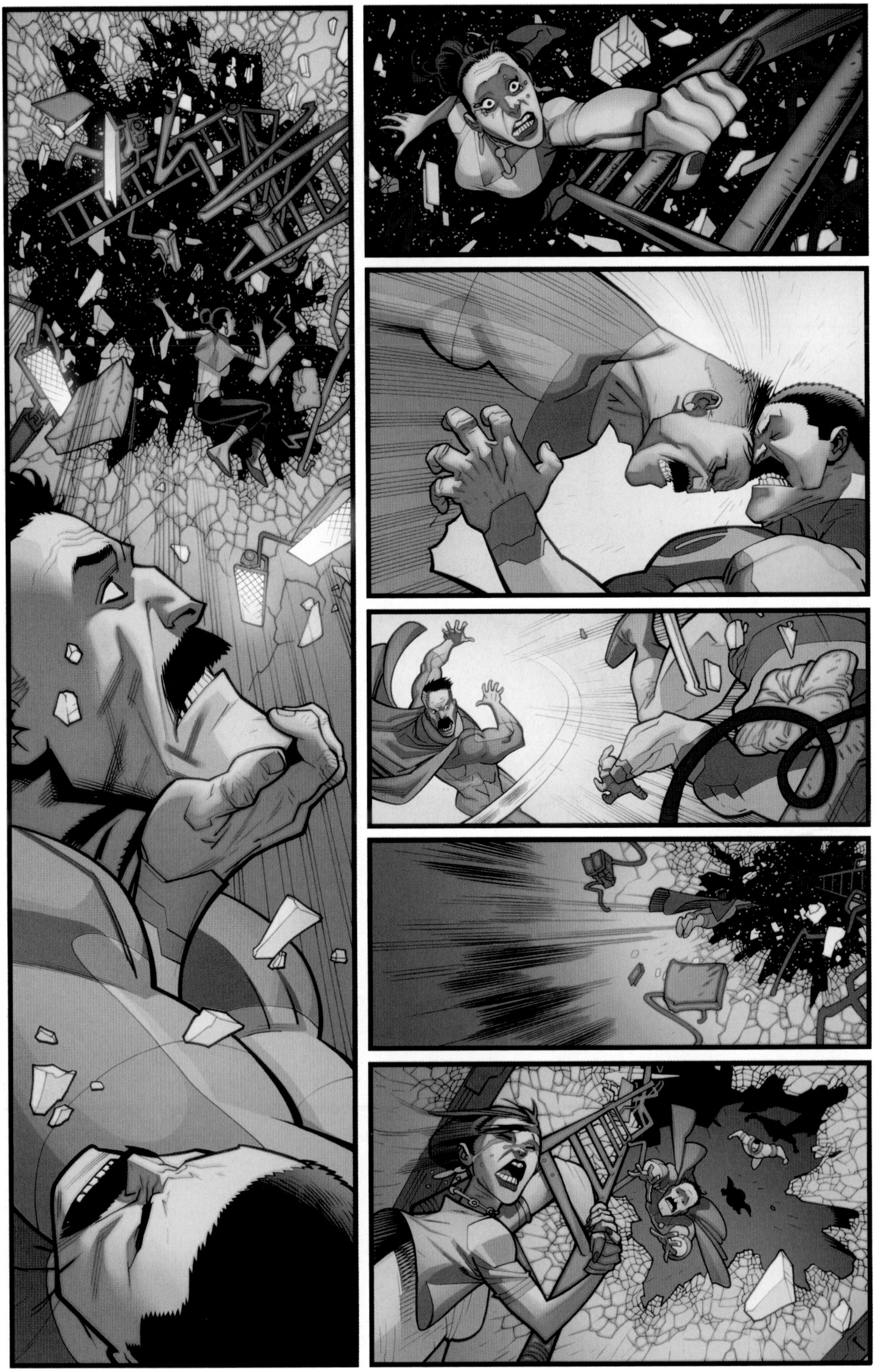

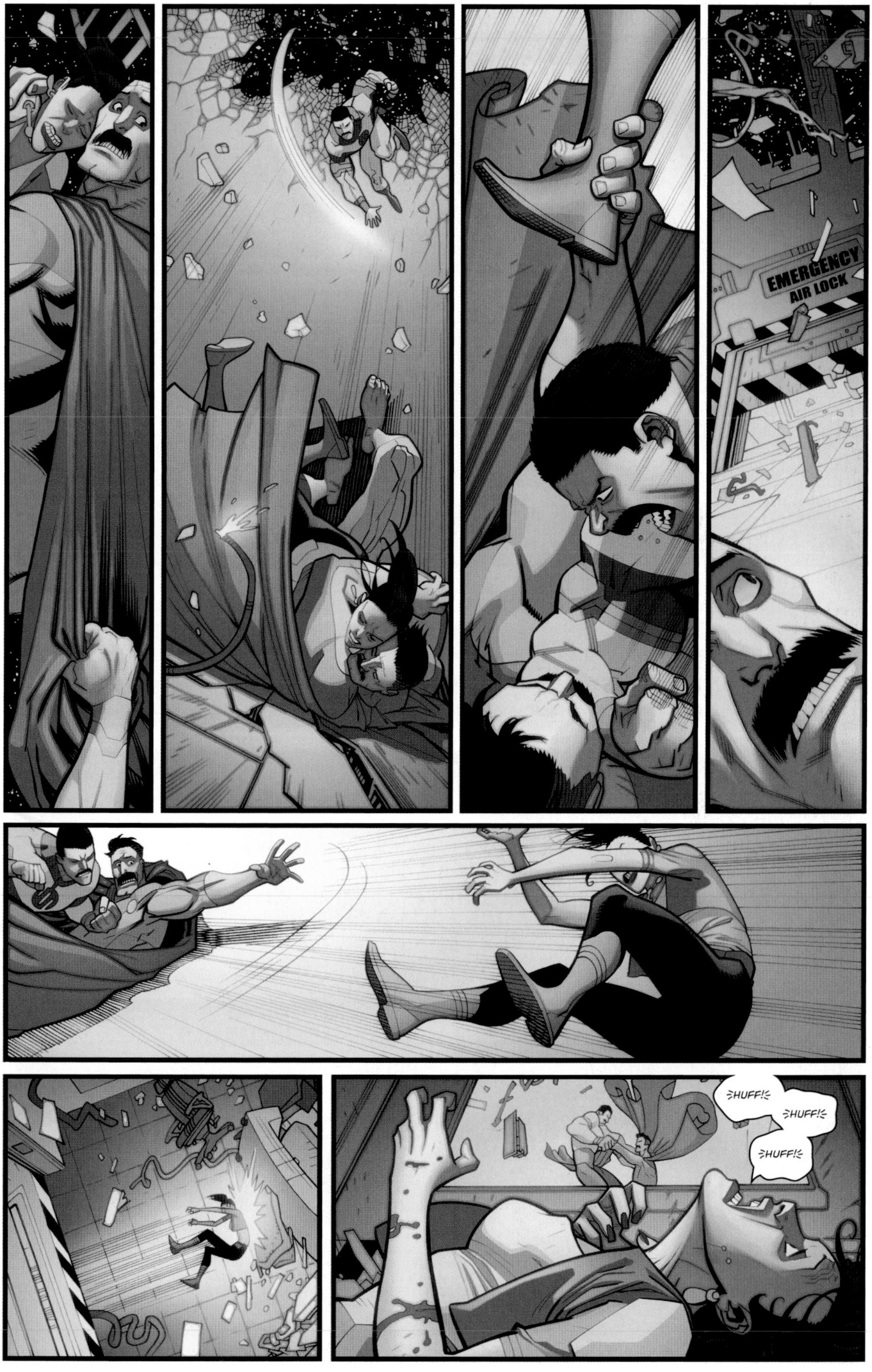
EMERGENCY
AIR LOCK
HUFF!
HUFF!
HUFF!

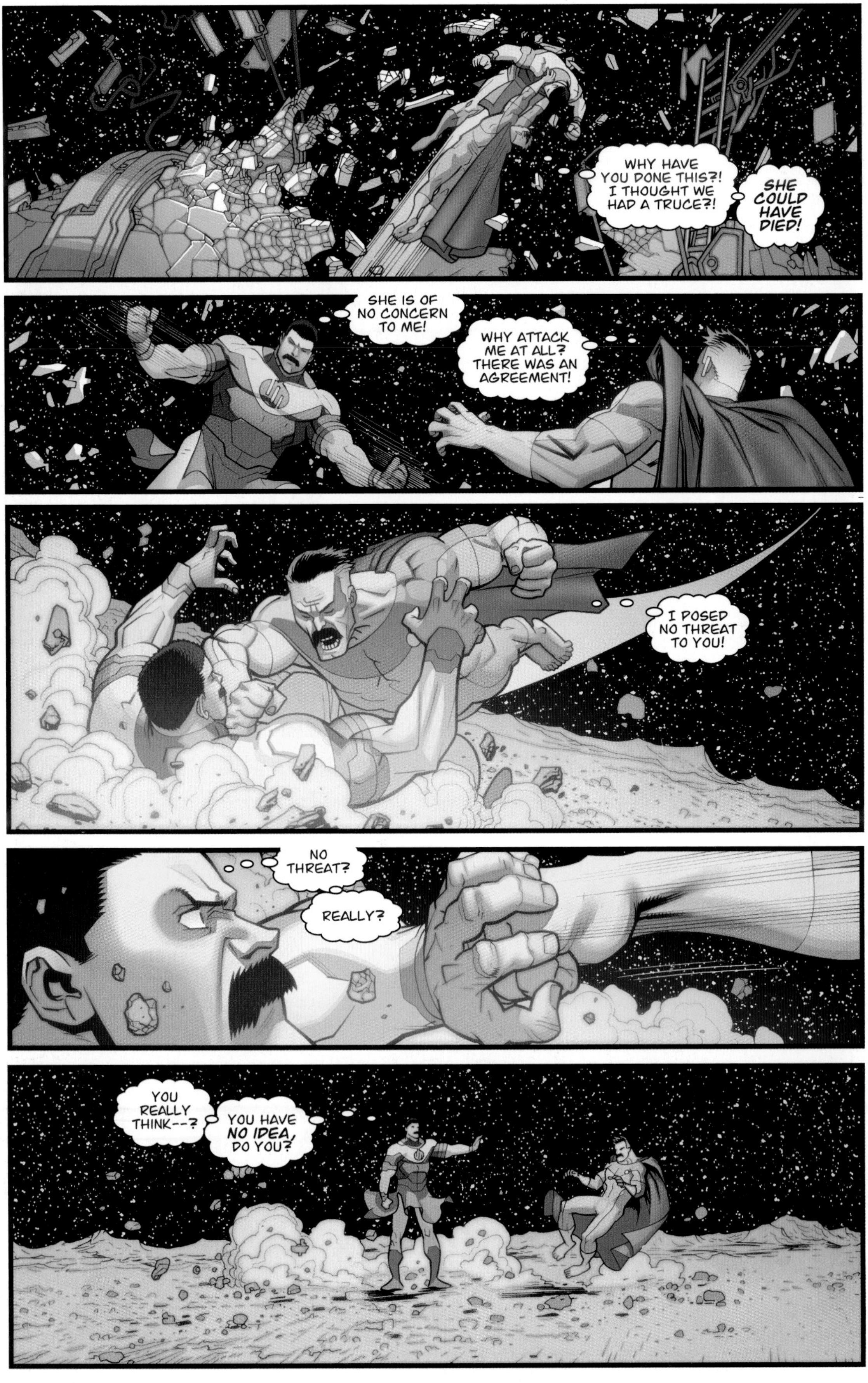
WHY HAVE YOU DONE THIS?! I THOUGHT WE HAD A TRUCE?!
SHE COULD HAVE DIED!
SHE IS OF NO CONCERN TO ME!
WHY ATTACK ME AT ALL? THERE WAS AN AGREEMENT!
I POSED NO THREAT TO YOU!
NO THREAT?
REALLY?
YOU REALLY THINK--?
YOU HAVE NO IDEA, DO YOU?

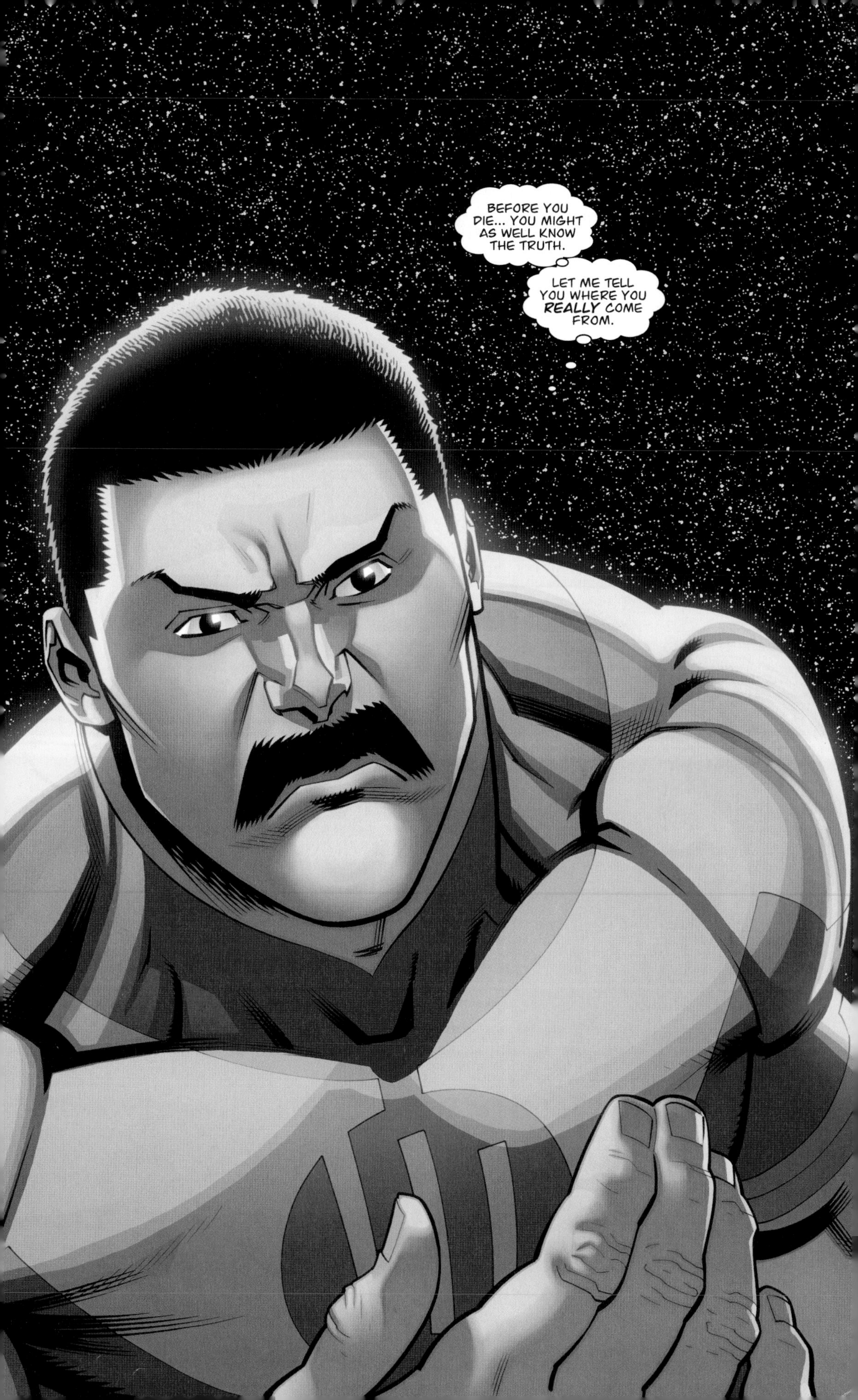
BEFORE YOU DIE... YOU MIGHT AS WELL KNOW THE TRUTH.
LET ME TELL YOU WHERE YOU **REALLY** COME FROM.

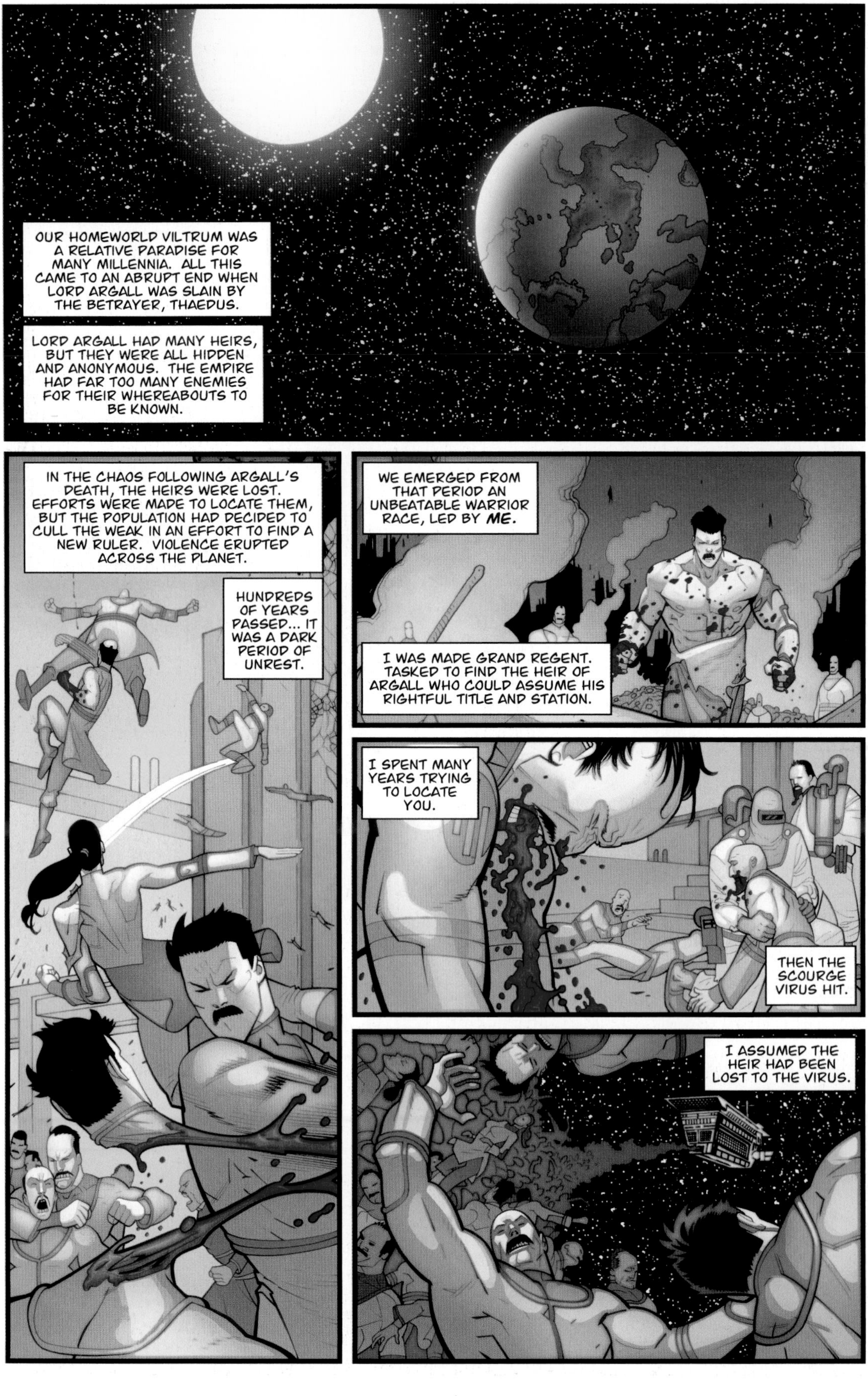
OUR HOMEWORLD VILTRUM WAS A RELATIVE PARADISE FOR MANY MILLENNIA. ALL THIS CAME TO AN ABRUPT END WHEN LORD ARGALL WAS SLAIN BY THE BETRAYER, THAEDUS.
LORD ARGALL HAD MANY HEIRS, BUT THEY WERE ALL HIDDEN AND ANONYMOUS. THE EMPIRE HAD FAR TOO MANY ENEMIES FOR THEIR WHEREABOUTS TO BE KNOWN.
IN THE CHAOS FOLLOWING ARGALL'S DEATH, THE HEIRS WERE LOST. EFFORTS WERE MADE TO LOCATE THEM, BUT THE POPULATION HAD DECIDED TO CULL THE WEAK IN AN EFFORT TO FIND A NEW RULER. VIOLENCE ERUPTED ACROSS THE PLANET.
HUNDREDS OF YEARS PASSED... IT WAS A DARK PERIOD OF UNREST.
WE EMERGED FROM THAT PERIOD AN UNBEATABLE WARRIOR RACE, LED BY ME.
I WAS MADE GRAND REGENT. TASKED TO FIND THE HEIR OF ARGALL WHO COULD ASSUME HIS RIGHTFUL TITLE AND STATION.
I SPENT MANY YEARS TRYING TO LOCATE YOU.
THEN THE SCOURGE VIRUS HIT.
I ASSUMED THE HEIR HAD BEEN LOST TO THE VIRUS.

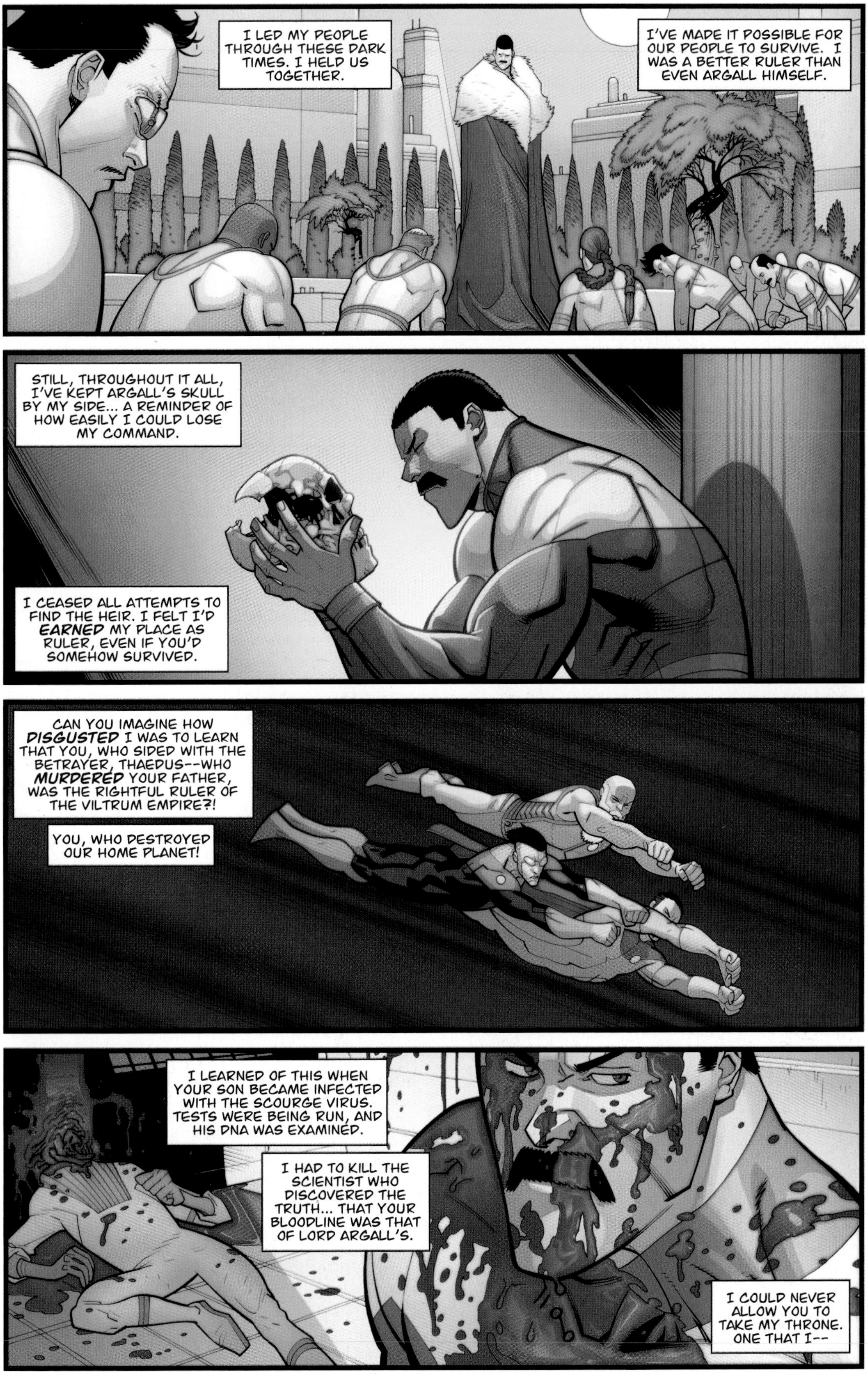
I LED MY PEOPLE THROUGH THESE DARK TIMES. I HELD US TOGETHER.
I'VE MADE IT POSSIBLE FOR OUR PEOPLE TO SURVIVE. I WAS A BETTER RULER THAN EVEN ARGALL HIMSELF.
STILL, THROUGHOUT IT ALL, I'VE KEPT ARGALL'S SKULL BY MY SIDE... A REMINDER OF HOW EASILY I COULD LOSE MY COMMAND.
I CEASED ALL ATTEMPTS TO FIND THE HEIR. I FELT I'D EARNED MY PLACE AS RULER, EVEN IF YOU'D SOMEHOW SURVIVED.
CAN YOU IMAGINE HOW DISGUSTED I WAS TO LEARN THAT YOU, WHO SIDED WITH THE BETRAYER, THAEDUS--WHO MURDERED YOUR FATHER, WAS THE RIGHTFUL RULER OF THE VILTRUM EMPIRE?!
YOU, WHO DESTROYED OUR HOME PLANET!
I LEARNED OF THIS WHEN YOUR SON BECAME INFECTED WITH THE SCOURGE VIRUS. TESTS WERE BEING RUN, AND HIS DNA WAS EXAMINED.
I HAD TO KILL THE SCIENTIST WHO DISCOVERED THE TRUTH... THAT YOUR BLOODLINE WAS THAT OF LORD ARGALL'S.
I COULD NEVER ALLOW YOU TO TAKE MY THRONE. ONE THAT I--

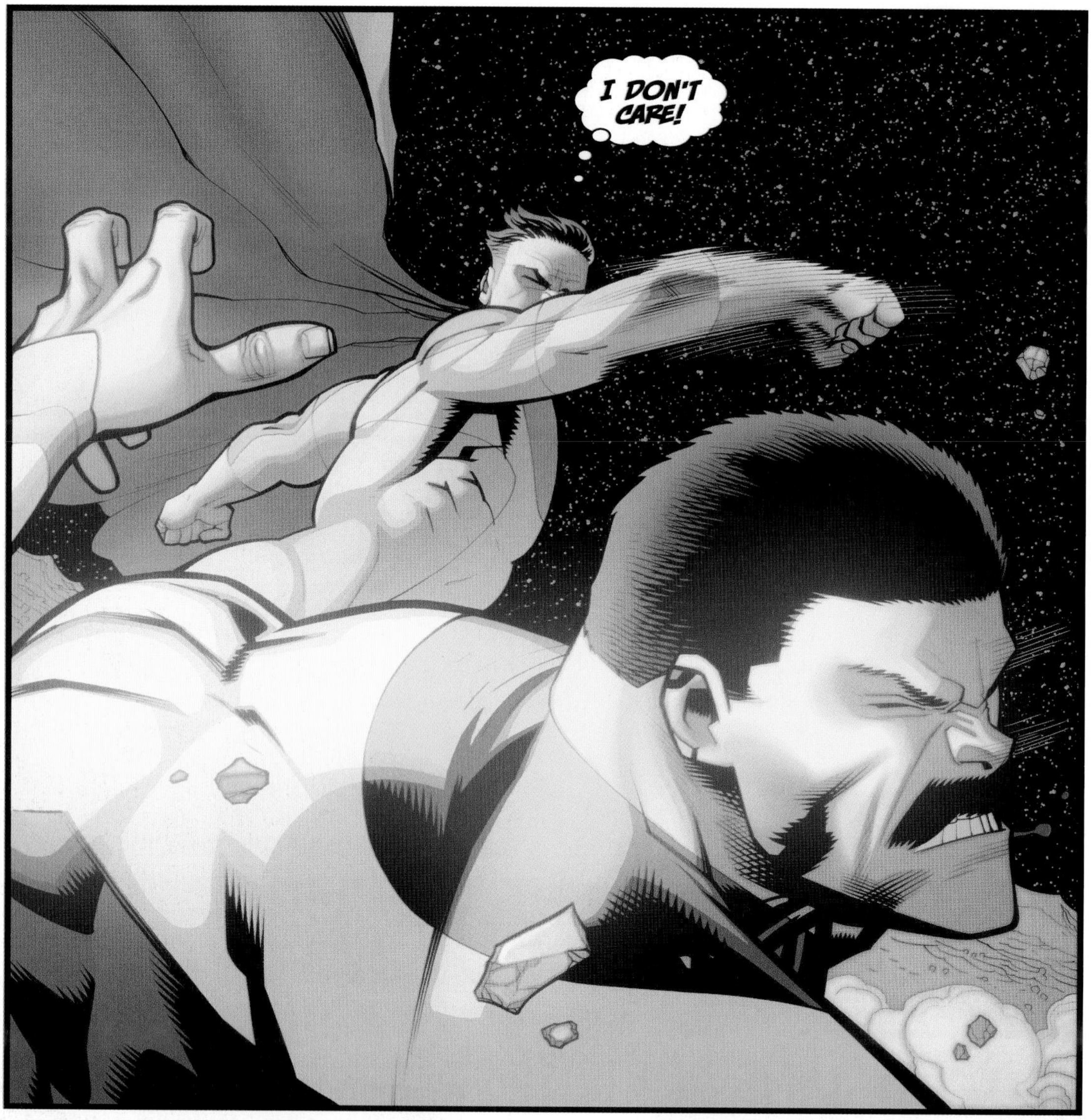
I DON'T CARE!

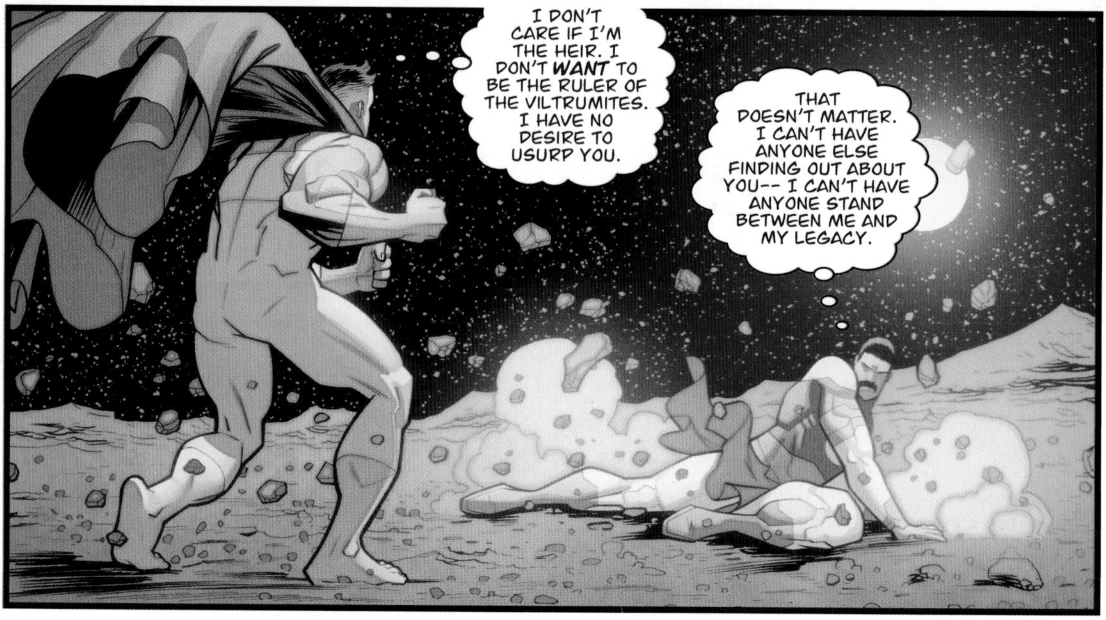
I DON'T CARE IF I'M THE HEIR. I DON'T WANT TO BE THE RULER OF THE VILTRUMITES. I HAVE NO DESIRE TO USURP YOU.
THAT DOESN'T MATTER. I CAN'T HAVE ANYONE ELSE FINDING OUT ABOUT YOU-- I CAN'T HAVE ANYONE STAND BETWEEN ME AND MY LEGACY.

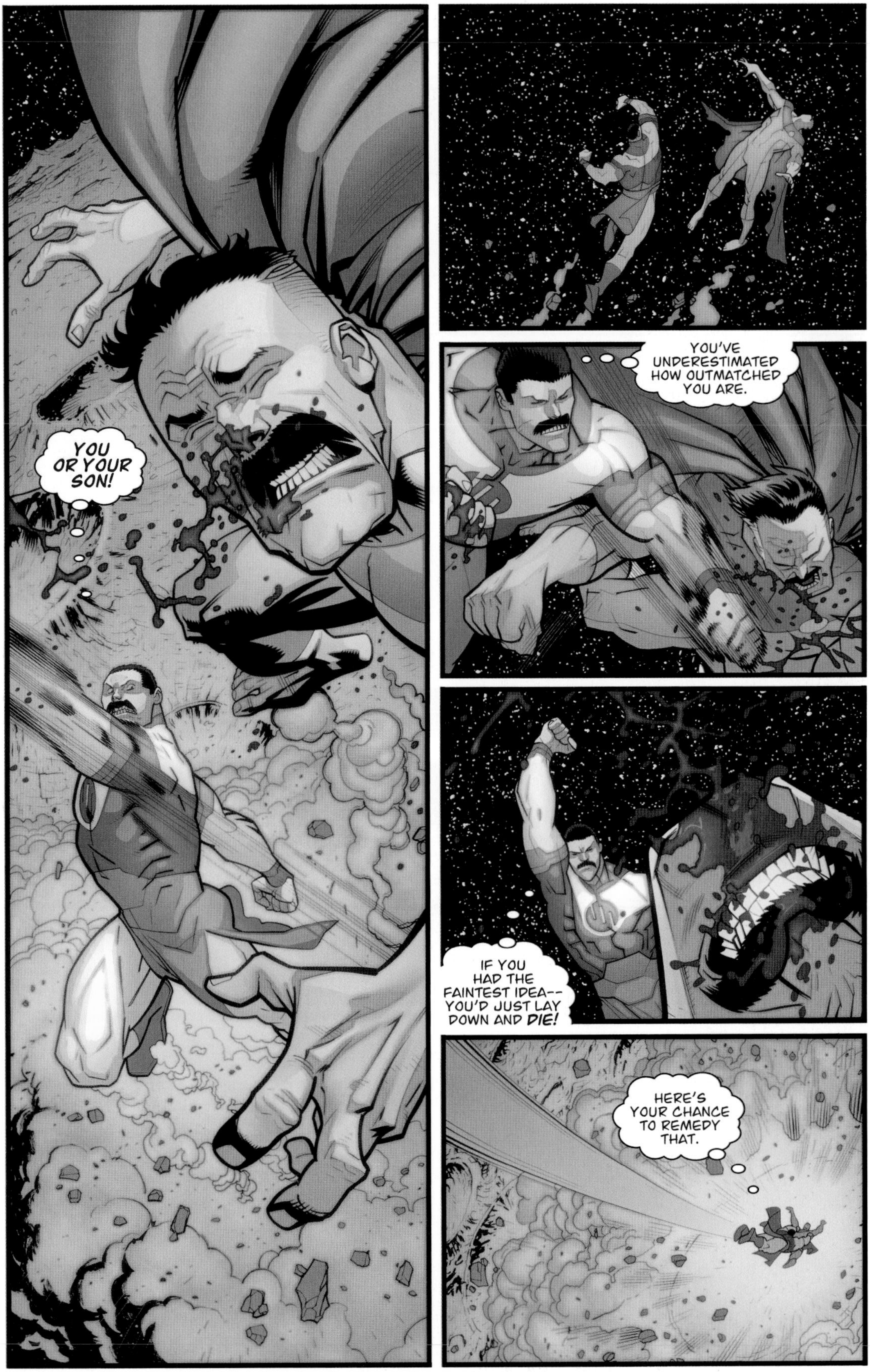
YOU OR YOUR SON!
YOU'VE UNDERESTIMATED HOW OUTMATCHED YOU ARE.
IF YOU HAD THE FAINTEST IDEA-- YOU'D JUST LAY DOWN AND DIE!
HERE'S YOUR CHANCE TO REMEDY THAT.

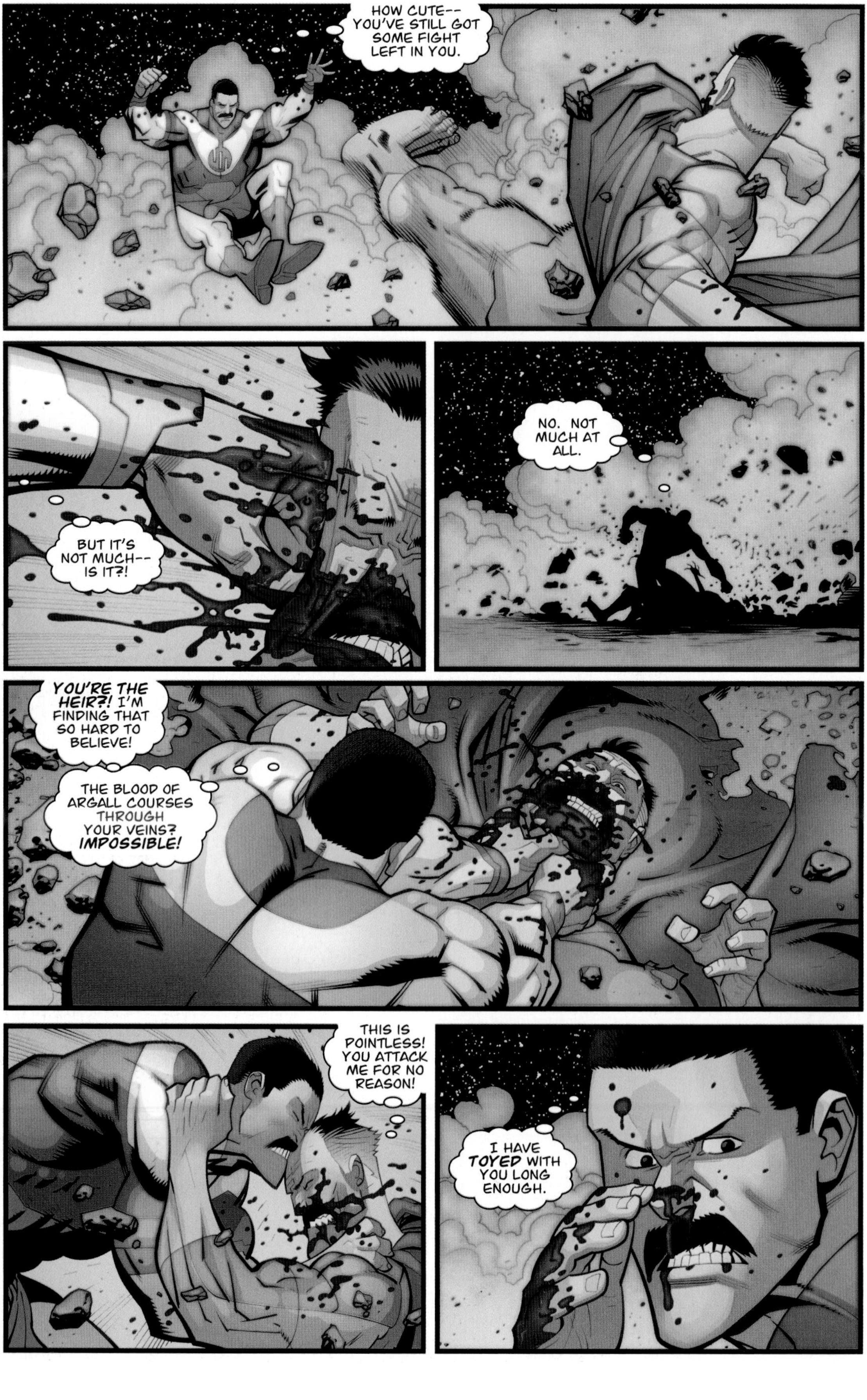
HOW CUTE-- YOU'VE STILL GOT SOME FIGHT LEFT IN YOU.
BUT IT'S NOT MUCH-- IS IT?!
NO. NOT MUCH AT ALL.
YOU'RE THE HEIR?! I'M FINDING THAT SO HARD TO BELIEVE!
THE BLOOD OF ARGALL COURSES THROUGH YOUR VEINS? IMPOSSIBLE!
THIS IS POINTLESS! YOU ATTACK ME FOR NO REASON!
I HAVE TOYED WITH YOU LONG ENOUGH.

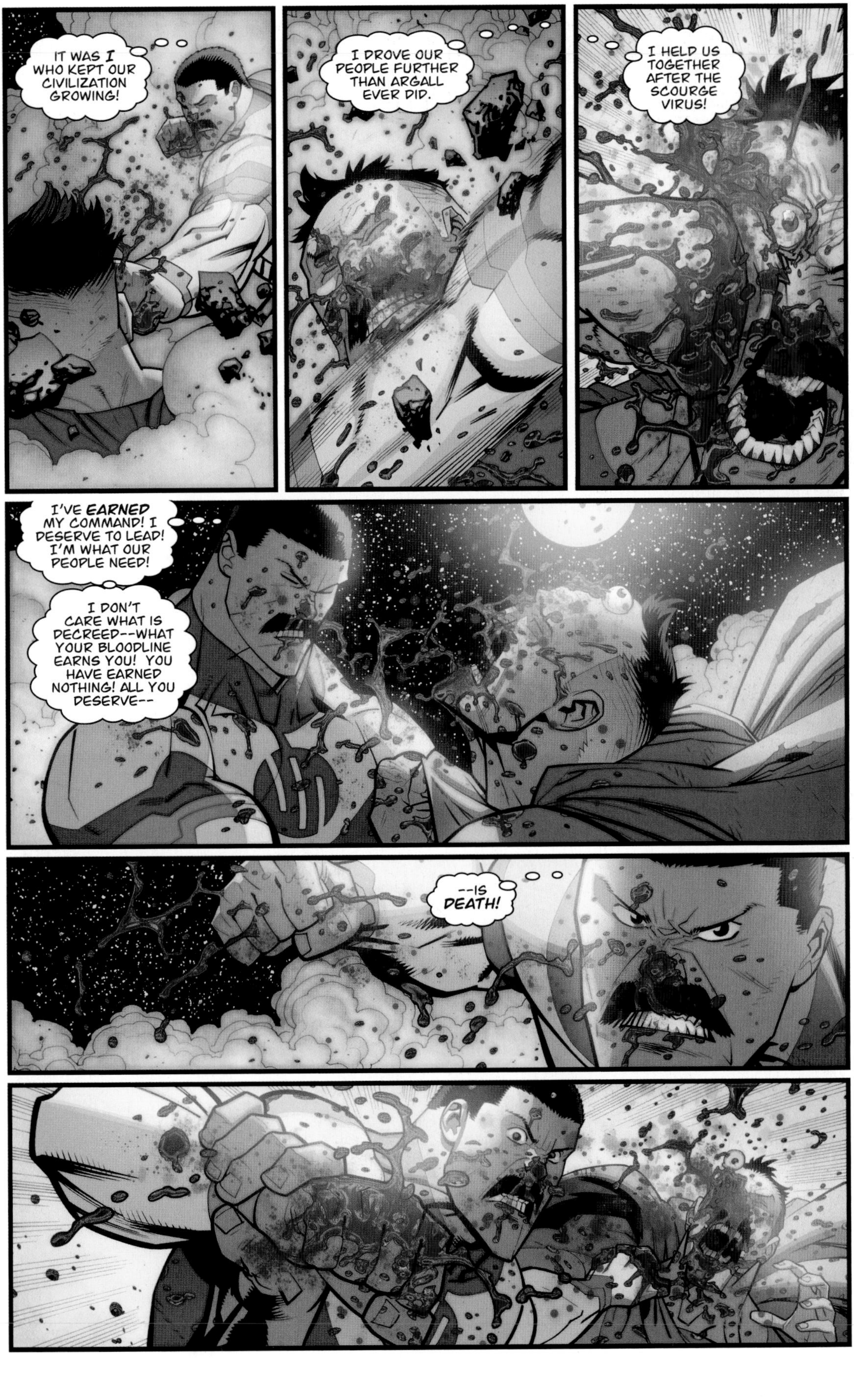
IT WAS I WHO KEPT OUR CIVILIZATION GROWING!
I DROVE OUR PEOPLE FURTHER THAN ARGALL EVER DID.
I HELD US TOGETHER AFTER THE SCOURGE VIRUS!
I'VE EARNED MY COMMAND! I DESERVE TO LEAD! I'M WHAT OUR PEOPLE NEED!
I DON'T CARE WHAT IS DECREED--WHAT YOUR BLOODLINE EARNS YOU! YOU HAVE EARNED NOTHING! ALL YOU DESERVE--
--IS DEATH!

WHAT?!

EXPLAIN YOURSELF, GENERAL KREGG!

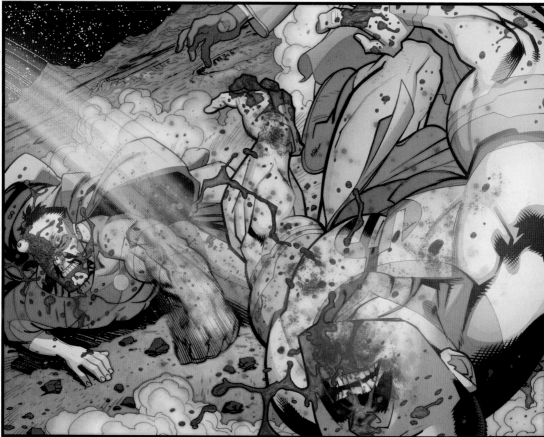

THIS MAN WAS TRYING TO TAKE MY THRONE-- THIS WAS AN ASSASSINATION ATTEMPT!

I AM YOUR REGENT!

YET YOU DARE TO ASSIST HIM--TO STAY MY HAND--PRESERVE HIS LIFE! YOU STAND AGAINST ME?!

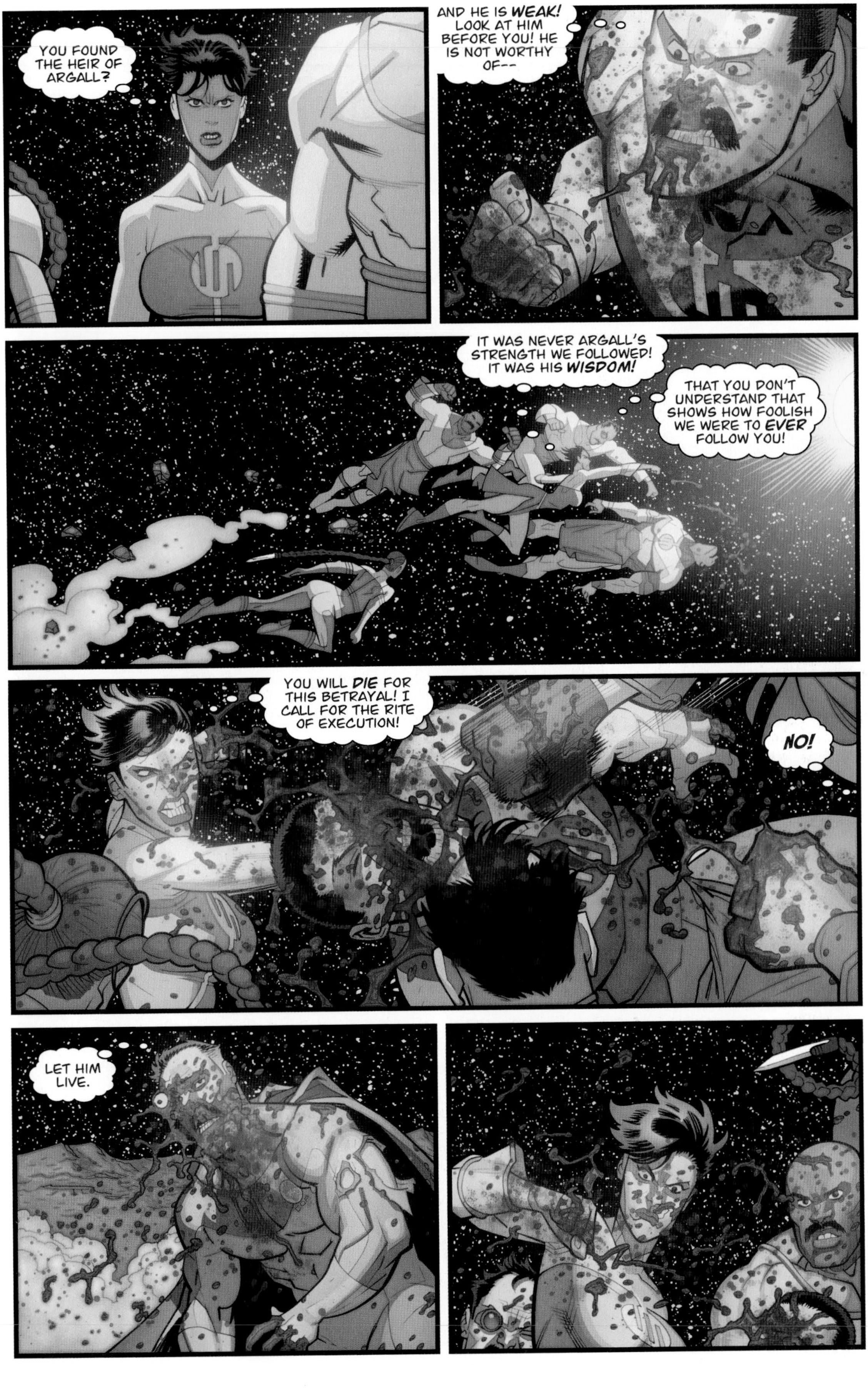
YOU FOUND THE HEIR OF ARGALL?
AND HE IS WEAK! LOOK AT HIM BEFORE YOU! HE IS NOT WORTHY OF--
IT WAS NEVER ARGALL'S STRENGTH WE FOLLOWED! IT WAS HIS WISDOM!
THAT YOU DON'T UNDERSTAND THAT SHOWS HOW FOOLISH WE WERE TO EVER FOLLOW YOU!
YOU WILL DIE FOR THIS BETRAYAL! I CALL FOR THE RITE OF EXECUTION!
NO!
LET HIM LIVE.

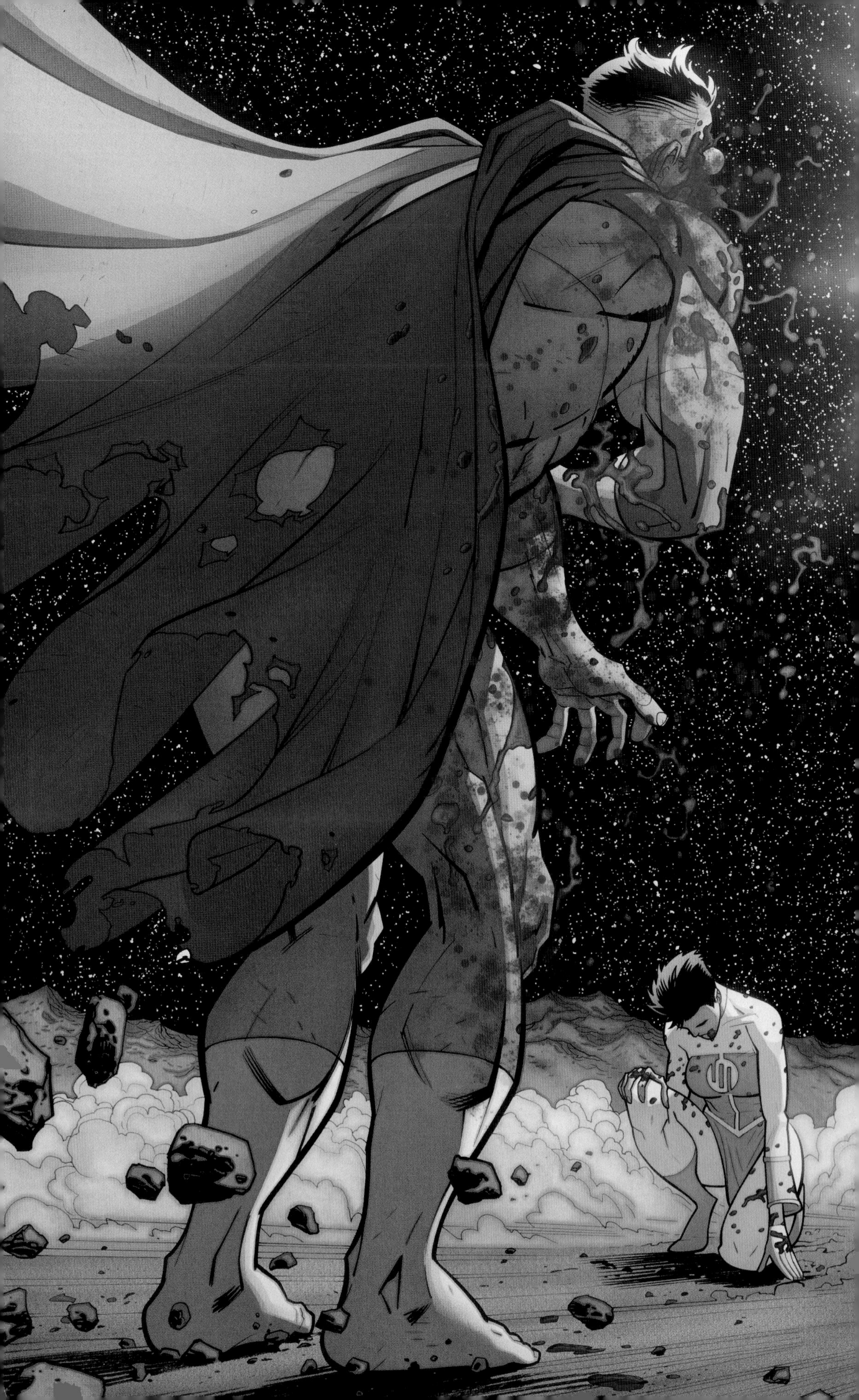

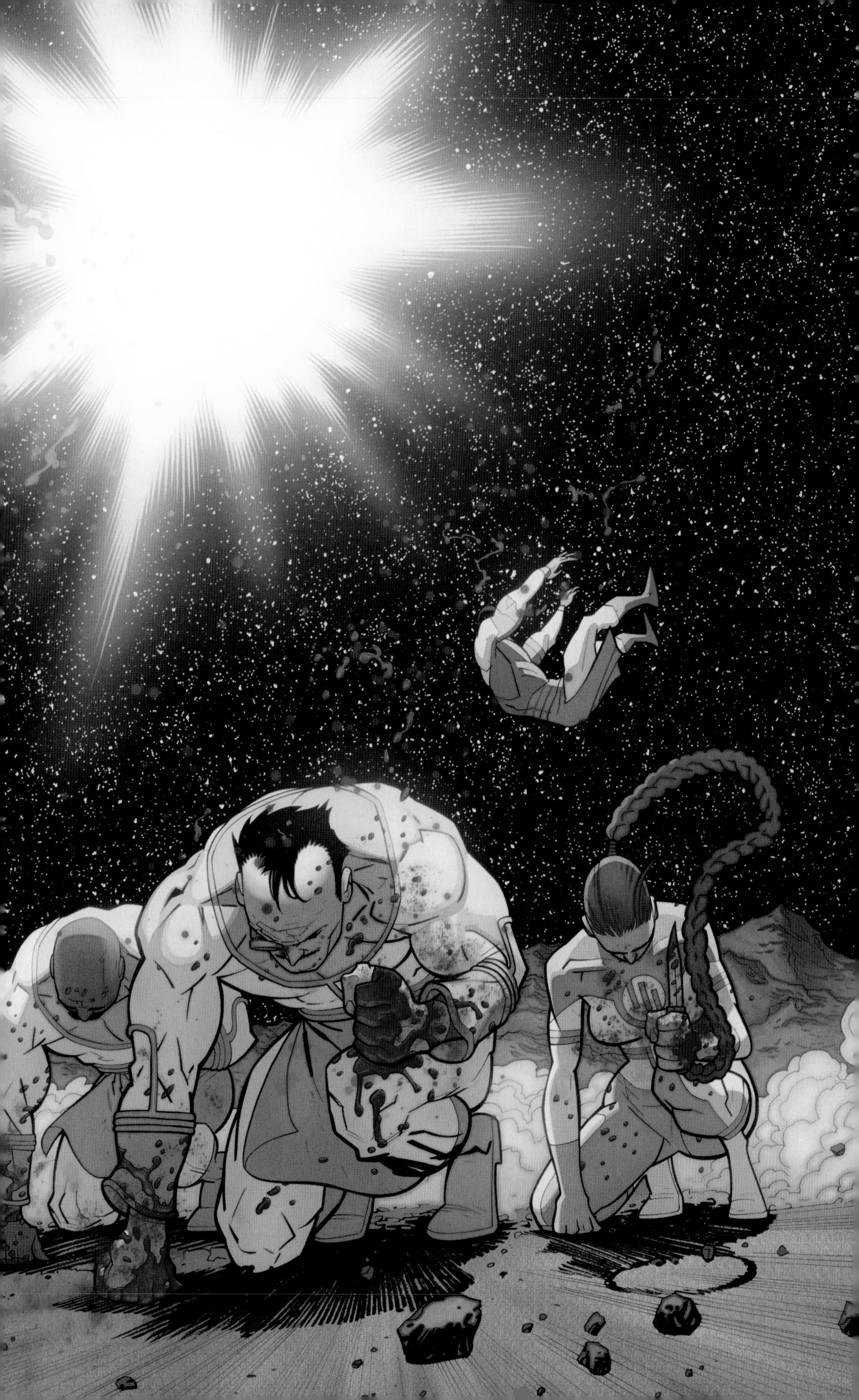

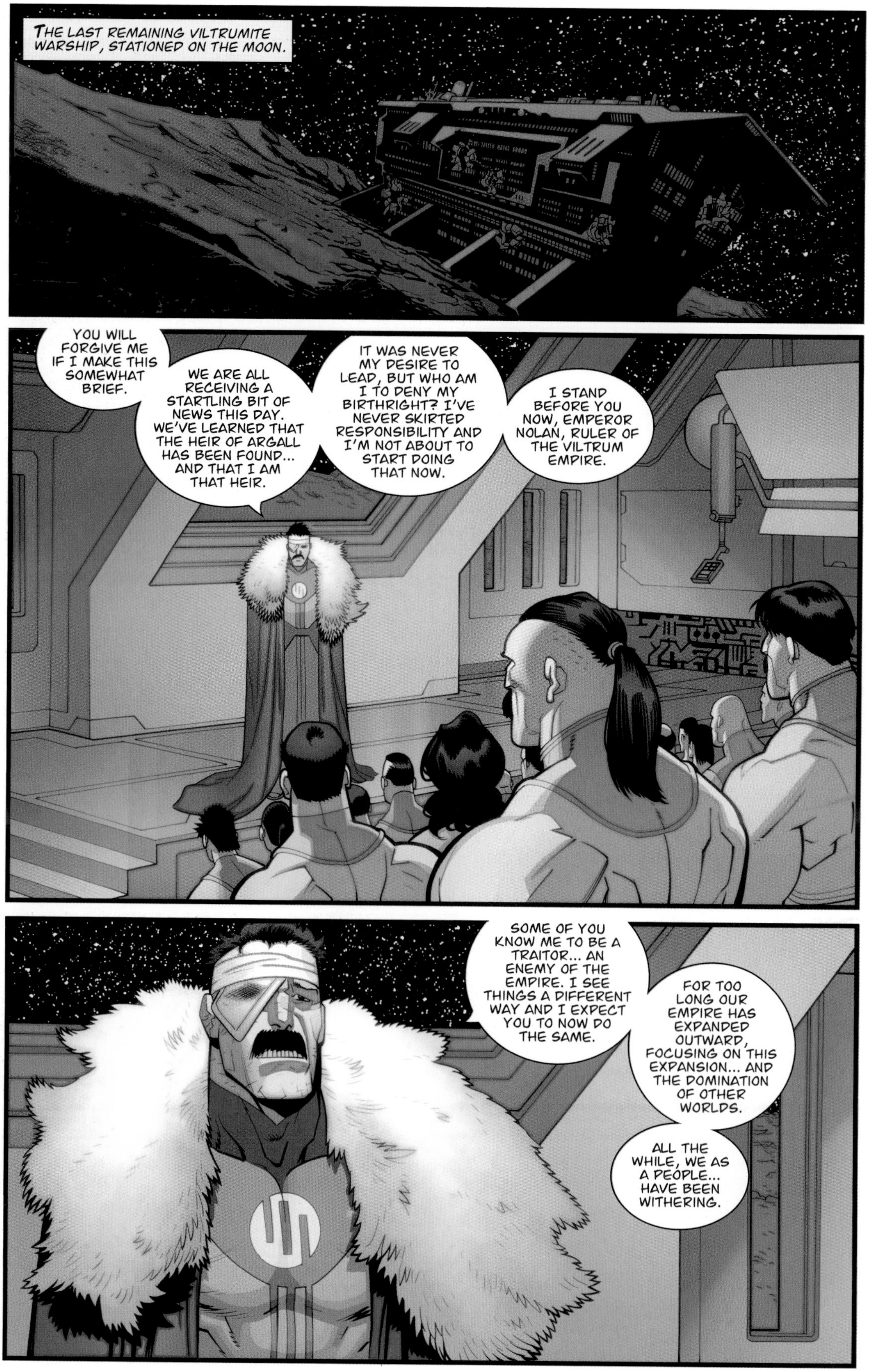
THE LAST REMAINING VILTRUMITE WARSHIP, STATIONED ON THE MOON.
YOU WILL FORGIVE ME IF I MAKE THIS SOMEWHAT BRIEF.
WE ARE ALL RECEIVING A STARTLING BIT OF NEWS THIS DAY. WE'VE LEARNED THAT THE HEIR OF ARGALL HAS BEEN FOUND... AND THAT I AM THAT HEIR.
IT WAS NEVER MY DESIRE TO LEAD, BUT WHO AM I TO DENY MY BIRTHRIGHT? I'VE NEVER SKIRTED RESPONSIBILITY AND I'M NOT ABOUT TO START DOING THAT NOW.
I STAND BEFORE YOU NOW, EMPEROR NOLAN, RULER OF THE VILTRUM EMPIRE.
SOME OF YOU KNOW ME TO BE A TRAITOR... AN ENEMY OF THE EMPIRE. I SEE THINGS A DIFFERENT WAY AND I EXPECT YOU TO NOW DO THE SAME.
FOR TOO LONG OUR EMPIRE HAS EXPANDED OUTWARD, FOCUSING ON THIS EXPANSION... AND THE DOMINATION OF OTHER WORLDS.
ALL THE WHILE, WE AS A PEOPLE... HAVE BEEN WITHERING.

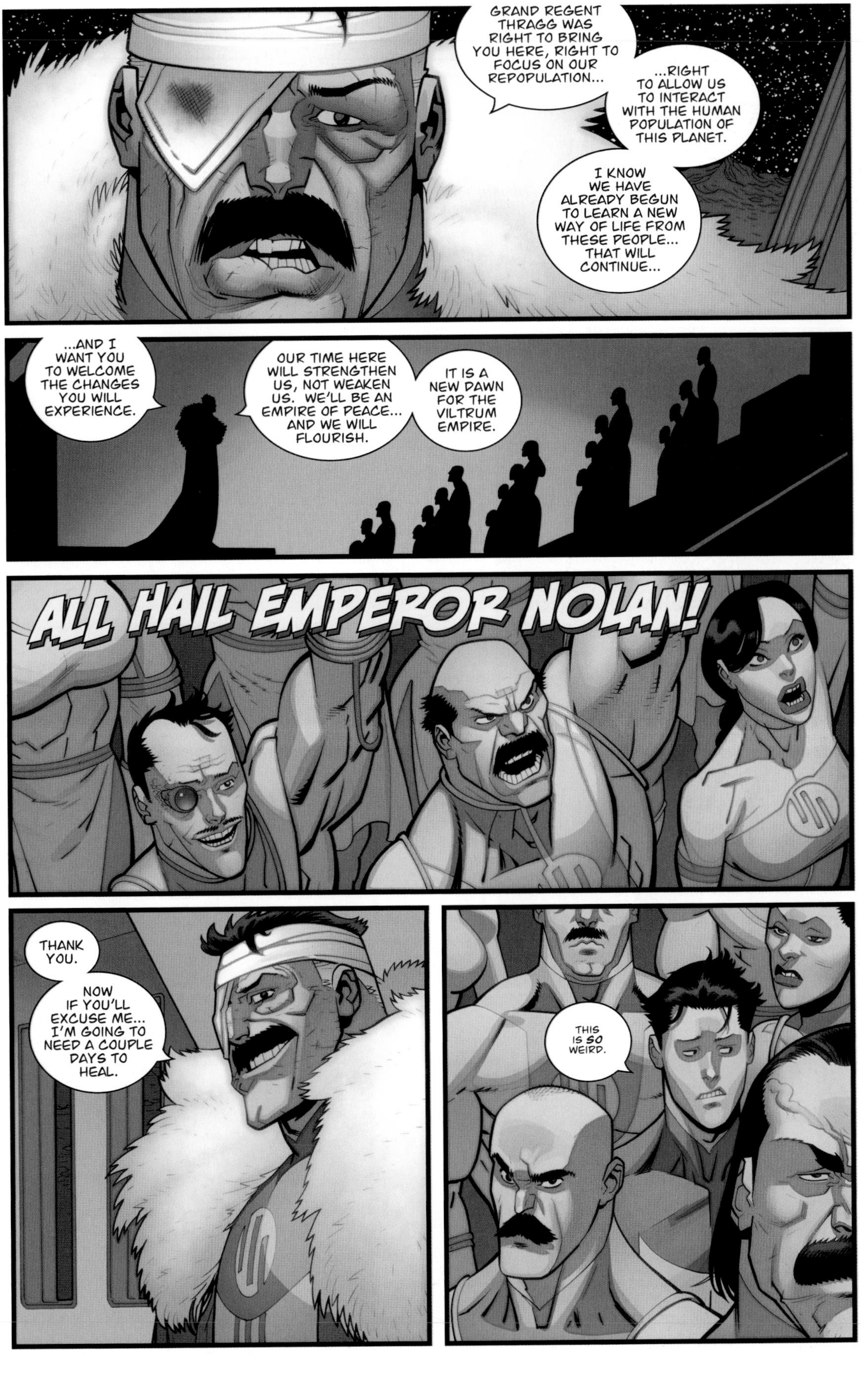
GRAND REGENT THRAGG WAS RIGHT TO BRING YOU HERE, RIGHT TO FOCUS ON OUR REPOPULATION...
...RIGHT TO ALLOW US TO INTERACT WITH THE HUMAN POPULATION OF THIS PLANET.
I KNOW WE HAVE ALREADY BEGUN TO LEARN A NEW WAY OF LIFE FROM THESE PEOPLE... THAT WILL CONTINUE...
...AND I WANT YOU TO WELCOME THE CHANGES YOU WILL EXPERIENCE.
OUR TIME HERE WILL STRENGTHEN US, NOT WEAKEN US. WE'LL BE AN EMPIRE OF PEACE... AND WE WILL FLOURISH.
IT IS A NEW DAWN FOR THE VILTRUM EMPIRE.
ALL HAIL EMPEROR NOLAN!
THANK YOU.
NOW IF YOU'LL EXCUSE ME... I'M GOING TO NEED A COUPLE DAYS TO HEAL.
THIS IS SO WEIRD.

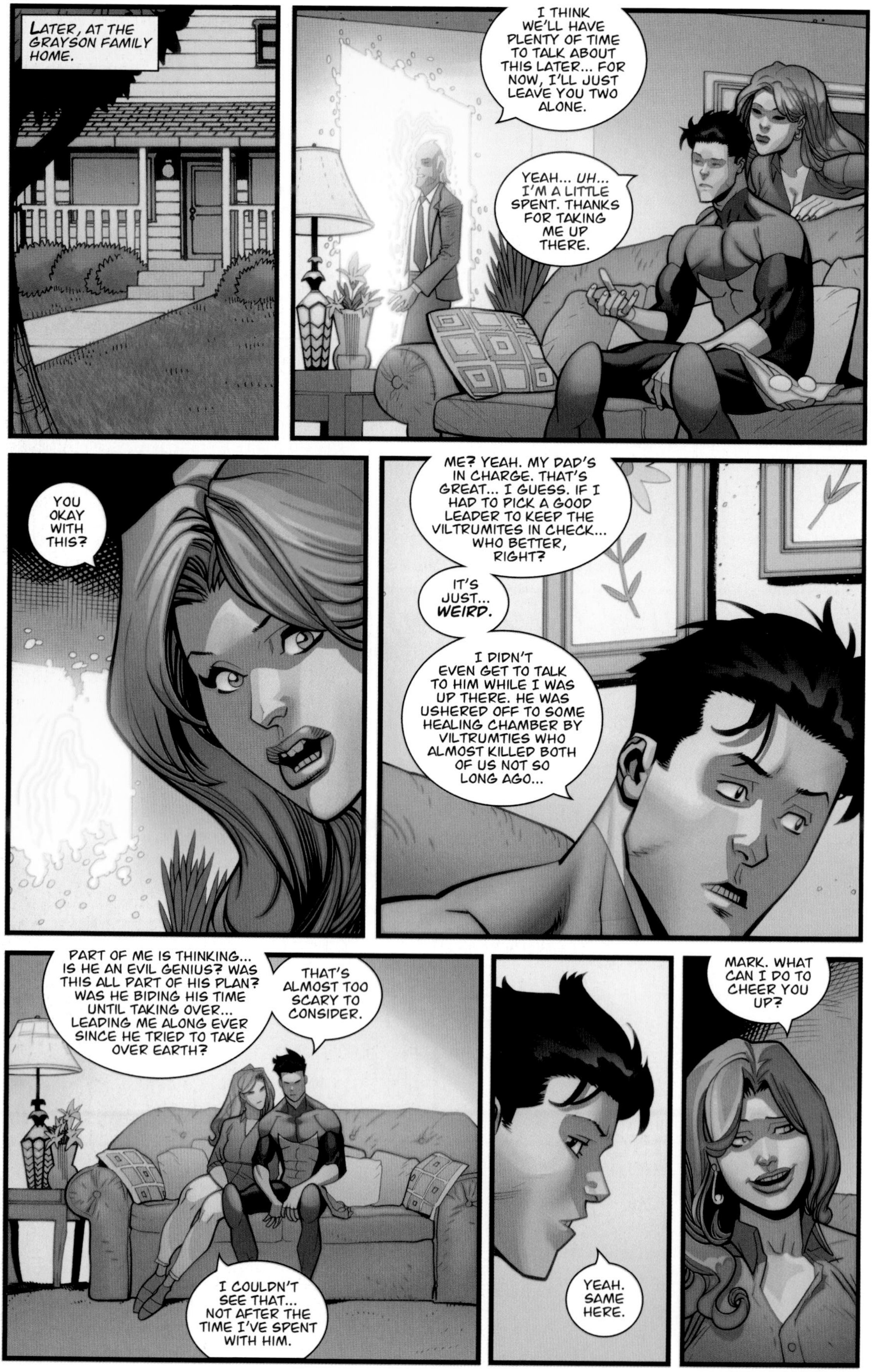
LATER, AT THE GRAYSON FAMILY HOME.
I THINK WE'LL HAVE PLENTY OF TIME TO TALK ABOUT THIS LATER... FOR NOW, I'LL JUST LEAVE YOU TWO ALONE.
YEAH... UH... I'M A LITTLE SPENT. THANKS FOR TAKING ME UP THERE.
YOU OKAY WITH THIS?
ME? YEAH. MY DAD'S IN CHARGE. THAT'S GREAT... I GUESS. IF I HAD TO PICK A GOOD LEADER TO KEEP THE VILTRUMITES IN CHECK... WHO BETTER, RIGHT?
IT'S JUST... WEIRD.
I DIDN'T EVEN GET TO TALK TO HIM WHILE I WAS UP THERE. HE WAS USHERED OFF TO SOME HEALING CHAMBER BY VILTRUMTIES WHO ALMOST KILLED BOTH OF US NOT SO LONG AGO...
PART OF ME IS THINKING... IS HE AN EVIL GENIUS? WAS THIS ALL PART OF HIS PLAN? WAS HE BIDING HIS TIME UNTIL TAKING OVER... LEADING ME ALONG EVER SINCE HE TRIED TO TAKE OVER EARTH?
THAT'S ALMOST TOO SCARY TO CONSIDER.
I COULDN'T SEE THAT... NOT AFTER THE TIME I'VE SPENT WITH HIM.
YEAH. SAME HERE.
MARK. WHAT CAN I DO TO CHEER YOU UP?

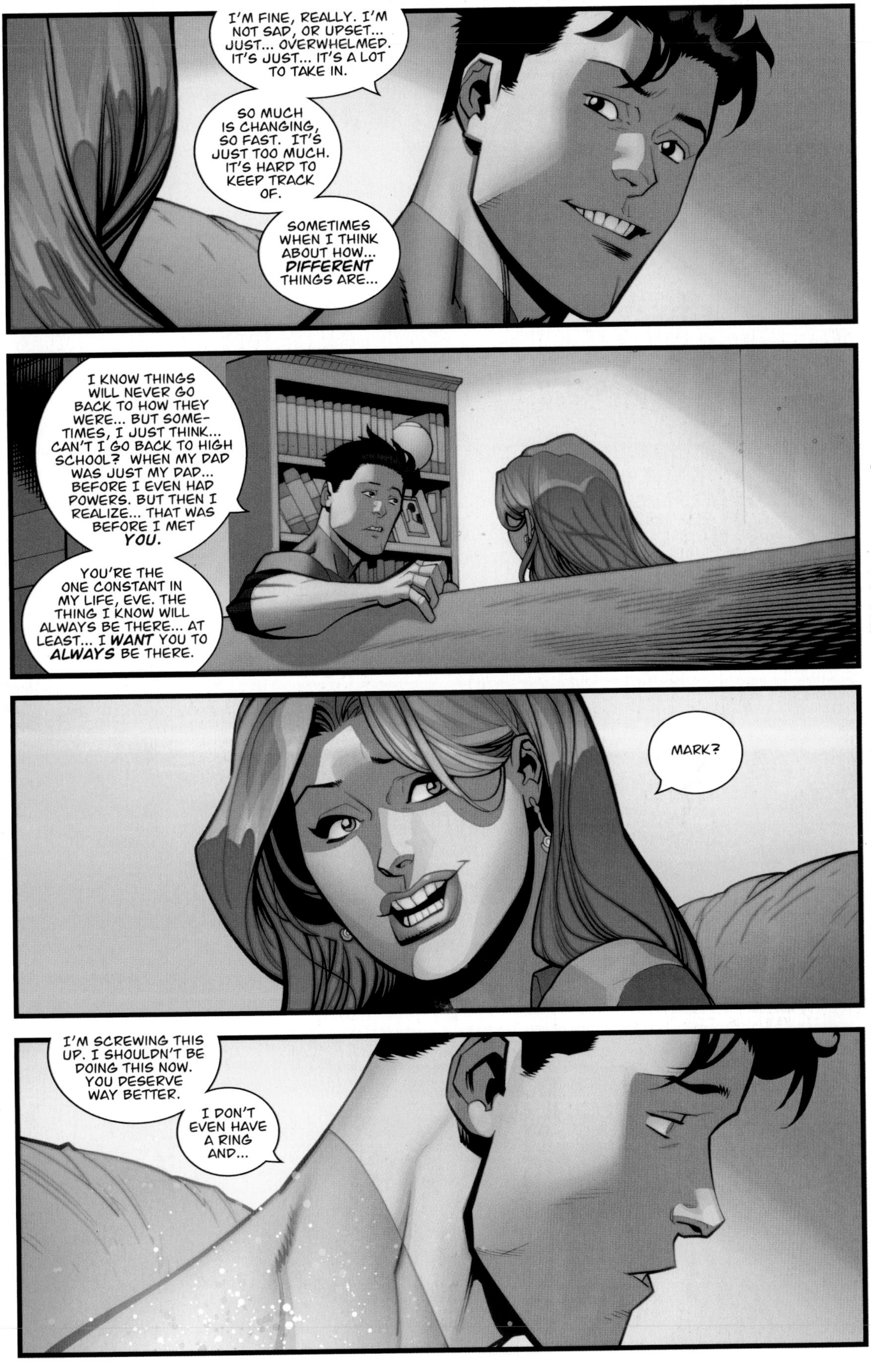
I'M FINE, REALLY. I'M NOT SAD, OR UPSET... JUST... OVERWHELMED. IT'S JUST... IT'S A LOT TO TAKE IN.
SO MUCH IS CHANGING, SO FAST. IT'S JUST TOO MUCH. IT'S HARD TO KEEP TRACK OF.
SOMETIMES WHEN I THINK ABOUT HOW... DIFFERENT THINGS ARE...
I KNOW THINGS WILL NEVER GO BACK TO HOW THEY WERE... BUT SOME-TIMES, I JUST THINK... CAN'T I GO BACK TO HIGH SCHOOL? WHEN MY DAD WAS JUST MY DAD... BEFORE I EVEN HAD POWERS. BUT THEN I REALIZE... THAT WAS BEFORE I MET YOU.
YOU'RE THE ONE CONSTANT IN MY LIFE, EVE. THE THING I KNOW WILL ALWAYS BE THERE... AT LEAST... I WANT YOU TO ALWAYS BE THERE.
MARK?
I'M SCREWING THIS UP. I SHOULDN'T BE DOING THIS NOW. YOU DESERVE WAY BETTER.
I DON'T EVEN HAVE A RING AND...

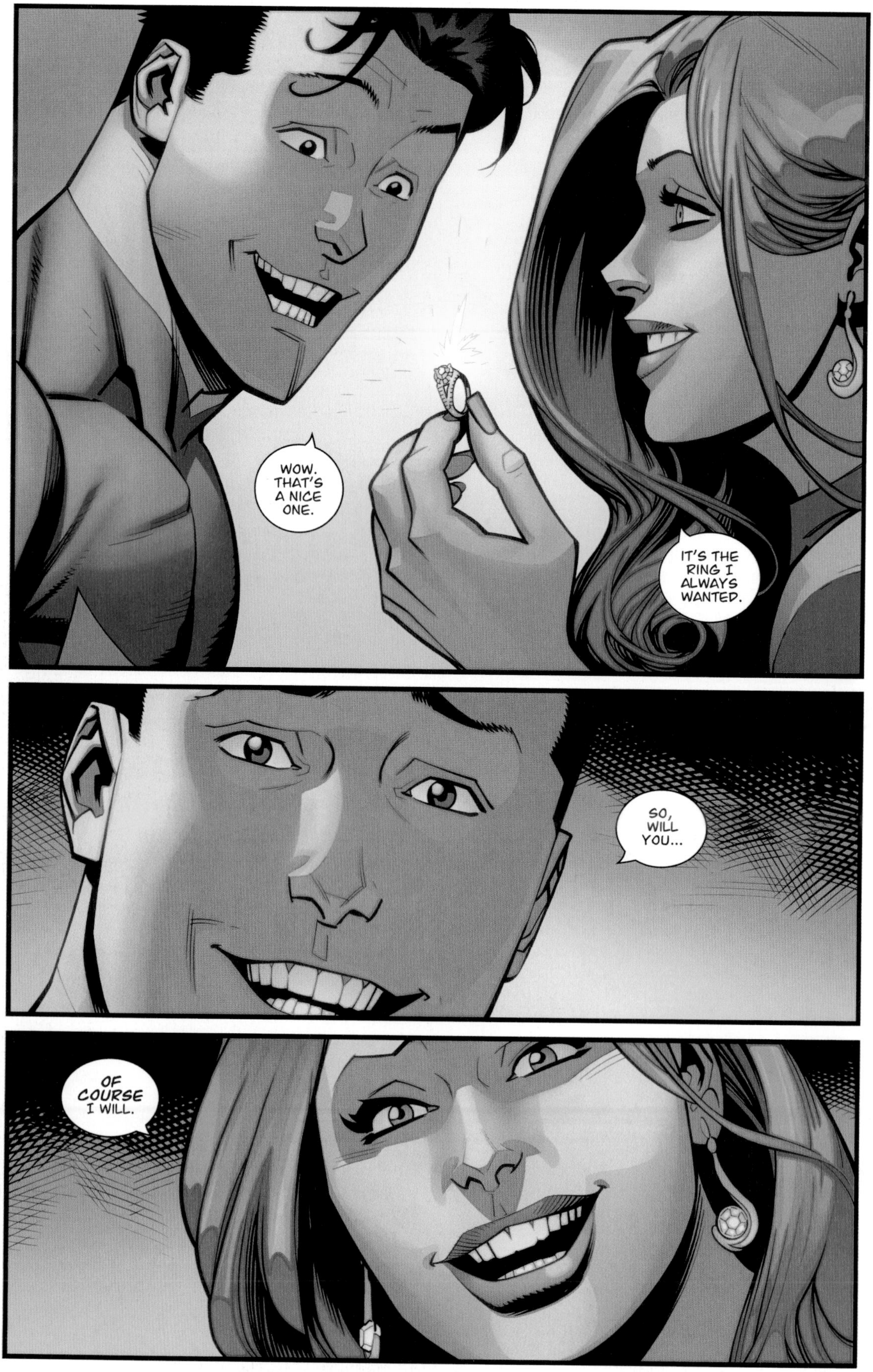
WOW. THAT'S A NICE ONE.
IT'S THE RING I ALWAYS WANTED.
SO, WILL YOU...
OF COURSE I WILL.

SKETCHBOOK

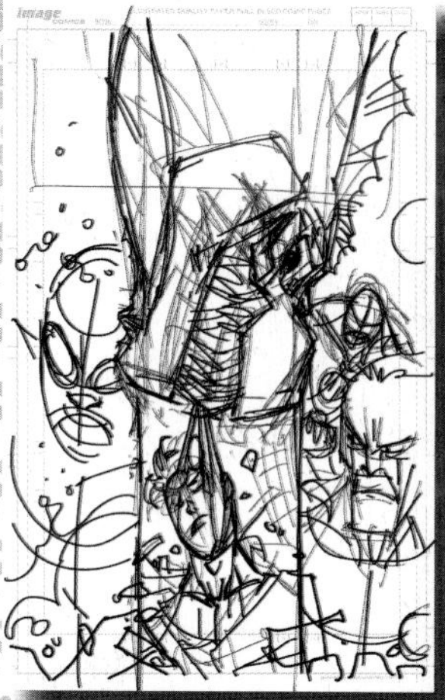

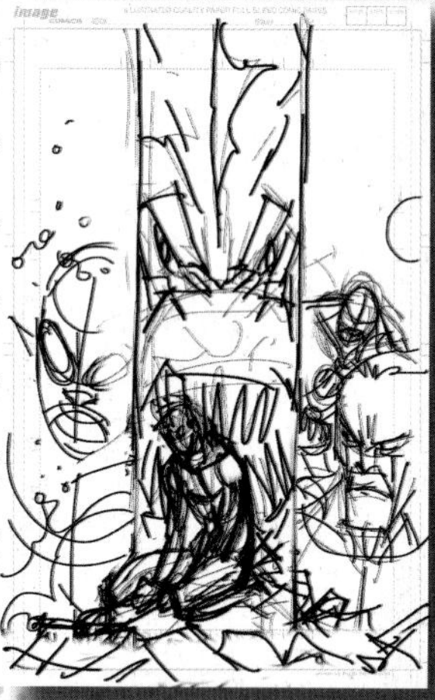

RYAN OTTLEY: So when this cover hit me, I was in a rush on a current issue to get it out the door, so I wanted to make it easy on myself and finish this cover in a day. The first two layouts I could have finished quickly, Robert didn't like the result and asked for a better one with full figures, so I did a new one which took much more time. Of course, I had to wait for the wounds on my back to heal from Robert's whip lashings. But eventually I turned in a cover we were all much happier with.

ROBERT KIRKMAN: I always feel like the wounds on your back make for a better comic. I feel like I'm not doing my job if they're allowed to heal before new ones are applied. It may not be a fun working process... but it's a productive one.

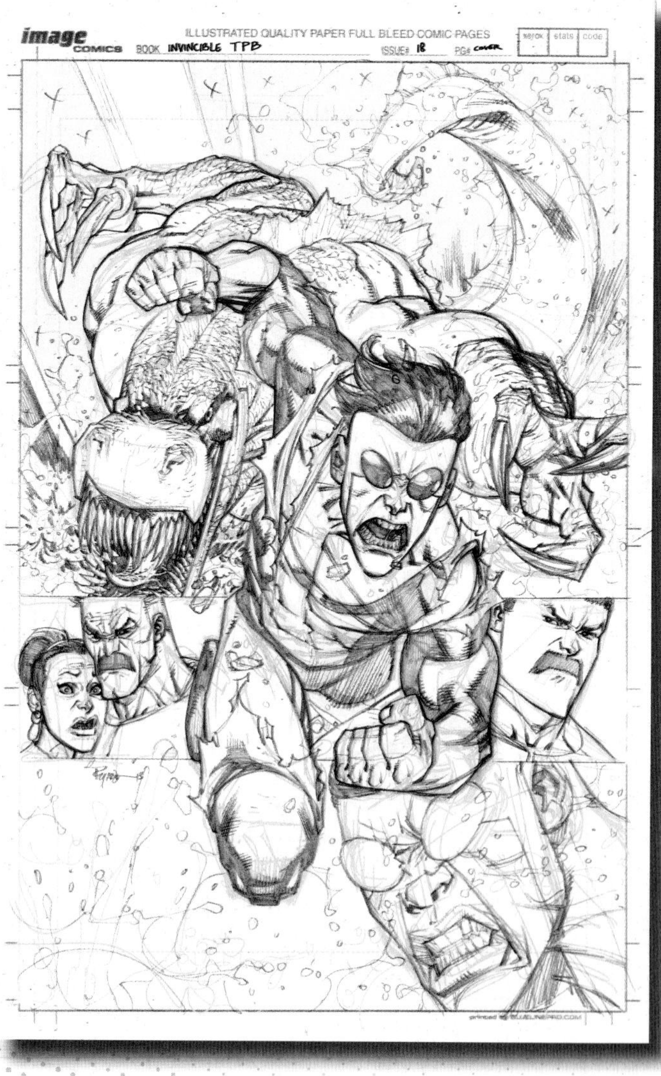

image COMICS
ILLUSTRATED QUALITY PAPER FULL BLEED COMIC PAGES
BOOK INVINCIBLE TPB
ISSUE# 18
PG# COVER
xerox stats code

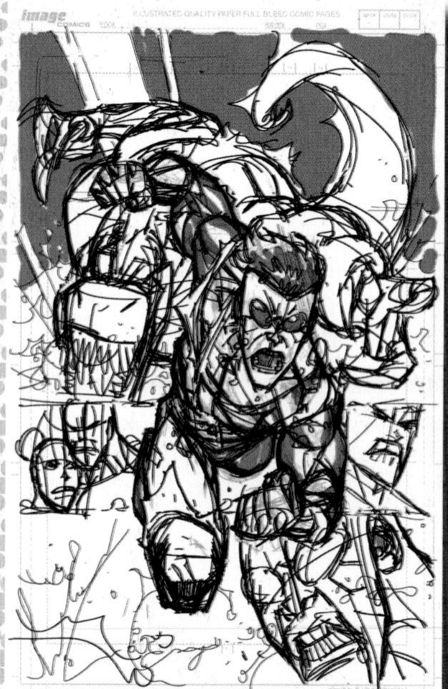

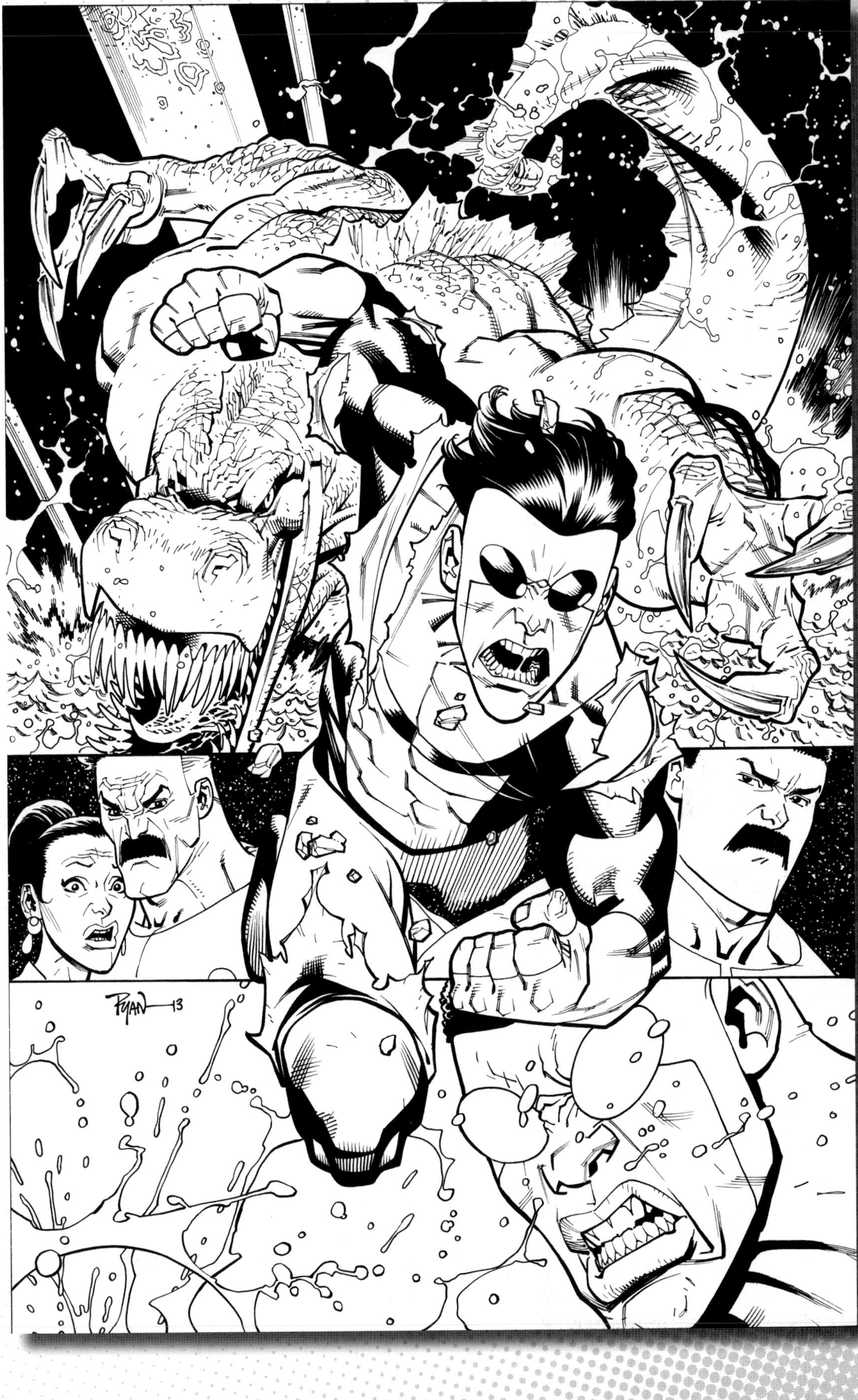
RYAN 13

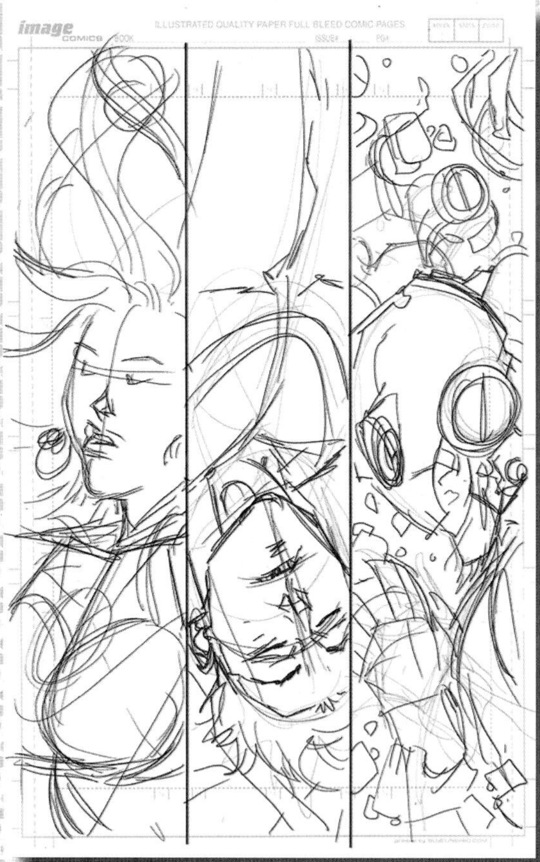

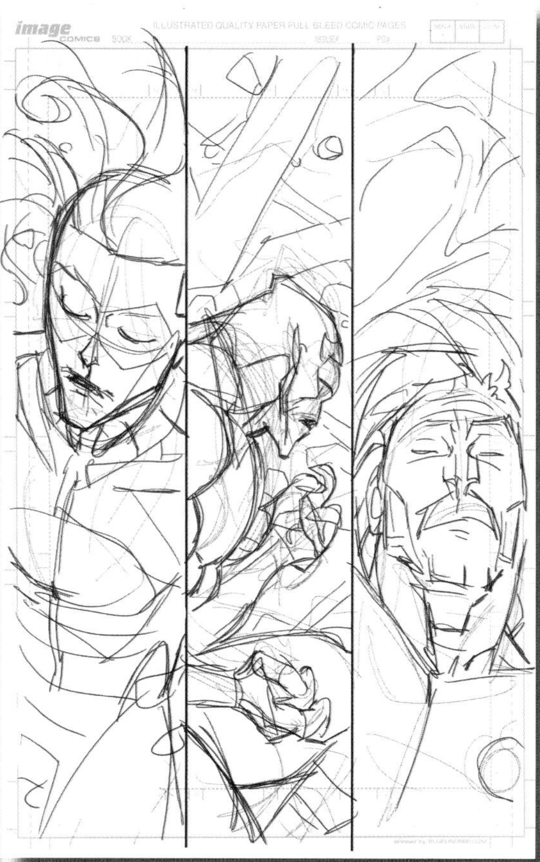

RYAN: These were drawn as teaser images to show the impact of issue #100. Eventually it was used for a variant cover for issue #99. You'll see the changes between the layout sketches and the finals. There were too many close-up images by each other, so I gave it a little variety and zoomed out for a few characters.

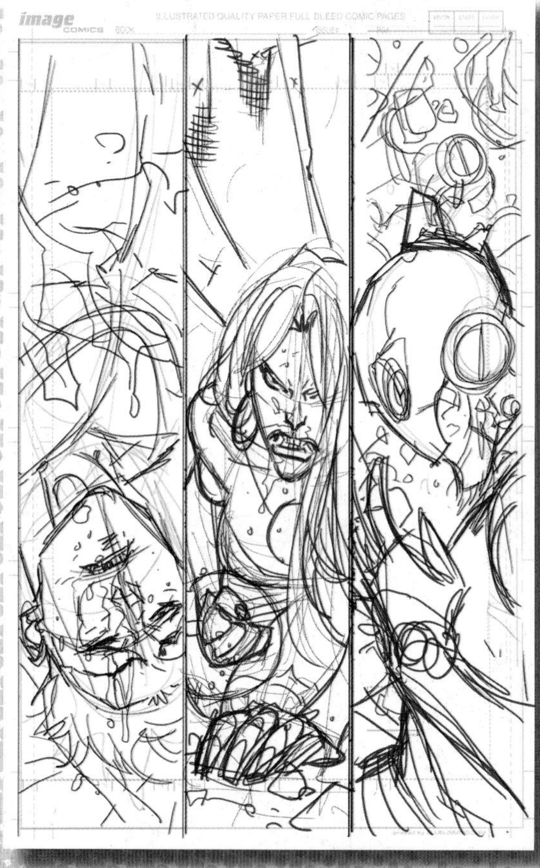

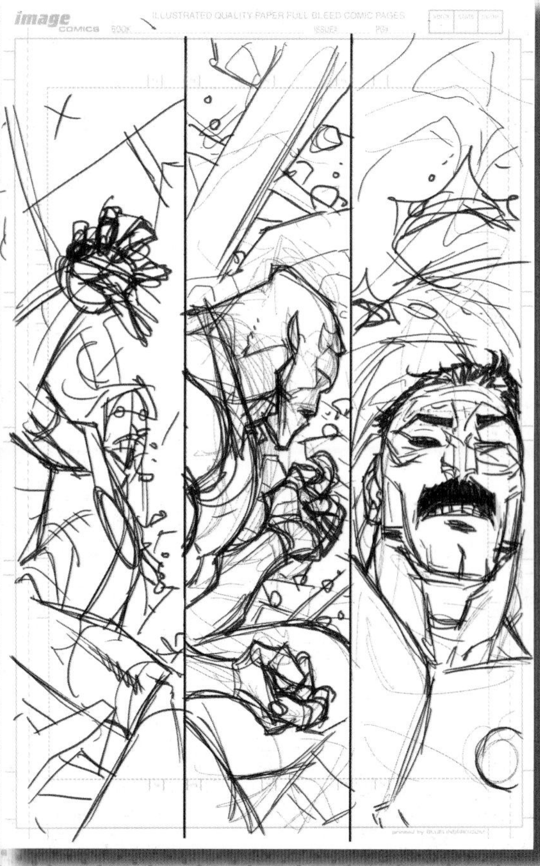

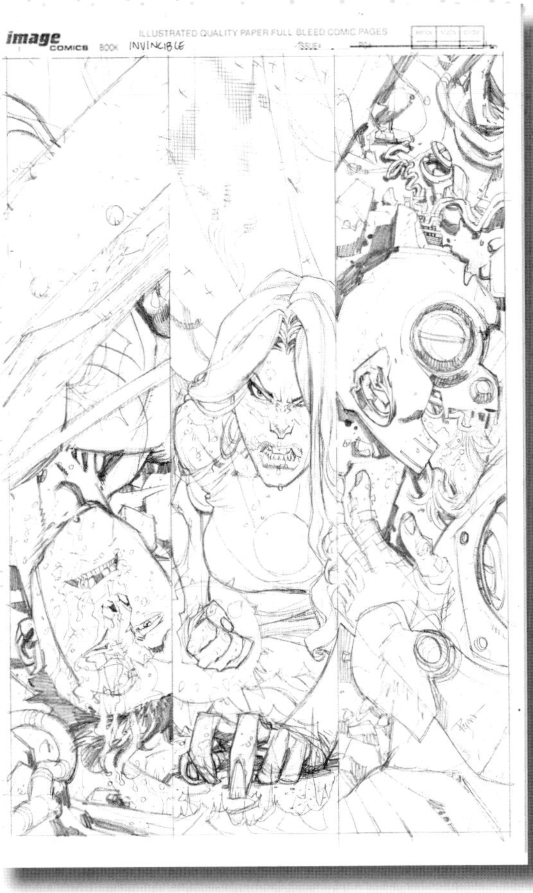
image COMICS
ILLUSTRATED QUALITY PAPER FULL BLEED COMIC PAGES
BOOK INVINCIBLE
ISSUE#
PG#

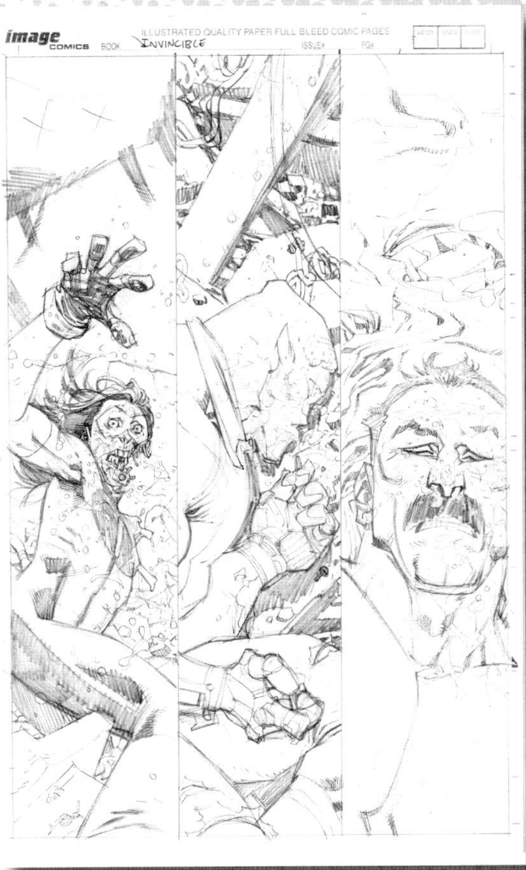
image COMICS
ILLUSTRATED QUALITY PAPER FULL BLEED COMIC PAGES
BOOK INVINCIBLE
ISSUE#
PG#

ROBERT: I really loved this thing. It's really cool when we have enough time (or decide to just make the time) to do completely original art just for marketing. This reminded me of the original ad for Youngblood #6, which I always thought was pretty cool.

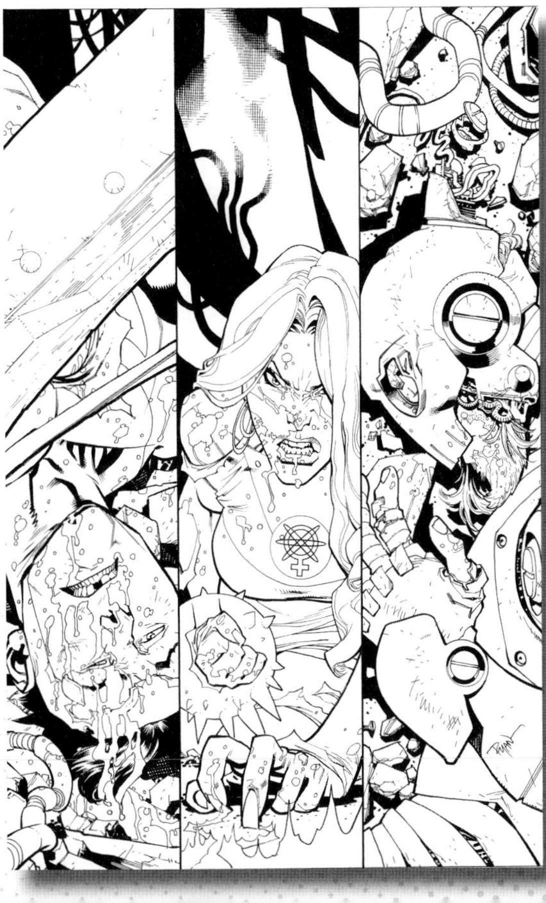

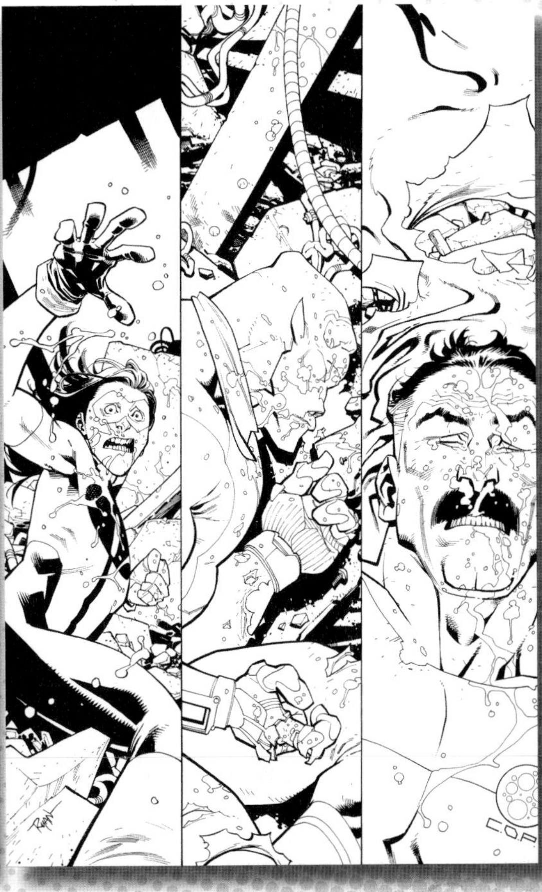

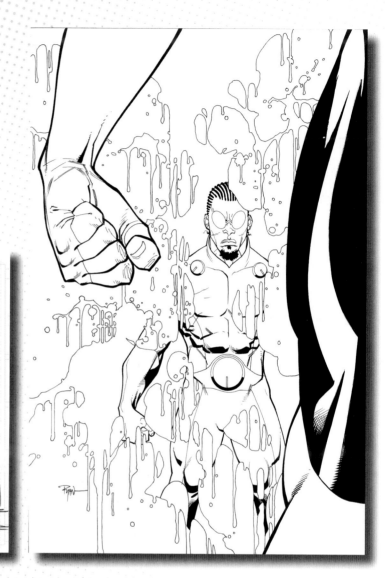

RYAN: *So here is another cover I needed to do in a rush. Luckily Robert liked the layout so he spared the whip and let me do the cover, which I finished, layouts/pencils/inks, in a day. And a glorious day it was!*

ROBERT: *I remember I had some stupid idea of this cover being from Zandale's POV as he looked down into a pool of blood on the ground and the cover would simply be an upside down reflection of him. I don't quite get what the blood is doing on the wall here, but it looked so cool I figured I'd let it go. It's a pretty great cover.*

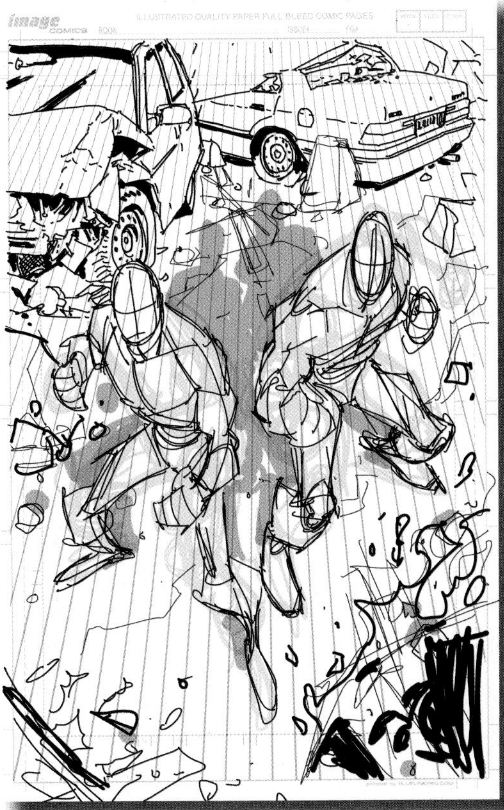

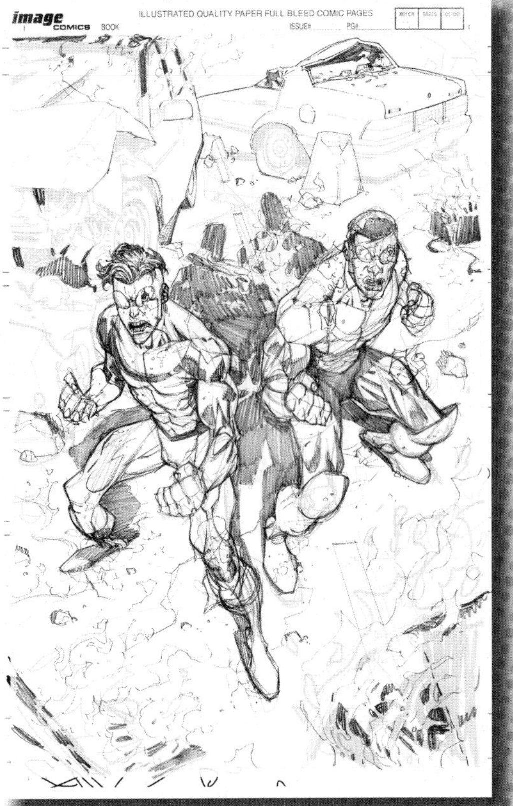
image COMICS
ILLUSTRATED QUALITY PAPER FULL BLEED COMIC PAGES

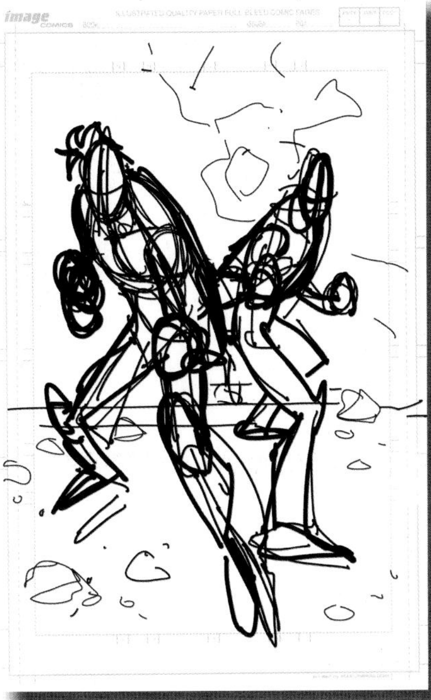

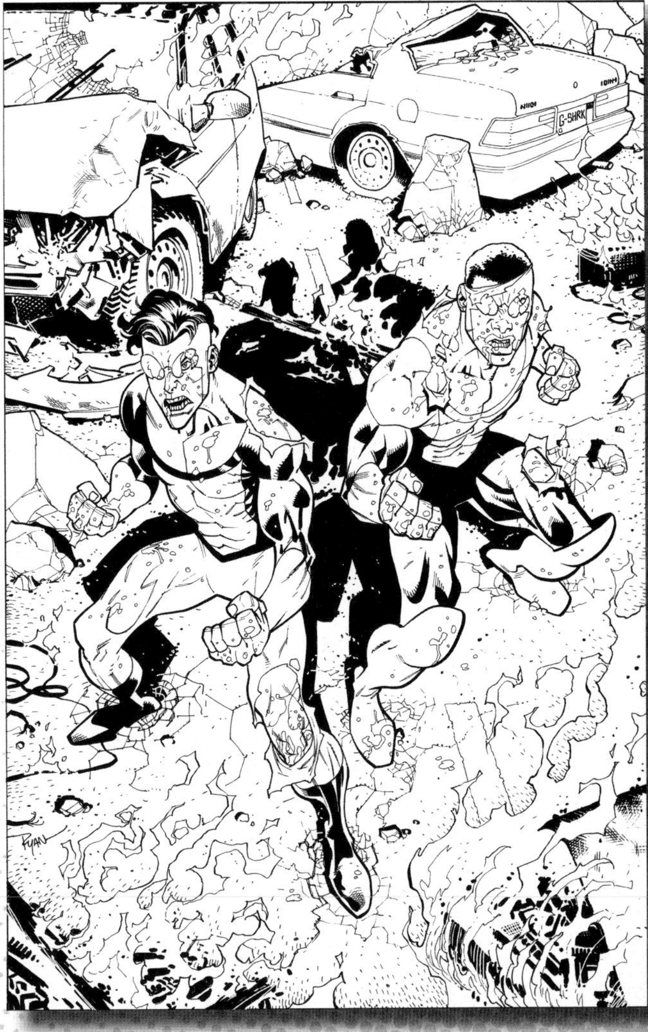
G-SHRK
RYAN

RYAN: Not my favorite cover. I overdid it, I made a few anatomy mistakes, it just feels cluttered to me. I mean there is tons of clutter and rubble and things on the page, I just mean it feels like I could have made better choices and a better composition and.... Blargh! I can't explain myself! Never mind, this is the best cover ever drawn by anyone ever!

ROBERT: Yeah, this cover blows. You suck.

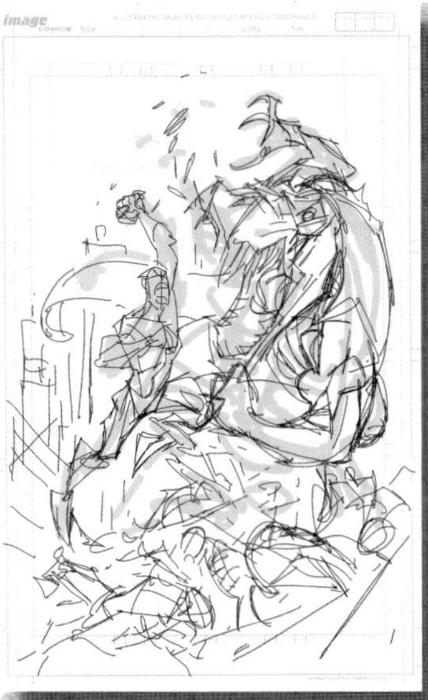

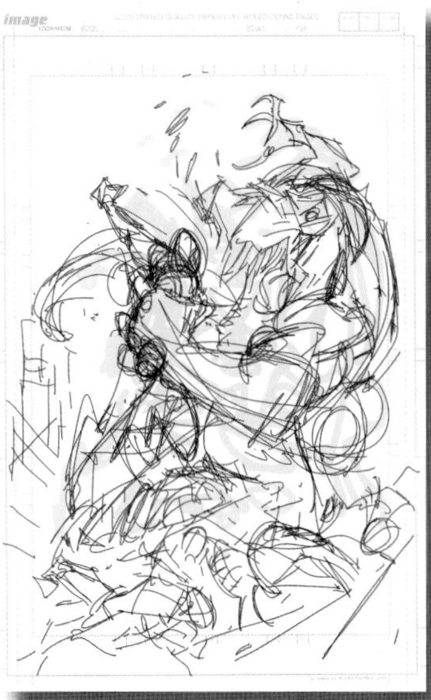

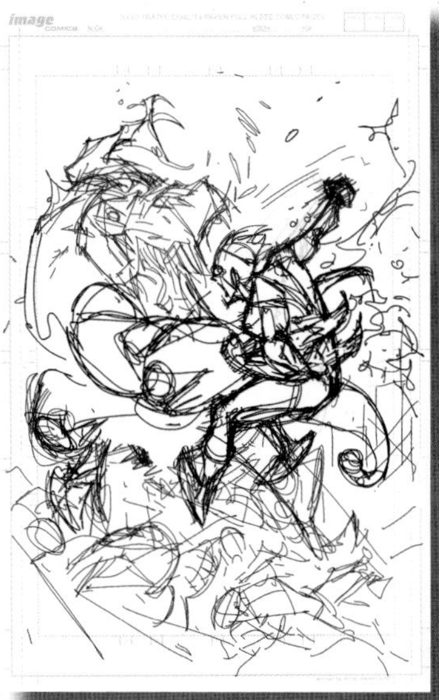

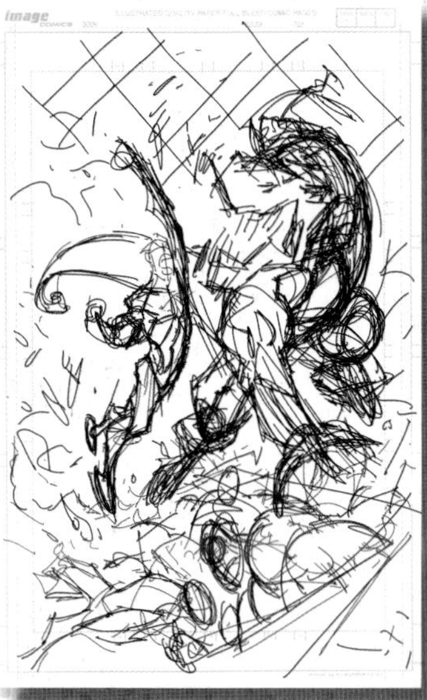

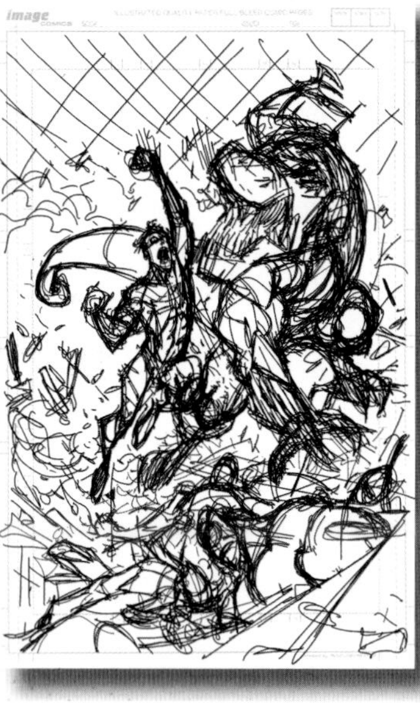

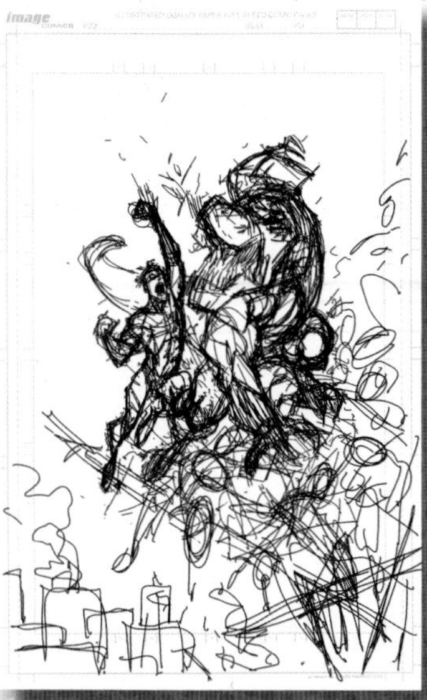

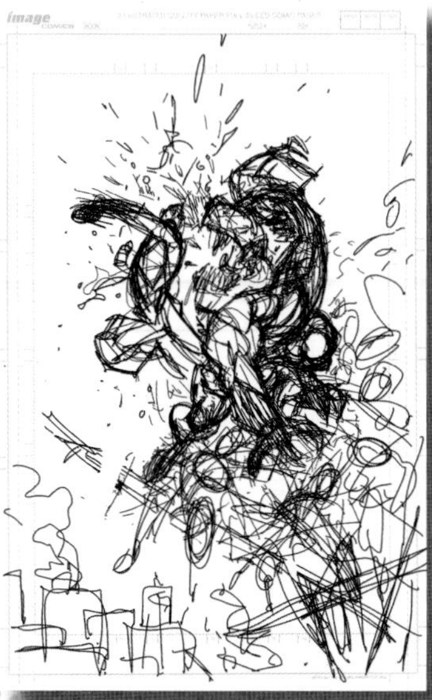

RYAN: Ahhhh, the issue #99 cover! Let's just sit back and watch me struggle with poses on this one! It was quite the doozie.

ROBERT: I quite enjoy this cover. You should struggle with poses more often.

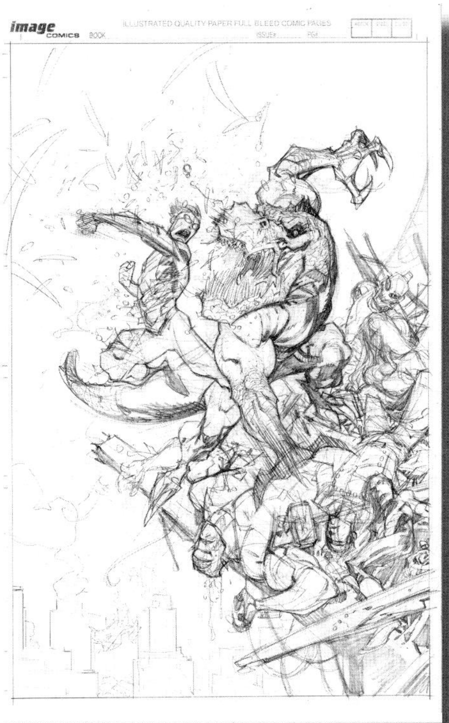
image COMICS
ILLUSTRATED QUALITY PAPER FULL BLEED COMIC PAGES
BOOK
ISSUE#
PG#

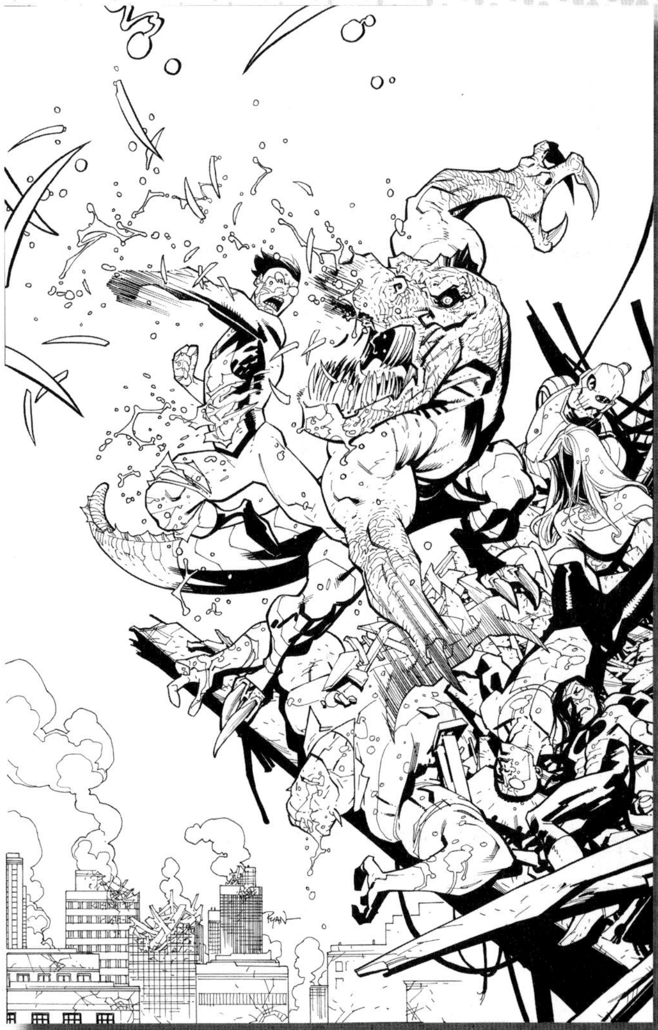
RYAN

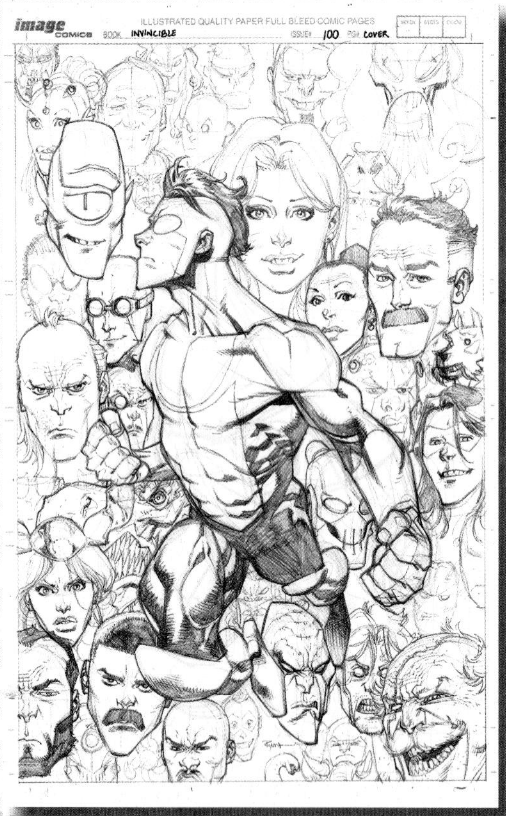
image COMICS
ILLUSTRATED QUALITY PAPER FULL BLEED COMIC PAGES
BOOK INVINCIBLE
ISSUE# 100 PG# COVER

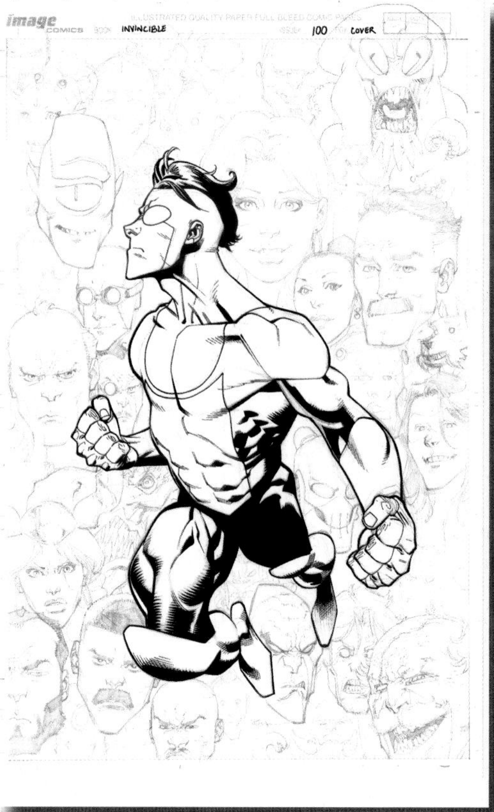
image COMICS
ILLUSTRATED QUALITY PAPER FULL BLEED COMIC PAGES
BOOK INVINCIBLE
ISSUE# 100 COVER

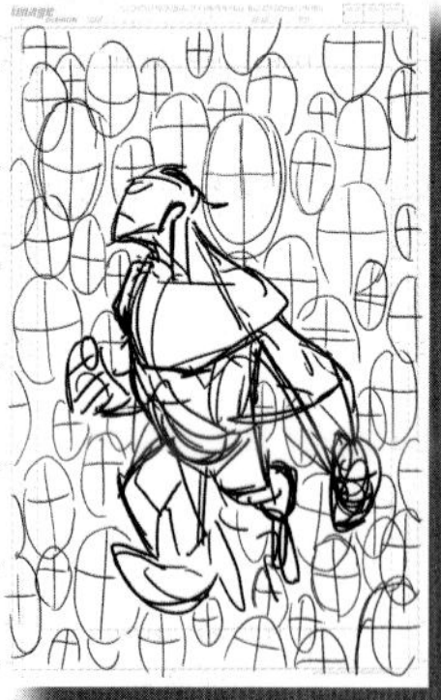

RYAN: So Robert asked for a cover with a figure of Invincible surrounded by heads, kind of an homage to Spidey #100 and Savage Dragon #100. Lots of fun to do! It's kind of a no-no to have your main characters looking right off the page, but I've drawn him looking forward on so many covers, and for some reason I really liked that gesture line in the layout from his head down to his fist. I just didn't want to break that by having his head turned.

ROBERT: I let it go, but that was a mistake. He looks like he's smelling Rex and looking at Allen. Boo! It did look really good on that cake, though... but I think everything looks good on a cake.

SEAN: To clarify, there was a #100 signing, and there was cake. And that cake was big and awesome.

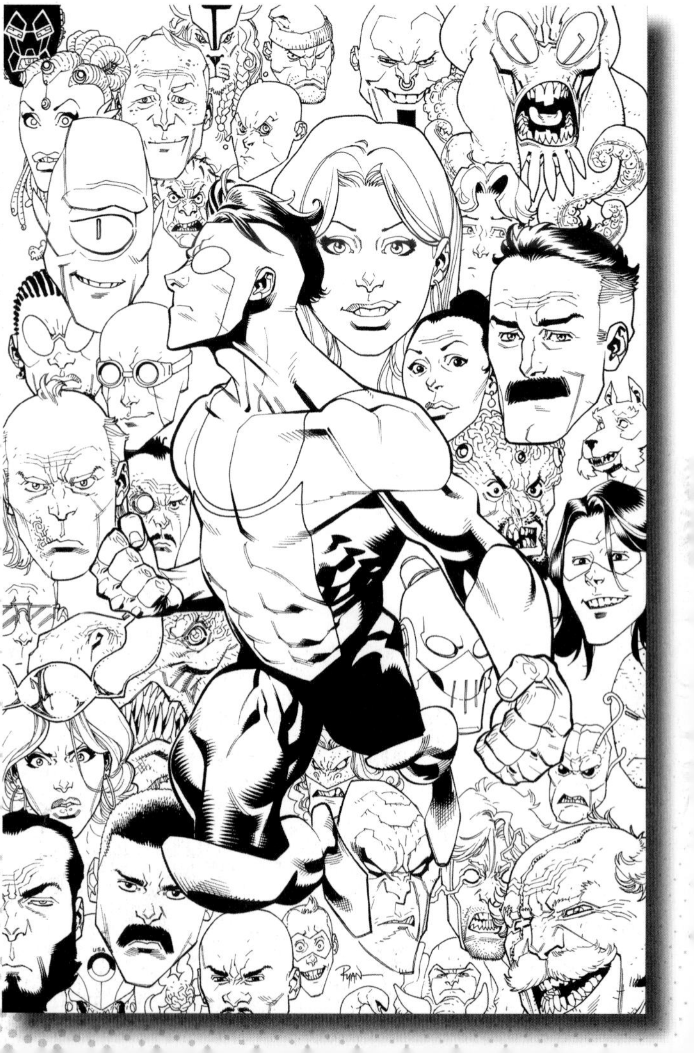

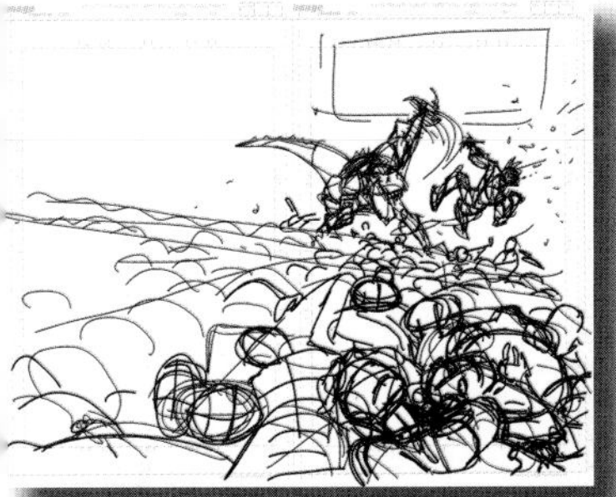

RYAN: I remember fighting Robert on this one a little bit. He loves those Erik Larsen fights where two characters are fighting and punching at the same time. He wanted that for this cover, it's what I did on issue #99 too, so I thought that would be redundant. And I figured we had ALL these characters dead on the ground, to have Dinosaurus laying in the finishing kill on Invincible adds to the OOMF of this cover. Makes it MORE dynamic and dire feeling and brings a nice "WTF" feeling to the viewer.

ROBERT: To be fair, those Larsen fights always look cool as hell. So shut up. This cover was also meant to be a homage to the wraparound cover of Walking Dead #100. The only difference is all the dead bodies on that cover were characters who were actually dead. We really should kill more characters in this book...

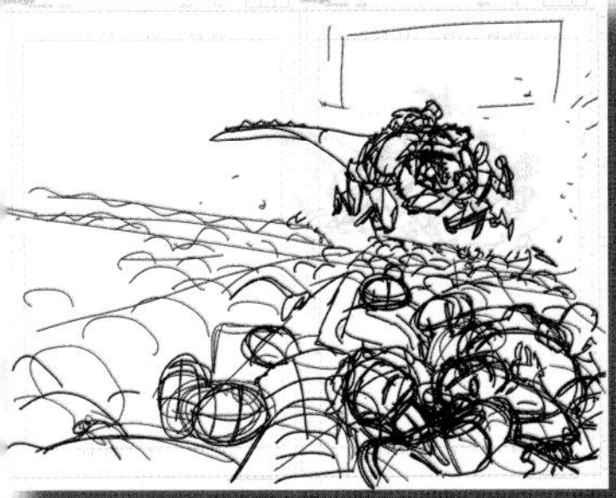

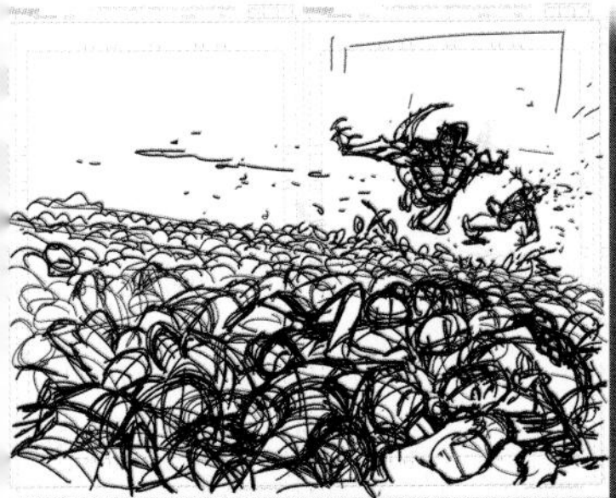

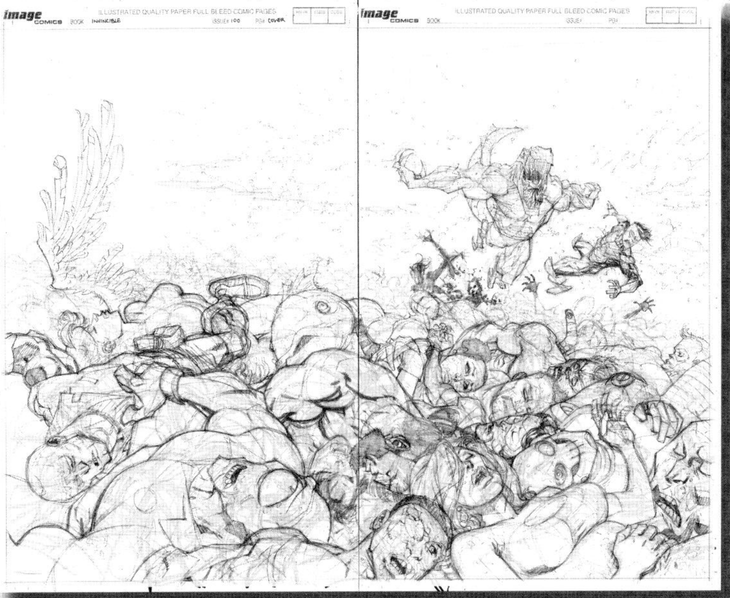

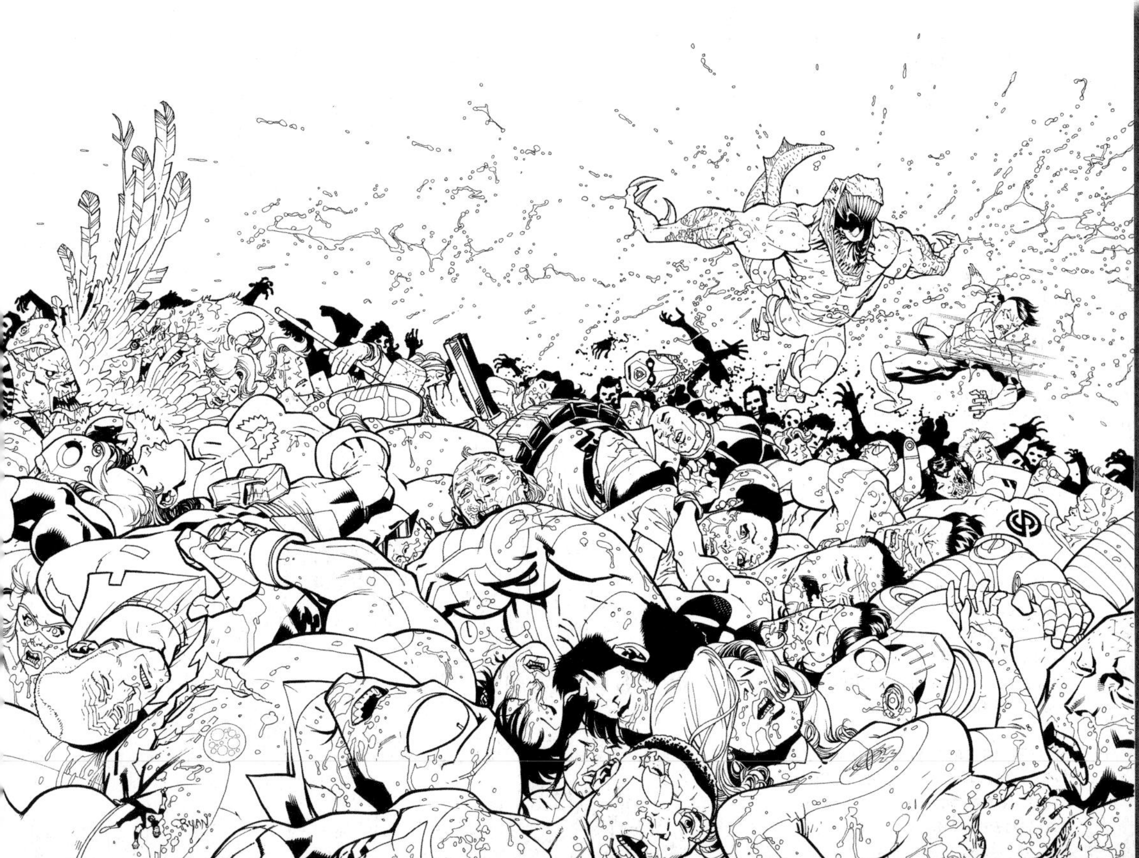

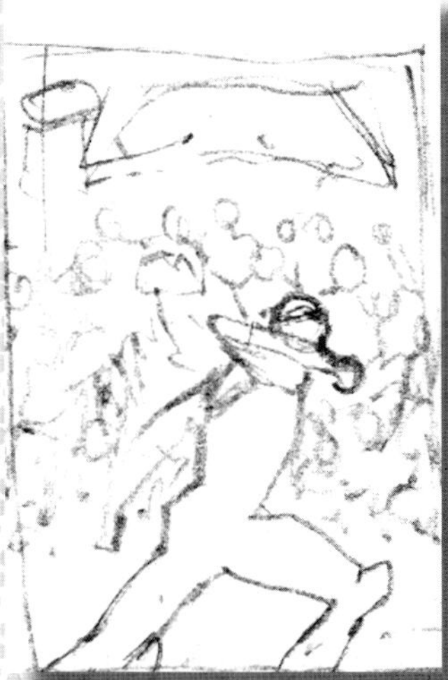

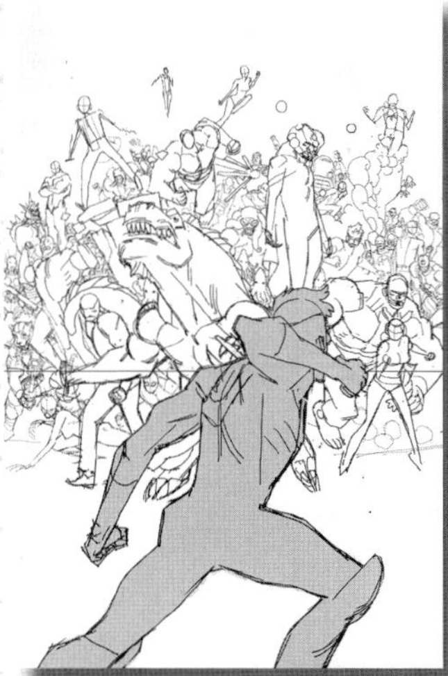

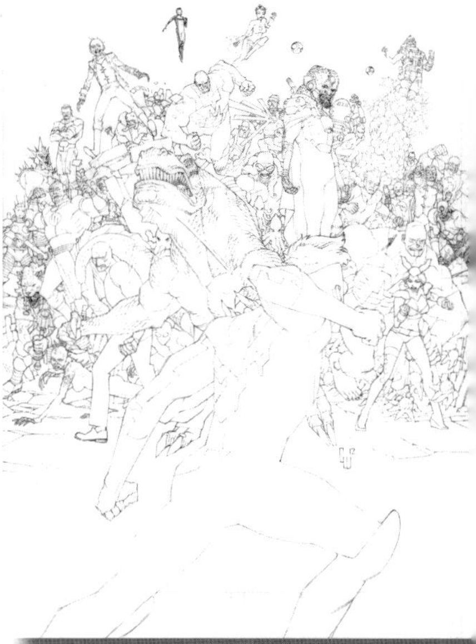

RYAN: Damn Cory. This cover wins the best cover award. For any cover that's ever been drawn by anyone ever!

ROBERT: I love that Cory will read that as sarcasm despite it being completely sincere. Cory actually didn't want to do a cover for this issue, and I sort of kind of made him. He wasn't too happy, but then he came up with the idea of reversing issue #1's cover to see all the villains he was fighting... it's just brilliant. I wish I could say it was my idea, but the fact is, a good majority of the good ideas on things Cory and I do together come from him. The guy is kind of brilliant. (Also not sarcasm, Cory.)

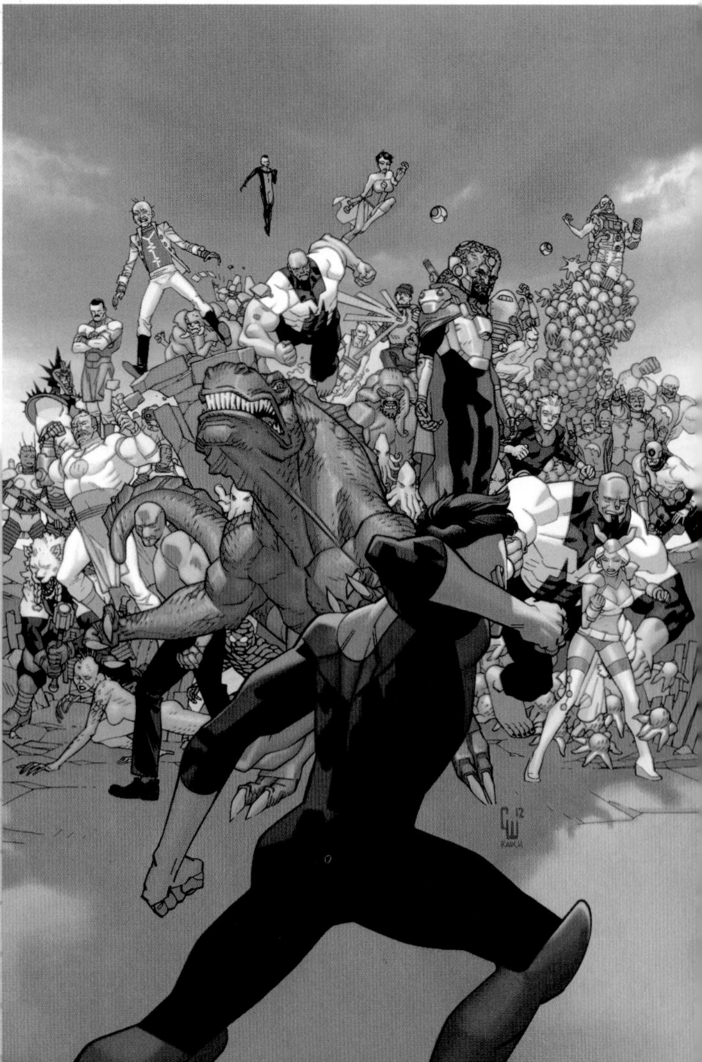

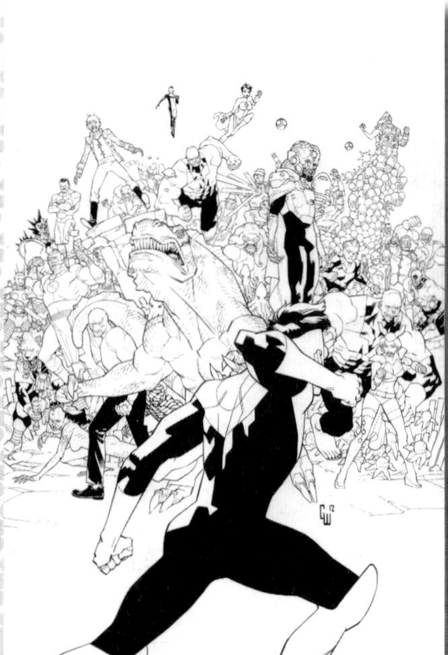

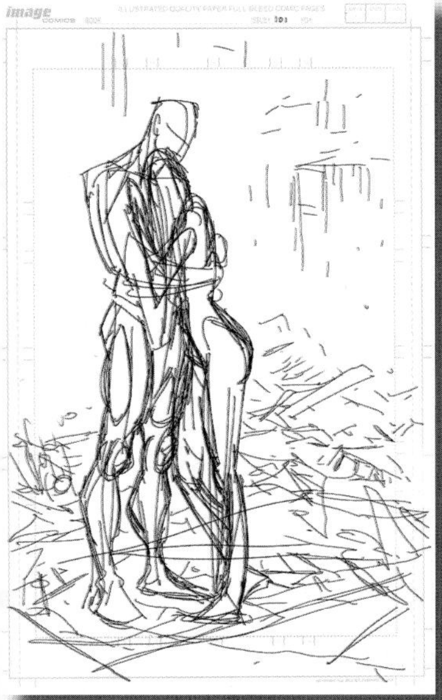

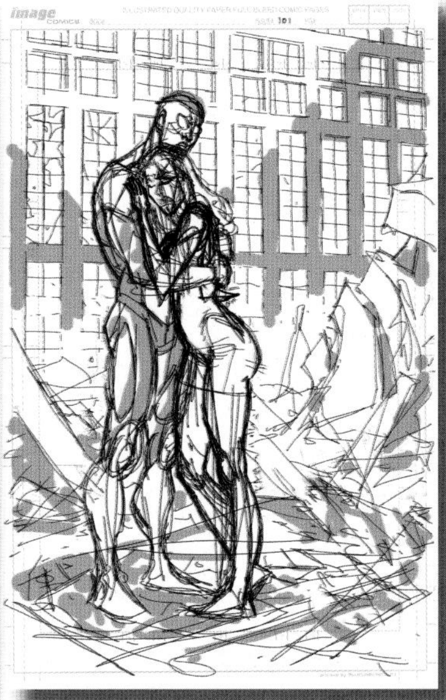

RYAN: So sweet.

ROBERT: It's always hard to do those few covers after an event where the main character could have died where you can't show that the main character actually lived... especially with the way we started issue #100. If you read that having SEEN the covers to #101 or #102 online and knew they had Mark on them... it would kind of ruin the story. Ryan always pulls it off though. This cover is dope.

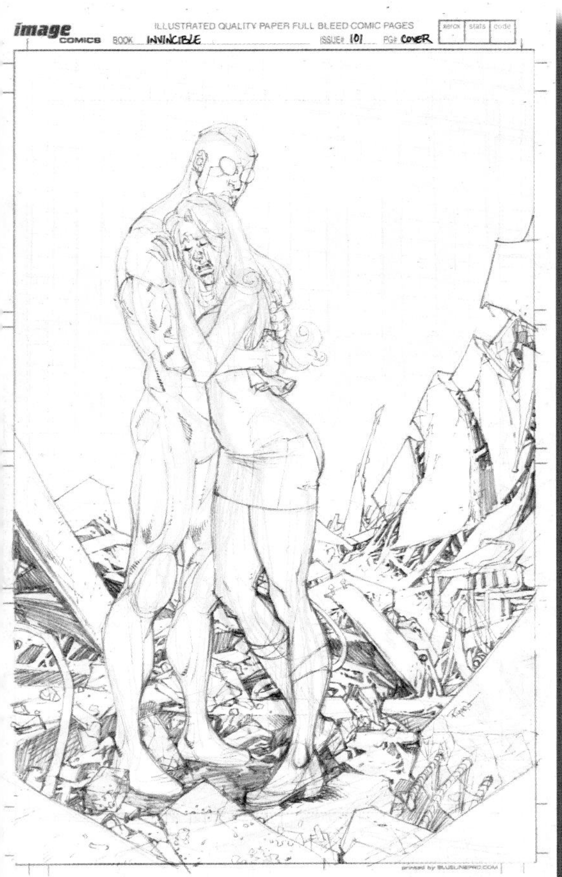
image COMICS
ILLUSTRATED QUALITY PAPER FULL BLEED COMIC PAGES
BOOK INVINCIBLE
ISSUE# 101
PG# COVER
xerox stats code
printed by BLUELINEPRO.COM

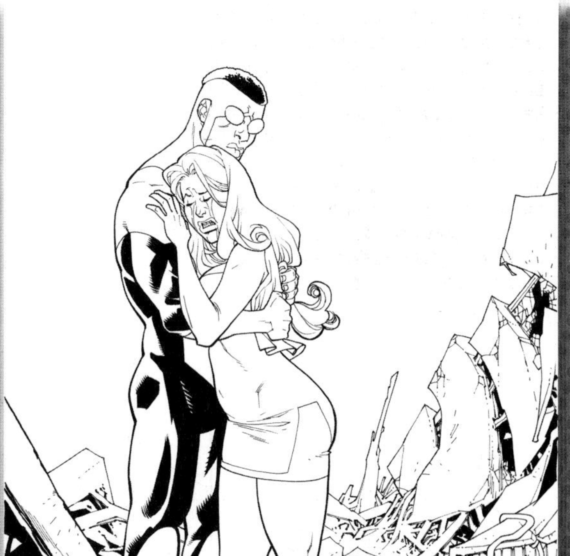

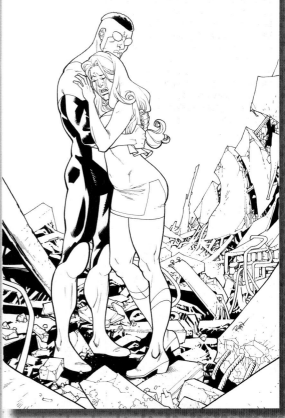

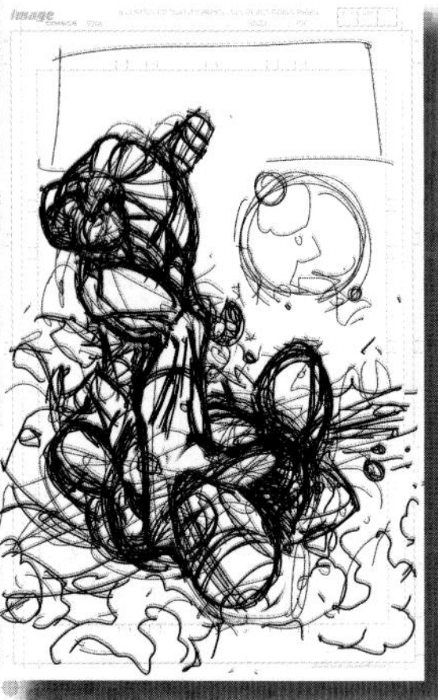

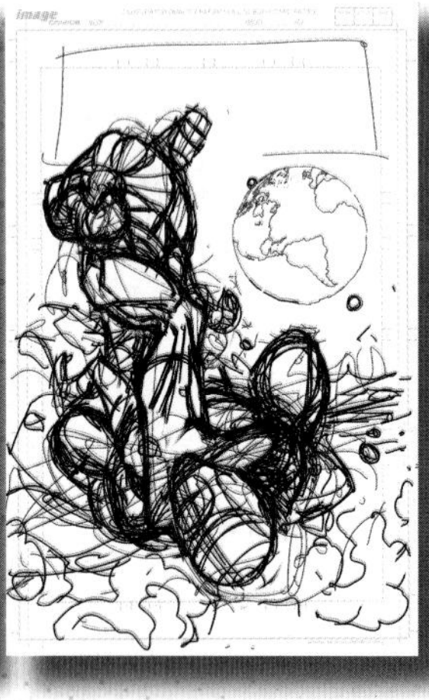

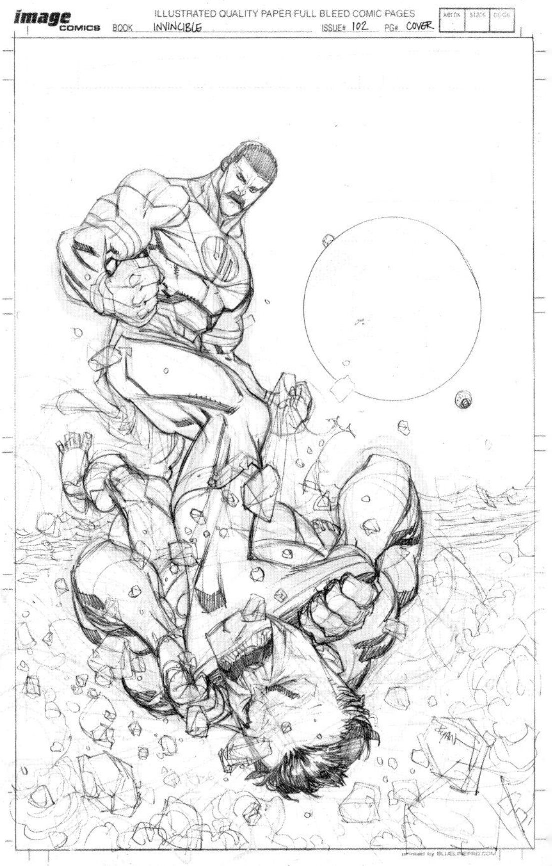
image COMICS
ILLUSTRATED QUALITY PAPER FULL BLEED COMIC PAGES
BOOK INVINCIBLE
ISSUE# 102 PG# COVER
xerox stats code
RYAN

RYAN: FIGHT! Thragg versus Nolan! Who will win?! Def Thragg. Dude's a monster, I love drawing him.

ROBERT: And Thragg did technically win... or he would have... but he kind of didn't... technically.

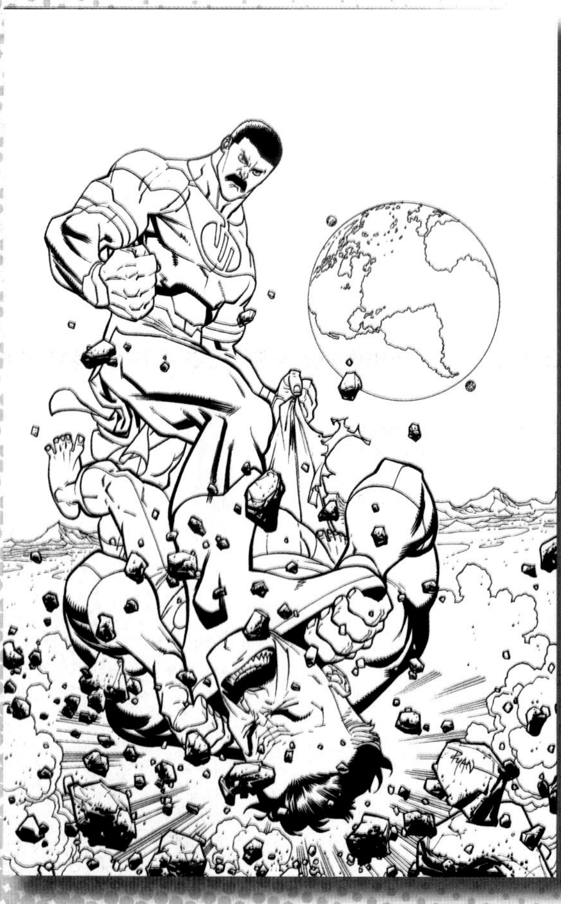
RYAN

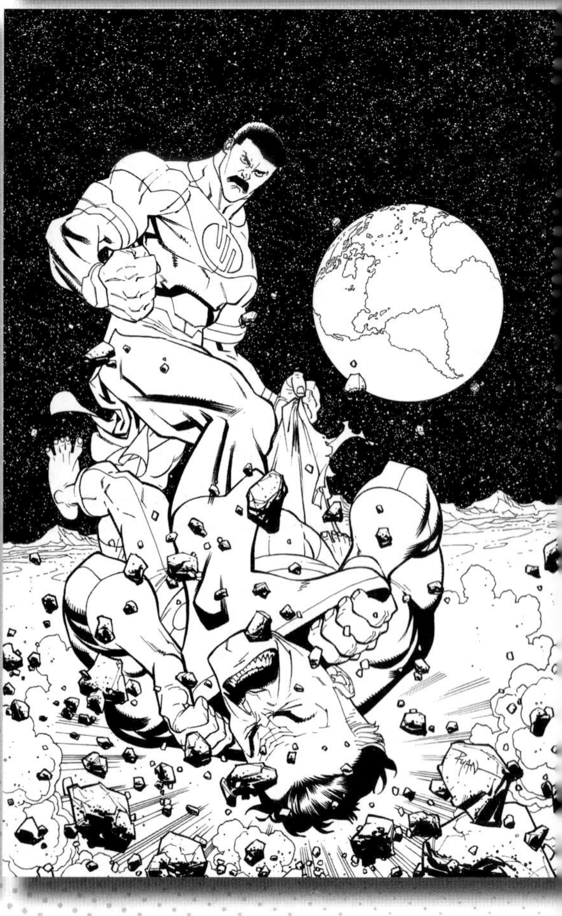
RYAN

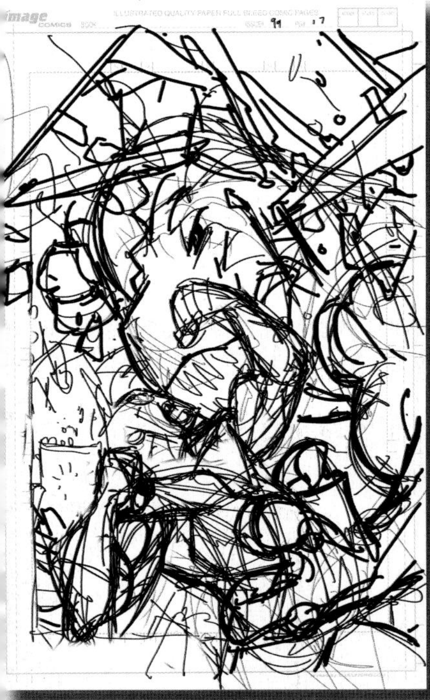

image
COMICS
99
17

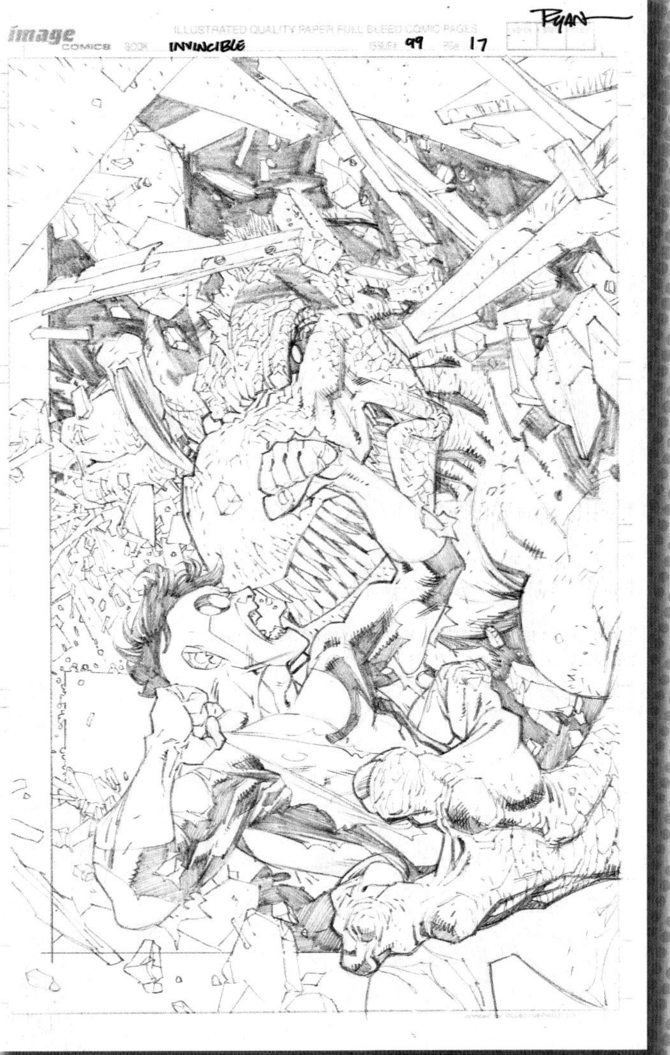

image
COMICS
INVINCIBLE
99
17
RYAN

RYAN: Such a fun issue to draw, all splash pages, I would so do that again. Dinosaurus will be missed! He was one of my favorite characters to draw.

ROBERT: We'll do another all splash page issue again... I promise... but Dinosaurus... he's pretty much gone forever.

MORE BOOKS FROM
ROBERT KIRKMAN
AND SKYBOUND!

TO FIND YOUR NEAREST COMIC BOOK STORE, CALL:
1-888-COMIC-BOOK

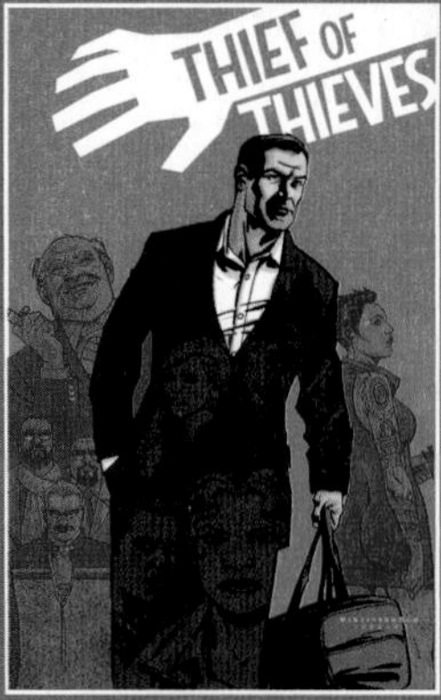
THIEF OF THIEVES

THIEF OF THIEVES
VOL. 1: "I QUIT."
ISBN: 978-1-60706-592-0
$14.99
VOL. 2: "HELP ME."
ISBN: 978-1-60706-676-7
$14.99

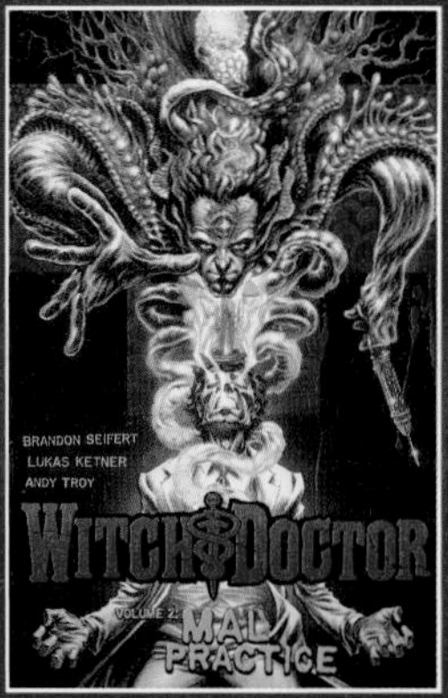
BRANDON SEIFERT
LUKAS KETNER
ANDY TROY
WITCH DOCTOR
MAL PRACTICE

WITCH DOCTOR
VOL. 1: UNDER THE KNIFE TP
ISBN: 978-1-60706-441-1
$12.99
VOL. 2: MAL PRACTICE TP
ISBN: 978-1-60706-693-4
$14.99

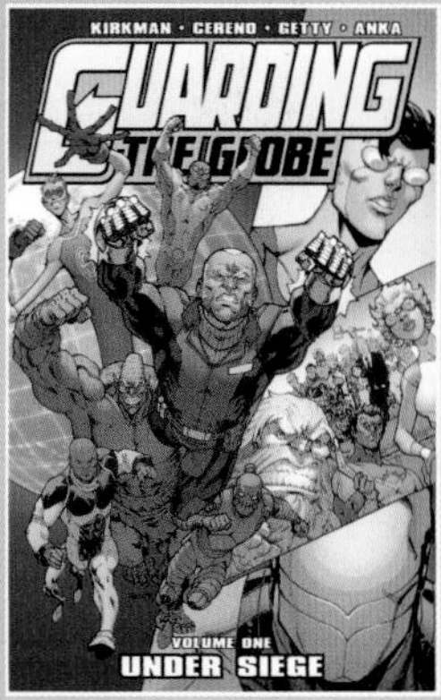
KIRKMAN · CERENO · GETTY · ANKA
GUARDING THE GLOBE
VOLUME ONE
UNDER SIEGE

GUARDING THE GLOBE
VOL. 1: UNDER SIEGE TP
ISBN: 978-1-60706-356-8
$16.99
VOL. 2: HARD TO KILL TP
ISBN: 978-1-60706-673-6
$16.99

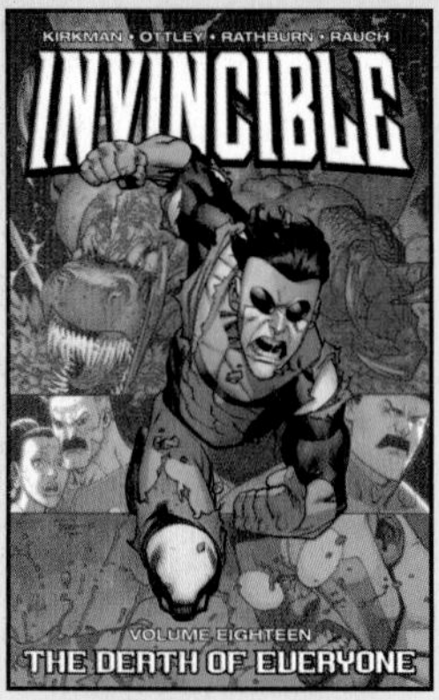
KIRKMAN · OTTLEY · RATHBURN · RAUCH
INVINCIBLE
VOLUME EIGHTEEN
THE DEATH OF EVERYONE

INVINCIBLE
VOL. 1: FAMILY MATTERS TP
ISBN: 978-1-58240-711-1
$12.99
VOL. 2: EIGHT IS ENOUGH TP
ISBN: 978-1-58240-347-2
$12.99
VOL. 3: PERFECT STRANGERS TP
ISBN: 978-1-58240-793-7
$12.99
VOL. 4: HEAD OF THE CLASS TP
ISBN: 978-1-58240-440-2
$14.95
VOL. 5: THE FACTS OF LIFE TP
ISBN: 978-1-58240-554-4
$14.99
VOL. 6: A DIFFERENT WORLD TP
ISBN: 978-1-58240-579-7
$14.99
VOL. 7: THREE'S COMPANY TP
ISBN: 978-1-58240-656-5
$14.99
VOL. 8: MY FAVORITE MARTIAN TP
ISBN: 978-1-58240-683-1
$14.99
VOL. 9: OUT OF THIS WORLD TP
ISBN: 978-1-58240-827-9
$14.99
VOL. 10: WHO'S THE BOSS TP
ISBN: 978-1-60706-013-0
$16.99
VOL. 11: HAPPY DAYS TP
ISBN: 978-1-60706-062-8
$16.99
VOL. 12: STILL STANDING TP
ISBN: 978-1-60706-166-3
$16.99
VOL. 13: GROWING PAINS TP
ISBN: 978-1-60706-251-6
$16.99
VOL. 14: THE VILTRUMITE WAR TP
ISBN: 978-1-60706-367-4
$19.99
VOL. 15: GET SMART TP
ISBN: 978-1-60706-498-5
$16.99
VOL. 16: FAMILY TIES TP
ISBN: 978-1-60706-579-1
$16.99
VOL. 17: WHAT'S HAPPENING TP
ISBN: 978-1-60706-662-0
$16.99
VOL. 18: DEATH OF EVERYONE TP
ISBN: 978-1-60706-762-7
$16.99
ULTIMATE COLLECTION, VOL. 1 HC
ISBN 978-1-58240-500-1
$34.95
ULTIMATE COLLECTION, VOL. 2 HC
ISBN: 978-1-58240-594-0
$34.99
ULTIMATE COLLECTION, VOL. 3 HC
ISBN: 978-1-58240-763-0
$34.99
ULTIMATE COLLECTION, VOL. 4 HC
ISBN: 978-1-58240-989-4
$34.99
ULTIMATE COLLECTION, VOL. 5 HC
ISBN: 978-1-60706-116-8
$34.99
ULTIMATE COLLECTION, VOL. 6 HC
ISBN: 978-1-60706-360-5
$34.99
ULTIMATE COLLECTION, VOL. 7 HC
ISBN: 978-1-60706-509-8
$39.99
ULTIMATE COLLECTION, VOL. 8 HC
ISBN: 978-1-60706-680-4
$39.99
COMPENDIUM VOL. 1
ISBN: 978-1-60706-411-4
$64.99
THE COMPLETE INVINCIBLE LIBRARY, VOL. 2 HC
ISBN: 978-1-60706-112-0
$125.00
THE COMPLETE INVINCIBLE LIBRARY, VOL. 3 HC
ISBN: 978-1-60706-421-3
$125.00
THE OFFICIAL HANDBOOK OF THE INVINCIBLE UNIVERSE TP
ISBN: 978-1-58240-831-6
$12.99
INVINCIBLE PRESENTS, VOL. 1: ATOM EVE & REX SPLODE TP
ISBN: 978-1-60706-255-4
$14.99

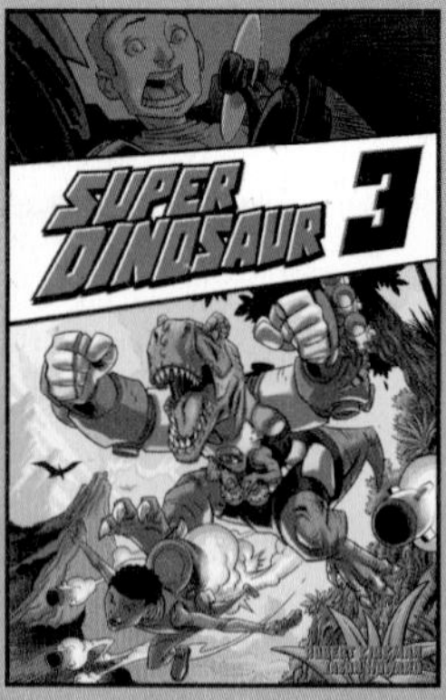
SUPER DINOSAUR 3

SUPER DINOSAUR
VOL. 1
ISBN: 978-1-60706-420-6
$9.99
VOL. 2
ISBN: 978-1-60706-568-5
$12.99
VOL. 3
ISBN: 978-1-60706-667-5
$12.99
DELUXE COLORING BOOK
ISBN: 978-1-60706-481-7
$4.99

THE ASTOUNDING WOLF-MAN
VOL. 1 TP
ISBN: 978-1-58240-862-0
$14.99
VOL. 2 TP
ISBN: 978-1-60706-007-9
$14.99
VOL. 3 TP
ISBN: 978-1-60706-111-3
$16.99
VOL. 4 TP
ISBN: 978-1-60706-249-3
$16.99

BATTLE POPE
VOL. 1: GENESIS TP
ISBN: 978-1-58240-572-8
$14.99
VOL. 2: MAYHEM TP
ISBN: 978-1-58240-529-2
$12.99
VOL. 3: PILLOW TALK TP
ISBN: 978-1-58240-677-0
$12.99
VOL. 4: WRATH OF GOD TP
ISBN: 978-1-58240-751-7
$9.99

BRIT
VOL. 1: OLD SOLDIER TP
ISBN: 978-1-58240-678-7
$14.99
VOL. 2: AWOL
ISBN: 978-1-58240-864-4
$14.99
VOL. 3: FUBAR
ISBN: 978-1-60706-061-1
$16.99

CAPES
VOL. 1: PUNCHING THE CLOCK TP
ISBN: 978-1-58240-756-2
$17.99

HAUNT
VOL. 1 TP
ISBN: 978-1-60706-154-0
$9.99
VOL. 2 TP
ISBN: 978-1-60706-229-5
$16.99
VOL. 3 TP
ISBN: 978-1-60706-552-4
$14.99
THE IMMORTAL EDITION, VOL. 1 HC
ISBN: 978-1-60706-241-7
$34.99

THE INFINITE
VOL. 1 TP
ISBN: 978-1-60706-475-6
$9.99

SUPERPATRIOT
AMERICA'S FIGHTING FORCE
ISBN: 978-1-58240-355-1
$14.99

TALES OF THE REALM
HARDCOVER
ISBN: 978-1-58240-426-0
$34.95
TRADE PAPERBACK
ISBN: 978-1-58240-394-6
$14.95

TECH JACKET
VOL. 1: THE BOY FROM EARTH TP
ISBN: 978-1-58240-771-5
$14.99